Oh God, she'd just hit someone with her car!

She felt the impact, the thud, saw the form bouncing off the hood of her car. She jammed her foot on the brake and jumped out of the car.

He moaned….

"Please be all right," she whispered. Amber opened her senses, probing his mind for pain. But what she found there shocked her so much she jerked away.

"You're a vampire!"

"That doesn't mean I'm not hurting like hell right now." He rose from the pavement with a limp.

Amber sucked in a breath so fast she hurt her lungs. It was *him!* The vampire in her dreams! Her mind screamed, *It's death he brings you….*

He closed the remaining distance between them and extended a hand. His touch was like a jolt of electricity.

"They call me Edge."

D0376990

MAGGIE SHAYNE

EDGE OF TWILIGHT

MIRA®

ISBN 0-7783-2022-7

EDGE OF TWILIGHT

Visit us at www.mirabooks.com

Printed in U.S.A.

This one is for you, though I've never known your
    name,
You, gentle-voiced spirits who whisper to me,
Who speak louder in case I didn't hear,
Who shout if I remain unmoved,
Who kick my shins until I either bleed,
Or take heed.

This one is for you.
You, eternal muses
Who shake me from the depths of sleep with an
    idea,
A scene,
A story that *must* be told,
You who drag my mind away from conversation,
And put that blank stare in my eyes, and silence my
    lips,
So that friends and family think me rude and
    inattentive,
Because suddenly, I can hear only you!

This one is for you,
Goddess of the Storytellers of old,
You who make me run stop signs,
And leap up from a public meal,
My exclamation nonsensical to any who might hear
As I race off to find a computer,
A pad and pen,
An eyeliner and paper napkin,
Anything!
Anything to capture your whisper, your breath,
My inspiration.

This one is for you.
Hell, they all are.

Prologue

Summer, 1959

"The guy actually pissed himself, I scared him so badly," Bridget said, laughing as they cut through the alley, jumped up onto the skeletal remains of a fire escape and swung inward through the broken window to land on the floor far below. The abandoned warehouse's floorboards were cracked from these oft repeated impacts. But it was home to the Gang of Five.

Edge loved the kid. But he wasn't happy with her right now. He tousled her Orphan Annie curls, knocked the matching barrettes askew. Twelve years old when she was made over; twelve she would remain, even though she'd been undead for more than a decade now. He'd found her on the street, wandering, alone. Orphaned by her maker, just as he'd been. Just as they all had been.

"So who the hell was he?" he asked.

Shrugging, Bridget climbed a ladder to the loftlike second floor, where they always met after a day of scavenging to divvy up the take. Edge didn't climb, he jumped. When he landed, a little cloud of dust rose up.

"Nice entrance," Ginger said without getting up from where she sat on the floor, her voice dripping sarcasm. She dressed all in black, kept her short hair and dagger-sharp nails that color, too, as if trying to live the cliché.

She brushed the dust from her black jeans as if he'd put it there deliberately.

"Quit your bitching, Ginger," Bridget snapped.

"Watch your mouth, pipsqueak."

Bridget spun on her, and Ginger leaped to her feet.

"Hey, hey, knock it off!" Baby-faced Scott got to his feet, as well, putting himself between them. "Come on, what's your problem, anyway?" He was skinny but strong. As strong as any of them were, at least, which was damn strong in comparison to humans. As vampires, they were kittens. "Fledglings" was the term Edge had heard older ones use. Both Ginger and Scottie had been undead for less than five years. She'd been eighteen, and he'd been a year younger, when the change occurred. Babies. But that was why they needed each other. And why they needed him.

Ginger and Bridget didn't show any signs of backing off. Scottie's blond, blue-eyed head and rail-thin build were hardly any more intimidating than his butter-soft voice.

"Settle down," Edge said. He said it sternly. *"Now."*

Blinking guiltily, the females parted. They always followed his orders. Edge hadn't applied for the job of leader of this little gang, it had just fallen to him naturally. He was the oldest. He'd been twenty-three when he was made over, which was older than any of them had been. And he'd been a vampire longer than any of them. Twelve years now. The hideout was his own. They'd just sort of…followed him home, one by one, until he had this gang of homeless vamps. A natural progression, he figured. He'd been part of a street gang in Ireland, the year he'd been transformed. Though that gang had been different. Homeless toughs, each trying to out-tough the others. This little group…damned if they hadn't become almost like—a family.

Edge loved them, every one of them. He took care of them. And they looked to him to lead, trusted him to protect them, for some reason. His age, his experience, he didn't know. It was just the way things had worked out.

"So where's Billy Boy?" Ginger asked. "He should have been back by now."

Bridget shrugged and opened her backpack. "I took a mark all by myself today," she said, dumping out the contents. A wallet, cuff links and expensive watch fell out onto the floor.

"And as I've already reminded you, Bridget," Edge began, "you're not supposed to—"

"Hell, Edge, I'm not *really* twelve, I only look it." She smiled, deep dimples in little-girl cheeks. "You should have seen this guy," she said to the others. "College student, I think. Young, maybe a freshman. Rich as hell and looking lost. Probably his first time in the big city, right? So I spotted him on the street, caught a glimpse of the Rolex on his wrist and decided it was too good to pass up. So I got ahead of him a little ways and ducked into an alley. When he came past, I called out in this sweet little girl voice." She softened her tone, raised its pitch to a plaintive, innocent whine. "Help me. Please help me, mister."

Edge frowned but saw the rapt attention on the faces of the others.

"So he comes walking into the alley, and that's when I jumped him." She shrugged. "Heck, I was hungry anyways."

"Bridget, you didn't kill him, did you?" Scottie asked,

while sending Edge a worried look. "We don't want to draw attention to ourselves."

"I didn't drink enough to kill him. Just scared the hell out of him. Quenched my thirst, too." She licked her lips. Then she smiled, falling back into her story. "I jumped onto his back, wrapped my legs around his waist and my arms around his neck and bit him hard. He was so scared he wet his pants! I laughed my ass off!"

Scottie muttered, "Oh, Bridget," shaking his head slowly. "What did this poor fellow ever do to you?"

"Leave her alone, Scottie," Ginger barked. "It's survival of the fittest out here. Kill or be killed. We do what we have to. Besides, she didn't hurt him."

"She didn't have to scare him that badly, either."

Bridget rolled her eyes. "All I took were his watch, wallet and fancy-schmancy cuff links," she insisted.

"You took a lot more from him than that, Bridge," Scottie said. "You took his pride."

Edge found himself agreeing. "Moreover, you put the rest of us at risk, Bridget," he told the girl. "What do you suppose this man is going to do now? What if he goes to the police or the press, and talks about a little girl with superhuman strength who stole his wallet and bit his neck?"

"He won't," she said with a smile. "He's a man, after all. He has his ego to think about. It's bad enough he has to live with the memory. He'd never dream of admitting it to anyone else. Besides, who'd believe him?" She grinned. "You should have heard him when I left him there, lying in the garbage with his pissy pants and bleeding neck. He starts screaming at me, swearing he'll get revenge. So I turn around and I say, 'Yeah, I'm real scared of a man who wets his pants in fear of a little girl with sharp teeth.' She threw her head back and laughed. "*That* shut him up in a hurry."

Edge sighed, a dark feeling creeping over his soul. Bridget was not developing any sort of empathy, nor any moral values, despite his efforts to instill a modicum of something like ethics. Take only what you need, don't harm the innocent unnecessarily, that sort of thing. Scottie had a heart as big as the night, but he'd been that way before the change, Edge suspected. Ginger had just been mean, and she'd only grown meaner, and Bridget hadn't been old enough to know what she would have become. She seemed to be modeling herself after Ginger, though, more than any of them.

He took the wallet Bridget had stolen, removed the driver's license from it and examined the photo of a rather handsome young man with dark hair and eyes. "Frank W. Stiles," he read. "He's twenty-one." He flipped through the wallet, finding little else of interest, other than a business card with a phone number on it and the letters "DPI" embossed in black on its surface. He didn't know what that was, but the name on the card was J.D. Smith, and the title that followed it was "recruiter." Apparently the young Mr. Stiles was being courted by some company. Must be a gifted student.

Sighing, Edge shook his head. "What's done is done, I suppose. But you and I are due for a long talk, Bridget."

Sighing, he put the license and business card back, and tossed the wallet onto the floor. "How did the rest of you do?"

"Got seventy-five in cash and three credit cards," Scottie said. "I used that mind control technique you taught us, Edge. If it worked, none of them will remember a thing. And since I only took a little cash and one card from each victim, they'll just assume they misplaced their missing cards. Probably won't even miss the cash.'' He looked at Bridget as he spoke, as if it would help her get the message. ''See, kid? It can be done without scaring them half to death and announcing our presence to the world.''

Bridget stuck her tongue out at him.

''I got three hundred bucks and a diamond bracelet,'' Ginger added, her expression smugly superior. 'One victim. I hid in the back of her limo, knocked the driver out and waited. She got in, and I snagged the purse and bracelet and hopped out the other side. She barely knew what hit her.''

''Poor little rich bitch, I hope she wasn't too traumatized,'' Bridget said.

Scottie knew the remark was directed at him. ''Just because she's wealthy doesn't mean she deserves to be harmed or frightened, Bridget.''

Edge sighed. ''Add the cash to the till. We'll hock the rest.'' He glanced at the Rolex, which had Frank Stiles's name engraved on its back. ''It'll be dawn in two hours. I'm going back out to look for Billy Boy. I don't like that he's this late.''

''Will we have enough to get out of here soon, Edge?'' Bridget asked.

She wanted a place in the country. A safe place where they didn't have to worry about being discovered some sunny day while they slept. Frankly, he thought it was going to take a lot more than the pittance they managed to take in from petty crime and picking pockets. He was going to have to think of something better, something bigger.

''Soon,'' he told Bridget. ''Real soon, hon.''

Then he went out. But he didn't find Billy Boy. Not

until he came back, just a little while before dawn, and found all of them.

They were hanging upside down from the beam that supported the loft. Ropes had been tied around their ankles and looped over the beam. The floor beneath them was soaked in their blood. Every one of their throats had been cut.

Ginger, Billy Boy, gentle, sweet spirited Scottie, and his precious little Bridget. Dead. Murdered. The sight knocked the breath out of him, made his body go limp, and Edge fell to his knees. He didn't need to check their bodies to know they were gone. The stench of death was powerful. He'd felt it from the moment he'd neared the warehouse, and he'd run full speed the last several blocks.

But he was too late. His little misfits, his fledglings who'd depended on him to keep them safe, had been murdered.

He closed his eyes against the pain, but that didn't ease it. And finally he had to face the grim task ahead. He had to take care of them one last time. He climbed up to the loft to cut them down. And there on the floor he saw the little pile of stolen wallets, cash and credit cards, right where they'd been when he'd left. A few new items had been added to the pile, Billy Boy's take, no doubt. The diamond bracelet glittered up at him. Apparently the killer hadn't been interested in it.

And yet, Edge noticed, there were a few things missing from the pile.

Frowning, he moved closer. The Rolex was gone. The cuff links, too. And the wallet that had belonged to the man named Frank W. Stiles.

Blinking slowly, Edge realized that the man had come back. He'd had his revenge, just as he'd promised he would. How he'd done it, Edge didn't know. One man against four vampires? It seemed impossible. And yet it had happened.

Edge closed his eyes, vowed vengeance on the man who'd murdered his family. "You'll pay, Frank Stiles," he said aloud. "If it takes me an eternity, I will find you, and you *will* pay."

1

Present Day

There was no way the woman could have known he was waiting in her apartment when she walked in that night. She couldn't hear him, because he made no sound. She couldn't detect his body heat, because he didn't emit any. He had all the advantages. He could see her just as well in the dark as he could have in full light. Maybe better. He could hear every sound she made, right down to the steady beat of her heart and the rush of blood through her veins. He could smell her. Strawberry shampoo, baby powder scented deodorant, aging nail polish, a hint of perfume, even the fabric softener scent that lingered on her clothes.

She stepped into the dark apartment, closed the door behind her and turned the locks, all without reaching for a light switch. She leaned back against the door and heeled off her shoes, shrugged the heavy looking handbag from her shoulder, along with her coat, and draped them both over a hook on the tree near the door. Still no light switch.

She sighed and padded across the carpet, sank onto the sofa, let her head fall backward. She worked as a nurse at an elementary school in rural Pennsylvania, spent her days wiping bloody noses and checking heads for nits. A far cry from her former career.

He waited until she'd closed her hand unerringly on the remote control and aimed it at the television before he spoke. "Don't turn that on."

The remote dropped to the floor, and she shot to her feet with a broken cry, her hands pressing to her chest as she searched the darkness with wide, frightened eyes.

"No need to be afraid," he said, stepping from the darker shadows near the door into the slightly lighter ones that surrounded her. She could see him now, just barely. A black silhouette in the darkness. To help her out, he shook a cigarette from his pack, put it to his lips, fired it up. He watched her fear deepen as the flame briefly lit his face. He took a long pull and released the smoke while she stood there with her heart pounding like a rabbit's. "I didn't come here to hurt you. I will, of course, if you make me. I'd probably enjoy it. But ultimately, it's up to you."

"Wh-who are you? What do you want?"

He rolled his eyes at the utter predictability of the questions. "Sit down. Relax. I only want to talk to you." He held out the pack. "You want a smoke?"

"N-no." She sat down, just barely perching on the very edge of the sofa, shaking from head to toe. "B-but…"

"But what? Go on, ask. The worst I can do is say no. What do you want?"

"Could you t-t-turn on a light?"

"No." He smiled, amused by his own little joke. "See? That wasn't so bad, was it?"

She let her head fall forward, catching her face in her palms. Crying now. God, he hated crying women. He reached out for a handful of the blond hair on the very top of her head, tugged her head upward. It didn't cause her any pain, but she whimpered anyway. "Come on, now. I'm going to need your full attention for this."

She sniffled, wiped her eyes, squinted through the darkness at him. If she could see him at all, he supposed she could probably see his hair. He didn't really care. He'd only refused to turn on the lights because she wanted them on. He needed her uncomfortable, afraid and off balance.

"So here's the thing," he said. "I've been hunting for this man for…oh, more than forty years now. And during the course of my search, I found that he had a connection to you. A recent one, in the scheme of things. So here I am."

"What man?" Her voice was only a whisper now.

"Frank Stiles." He saw the way she jerked in reaction, then tried to hide it.

"Why is it you're looking for this…Stiles?"

He didn't have to answer. But he answered anyway. "He's a vampire hunter. I'm a vampire, you see. Thought it might be fun. Turn the tables, hunter becomes the hunted and all that."

"Oh God, oh God…"

"I understand you worked for Stiles five years ago or thereabouts." He took another drag, blew a few smoke rings. "That true?"

"No. I…I never heard of him."

He moved his hand too fast for her to follow it, gripped her throat and squeezed. He kept the pressure light, just enough to cut off the air supply and reduce the blood flowing to her brain, enough to make her panic. Not enough to crush her larynx. She would be no good to him dead. He lifted her right off the sofa by her throat, while taking another drag from his smoke with the other hand. Then he let her go. She fell sideways onto the sofa, and her hands shot to her throat as she gasped for breath.

"You're going to tell me what I want to know before this night ends. It really doesn't matter to me how much pain you want to withstand before you talk. As I said, I'll probably enjoy it more if you make me hurt you. It's all the same to me." He sat down on the easy chair near the sofa, smoking and giving her time to catch her breath.

"Your name is Kelsey Quinlan," he said at length. "You are a Registered Nurse. You work at Remsen Elementary. Is all of this correct?"

Dragging herself upright again, still pressing a hand to her throat, she nodded.

"And five years ago, you worked for Frank W. Stiles as a research assistant. Is *that* correct?"

"Yes. I did. B-but—"

"Shhh. Just answer my questions. I'm not here to punish you for your crimes, whatever they may be."

She lifted her head, swallowed hard. It hurt when she did. He felt it. "He's the one you want to punish, isn't he? What are you going to do with him when you find him? Kill him?"

"Oh, I've already killed him. A couple of times, actually. Oddly, the man keeps recovering."

The hand that had been rubbing at her throat went still, and the woman's face paled in the darkness. "That's... not possible."

"That's what I thought. But I killed him really well the second time. Honestly. He was very, very dead. And then...well, then he just wasn't." He shrugged. "So what I need to know from you is just what kind of research he was doing when you worked for him?"

Her eyes shot wider. He smelled her fear.

"I'm not going to punish you, Kelsey. I already told

you that." Again he shrugged. "Unless you're into that kind of thing, in which case—" As he said it, he reached for her.

"I didn't do anything to the girl! It wasn't me. It was all Stiles. I swear it."

He didn't touch her, lowering his hands slowly now that he had her talking. The taps were turned, the pump primed. The information would flow now. "What girl would that be?"

She blinked slowly. "The captive he held five years ago. The half-breed vampire."

He nodded slowly. This was in keeping with what the soldier-for-hire who'd worked on Stiles's security force had told him—after a lot of persuasion.

"Did this…half-breed have a name? Or did you just assign her a number?"

"She called herself Amber Lily Bryant. In the files she was Subject X-1."

Amber Lily. The Child of Promise. Then she did exist. He'd heard stories, of course. What vampire hadn't? But he'd pretty much dismissed them as legends. And the soldier he'd questioned had been ill-informed about what went on inside the old house in Connecticut where Stiles had conducted his "research." Still, he needed to test his witness, to make sure.

"This girl—she was a half-breed vampire, you say?"

The woman nodded.

"I think you're lying. There's no such thing. You're making up tales to distract me from my purpose here. Everyone knows vampires are infertile."

"Only the males. The females seem to ovulate for the first few months after being transformed. I thought—I thought you already knew. I thought all of you knew about all this."

Her eyes were adjusting to the darkness now, he thought. She was staring at him as if she could see his face. "Why don't you pretend I don't and fill me in?"

Nodding rapidly, she seemed to search her mind. "There was a mortal, one of the Chosen. You know about them—the only humans who can become vampires. They all have the same rare Belladonna antigen in their blood."

"And they all tend to die young if they aren't transformed. I know all that, go on."

She nodded. "Well this mortal, a male, was mated with a newly transformed vampiress, and X-1 was the resulting offspring."

He pursed his lips. "This was a DPI experiment, I take it?"

She nodded. "Yes. It all took place before the Division of Paranormal Investigations was dismantled. Stiles worked for them then. I believe he was directly involved with the experiment. But a group of vampires attacked the research facility—"

"Research facility." He snorted. "Extermination camp, you mean."

"The parents escaped with the child." She lowered her head. "That's all the background I was given on her."

He nodded slowly. "So even though DPI was never restored as a functioning government agency, Frank Stiles continued the work on his own. And part of that work included hunting and capturing this half-breed child who'd escaped them years before?"

"Apparently so. But she was hardly a child by then."

"No?"

She shook her head. "Eighteen when he held her in Connecticut." Her eyes shifted, downward and then left.

"I did my best to protect her while he kept her. And she was still alive when the vampires came and broke her out." She met his gaze again and maybe saw the doubt in it. "They didn't kill me when they came for her, surely that should tell you something."

"As a rule, my kind tend to get squeamish about cold-blooded murder—even when it's deserved. That they left you alive tells me nothing other than that they had weak stomachs." He shrugged. "I'm something of an exception to that rule, myself."

She sat very still, holding her breath.

"Stiles held the girl for how long?"

"I...don't remember exactly. A few days. No more."

"And he performed experiments on her?"

She lowered her head. "Yes."

"Details, Kelsey. I need details." He reached for her chin, tipped her head up so she faced him. "And I'll know if you're lying. I know you were lying about trying to protect her. You were as cruel to her as any of them. Fortunately for you, I don't give a damn about that. My interest is in Stiles. So tell me—and tell me everything."

The woman licked her lips, and he knew she believed him. She should.

"He wanted to know what kinds of powers she had. Whether she was immortal or not. What could kill her. That kind of thing. He kept her drugged, though, so she wasn't aware of most of the experiments. She probably didn't feel a thing."

"Really." His belly knotted just a little. "And what kinds of things didn't she feel, Kelsey?"

She drew a breath, had the decency to look ashamed. Her voice a bare whisper, she said, "Electric shock, enough to stop her heart, just to see if it would start again. Drowning, to see if that would kill her. Various toxins introduced into her bloodstream at fatal doses. Blood letting. Blows to the head.''

"Jesus," Edge muttered.

"She revived every time, and she was long gone before he could try things like bullets to the brain or wooden stakes to the heart.''

Edge rolled his eyes. Stakes indeed.

"She seems to age like a human. At least, she had the appearance of a normally aging eighteen-year-old, but she revivifies like an immortal.''

"And what else?''

She shrugged. "He took the usual samples. Blood, lots and lots of blood. Tissue, hair, bone marrow.''

"What did he do with them?''

She looked at him hard. "I don't know. I thought he was trying to map her DNA, but he kept a lot of his work secret. Used to lock himself in a private lab for hours on end. One of the others who worked for him thought he had two sets of notes, one we could see and the other for his eyes only.'' She shrugged. "I caught him once, injecting himself with something. But I never knew what it was.''

He pursed his lips. He suspected that Stiles had been trying to imbue himself with whatever it was that made the girl immortal—trying to steal her immortality, and whatever other powers she possessed, for himself. And it looked as if his suspicions were true. The bastard wanted to find a way to live forever without becoming a vampire, without being one of the Chosen, possessing the antigen. And maybe, Edge thought, he'd succeeded.

"In all the experiments, did Stiles ever find the girl's weakness? Did he ever find out what would kill her?''

She closed her eyes. "Not to my knowledge, no. If he had, she wouldn't have been alive to escape.''

It didn't matter, Edge thought. He would. He would find Amber Lily Bryant, and when he did, he would find her vulnerability. Her poison. Her kryptonite. Because whatever it was, it would be the weapon he needed to kill Frank Stiles.

And for more than four decades, his one goal in life had been to kill Frank Stiles.

No half-breed vampiress was going to stand in his way. Not even the so-called Child of Promise.

He dropped the burned out butt of his cigarette onto the carpet, ground it under his heel as he got to his feet. "You've been very helpful, Kelsey."

She closed her eyes, sitting very still. "And now you're going to kill me, aren't you?"

"Thanks, but I've already eaten." He smiled at his own joke, but she didn't seem to pick up on the humor. "You're no threat to me, Kelsey Quinlan. You've told me what I need to know, and I doubt you're stupid enough to try to warn Stiles, even if you knew where to find him, which you do not. I've been reading your thoughts all evening. So given all that, why do you think I would kill you now?"

"For my crimes against…your kind."

He shook his head as he strode toward the door. "I don't give a damn about my kind."

Amber pulled her low-slung black Ferarri into the driveway of her parents' palatial home—no matter where they lived, it was always palatial—at midnight. This one was a Georgian red-brick mansion in an isolated little inlet of Lake Ontario's Irondoquoit Bay. It had come complete with secret passages and hidden escape routes and was one of their more recent acquisitions. The house on Lake Michigan had had to be sold five years ago.

Secretly, Amber loved it here far more. Maybe because, for the first time, she'd begun declaring her independence.

"So what do you suppose this 'family meeting' is about?" Amber asked, glancing across the seat at Alicia. "Another reasoned attempt to get us to move back in with them?"

Alicia released her seat belt and opened her door. "So far they've kept their promise not to pressure us on that."

"Yeah, in exchange for us staying within a twenty-mile radius."

"After our little adventure in New York, Amber, we're lucky they didn't have us imprisoned in a convent somewhere."

"God, it's been five years already." Amber opened her door, and they both got out. She closed the door and hit the lock button on her key ring. "What do you suppose the statute of limitations is on something like that, anyway?"

"For normal families, or ours?" Alicia asked. She shrugged, running a hand along the smooth shiny black fender of the Ferarri. "Still, I don't suppose normal families buy such nice presents for their wayward daughters." She wiggled her brows. "Though I still think you should have gone with the little red 'vette. Then we could match."

"That would just be too cute, 'Leesh." Amber rolled her eyes, flung back her hair and walked side by side with her sister—and she didn't much care how official or unofficial it was, Alicia was her sister. It was an odd family, an odd, overprotective, obscenely wealthy family. The girls had two mothers, always had. One vampire, one mortal. And Amber's father watched over and protected all of them—even though he looked young enough to be their brother.

Which was why she hadn't told him about the dream that had been plaguing her for more than a year now. A dream that intrigued her—and terrified her, though she wasn't sure why. Her dreams tended to be precognizant, and everyone knew it. So there was no reason to trouble the entire tribe until she'd figured out what this one meant.

Just who the hell was the blond-haired vampire with the fiery eyes that made every part of her being turn molten when they locked with hers? And what was in the ornately carved box he handed to her that made her heart turn to ice with dread? She could never remember. Never. But there was a cold certainty in her mind that what the box contained…was death. She didn't understand what that meant. But she believed it. The tear in the vampire's eye as he handed her the box was too real to be denied. Death. Whoever he was, he would bring her death.

Amber closed her eyes and focused her mind on her mother, ordering herself to lock the dream away and keep it entirely to herself. *We're here, Mom.*

By the time the two were on the steps, Amber could hear the locks turning. The door was flung open, and Angelica, beautiful and forever young, was wrapping her arms around both of them. "Oh, I'm so glad you're here. You just don't know."

Amber hugged her mother hard, then stepped away. "Mom, we're here every weekend. How could you possibly miss us already?" And that was when she picked it up—the tense, sad vibe her mother couldn't have hoped to hide from her. Worry. Grief, even. She felt her blood rush to her feet and searched her mother's face. "God, what is it? Has something happened to Dad?"

"I'm fine, Amber," Jameson said. He stepped into the foyer with Susan at his side and held out his arms. Amber went to hug him, while Alicia hugged her mother, then they switched places and repeated the heartfelt, if obligatory, embraces.

Wringing her hands, Angelica hurried into the living room, with the others following. Amber kept looking at her father, asking him silently what was going on. He told her without a word to be patient and to brace herself for tragedy.

Amber was on the verge of tears even before she made it to the living room and settled into an overstuffed chair. Alicia, though unable to read minds with the accuracy of a vampire, was adept at reading faces and at feeling emotions. She, too, had picked up on the grief in the air. She sat in a rocking chair, reached out to clasp Amber's hand. Susan sat on the sofa, and Angelica sat beside her. Over the years, as Susan had aged like any normal woman, she'd taken on an almost motherly role with Angelica. She protected her, loved her, and kept one hand on her shoulder now.

Jameson remained standing, seeming to gather his words in his mind.

"Father, for God's sake, say something!" Amber exploded at last. "Has someone died? Are Eric and Tamara all right? God, is it Rhiannon? Or Roland? What's happened?"

Jameson licked his lips and shook his head. "No one has passed, Amber. But it's…it's Willem."

Amber blinked in shock. Five years ago, Willem Stone had saved her from the hands of a ruthless scientist who'd been treating her like his own personal guinea pig.

Since then, he and the vampiress he'd fallen in love with, Sarafina, had become a part of her odd little family. But unlike the rest of them, Willem was a mere mortal. Not one of the Chosen, not one who could be transformed. Just a mortal man. The most exceptional, incredible mortal man Amber had ever known.

Almost afraid to ask the question, she forced the words out. "What's happened to Willem?"

Alicia's hand squeezed hers tighter when Jameson said the single word.

"Cancer."

It was as if he were speaking a foreign language. She felt her brows bend into question marks. "What?"

"He has a brain tumor, Amber. It's inoperable. And it's…terminal."

"No." She searched her father's eyes, then her mother's and Susan's. "There has to be something we can do. There has to be something—"

"He's a mortal," Angelica whispered. "Mortals… die."

As she said it, Alicia and her mother exchanged a knowing look, one of sad acceptance, but it wasn't lost on Amber Lily. She wasn't used to dealing with death. She refused to accept it as the inevitable end to those she loved. Even the mortals.

"It can't happen. Not now, not yet," she said, as if saying the words emphatically enough could make them true. "God, Sarafina only just found him. How can he be taken from her like this? They should have had years together. Decades!"

"It's not fair," Alicia whispered. Then she licked her lips, shook her head. "But, it won't kill him. Will's the strongest man I know. He'll beat it. He will."

Amber nodded. "'Leesha's right. God, he withstood

torture in the desert, he was given medals for protecting all those men who would have died if he'd talked. He's a hero. He faced down Stiles, he even faced down Aunt Rhiannon and Sarafina and lived to tell the tale!''

"This is different, Amber," Susan said softly. "I know it's not fair, but it's the way life works. Death is— it's a natural part of the cycle for some of us, honey. It's just the way of things—part of being human."

Amber lifted her head, staring for a long time at Susan, noticing her gray hairs, extra weight, the wrinkles around her eyes. She looked at Alicia, who'd changed in the past five years in far more subtle ways. She'd lost the look of a teenager, looked like a woman now. While Amber hadn't changed at all. Not since that house in Byram, Connecticut. Not since Frank Stiles and his experiments.

She lowered her head. "Sarafina must be devastated."

"Rhiannon is with them right now at their place in Salem Harbor," Jameson said. "Eric's doing research at the lab at Wind Ridge, but..." He shook his head. "There's not a lot of time."

Amber's brows drew together. "How long?"

"Six months, at the outside."

Her eyes fell closed even as the words were spoken, and tears flooded them. God, six months. It was less than a heartbeat. She sniffed and knuckled away her tears. "I need to go to him. I need to see him—both of them. How is he? Have you spoken to him?"

"It was Rhiannon who phoned with the news," Angelica said softly. "She specifically asked for you to come."

Amber nodded. "And what about the rest of you?"

"We'll be coming later. First we're heading down to Eric's. Roland is already there. They need all the help they can get with the research," Jameson said.

"Besides," Angelica added, "we don't want to over-whelm 'Fina and Will. All of us descending on them at once might be a little too much."

"They'll want time alone, too." Amber swallowed her tears, though they nearly choked her. "Coming with me, Alicia?"

"One of us needs to stay and keep the shop open, hon. Pandora's Box can't run itself. But if you need me, call me, and I'll be there like lightning."

"Alicia, I'd feel better if you went along," Angelica began.

Amber interrupted her. "Mom, I'm twenty-three and perfectly capable of getting to Salem Harbor on my own."

Angelica thinned her lips.

"We both learned from our mistakes, Angelica," Alicia said softly. "We're not teenagers anymore. We own a business now. The Box is already turning a profit. We're responsible adult women. Both of us."

"I know that." Angelica shot a look at Jameson, and he gave her a silent nod.

Amber drew a breath and sighed in gratitude. Alicia was giving her time and space to do this on her own. Amber and Will—they'd formed an odd bond when he'd saved her life five years back. He was like the big brother she'd never had. She loved him madly, and maybe part of that was because he was an outsider, too. Part of this extended family of the undead, even though he wasn't one of them. Just like Susan and Alicia. Just like she was herself. Well, not *just* like, she thought slowly. She wasn't mortal, either. She didn't know exactly *what* she was.

Nodding hard, her mind made up, Amber said, "I'll pack up tonight. Leave early in the morning."

"Should I call the airlines for you, Amber?" Susan asked.

"No, I...I think I'll drive. It'll give me time to...process all this."

"Sounds like a good idea." Alicia got to her feet. "Are you guys all right?"

"We're dealing with it as best we can," Angelica said. "It's not easy on any of us. But Eric's refusing to give up hope, and maybe there's some chance he's right."

"But you don't really think so, do you?" Amber asked.

Her mother lowered her eyes, but Amber heard the hopelessness in her heart.

Alicia said, "Amber, let's get back. I'll help you pack, maybe even make you a few snacks for the road, huh?"

Smiling her thanks, Amber nodded. She got to her feet, let her father hug her hard. "When you go out there, Amber, forget your own pain. Think of easing theirs."

"I will."

"I know you will."

Edge was staked out in the shadows outside the kitschy little New Age-slash-magic shop in one of Rochester, New York's suburbs, a town called Irondequoit. The sign in the window read Pandora's Box, and included a stylized drawing of a treasure chest with its lid open and purple sparkles spiraling from within. The apartment where Amber Lily Bryant lived with her mortal roommate Alicia Jennings was on the second floor, and his research showed the two were joint owners of the shop, which they'd purchased from its former owners two years ago.

Why the Child of Promise was sharing an apartment and a business with a mortal, rather than living under the constant protection of a dozen vampiric bodyguards, he couldn't begin to guess. None of the vampires he'd questioned in order to track her down had offered a reason. The information he'd been able to glean had been piecemeal at best, but he'd been persistent, nosy, less than ethical, and he'd picked up the occasional unguarded thought. Taken together, the pieces had led him here...where she lived in an ordinary apartment with an ordinary mortal girl. She must be the most sought after prize of every vampire hunter in existence—and he had heard of many, besides the rogue DPI agent Frank Stiles. And yet she lived like a mortal. Unprotected.

If she had guardians, he thought, they ought to be taken out and beaten.

There had been no one at home when he'd first arrived, but the two woman returned around 2:30 a.m. in a car that made his mouth water even more than the red Corvette in the garage had done. A black Ferrari. Not that he would trade his '69 Mustang for anything in the world, but hell, a man could look.

They pulled into the driveway, but not into the two-car garage that was attached to the rear portion of the shop.

He took great pains to mask his presence from the Child of Promise, to shield his mind, his thoughts, his very existence, from her. He had no idea what powers she might possess, whether she had the ability to detect his presence or not, so he was taking precautions.

Not that she would have noticed him anyway, he realized once he took in her state. She got out of the car, took two unsteady steps toward the two-story building where she lived, and then stopped, braced one arm on the brick wall and lowered her head. Her hair was long, perfectly straight, and so dark he'd thought it black at first. But it wasn't. It was the darkest shade of auburn imaginable, deep shades of burgundy that gleamed in the glow of the streetlights. If pressed, he would describe her hair as black satin, rinsed in blood. It hung forward, so he couldn't see her face. But he could feel her—sense her, the way he could sense any other living creature. She didn't *feel* like a mortal, but not quite like a vampire, either. There was an electric energy about her, a static charge that made his skin prickle, his groin tighten and the fine hairs on his arms stand erect.

She made a sound, a sob that caught in her throat, and he realized she was crying.

Edge took an instinctive step closer, jerking into motion like a kneecap tapped by a doctor's mallet, before stopping himself. He dismissed the gut reaction, covering it with his more characteristic sarcasm. Just what he needed, he told himself. More blubbering females. What the hell was wrong with this one?

The other one was beside her a second later, and then the two hugged each other fiercely, both of them sobbing. The other girl was clearly the mortal one. She had short hair, as blond as his own. It would be curly if allowed to grow long, but in its present state it shot out in all directions in a stylized mess that looked good on her. She was attractive. She smelled faintly of magic. He thought she'd been doing more than stocking the shelves and managing the register in that shop of hers. She'd been studying, experimenting a bit, and keeping it to herself, he thought.

"I can't wait until morning, Alicia," Amber said, when she could control her sobbing enough to speak. "I need to leave sooner. As soon as I can get ready." She sniffled, wiping her eyes and stepping out of the other woman's arms. "I didn't see any sense in giving Mom a reason to object."

"And she would have. She's trying, Amber, but she can't help but be overprotective. Throw a few things in a bag, hon. I'll go online and get the directions while you pack."

Amber nodded, and the two went up the exterior stairs to the second floor apartment, arm in arm, locking the door behind them.

Not that a locked door had ever been a problem for Edge.

2

Edge couldn't take his eyes off the woman, and she was that, a woman, not a girl, and not a child—of promise or anything else. Twice, she stopped what she was doing, went very stiff and alert. She felt his presence, despite all his efforts to conceal it. She felt his eyes on her.

He leaned against the bricks on the little balcony outside her bedroom, watching her through the sheer black curtains as she packed clothing into a suitcase. Every now and then she would pause as grief swept over her. He could feel it. She wasn't shielding herself tonight—either because she thought there was no one around who could read her, or because she didn't care. He rather thought it was the latter. He wasn't certain what had happened to her tonight; he thought perhaps someone had died. It was that kind of grief. And yet, there was something else lying beneath it. Something she was struggling to ignore. A kind of stubborn denial. A streak of rebellion he recognized. A fighter looking for a fight.

It was buried under all that grief, but it was there. He would know it anywhere.

As she moved around her bedroom, adding items to her suitcase, he was finally able to see her face. She had these huge, deep, wide-set eyes, oval and thickly fringed. They were stunning, her eyes—such a dark shade of blue he'd thought at first they were ebony. The rest of her face was beautiful, pale and delicate and finely boned.

He'd never been overly fond of beautiful women. Wouldn't have given this one a second look—if he'd had any choice in the matter. But it didn't seem as if his mind or body were obeying his personal preferences here. She drew him on so many levels his head was spinning.

It must be one of her powers, he decided.

He turned away. But he had to watch her, had to figure out what she was doing, how he could best get her to tell him what he needed to know. So he looked back again, just in time to see her glancing out her bedroom door into the hall, before closing the door and locking it. She was trying to be quiet, acting…sneaky.

Frowning, he watched, riveted.

She climbed up onto a chair and, reaching above her head, pushed one of the ceiling panels upward. Now *this* was interesting. Reaching into the opening, she tugged out a large file box, one of those cardboard numbers for storing documents and file folders. Edge moved closer to the glass, riveted as she climbed down, set the box on her bed and removed the lid. Her lips pursed, she tugged something out of it: a black three-ring binder, with a white label on its spine.

Squinting until his eyes watered, Edge focused on that spine and eventually managed to read the words on its label.

X-1: Volume A.

"X-1," he whispered. It was Stiles's name for her. Then those binders—the box was full of them—had to be his notes. "I'll be damned," he muttered. "She's got everything he learned about her—all of it, right there."

And maybe the answers Edge needed. The key to Stiles's vulnerability.

She skimmed pages for a while, and Edge slipped inside her mind, trying to listen in. Her parents thought these notebooks were still locked in the safe at their home, he heard her thinking. She felt a little guilty about that. Someone called Eric had made copies of everything and taken them to his lab, while the originals had been secured in the house at Irondequoit Bay. Only they weren't. They were here, hidden in her bedroom. He couldn't get deep enough to read through her eyes, to see what she was seeing—but he felt her frustration before she slammed the book closed.

Whatever she was looking for, she wasn't finding it.

She dragged another suitcase from underneath her bed, slung it onto the mattress and opened it. Then she piled the notebooks into it, lining them up carefully, side by side, then adding a second layer, narrow front to wider spine. Finally she laid a few articles of clothing over the top and then zipped the bag. She put the empty cardboard box under her bed, double-checked the ceiling panel to be sure it was in place, and then unlocked and opened her bedroom door.

"I'm about ready," she called, snagging the two suitcases from the bed and heading into the hallway.

Edge left his post then, jumping to the ground, and creeping around to the front of the apartment again, where she'd left her car. The trunk popped open before she even exited the house. Remote control, he guessed. Then she was hurrying from the apartment, with her friend on her heels. She slung the cases easily into the trunk and slammed it, then went to the driver's door.

The blonde handed her a sheaf of papers and a grocery bag. "Here are your directions. And a few snacks for the road."

Amber Lily—God, the name was ill suited to her, Edge thought. She was more vibrant than amber and far tougher than any fragile lily. At any rate, she took the bag and peered inside. Then the other one took it back from her, opened the passenger door and set it on the seat. She laid the sheets of paper on the dashboard and turned to Amber again. "I love you, you know."

"I know. And I know why you're not going with me."

"Do you?"

Amber nodded. "I do. And I'm grateful. You're right, Alicia. I need to go alone."

"I'll come later. Give you a few days to be alone with Will."

Who the hell was Will? Edge wondered. And he wondered it with a passion that surprised him.

"I don't know how alone I'll be. Aunt Rhi's there. And don't forget 'Fina. I'll be lucky if she lets him out of her sight."

"She's not going to handle this well."

"I can't imagine her handling it at all," Amber said. She lowered her head. "God, they're so in love. I just don't know how she'll go on if he dies."

"I'm afraid…she might decide not to try," Alicia said softly.

Amber stared into her friend's eyes. "Let this be a lesson to us both. A girl can't afford to fall so deeply in love that she can't live without a guy. It's too risky." She shook her head. "God, when I see how desperately my parents need each other it scares the hell out of me. If one of them should lose the other…"

"I know. I know. But that's not going to happen."

"It could. But not to me. Never to me."

"You wouldn't know it to see how you're reacting to this news about Will."

Amber lowered her eyes, sighed. "It's different with Will, and you know it." She sighed softly. "Will saved my life. I just can't help thinking there might be some way I can…return the favor.''

"Oh, Amber, don't," Alicia said softly. "Don't get your hopes up. You may be Superchick, but you're not a goddess. You don't have the power to cure cancer."

"I know that," she said.

But Edge got the feeling she didn't really mean it. He felt that stubborn determination, that fight, kicking its heels up somewhere inside her again. She tamped it down and wrapped the other woman, Alicia, in her arms. "But if there were anything I could do, I would. I owe him my life, you know. If I could give it to him, I'd do it in a minute."

"He wouldn't take it if you offered." Alicia kissed Amber's cheek, then brushed her fingers over it, maybe to wipe away a tear. "Go, and be careful."

"I will."

Amber got into the car, put in the key. Alicia pulled something from a pocket and handed it through the window to her.

"A CD?"

"My favorite traveling mix. Stroke-9. Matchbox-20." She frowned. "Ever notice all our favorite bands have numbers in their names?"

"Sum-41 on there?"

"Actually, they are." The two of them laughed. Amber took the CD from its case and slid it into the player. Music, smooth and mellow, wafted from the car. Amber put the car in gear, pulled it slowly away from the curb.

Alicia stood there for a long time, watching her, waving.

Edge tore himself away from the emotional goodbye long enough to dash into the apartment—the two women had left the door unlocked, and the one who might sense him there was gone. He moved through the apartment far too fast for human eyes to detect him and found the computer easily—it was in Alicia's bedroom, and its screen still showed the driving directions the girl had printed out for her friend. He read the screen quickly. She was heading to some place called Harbor Rock, in Salem Harbor, just outside Salem, Massachusetts. He memorized the route, all of ten hours by car. He was slightly surprised that it tended to avoid the Thruway, which would have been faster. Then he ducked into Amber's bedroom when he heard Alicia coming back inside. He exited through the same window he'd been looking through moments ago, closed it behind him, and then headed away from the apartment, into the darkness.

A few blocks away, he found his Mustang. It had been glossy and black in its youth. Now it was dull and faded, and he owed the little car a paint job in return for its years of loyal service. It would do until he got where he needed to be, though. He planned to be riding in a fancy little Ferrari within a few hours.

Amber Lily was as soft hearted as they came—she'd revealed as much. Going by the neighborhood and what he'd seen of the apartment, not to mention the car, he would say she was fairly well spoiled, too, used to being pampered. Softhearted and sheltered.

This would be like taking candy from a baby. He would just have to be careful—because despite appearances, she was no baby.

Amber had been driving for two hours, and it was after 5:00 a.m. when she hit something. She felt the impact, the thud, saw the form bouncing off the hood of her car. A person! God, she'd never seen him! Her stomach lurched as her foot jammed the brake pedal to the floor.

Tires squealed, and the stench of hot rubber assailed her. "God almighty, where did he come from?"

She wrenched her door open and lunged from the car, only to be jerked back by the force of the seat belt. Fumbling, impatient and clumsy, she got it unbuckled and scrambled out of the car, racing to where the man lay very still on the pavement.

"God, are you all right? I'm sorry, I'm so sorry. I just didn't see you." He was lying facedown. She knelt beside him and touched his shoulder. "Please," she whispered. "Please be all right."

He moaned, and Amber opened her senses, probing his mind for pain, for injuries. But what she found there shocked her so much that she jerked her hand away from him, shot to her feet and backed rapidly toward her car. "You're a vampire!"

Slowly he brought his hands upward, pushed his upper body off the pavement, and lifted his head. "That doesn't mean I'm not hurting like hell right now."

He turned over, the better to look at her, and she sucked in a breath so fast she hurt her lungs. My God, it was *him!* The vampire from her dreams!

She stopped backing up, but she didn't move any closer, either. She watched him like a hawk as he got himself upright, brushed the dirt from the front of his leather jacket and jeans. He wiped the blood from his scraped cheek, then stared at a smear of it on his thumb.

"How do you know what I am?" he asked, as if he'd just thought of it. Then he widened his eyes a little, lowered his hand. "Was it an accident at all, you hitting me? Or are you one of those vamp hunters I keep hearing about?"

She relaxed a little. If he was afraid of her, she probably had no reason to be afraid of him. Other than the dream, at least. The one where she felt certain he was bringing her a gift—death in a pretty box. Whatever the hell that meant. "I'm no vampire hunter."

He frowned at her, took a step closer. She didn't back away, so he took another. He was limping a little. He had the posture of a wolf sniffing the air, but he wasn't sniffing. He was feeling. Sensing. "You're one of the Chosen—and yet, not exactly. You're not mortal. But you're not one of us, either."

She pursed her lips, lowered her head. "Look, it doesn't matter what I am. I'm no threat to you."

"Not unless you're behind the wheel, at least." He tempered the words with a smile, and when he smiled, a dimple cut into his cheek. He held her gaze, and her heart turned a somersault.

My God, she thought. Looking into his eyes had the same impact on her as it did in the dream. It was like electrocution. It made her heart race and her stomach feel tight. It heated her blood and tingled her skin. Who was he?

He closed the remaining distance between them, still limping, and extended a hand. "They call me Edge."

She took his hand. It was large and very strong. She liked the slight pressure it exerted around hers, and the way her blood warmed and pooled somewhere in her center at his touch. "Edge, huh? That a nickname?"

"What, you don't like it?" He pressed his free hand to his heart, keeping his other one around hers a second longer. "I suppose yours is better?"

He was asking her name. "Amber Bryant."

He blinked and drew his brows together. "Not Amber *Lily* Bryant?"

With a sigh, she nodded. It was tiring, being something

of a legend, at least among the undead. "Guilty, I'm afraid."

"Well, that explains the mixed vibes you send out. You're the Child of Promise." Shrugging he said, "But I'm afraid it doesn't suit you at all."

"What? My name?"

He nodded. "No more than mine did, originally. It sounds like something fragile and delicate. A hothouse flower afraid to go outside. You don't look like a hothouse flower to me. Exotic, yes. But wild. Tough."

"So you're saying I need a nickname?"

He nodded. "Amber Lily." He *snapped* his fingers. "Al."

"Al? That's exotic and wild?"

"No, but it's tough. How about Alby?" He smiled. "Yeah. Alby."

She lifted her brows. "I could get used to it." In truth, it made her skin tingle when he rolled it off his lips.

He finally released her hand and ran his own over his side, wincing a little as he did.

"I'm sorry about hitting you. Are you hurt badly?"

"A broken rib, I think. Nothing major. It'll heal with the day sleep. Guess I just won't make as many miles as I'd hoped tonight."

"You're…traveling on foot?"

"Only since the car died a few miles back."

She licked her lips. How many times had her parents warned her not to trust strange vampires? But so far, every vamp she'd ever met had been decent—especially to her, their legendary Child of Promise. "Where are you heading?" she heard herself ask.

"Salem. You?"

She blinked. If Alicia were here, she would say it was a sign. No such thing as coincidence, she would insist.

Synchronicity didn't happen by chance. She'd been doing too much reading about magic and Wicca lately, Amber had decided. Still, there was some part of her that agreed with her friend's logic.

"Salem," she said softly. "That's a long walk, even for a vampire."

"Too far to sustain any sort of speed," he said, nodding.

"You, um…want to ride with me?"

"Are you kidding? I'd pay to ride with you." He licked his lips, lowered his head. "If I wasn't broke, I mean."

"It's okay. I don't need money."

"Kind of guessed that from the car you're driving." He looked past her at the car. "You must be rolling in it."

"My parents are. It was a gift from my father."

He smiled at her. "Spoiled, then, are you?"

She smiled back at him. "Rotten."

"Must be nice."

"You wanna drive it?"

He sent her an astonished look. "Really?"

"It's the least I can do after running you over." She tossed him the keys, and he caught them. He seemed to forget about his limp as he walked to the driver's door and got in. She got in the passenger side, fastened her seat belt. He ignored his own.

"You're actually…*nice,* aren't you, Alby?"

"I try to be. Why, aren't you?"

"No," he said, shifting the car into gear, straightening it out and then stomping the accelerator. "No, I don't think anyone who knows me would call me nice."

He shifted, pressed the gas pedal down until the engine roared, shifted again. The car flew through the night in the way she guessed it was designed to do. She'd never driven it that way in her life. The car came to life under his expert touch, seemed almost to sit up and purr in response to being driven so hard.

She was a little bit jealous.

Reaching forward, she hit the play button on her CD and was surprised as hell when Edge began singing along.

He drove like an expert, faster than she would have done herself, but so professionally that it didn't make her nervous at all. He exuded confidence. And danger.

And yet she wasn't afraid of him, even though she probably should have been. Especially given the dream. But that was kind of the point of letting him ride along, wasn't it? To find out what the hell that dream meant, what it was that tied this man to her psyche and her subconscious.

After the song ended, Edge reached out to turn the CD player off and glanced her way. "So why is it you're heading for Salem? Vacation?"

"I wish. No, a friend of mine is sick."

"A mortal friend, then?"

She nodded. "Yes. A very good one."

He frowned a little, looking her way often, as if he enjoyed it. "It's unusual, a vampire having good friends who are mortals."

"I'm not a vampire," she told him. "And most people would describe me as somewhat unusual." She tilted her head, studying him in profile. He had the bone structure of a work of art, she thought. Broad, angular jawline and cheekbones to die for.

"What?" he asked, looking at her. "I have someone in my teeth?"

She smiled at the joke. "So you don't have any mortal

friends?'' she asked, just to change the subject from her reasons for staring at him.

''Mortal or otherwise.''

She blinked. ''You don't have friends at all, is that what you mean?''

''That's what I mean.''

''Don't you get…lonely?''

''Depends on how you define loneliness, love. Do I get to wishing I had a group of well-meaning busybodies prying into my shadows and meddling in my life? Not on your life. Do I wish I had a pile of others depending on me to take care of them? No way in hell. Been there, done that. It's far too much responsibility for any sane person to take on. I'm not up to the task, anyway. Do I sometimes crave a body besides my own in my bed? You bet I do. But that's easily remedied. And friendship doesn't have to enter into it.''

She didn't imagine he'd ever had too much trouble finding willing women to share his bed. The man was hot. And just enough of a bad boy to whet any female's appetite.

''Do you ever…just wish for someone to talk to? Someone who gave a damn what you had to say?''

He tilted his head. ''Is that the kind of friends you have? The kind who listen and give a damn what you have to say?''

She smiled. ''Sure. But they're also the kind who pry into my shadows and meddle in my life. I think it's tough to get the one without the other.''

''I think you're right there.'' He sighed. ''You have lots of them? Friends, I mean.''

''Mmm. Friends, family. Guardians and protectors. Mostly vampires, but some mortals, too.'' She looked at him and suddenly smiled. "Hell, I have so many I can afford to share them with you."

"Whoa, no thank you. I don't need them." He studied her face for a moment before turning his gaze back to the road. "Doesn't look as if it's been doing you much good. Not lately, at least."

"What do you mean?"

"You've been crying tonight."

She ought to be used to the sharp observations of vampires, she supposed. The talent shouldn't surprise her. And yet he had taken her off guard.

"The sick friend?" he asked.

She nodded.

"What's wrong with him, exactly?"

Blinking, she frowned at him. "How do you know it's a him?" She'd erected a shield around her thoughts from the instant she'd realized he was a vampire and able to read them. So he couldn't be picking things up from her mind.

"Rarely see a pretty woman crying over a girl. This fellow in Salem—your lover?"

She smiled broadly. "No. More like a beloved older brother. He saved my life once."

"Did he really? An ordinary mortal?"

"Will is probably the farthest thing from ordinary you'll ever come across. He was a colonel in the Army. Special Forces. Captured in the desert, tortured until he escaped, and he never told them a thing."

He lifted his brows, turning slowly to face her as she spoke. "Are you *sure* you're not in love with him?"

"I'm sure."

"Not even sleeping with him?"

"Never."

"Never?"

"I meant I would never sleep with Willem."

"Oh." He grinned at her. "I thought you meant you were a virgin."

She turned her head toward the window. "You're getting a little personal for someone I only met an hour ago, Edge."

"You let me drive your car. I figure that puts us on intimate terms."

"You figure wrong."

"So are you, then?"

She frowned at him.

"A virgin?"

"Why do you care?"

"Curious, is all."

"Well, I'm not going to satisfy that curiosity. So stop asking."

"Mysterious, aren't you? I like that." He reached across the seat, trailed a forefinger down her cheek, making her shiver. "I like a lot of things about you, Alby."

She lowered her eyes, tried not to let her face turn red or her heart start racing, because he would hear it. But God, his touch sent a thrill through her, right to her bones.

"You never answered my question."

She swung her eyes to him, shocked he was still asking.

"About your friend, I meant. Will. What's wrong with him?"

"Oh." She let her anger fade. "Cancer."

"Terminal?"

She shrugged. "That's what they're saying. But I'm not ready to give up on him just yet."

"Really?"

She nodded.

"I don't suppose...no, never mind."

"No, go on. What were you going to say?"

He slanted his eyes toward her. When he looked at her, she could feel them touching her, and this time they slid from her face down to her neck, over her chest and hips and legs, all the way to the floor. "It's just, well, you must have different—powers, for want of a better word—than the rest of us. Is healing fatal diseases one of them?"

"I don't think so."

He frowned at her, and she knew what he was asking. "I don't know everything about myself, Edge. It's not like there's ever been anyone like me before, anyone I could ask."

"Surely you've tested them. Are you immortal?"

"I think so."

"But you age like a mortal?"

"Used to."

"Used to?"

She pursed her lips and said nothing.

He slid a hand over hers, where it rested on her leg. "Poor lamb, you're rather lost, aren't you? In spite of all your friends and their meddling?"

"I'm perfectly fine."

"No, you're not. You don't even know who you are. Or who you want to be."

She met his eyes. He held her gaze, smiled gently, and looked like a fallen angel. "Stick with me for a while, Alby. I'll help you find yourself."

She frowned, amazed at how her body responded to the touch of his hand, surprised that she let him turn her hand in his own, lace his fingers with hers. He had to draw his attention to the road again, but he kept on holding her hand.

"How?" she asked. "You don't even know me."

"I'd like to, though. I'd like to explore every part of you, inside and out. And while I'm at it, you might as well do the same. Who knows what discoveries you might make?"

When he looked at her again, his eyes made it clear that she had not misunderstood him. He'd meant for his words to sound as sexual as they had. To rub over her senses like velvet over satin. Like his finger over the very center of her palm.

"It'll be daylight soon," he told her. "We should find a place—a dark, private place, where the sun can't touch me."

She had never been so turned on in her life, she thought wildly. "I know just the place. Pull over, right up here."

With a smug half smile, he pulled the car off onto the shoulder of the road. Amber reached to the dashboard and hit the trunk release button, then got out while he was frowning at her. She went to the rear of the car, looked into the open trunk and waited for him to join her there.

He glanced at her, then at the trunk. "Not very romantic, love. And not a lot of room for...movement."

"Then I suggest you lie still."

She'd moved around behind him while he spoke, and as she delivered her reply, she pressed both hands to his back and shoved hard.

He flipped right into the trunk, taken off guard by the sudden attack, and even as he rolled onto his back with a shocked expression on his face, she looked at the lid, flicked her eyes downward. It slammed closed.

He swore, a stream of profanity issuing from beyond the trunk.

"You deserved worse. You ever hear of manners, Edge? You were way out of line."

"You were loving every minute of it." He hit the trunk, a halfhearted punch that didn't even dent it. "Open it up or I'll kick your pretty car full of holes."

"You do that, you'll be walking the rest of the way to Salem. It's twenty minutes to sunrise. Just be still and go to sleep. When you wake, we'll be in Salem."

"Spoiled, evil little…"

"Watch it, Edge, or you'll wake to find yourself dumped on the roadside in a nice sunny spot around noon."

He was still muttering under his breath when she walked to the driver's door and got behind the wheel.

3

As soon as the sun was fully up, Amber found a place to pull off and took a much needed nap. She supposed her exhaustion was more emotional than physical. The shock of learning about Will's condition, the grief. And then to literally run into the man she'd been dreaming about for a year... She was overwhelmed. She told herself she only needed a nap; an hour would be plenty.

The dream came again.

She lay in a bed, and Edge came slowly toward her. He held a box in his hands, and his eyes were locked with hers. Her stomach was roiling in the dream, her heart bursting with a mingling of emotions too powerful to bear. Passionate feelings that all revolved around the man—and whatever was in the box he held. She couldn't look away from his face, or from the tear that welled in his eye and spilled over to roll slowly down his beautiful cheek. He knelt, lowering the box so that she could look inside.

Don't look! her mind screamed. *It's death he brings you! It's death!*

Amber woke suddenly, sitting up so fast she banged her elbow on the car door. Slowly she shook herself free of the paralyzing fear the dream had left in its wake. God, what did it mean? Was she making a huge mistake by having anything to do with him?

Sighing, wondering if she would have the willpower

to send him packing even if she decided it was the best thing to do, she looked at her watch, then blinked and looked again. It was after 11:00 a.m. She'd slept for more than five hours.

Hell.

She started the car and pulled it into motion again. After two hours, she stopped for a veggie sub and a bathroom break, freshening up in the rest room and wishing for a shower. Then she drove straight through. Still, the sun was sinking behind her when she finally pulled onto the winding country road that led from Salem to Salem Harbor and followed its meandering path to the house on Harbor Rock. Sarafina and Will had bought the place five years ago, and Amber had been there several times but still hadn't managed to memorize the driving directions. She supposed that meant a photographic memory was not among her special abilities. Cross one more off the list of things to wonder about, she thought.

The house was modern, a giant log structure at the tip of a peninsula surrounded by boulders and sea foam. Its windows were large and looked out on the sea. No one would ever suspect a vampire lived there with her mortal lover. Her all too mortal lover.

Amber pulled the car to a stop, shut off the engine and sat there for a long moment, staring at the rich wood tones of the house, trying to get a handle on her emotions. Her mother was right; she shouldn't show up grieving. Will was alive. Surrounding him in tears wasn't going to help him, and it would do nothing for Sarafina, either. She closed her eyes, called up the toughest part of herself, focused on control.

A loud thump from the back of the car jolted her right out of her meditation. "It's night again, and yet I find myself still locked in a suffocating trunk."

She lowered her head, shook it slowly.

"Alby, are you out there?" *Thump, thump.*

Pursing her lips, she reached out and hit the trunk release. It flew open, and she felt the car move as Edge climbed out. Amber opened her door and got out, turned and found herself face-to-face with him, nose to chin.

"That wasn't very nice, you know."

She smiled. "I was trying to make a point."

"I got the point," he said.

"Did you?"

He nodded. "Yeah. You're one of those girls who's into making men beg."

Her jaw dropped. "You're deluded."

"*I'm* deluded? Come on, Alby, you're as into me as I am into you. Admit it."

She pursed her lips and searched for patience. "You're attractive enough, I suppose. That's not what I would call being 'into' you, though. I don't even know you."

He leaned closer, his eyes fixed on her lips. "You're saying this magnetism between us is purely physical, then?"

She blinked. "You're putting words into my mouth."

He looked at her mouth. "I'd like to—"

"Don't even."

He smiled at her, that dimple digging into his cheek and making her go soft and tingly all over. "All right, I'm coming on like a rutting buck, I suppose. I'm not used to dealing with sheltered virgins, is the thing."

"I never said I was—"

He held up a hand to stop her speaking, then glanced at the house. "So this is where your friends live?"

She nodded.

"I should take off." He turned to walk away.

"I'm sure they wouldn't mind…my bringing a guest."

He went still, his back to her. "Don't worry, Alby. I'm not walking away for good. I'll come around again, once I get settled in."

"You're so full of yourself, you know that?"

"Yeah. You play your cards right, you might get to be full of me, too." She aimed a foot at his backside, but he felt it coming and dodged it, then turned to face her. "Violent little thing, aren't you?"

"You seem to bring it out in me."

He let his heated gaze move down her body. "You knocked me into that trunk like a vampire. Just how strong are you?"

"Stronger than you think."

"Stronger than me?"

She shrugged. "I don't know. Why?"

"Just wondering if you're going to kick my ass for kissing you."

"But you didn't—"

She gasped as he snapped an arm around her waist, tugged her hard against him and, cradling the back of her head with his other hand, captured her mouth with his. He kissed her with his mouth open, moving it over her lips and drawing on them. And just when she let her body relax against his, let her jaw relax so her mouth fell open, just as she wished he would use his tongue and keep on kissing her for a long, long time, he released her and lifted his head away. He sent her a wink, then turned and walked back along the driveway toward the road.

He didn't look back. She stood there watching him out of sight, the sea wind blowing cool and damp over her heated skin.

"*What*," Rhiannon asked, "was that?"

Sighing, turning to face her unofficial aunt, Amber said, "That was Edge." She slid a look at Rhiannon.

She stood there, her long, jet-black hair dancing in the sea wind, arms crossed over her chest, stern faced. "What kind of a name is 'Edge'?"

"A fitting one, I think. Where's Pandora? I don't see her."

Her attempt at changing the subject was a lame one, and she knew it. Her aunt's pet panther was nowhere in sight, and would have been had she been with Rhiannon.

"She's getting old. Long trips do her very little good these days. She stayed behind at Wind Ridge, with Eric, Tam and Roland. And she thanks you for naming your little shop in her honor. Now, if we could get back to the subject at hand?"

"Will?"

"Edge," she said flatly. "Just what is going on between you and this character, Amber Lily?"

"It's too soon to tell, Rhiannon. But he'd better not turn up dead before I have a chance to decide."

Rhiannon smiled then, picking up on Amber's teasing tone. "Then you'd better decide soon. Having kissed my niece right under my nose, he might not have much time." She opened her arms, and Amber went to her, hugged her gently. "How are you, darling? I've missed you. It's been months."

"I thought I was fine, until I heard the news about Will."

Rhiannon thinned her lips. "He's out right now. Yet another appointment with yet another doctor."

"And 'Fina?"

"Said she needed a few moments alone, so I drew her a steaming, scented bath and told her I was going for a walk along the beach. I knew you were close, and I wanted a chance to speak to you alone before you saw her."

"How's she doing with all this?"

"Amazingly well," Rhiannon said. "Too well. It worries me."

Amber licked her lips, lowered her eyes.

Rhiannon drew a breath, clasped Amber's arm. "There's no need to shield your thoughts from me, Amber, I've been consumed with the same notion."

"I don't know what you mean."

"You know exactly what I mean."

Amber pursed her lips, lowered her head.

"Did you bring the notebooks?"

Frowning, Amber brought her head up fast. "What notebooks?"

"Oh, please, child, we have no time for this. Stiles's notebooks. The ones your parents think are locked up in their safe. You took them, of course."

"How do you know that?"

"It's what I would have done," Rhiannon said.

Amber sighed. Dammit, her aunt knew her far too well. "Yes, I took them, but that doesn't mean we'll find any answers in their pages. God knows I've looked, but so far—"

A blood chilling shriek cut the night, and stopped Amber in midsentence. Even as the two women tore free of the shock and raced toward the house, there was a crash and a howl. "Gods. 'Fina," Rhiannon whispered, pouring on more speed, until she simply vanished in a blur of black.

Amber ran at a closer to mortal pace. She hadn't been there in some time, and she didn't want to collide with anything on the way.

When she arrived in the house, she hurried up the stairs and into a bathroom, the door of which stood wide. Sarafina stood in the room's center, dripping wet, naked except for the white towel she held to her chest. The glass topped vanity was shattered; makeup and hair products lay everywhere.

"'Fina, honey? What happened?"

Rhiannon, who'd already sized up the situation and vanished from the room, appeared beside Amber, a thick terry bathrobe in her arms. "Let's get her out of here before she cuts herself to ribbons," she said, and she moved to Sarafina, her feet crushing glass on the way. "Stay still, 'Fina. Don't move."

Sarafina was shaking, staring but not seeing either of them. As Rhiannon tried to slip the plush robe onto one arm, 'Fina jerked away with a strangled cry, then sank to her knees amid the broken glass, tipping her head back and moaning like a wounded animal.

"By the Gods," Rhiannon whispered.

Tears sprang to Amber's eyes, and her throat closed tight, but she swallowed the urge to break down and cry, and instead joined Rhiannon. They crouched on either side of Sarafina, each of them pulling one of the woman's arms around her shoulder, sliding their free arms beneath her thighs. The towel fell away as they lifted her straight up, doing their best to avoid the glass, and carried her out of the bathroom while she dissolved in uncontrollable tears and racking sobs. They lowered her onto a large canopy bed swathed in sheer black curtains. Amber glimpsed blood but wasn't sure of its source.

"See to her. I'll take care of the mess," Rhiannon said. She retrieved the robe, which had fallen to the floor halfway between the bathroom and the bed, and tossed it to Amber. Then she returned to the bathroom.

Amber slid onto the bed beside the woman, sliding the soft robe easily onto her. Sarafina didn't fight. She wept, her entire body jerking as the flood of emotion battered her like a storm.

"It's all right, 'Fina. It's going to be all right." She pulled the robe together in front, letting the bottom half drape over Sarafina's long legs, loosely tying the sash, then leaning close to brush black curls from tear-wet cheeks. "It's okay to cry," she whispered. "You're not made of stone." She blinked back her own tears, but fighting them was nearly impossible.

'Fina's face pulled into a painfully twisted mask. "H-h-he can't...I can't do this. I can't—"

"I know. I know." Amber embraced her quaking shoulders, pulled her gently close and found it surreal to be comforting one of the two toughest, strongest women she had ever known. The other one was in the bathroom, and if Amber's senses were on target, she was weeping, as well.

"It's too cruel," Sarafina whispered. "It's too cruel. How can he be taken from me? How?"

"I don't know."

Sarafina shivered, pulling free of Amber's arms to lie down, curled on one side in the fetal position, her back to Amber. "I knew I should never have let myself love him."

"You know you don't mean that." Amber closed her eyes and told herself this was exactly why she would never lose herself to a man this way. Never.

"Everyone I love leaves me. My mother died giving me birth. My sister hated me for that, all my life. My first love, Andre, plotted against me and turned the entire clan against me. Bartrone, my sire, walked into the sunlight one dawn." Her shoulders stilled from their trembling. "For the first time, I understand what drove him to that."

"Don't talk that way, 'Fina. You have to be strong."

"I'm tired of being strong. I'm so…so very tired." She sniffed. "If Willem must die—"

"Willem isn't dead yet, woman." It was Rhiannon's voice, stern and harsh. She'd apparently finished with her work and now stood in the bedroom. "If it is his fate to go, then you'll have time enough for hysterics when it's over. In the meantime, don't be so quick to give up on him."

Sarafina rolled onto her back, glaring at Rhiannon. "The doctors say there's no hope."

"Mortal doctors. Humans. Fools. What do they know about us? About our kind? We can do things they've never dreamed, Sarafina. We're gods compared to them."

"Will's not a god. He's not one of us. He's just a man."

"He's far from that, and you know it." Rhiannon came closer, pulling something from the deep pocket of her silk skirt, a glass vial with a cork in the top. "Drink this."

"What is it?"

Rhiannon pulled the cork free. "A modified version of that delightful tranquilizer DPI invented to use on us. Eric's been toying with it. It has many uses for our kind. Helps with pain. It'll make you sleep."

"I don't want to sleep. I want to be with Willem when he gets back."

"He'll be hours yet. You'll be awake by then, I promise."

Rhiannon pushed the vial to Sarafina's lips, and she swallowed the contents and made a face. She licked her lips and met Amber's eyes. "It's good to see you."

"It's good to be here."

"I'm sorry about—all of that."

"Don't be. I'd have torn the house apart in your place by now."

She blinked slowly. "It's not as if I didn't know the risks. Risk—that's not even right. When an immortal falls in love with a mortal, the outcome is certain." She looked at Rhiannon. "It's not as if I wasn't warned."

"It's not over yet, Sarafina," Rhiannon said. "Sleep now. Give me time to do what I do best."

'Fina lifted her brows. "What's that? Terrorize people?"

"Play goddess, of course." She slid a look at Amber, and Amber knew exactly what she was thinking.

The two of them stayed there until Sarafina slid into a deep, still slumber. Then Rhiannon touched Amber's shoulder, tipped her head toward the door and led the way back down the stairs.

Edge sat outside the house, in the darkness, keeping his presence to himself. He'd heard the scream right after he'd left Alby's side, heard the crashing, breaking glass, and he'd immediately thrown his senses wide-open, even as he raced back to the house on the seashore.

He didn't go inside. He didn't need to. He could see what was going on just as easily from outside, just by probing and prying. It was bad form among his kind to eavesdrop this way, but he didn't really give a damn about the protocol and etiquette of being undead. Never had. Normally this kind of snooping wouldn't go undetected, but the women inside were far too distracted to pay him any mind.

The woman they called 'Fina was grieving over a dying mortal. Willem. She was his lover, Edge deduced.

He felt her pain and had to shut it out because it was too intense to bear. Nearly paralyzing.

He wasn't sure whether the Child of Promise and her "aunt" Rhiannon were aware of it or not, but it was clear to him the Gypsy Sarafina would not go on once Willem was dead. It was coming through his senses as clearly as the images of her dancing around a fire amid a village of painted wagons and reading palms in exchange for silver in some long-ago time.

It was, of course, nothing to him. He had a feeling she'd known once what he knew now. How foolish it was to care for anyone other than herself. How utterly stupid and self-destructive it was to put anything or anyone above your own well-being.

Stupid. She'd known it once. She'd put it aside. And now she was paying the price. She would die. There was no question. Within a few days—maybe hours—of her mortal lover's death, she would be gone.

He felt a little twist in his gut when he thought how much that was going to hurt Alby. Then he reminded himself that it was nothing to him. *She* was nothing to him.

He focused again. The one called Rhiannon—with her he got a feeling of age and extreme power, and he saw flashes of desert sands and pyramids, Egyptian temples and pharoahs—had drawn Alby into a lower level room, and the two were sitting now. He opened his senses, witnessed it all in his mind.

Rhiannon, seated in a thronelike chair, looked at Alby and said, "We are not going to let this happen."

"I'm not sure there's anything we can do to stop it."

"Nonsense. There's one thing. And you know it as well as I do."

"Rhiannon, I don't know—"

Rhiannon flung up a hand, and Amber fell silent. "You saw it. I saw it. Five years ago, Willem flung Frank Stiles from a cliff to the rocks below. The man should have been dead. But he wasn't. He took a boat and he rowed away."

"We can't be sure that was him," Amber said softly, even though she knew that it was. Edge felt the knowledge in her mind, and knew Rhiannon did, as well. "The man in the boat was too far away to see clearly, even for us. Stiles's body could have been swept out to sea."

"But it wasn't. It revived, he survived, and he lives still."

"Maybe…"

"An ordinary mortal, Amber. Not even one of the chosen. The rumors, the whispers, they're true. He made a serum from your blood, and he made himself indestructible. If it could be done once, it can be done again."

The pretty one lowered her head. "We don't know how he did it. There's no formula in his notes. He told no one, not even his most trusted assistants, what he was doing. No one knows how he accomplished it—*if* he accomplished it—other than the man himself."

Rhiannon seemed to consider that for a long moment. Then she said, "If you had the formula, would you let yourself be used in such a way?"

"I'd give anything to save Willem. How is this any different from offering a kidney or a bone marrow transplant? Of course I'd do it."

Edge was stunned. Why would anyone be so willing to do so much for someone else? It made no sense to him. A small voice inside whispered that he would have done the same once, a long, long time ago. For his fledglings. For little Bridget. But God, he'd learned how foolish it was to care that deeply. All the caring in the world couldn't prevent death when it came.

Rhiannon slid a hand over one of Amber's. "Eric wants me to send all of Stiles's journals down to him, along with a pint of your blood. He's working tirelessly to unlock the formula."

Amber nodded. "But he has copies of everything."

"I know. I think he believes there may be something he's missed, something a copy machine might not have picked up. A special ink, or perhaps some notes in the linings of the books. I don't know."

"Then we'll send them. The blood, as well. But... what if he can't do it in time?"

Rhiannon nodded. "I'm working on that. I'm going to find Stiles. And believe me—when I do, he will tell me his secrets."

A little shiver rippled through Amber—Edge felt its echo in him. He also felt a rush of excitement. If Stiles's immortality was the result of a serum made from the young woman's blood, then the key to his weakness lay within her, as well. Everything the nurse had told him was true. He had to learn the girl's secrets, even the ones she didn't yet know herself. He had to learn what could kill her.

And he had to be around when they located Stiles.

So he could kill the man.

He didn't think the imposing Rhiannon would be willing to take him along on her hunt for the man. But that didn't matter. Rhiannon wasn't going to find Stiles, he decided in that moment. Because Stiles was going to come here. Right here.

He had never had the chance to finish his experiments on the Child of Promise. It must have driven him to madness when she'd escaped. Like Amber Lily herself,

Stiles might not yet know the full range of his powers. He might not even know his vulnerabilities. And that was something he would be burning to know.

Imagine, being unaware of what—if anything—could kill you.

No, Stiles was going to come here, because Edge had the perfect bait to bring him here. Amber Lily Bryant.

Alby.

He would win her trust. He would learn her secrets. He would put out the word that she was here, and then he would use her to lure the man he hated more than any other.

And then he would kill Frank Stiles. It would be easy.

"Rhiannon," Amber said softly, as the older woman got to her feet. "You'll have to be very careful with him. If you kill him, we'll never learn his secrets."

"Oh, I won't kill him. I might make him beg me to kill him, but I won't."

Amber nodded.

"You're needed here, Amber. Dante and Morgan are on their way, but Sarafina needs you here. So does Willem. There's no one for him during the daylight hours. It's not good, when he's ill."

Amber nodded.

"I'll take the blood and the journals to Eric myself."

"My parents are on their way to him, as well, in hopes they can be of some help."

"Good. We'll need all the help we can get." Rhiannon lowered her head, smiling slightly. "If someone had told me I would one day be so desperate to save the life of a mortal, I'd have laughed in their face," she said. "And yet, I cannot bear to see that bitch of a vampiress in this much pain."

"It's because she reminds you of yourself," Amber said.

"Please, she doesn't come close to me. I'm the daughter of a pharoah. A princess of Egypt."

"She's tough as nails, arrogant and slightly ruthless."

Rhiannon lowered her head. "And yet she's reduced to..." She cast a glance upward, toward the second floor bedroom. "I can hardly bear to see her this way."

"I know." Amber lowered her head. She sighed. "So when do you want to leave?"

"As soon as Willem returns." She sighed. "I suppose it's a good thing that stubborn mortal insisted on going to tonight's appointment on his own. He must have known Sarafina needed to vent some of this."

"And that she would never do it in front of him," Amber added with a nod. "Do you know how to draw blood, Rhiannon?" Amber rolled up a shirtsleeve as she asked the question.

Rhiannon laughed softly, and Amber, realizing the irony of asking what she just had of a vampire, laughed, as well. Then her aunt nodded. "Eric gave me rather detailed instructions. I have everything we need in my room. Paid a late-night visit to a medical clinic in Salem."

"Let's get it done, then," Amber said, getting to her feet.

Edge, drawn against his will, had to see this for himself. He crept up to the house, opening his senses to determine their location within. Then he crept inside, up to the bedroom, and watched while Rhiannon tied a rubber tourniquet around Amber's upper arm. She inserted a needle in the crook of Amber's elbow, then released the band.

Scarlet nectar flowed from her pink, healthy flesh, filling the tube and spilling into the plastic bag at its end. It ran in time with her pulse, increasing in pressure each time her heart beat. Edge's hunger gnawed at him, and his eyes would not move away from the rush of blood into that bag. He licked his lips. His passion stirred. How he would love to taste her. Just once.

"That should do," Rhiannon said when the bag was full. She removed the needle, pressed a cotton gauze pad to the tiny pinprick and bent the girl's arm over it. Then she gathered the other items. "Lie here for a while. I'll put this away and bring you some juice."

Edge ducked around a corner as Rhiannon left the bedroom. She paused in the hallway, looking this way and that, a frown etching her brow. He tried to draw himself inward and erect shields. He must have slipped, turned on by the blood.

When she continued on her way, Edge moved into the bedroom.

Amber saw him, and her eyes widened. "What are you doing here?"

"I told you I'd be back." His stomach knotted. "I felt as if you needed help, felt your blood being drained. But I see I misread the situation." He moved closer to the bed where she lay.

"Everything's fine, but it's nice to know you would have come charging to the rescue if it hadn't been."

He took her wrist in his hand, unbent her arm and gently peeled the gauze away from the tiny pinprick. "I'm just heroic that way, I guess," he whispered. Then he bent his head and pressed his lips to the wound. He tasted the barest hint of her blood, and his mind caught fire.

He heard the breath whisper out of her, and he couldn't resist letting his tongue dart out, licking a hot path over the crook of her elbow, tasting a tiny ruby droplet that lingered there. A shiver worked through his very bones at the taste of her.

She didn't taste like a mortal woman. She didn't taste like a vampire, either. She tasted different, exotic, and the jolt that hit him when her blood touched his tongue was far more powerful than anything he'd ever felt before.

Her fingers curled in his hair. She almost pressed him closer. Almost. Her hand was shaking with the effort she had to make not to. He felt it—everything she felt whispered through him.

Forcibly, he lifted his head away, wondering silently just what the hell kind of power this woman had. He'd never felt anything like her—and he hadn't heard anything about this part of her in the legends. No one had ever whispered that touching her could cause shock, that tasting her could be addictive, or that looking into those deep, dark eyes could prove fatal.

He had to avert his eyes and pull his insides back together, so he turned to take a little bandage from the bedside stand. He peeled off the wrapping, tried not to let his hands shake too badly as he applied it to her wound.

"Th-thanks," she whispered.

He met her eyes quickly, knowing that his tasting her had shaken her as much as it had him. He thought about kissing her then. Not to further his plan, though it would certainly do that. But just because he wanted to. And Edge had never been one to deny himself anything he wanted. So he leaned a little closer.

"Well now, what have we here?" Rhiannon asked from the doorway.

4

He stopped in midmotion, seeing the alarm in Amber's eyes at the sound of the other woman's voice.

She cleared her throat. "Aunt Rhiannon, this is Edge."

Rhiannon came forward even as Edge got to his feet, turned to face her and put on his most charming smile. He extended a hand. "It's a pleasure to meet you. I've heard of you. Princess of Egypt, right?"

The beautiful woman's stern expression softened just slightly. "Yes." She took the hand he offered, shook it. "And how did you meet my Amber Lily?"

"She hit me with her car."

Rhiannon blinked, shot a shocked look at Amber on the bed.

"It was an accident," she said. "But I figured the least I could do was give him a ride. He was coming this way anyway."

Her brows went up. "Really? And what brings you to Salem Harbor, Edge?"

"Amber's Ferrari."

She made a face, not embracing his humor.

"Actually, I just always wanted to see it."

She didn't seem to believe him. "Well, now you can."

He licked his lips. "I, um—I heard the commotion. Is there anything I can do?"

"We have things under control."

He nodded, then cast a glance at Amber in the bed. "I suppose I should go, then. Leave you to it."

"It was nice meeting you," Rhiannon said, stepping to one side of the open doorway.

Amber sat up on the bed, swinging her feet to the floor. "Do you have somewhere to stay?"

He smiled at her. "I'll find a place. I always do."

She sent Rhiannon a pleading look, to which the other woman responded with a scowl. But then, from outside the room, another voice came.

"That's the problem with royalty. They can be so rude." A third woman came into the room. She wore a plush robe and looked drained of energy. Her feet dragged a little when she walked, and her eyes were red, as if she had been crying or was suffering a hangover.

Amber shot to her feet, and Rhiannon turned to reach for the woman, but she held her hands up and stopped them both. "Don't."

Rhiannon sighed, but lowered her arms to her sides. "You should be sleeping."

She shrugged. "Tell your friend Eric his vampire-tranquilizer needs tweaking. It might have put you out of commission, Rhiannon, but for a vampiress as powerful as I am, it only produces a slight buzz."

"If you were yourself, Gypsy, I'd show you the meaning of powerful." Rhiannon said the words gently, though. It wasn't a real threat.

The "Gypsy" crossed the room, gently embraced Amber. "I didn't exactly give you a proper greeting, did I?"

"It's understandable," Amber said, hugging her back.

As they pulled apart, the vampiress studied Amber, stroked a hand over her hair. "It's redder than last time I saw you."

"More burgundy than red," Rhiannon said.

Amber shrugged. "It always seems to be changing. Mom says I have raven hair with bloody highlights."

She was all about highlights, Edge thought in silence. Her ebony eyes turned darkest midnight-blue if you looked closely enough. He wondered if they had changed, as well, or if they'd always been that way. Not that it mattered in the least to him.

The third woman was facing him now, offering a weak smile and a hand. "I'm Sarafina."

He took her hand. Her grip wasn't as strong as he would have expected in one as old as she was. The power of a vampire floated around them like a nimbus. It grew with age, and he sensed a depth of it in this woman— nearly as much as he felt wafting from Rhiannon. But it was hiding now, or dormant.

"They call me Edge."

"And you're a friend of Amber Lily's?"

He glanced her way. "I'd like to be."

"Then you're more than welcome to stay here with us."

"'Fina, a word, please?" Rhiannon whispered.

Sarafina shot her a look. "There's no need for secrecy, Rhiannon. I imagine Edge has figured out by now that you don't trust him, and that you guard Amber Lily like your Pandora would guard a freshly downed antelope."

Pandora? Edge sent the mental whisper to Amber, wondering if she could hear and respond.

Her pet black panther, she thought back at him.

He was impressed with her telepathic skills and not sure how to respond to the likening of Rhiannon to a predatory feline, so he said nothing at all.

Sarafina moved closer to him, studied his face. "Not that she's overprotective, by any means. There are a lot of ruthless sons of bitches who'd give anything to get their hands on our Amber Lily.''

"And you think I might be one of them?'' He tried to look shocked, glancing from her to Rhiannon to Amber. "I'm a vampire, ladies. I'm one of you.''

"You're a vampire. Not one of us,'' Rhiannon said, her voice soft, dangerous.

He held up both hands. "I didn't come here looking for free room and board.''

Sarafina shrugged. "Still, I can't think of a better way to keep an eye on you than to have you stay right here, with us.''

He smiled at her. "Not on your life, lady.'' Then he turned to Amber. "I'm out of here, Alby. But I won't be far.''

He started for the door, and Amber came up behind him. "Edge, you don't have to—''

She stopped speaking when he turned around, snapped an arm around her waist, tugged her hard against him and kissed her mouth. It wasn't a long kiss. It wasn't meant to be. It was a message. And he thought the vampires received it loud and clear.

When he let her go, she frowned at him, almost as if she knew exactly what he was doing. Damn, she was supposed to be weak-kneed and confused. Instead she looked as sharp and nearly as mistrusting of him as the vampires were.

He said, "I'll see you again.'' Then he turned on his heel, walked into the hall, down the stairs and out of the house.

Amber closed her eyes, squared her shoulders and turned to face the two women. "Don't even start.''

"I don't like him,'' Rhiannon said.

"He's up to something," Sarafina agreed.

"Of course he's up to something." Amber stalked down the stairs, with the two women right behind her. She headed to the kitchen, put on a kettle, dug in a cupboard for the herbal tea blend she and Willem both favored. Only then did she turn and face the women again. "Sit."

"Amber..." Rhiannon began.

"Just sit. Sarafina, you're going to fall down if you don't get off your feet." She took 'Fina's arm, pulled out a chair for her.

Sarafina sat down. Rhiannon didn't. She folded her arms over her chest and speared Amber with her eyes. "Amber, he's handsome, I'll grant you that," she said.

Sarafina agreed. "Devastatingly handsome."

"Hottest man I've ever seen in my freakin' life," Amber put in.

The two looked at her, wide-eyed.

"Look, I wasn't born yesterday, you know."

"No. Just twenty-three years ago," Rhiannon said. "Which really isn't much longer than yesterday."

"Not to you, maybe. But I'm not stupid."

"I never said you were stupid, Amber, just...inexperienced."

"With men, she means," Sarafina put in.

"Not so inexperienced I can't spot a con a mile away. God, do you think I believe any of this? He appears out of nowhere on a dark road and I don't sense him there? He had to be shielding." She shook her head slowly. "I've been mulling this over all the way out here. The only answer I can come up with is that he didn't want me to see him before I hit him."

Rhiannon blinked, glanced at Sarafina, then looked back at Amber.

"And that he just happened to be going to Salem? Come on, I'd have to be a dimwit to fall for that."

"But you brought him here all the same," Sarafina whispered.

Amber nodded, moving behind her to squeeze her shoulders. "Yes. And I'm sorry if it added any more tension to a situation that's already unbearable, Sarafina. I didn't want to make things worse for you."

"Then why did you do it?" Rhiannon asked.

Amber met her eyes. "I think…I was supposed to."

"What do you mean?"

Sighing, Amber shook her head. "No. Look, this is my deal, okay? I'm not ready to talk about it, not yet. And certainly not when there's so much else going on." She leaned closer to Sarafina. "Don't burden yourself worrying about this. I can handle Edge. And don't give up hope on Willem."

Sarafina jerked her head around to stare into Amber's eyes, then she turned her gaze on Rhiannon. "You're planning something, aren't you?"

Amber nodded.

"Amber, don't—" Rhiannon began.

"She has a right to know." Amber moved to the chair nearest Sarafina's, took her hands, held her eyes. "You remember when Will saved you from Stiles and threw him from that peak into the sea?"

She nodded. "We never found his body."

"I don't think his body was there. Rhiannon and I— we think he survived."

"But how…?" Then she blinked, and her eyes widened. "The experiments? You think he was successful?"

"We can't know that for sure," Rhiannon said.

"But we're going to find out." The teakettle started whistling, long and slow. Amber got up to shut it off.

"The importance of our new friend Edge and his motives for coming here pale in comparison to this."

Rhiannon sighed. "On that, I suppose I have to agree."

Amber put a tea bag into her mug, poured the steaming water over it. "Rhiannon is taking a sample of my blood to Eric at Wind Ridge. My parents are going to meet her there. You know Eric and his science. If there's anything to be found, he'll find it. It's just a matter of time."

"Time." Sarafina sighed, lowered her head. "That's something we don't have in abundance."

"Dante and Morgan are on their way, Sarafina," Rhiannon said. "They're going to work from this end on tracing Frank Stiles. If he is still alive, they'll track him down. And once we know where he is…" Rhiannon didn't finish. She didn't have to.

"It might not matter," Sarafina said softly. "Even if we found some way to—to do this thing—"

God, Amber thought. She couldn't even say it.

"I'm not sure Willem would surrender his mortality."

Amber frowned. "Is this something you've discussed, then?"

She shook her head. "We try not to. He's so determined that we live in the moment—so determined to keep me from torturing myself by thinking about the inevitable." Lifting her eyes, she said, "Or what we thought was inevitable."

"Then you don't know," Amber said. "And you won't, not until you ask him."

"He's such a stubborn man."

"Aren't they all?" Rhiannon asked. She swallowed hard, facing Amber again. "Still, I don't like the idea of leaving here with that Edge character lurking around."

"I told you, I can handle Edge," Amber said.

"We'll watch over her," Sarafina said. Then she bit her lip. "Though I don't suppose that's very comforting to you, given what happened the last time Amber was in our care."

"Amber doesn't need to be in anyone's care," Amber said.

Rhiannon sighed. "Dante and Morgan will be here soon. I suppose between the four of you…" She let her voice trail off.

Amber didn't argue that she could take care of herself, knowing it would fall on deaf ears, anyway. How did a twenty-three-year-old tell a pair of centuries-old immortals that she was a mature adult? It was impossible. She returned to the table with her tea, sat down, sipped it and prayed for patience.

Edge smiled at the irony of it as he eyed the abandoned church. He'd stuck close to the peninsula's shoreline, because he liked it. It had been a while since he'd spent any time near the ocean. The sea was dark tonight, moody, mysteriously hiding whatever it held in its depths. It reminded him of Amber Lily's eyes. And for some reason, he needed to keep it in sight. So he walked along the shoreline, covering several miles of distance in very little time. And then he spotted it. The tall steeple had bare patches of ribbing, where the shingles had been torn away by the storms and whims of the sea. Its once white paint barely qualified as a decent shade of pale gray anymore. It wasn't a large church. Just a simple rectangle, slightly longer than wide, with its back to the sea.

As he walked around the sad little church, he noted the tall windows, arched at the top, fitted with once red wooden shutters, all of them closed now with planks of wood crisscrossing them to keep them secure. At the front, the double doors were similarly boarded up. There had been steps once, but the weather had rotted them away. Only scraps of rotten lumber remained, surrounding a six foot square of black earth underneath the doors like an ugly scar.

Copses of trees stood on either side of the church, but in front of the building, scraggly weeds and a handful of saplings made for thinner cover. Edge walked that way and found the narrow dirt road that probably didn't see much use these days. It had grass growing in the middle, barely worn tracks on either side. It had probably been replaced with a paved, straighter road several decades ago. Maybe a newer church was built somewhere along it. But this one—this one hadn't seen use in a long, long time.

Moving to the side with the most coverage, he easily tugged off the boards, opened the shutters to look in at the broken window. Just as well it was busted, he would have had to break it anyway. He sure as hell wasn't going to yank the boards off the back windows, where beach walkers might notice. And the front doors would be more easily glimpsed, as well, should someone happen by. It was this side or nothing.

He brushed aside the broken glass, careful not to slide his hands over it—he didn't want to bleed to death before dawn. Then he held to the bottom of the window and easily jumped through, landing on his feet on the inside.

Brushing dirt off his hands, he took a look around.

There were crumbling plaster walls, broken floorboards, and cobwebs enough to weave a blanket. He brushed them aside as he walked through the place. A handful of pews remained, like the few remaining teeth in an old man's head. At the front, the floor was raised, but no altar stood there. He saw a door beyond the dais and went to it, forced it open, admiring the intricacies of the brass doorknob—an antique, no doubt, but tarnished to near black. The door had swollen, didn't want to budge, but he was a vampire and not in the mood to play. He shoved, and it popped open, immediately sagging to one side due to a missing hinge.

Edge stepped through. The room in the back was small, just a storage space, probably. There were shelves on the back wall, even a stray box or two, mold growing on the outsides of them. He reached for one of them, tugging it from the shelf. The wet bottom gave, and the contents spilled over his feet.

Candles.

He smiled. Perfect. Everything a vampire needed to feel at home. A trap-door in the floor led to the small basement. Barely room enough to stand. Dirt floor, stacked stone walls without a hint of cement to hold them together. Just flat stones piled atop one another on all four sides. He nodded in approval and moved back to the upper floor, slung his duffel bag onto a pew. Then he tugged one of the two remaining pews from its place, took it to the front, where the dais was, and set it dead center.

Returning to his duffel, he opened it and removed a smaller sack, carrying it with him. From the sack he took several small items and carefully, lovingly, set them in a circle on the surface of the pew. A bone-trimmed switchblade with Billy Boy's initials carved in the side. The silver crescent moon that Ginger had worn in her ear. Scottie's gold pen. He'd had the soul of a poet. And the opal barrettes Bridget had worn in her hair.

Edge retrieved a handful of the candles from the back, used his lighter to set the wicks aflame and dripped wax onto the pew, then set them upright in it, so they wouldn't tip easily. He placed them in a circle around the objects and watched their fiery light dance over his odd little collection of keepsakes.

His family. These items represented his family. The only one he'd ever had. The only one he wanted, because God knew he wouldn't put himself through that kind of pain again. The people they represented were long gone. Hunted down and executed by a man named Frank W. Stiles. And Edge was closer than ever to finding him and, finally, exacting revenge.

"You look wonderful," Amber told Will when he returned to the house.

"What, you were expecting otherwise?" He set his walking stick aside and gave her a hug, and she noted that his arms felt strong around her, powerful.

She smiled and hugged back, never admitting that she *had* expected otherwise. He had cancer, had been given a death sentence—she'd expected him to be pale and weak, to have lost weight. Not so. His hair hadn't turned gray. His face was harsher, more lines had appeared around his dark eyes, but they seemed more like laugh lines than age. And while his limp was more pronounced than it had been before, that could have been for any number of reasons besides the cancer.

"Don't look terminally ill at all, do I, kid?" he asked.

She winced inwardly but kept her smile in place. "You look healthy as a horse. Guess it takes more than a little cancer to bother a Special Forces colonel."

"Retired," he said, retrieving his intricately carved and painted walking stick—one Sarafina had bought him on their recent trip to Africa—and limping to where his beloved sat. He leaned over 'Fina, slid his hand over her shoulder, bent to kiss her neck. She closed her eyes. They'd been all around the world, the two of them. Privately, Amber thought it the most romantic thing she could imagine. And thank God, she thought. Thank God they'd had the time they had, to be together. Just in case they were nearing the end.

Amber moved around the table, pulled out the chair next to 'Fina's. "Sit down, Willem, have some tea with me."

He smiled at her. "It's been a while since I've had anyone to share tea with." 'Fina sent him a playful pout, and he patted her hand. "Not that I'm complaining."

Amber poured, and Willem sat. His sharp gaze slid carefully over Sarafina's face, and Amber knew he saw something there. Maybe some clue of the emotional breakdown she had experienced during his absence. God love her, she'd pulled herself together in a hurry. Fixed her hair, her face, put on clothes. But Will knew her too well not to notice something was off.

Rhiannon sat, as well.

"So are you going to tell me, or do I have to guess?" Willem asked when Amber set the tea in front of him.

Amber frowned. "Tell you what?"

He made a face, shook his head, sipped the tea and set the cup down. "Come on, kid. I know you. I know your so-called aunt there, and I know my wife. You've been plotting strategy."

Amber licked her lips and averted her eyes.

"Don't do it, Amber," he said softly. "Don't try to find Stiles." Turning his gaze to Sarafina and then Rhiannon, he went on. "If he finds out where Amber is, he'll come for her. You both know he will. It's not worth risking her life on the slim chance you can save mine."

"Don't you think," Amber asked, "that decision should be left up to me?"

He met her eyes. "Suppose it works, but you get yourself killed? You expect me to live with that?"

"You risked your life to save mine, Will. I'm only returning the favor."

"You're only a girl."

She glanced down at the walking stick, where it leaned against the table beside his chair. Then she jerked her gaze up and across the room. The stick flew like a well-aimed spear, at a speed so fast it hissed through the air. Just before it sank into the wall, Amber flicked up a hand, and it stopped dead. She flipped her hand over, and the stick turned vertical, then sailed easily back across the room and right into her palm. She set it down on the floor, leaning it against the table.

"I'm not *only* anything, Will. I may look young. I may *be* young, chronologically. But I'm a direct descendant of the most powerful vampire I know." When she said it, she looked to Rhiannon. "You sired Roland, he sired Eric, Eric sired Tam, and all of you, together, saved my father from certain death when you gave him your blood to transform him into what you are. That blood runs in my veins. And I may not be a vampiress, but I'm not a human, either. And I'm stronger than any of you know."

Will nodded slowly. "I know you are. But you've been sheltered, protected. You've never had to fight to survive, to kill or be killed, Amber. It's not something you pick up overnight, and it's not easy. No matter how strong you are. Experience is worth as much as power. And while you have the latter in abundance, you have very little of the former."

She held his gaze. He held hers right back, stubborn as ever. She said, "Rhiannon is taking some of my blood to Eric and Tam's tonight. They'll work on it in Eric's lab, with help and input from my parents and Roland. They might find the answers there. We don't necessarily have to bring Stiles into this at all, if he's even alive."

"Oh, he's alive," someone said. All eyes turned toward the doorway, where the two newcomers stood: strong, powerful Dante and his small, frail-looking companion, Morgan.

Dante's eyes went straight to Sarafina's, and their gazes locked. She trembled a little, rising to her feet, and Amber knew it was harder than ever for her to keep her emotions in check, now that her beloved Dante was here.

He swept forward, wrapping her in his arms. "I'm here for you, my precious 'Fina. I always will be."

"Don't make promises like that, Dante," she whispered. "You know life is uncertain at best, cruel at worst."

He closed his eyes, no doubt feeling her pain. Sarafina was a relative of his, an aunt or great-aunt, Amber thought, from the same Gypsy band. But in truth, they were more like siblings. They loved one another, fought with each other, then made up again, just as a brother and sister might do.

Amber waited until they'd parted. She'd never met Dante and his bride, though she'd seen all of Morgan's films. They were still being made today, even though she was supposed to be dead. Her sister had allegedly found trunks full of unproduced scripts, and Morgan had collected more awards posthumously than most screenwriters did while alive.

The films were great, too.

When the introductions were complete, Willem said, "What did you mean about Stiles being alive?"

Pulling out a chair for Morgan, Dante remained standing. "You know, of course, that Morgan and I are silent partners in her sister's investigations agency in Maine. We have…sources. On both sides of mortality. Stiles has been sighted numerous times since your encounter with him five years ago."

"You have proof it was him?" Will asked.

"No. But there's enough circumstantial evidence to convince me."

Will thinned his lips.

"You have doubts as to whether we should pursue him?" Dante asked.

"Of course he has doubts," Morgan said softly. "Stiles is deadly, a threat to every one of us in this room. He nearly killed you twice, Dante. But he's most dangerous to Amber."

Will met Morgan's gaze, nodded. "Thank you. I'm glad someone here sees the risk besides me. I really prefer we give Eric some time to work in his lab with Amber's blood samples before we even consider bringing that monster into this."

"But you'll let us go after Stiles as a last resort?" Sarafina asked, her voice filled with hope.

"Don't even answer, Will," Amber put in. "It doesn't matter if you decide to *let* us. If Eric can't recreate Stiles's formula, we're doing it."

Will lowered his head. "Stubborn woman."

He'd said "woman," Amber noticed. Not "kid." She appreciated that. "As stubborn as you are, Will. And far from ready to give up on you."

"Even if we don't go after Stiles right away," Morgan said, "we can still begin doing some of the work of tracking him down. We've brought our files, everything we've been able to dig up on the man, and if you don't mind, we can set up a computer here, hook up to the 'net and continue following the leads we dug up at home.''

Sarafina nodded enthusiastically, only to pause and look at Will. He nodded as well, sighing deeply. "Just be careful. I do not want word leaking out that Amber is here. It would put her at too much risk.''

Amber rolled her eyes when Dante said, "Agreed.''

"Now that you're all here,'' Rhiannon said, "I suppose it's safe for me to be on my way. I will trust Sarafina and Amber Lily to fill you in on our *other* little complication.''

"We don't know he's a complication,'' Amber said quickly.

"But we *will* find out,'' Rhiannon replied.

As goodbyes were said, Rhiannon hugged Amber fiercely and whispered in her ear, "Do not let your guard down with that Edge character. He's powerful, child. Not old, but powerful all the same. And dangerous. I feel it wafting off him in waves.''

"He must be related to you, then.'' Amber walked her outside to the waiting vehicle.

Rhiannon scowled. "If he wasn't up to something involving my favorite female in the universe, I might actually like the man.''

"I promise I'll be careful. And, Rhiannon?''

The vampiress looked at her, one brow cocked. "Oh, no,'' she said. "You're *not* going to ask me to keep my knowledge of Edge from your parents.''

"I'm not going to ask you,'' Amber told her. "I'm going to insist on it.''

Rhiannon thinned her lips, crossing her arms over her chest. "Amber...''

"They'd come with flamethrowers and machine guns

firing garlic-coated wooden stakes shaped like crosses, if they knew. You know they would.''

Rhiannon smiled a little at Amber's use of every cliché, including those that had no more effect on the undead than on the living. But her smile died slowly. "They're going to have to know sooner or later, Amber.''

"I prefer later.''

"They'll hate him on sight, you know. Just on principle.''

"Then the later, the better,'' Amber said.

"I don't know...''

"Rhiannon, Will had a point about my lack of experience. Let me do this. Let me figure out on my own just what Edge is up to and why he's homed in on me as his tool to get it.'' She shrugged. "Besides, there's always a slight chance he might just be smitten. Bewitched by my beauty, captivated by my sharp mind and entranced by my infinite charms.''

"Oh, I have no doubt of that,'' Rhiannon said, smiling. "As you pointed out inside, my blood *is* running in your veins.''

Amber rolled her eyes and watched as Rhiannon got into her Mercedes and drove away into the night. Then she turned toward the doorway, where Dante and Morgan waited—two vampires who had not, thank God, known her from birth and who did not, therefore, see her as a child but as she was.

She joined them inside, and being one of the only two mortals in the house, claimed she was tired and needed some rest. It made as good an excuse as any to slip out and stroll along the beach.

She rolled up her jeans, kicked off her shoes and waded through the ice-cold waves that washed up onto the sand and rock shore. But it wasn't a walk she wanted, and it wasn't solitude she sought, and she knew it.

She quieted her mind, then opened it, and put Edge's face before her eyes. It wasn't as if she didn't know his face intimately. She'd been seeing it for a long, long time now, in her dreams.

Silently, she called to him.

Immediately, he answered. And she got the feeling he'd been expecting her summons.

5
_____

"Has all the comforts of home, don't you think?"

Edge was standing in the window of an abandoned, falling-down church. He'd pushed open the shutters, spoken softly to her as she'd followed her sense of him along the beach. She turned, scanning the darkness. She saw well in the darkness, not as well as a vampire, but far better than a human.

It was always this way, Amber thought as she spotted him there and altered her course, turning toward the church. Everything she did, every talent she had, she weighed against the norms of the undead and of the living, trying to figure out where she fit.

She walked up to the window, stood on the ground looking up at him, six feet above her. "So does this luxury beach house have a door, or...?"

He reached down, bending low. She took his hand, and he easily pulled her up and inside. Her body slammed into his as she landed, and he wrapped his free arm around her waist as if to steady her, and kept her there.

She lifted her head, saw the mischief in his eyes and the heat around the edges of his smile. She felt the firmness of his body against hers and the power of his arms around her. It felt far too good, made her want far too much more.

He let her go all too soon and turned to walk around

the crumbling ruin. She scanned the place, taking in every detail. The duffel bag slung on one of the pews, the other pew that had been placed on the dais, and the odd items that sat upon it among some candles that had been recently snuffed. He watched her look around the place.

"Well?" he asked. "You approve?"

"It's a hovel."

He shrugged. "Yeah, but it's home." He brushed a layer of dust off an empty pew, and she sat down.

"You should have stayed with us at the house. Could've had your own room, a soft bed, indoor plumbing...."

"Here I have my own bell." When she frowned, he pointed upward, and she saw the rope hanging from a hole in the ceiling. "Up above, it's open clear to the steeple. There's a bell at the other end of this rope."

"If you ring it, you'll blow your cover."

"It *is* a dilemma."

She smiled at him. "So what's with the little altar?" As she said it, she nodded toward the pew with the candles and other items. "You into Voodoo or something?"

"It's only a few mementos."

Sliding off her pew, she moved closer to take a better look. "You mind?"

He shrugged, so she examined the items more closely, even picking up one or two. An earring, a pair of barrettes. "So you wore an earring and barrettes when you were alive?"

"Not exactly."

She handled the switchblade, examining the initials engraved in the bone handle. B. R. "These aren't yours, are they?"

"Are now."

He was shifting his weight, his eyes moving rapidly from his keepsakes to her hands on them. It made him uncomfortable, her handling these things. She put the blade down carefully. "If you don't want to tell me, just say so."

Again, he only shrugged, then turned away. "So what's the deal? Back at the mansion, I mean?"

It was hardly a mansion. She averted her eyes. "I told you about Willem. He's mortal, and he's sick."

"Dying," he said.

She sighed. "Not if I have anything to say about it."

"There's the rub, though, isn't it?" She looked at him sharply. "You don't have anything to say about it. Do you?"

She shrugged. "You might be surprised."

He licked his lips. "That Egyptian Princess—she bled you, didn't she?"

Amber frowned. "With my full consent."

"I thought as much. Otherwise I'd have torn into her."

That brought a smile to her face. He saw it and tipped his head. "What, you think I'd have trouble with her?"

"I don't think, I know."

He rolled his eyes. "I'm tougher than I look, you know."

"You look plenty tough. Don't get all offended."

He sighed. "Doesn't matter. If I'd thought she was harming you—"

"You'd have fought to defend me, huh?"

"Do you doubt it?" He was serious now, his eyes darkening, taking on a look of intense emotion. She got the feeling he was lying but decided to believe. He moved closer, cupped her cheek in one hand and bent toward her. He was going to kiss her. And she wanted him to, but she knew damn well she was going to lose her focus the minute his mouth touched hers. So she spoke just before it did, while his eyes were closed and his breath was fanning her face.

"What do you really want from me, Edge?"

It caught him off guard. His eyes popped open, and they held the expression of a kid caught with his hand in the cookie jar. But he caught himself fast, banished the guilty look and replaced it with a lecherous one. "I thought we'd start with the kissing. From there, I have all sorts of ideas."

Her stomach knotted a little at the suggestion of sex, even though he hadn't actually said it. He didn't have to say it. He practically oozed it. "Beyond that, I mean," she managed, her words emerging hoarsely from a throat that had gone tight. "Why did you fling yourself in front of my car last night? Why are you pretending to be interested in me now?"

He blinked at her as if in confusion. "Do you cast a reflection, Alby?"

Frowning, she nodded. "Yes. Why?"

"Just wondering if you've ever seen yourself in a mirror."

She rolled her eyes, told herself not to let his smooth, slow words make her lose track of her mission here, and gently extricated herself from his full body embrace.

"If you have, why would you accuse me of pretending to want you?"

"You've only known me for twenty-four hours, Edge, and half of those you were resting."

"I wanted you in the first ten seconds," he said. Then he shrugged. "Being female and half mortal, I suppose you're one of those who believes it's necessary to get to know a person before indulging in an exchange of mutual ecstasy."

"Well, yeah. Especially with someone who's being less than honest about his motives."

"I'm being perfectly honest, Alby. I'm not declaring eternal love, and I'll tell you up-front that I never will. Hell, I'm not even sure I like you much at this point. This—" he ran a finger along her cheek until she shivered "—is purely physical." He ran his hand slowly down her neck, to her shoulder, from her shoulder down her back, following the curve of her spine. His fingertips left a tingling wave of sensation in their wake. His hand kept sliding lower, until she stepped away from his touch. "I don't believe in self-denial," he said softly.

"Then I'll do the denying."

"Hell." He heaved a sigh and flung himself onto one of the pews, sitting heavily. "So why are you here, Alby? If you didn't come to let me ravish you, what are you doing here?"

She bit her lip. "I already told you, I want to know why you're interested in me. What were you doing on that road?"

"Walking to Salem."

"Why?"

"Because my car died. I told you that."

"And why did you throw yourself in front of my car and pretend I hit you?"

He pursed his lips, lowered his gaze to the floor, sighed. "All right. All right, you're too smart for me. I did do that. I thought it was my best shot at getting a ride." He licked his lips and searched her eyes. "I had no idea who you were, though. Not until after the fact. And I've got no reason to try to fool you now. I already got the ride I was after."

"Not the only ride you're after," she muttered.

"Well, that goes without saying." His smile was one

of pure mischief, and it turned her on like nothing she'd ever seen. "The only question now is, how am I going to get you to change your mind?"

She averted her face, felt the blood heating her cheeks.

"How long are you staying in Salem Harbor, Alby?"

She shrugged. "It really depends. There's a...a man who might be able to help me save Willem. If I can find out where he is, I'll leave immediately."

He nodded slowly. "Then we'll have to make the most of our time together, won't we?"

She felt her brows rise, turned to him in surprise.

"Don't tell me you've forgotten our conversation in the car? I promised I would help you figure out who and what you are." He shrugged. "It'll give me a chance to charm you out of your clothes, while I'm at it."

"Right." She sighed. "So how do you plan to do that?"

"Charm you out of your clothes?"

"Help me figure out what I am." If she were honest, she would admit she was more interested in the other. She was half afraid he could do it. Half *hoping* he could.

"You come back here tomorrow night, and I'll show you."

She licked her lips, nerves jumping. "Don't expect anything in return, Edge."

"Oh, I don't expect—I demand something in return."

She lifted her brows. "Do you?"

"Mmm-hmm."

"What?"

"This." He rose from the pew, walked slowly toward her, holding her eyes with his. She didn't move away, didn't even think about it. He pressed his palms to hers, at her sides, pressed his body to hers, rubbing, and she didn't pull back. No, she stood firm when he pressed himself against her, even, maybe, pressed back a little. He tipped his head to one side, she tipped hers to the other, and he lowered his mouth slowly, slowly closer to hers. Just before his lips touched her, he whispered, "Of course, I won't collect until I've delivered on my promise."

He started to lift his head away. And Amber heard herself saying, "The hell you won't." She tugged her hands from his and pressed them instead to the back of his head, pulling him to her, kissing his mouth. She felt his lips trying to pull into a smile as she kissed them; then they trembled and parted, and his arms slid around her waist and pulled her even closer. He pushed her mouth wider, digging inside with his tongue and feeding from her like a man starved to death. She heard a moan, wasn't sure if it was his or hers, and felt as if her very blood were blazing—molten lava crawling beneath her skin.

Finally, when the shaking was so intense she could barely stand and her mind was spinning, he lifted his head away and whispered, "God, Alby, I could eat you alive."

The words, combined with the blazing hunger in his eyes, sent a jolt of fear through her. She'd never been bitten by a vampire before. She had no idea what it would be like, but she knew he could easily lose control and drain her to the point of death.

His hand pushed her hair from her face. "No, Alby. That's not what I meant." He shrugged. "Though that would be good, too. I'll do both before I've finished with you."

She swore under her breath at the rush of desire his words shot through her. "I have…I have to go."

"But you'll come…here…tomorrow night," he told her. Then he smiled slowly, devilishly. "I promise."

Blinking, Amber turned and went to the window, leaped out, landing hard on the ground, and then ran all the way back to the house.

Edge had, the way he saw it, two options. He could screw the woman's brains out and wait for her and her friends to get a line on Frank Stiles, then follow them to the man. Or he could screw the woman's brains out and move forward with his plan to leak word of her presence in the Salem area to some of the underworld figures he knew, using her as bait to lure Stiles right here.

Either way, he was going to have her. He'd intended to seduce her all along, from his very first glimpse of her. But what he hadn't foreseen was the fire in her and the impact it had on him. By God, he'd never wanted like this. He hoped she was as strong as she claimed to be, because otherwise, he was liable to hurt her. Having her would be an unplanned bonus. Might feel almost as good as killing Stiles was going to feel.

He wondered if he should wait just a few days. Give her friends time to do their digging. Give himself more time to explore every inch of her, fulfill her every fantasy and violate her every inhibition. If he had to use her as bait, it would, after all, put her at some risk. He didn't care, of course. His goal was all that mattered to him.

And to prove that, he had to move and move now. But he would be sure he nabbed Stiles before the man got within a mile of Amber Lily. It would be a crying shame if anything happened to her before Edge had his fill.

The house was quiet. The sun had risen half an hour ago, and everyone except for Amber had slipped quietly into the comalike day sleep of the undead. Even Will had gone to bed. Amber looked in on him, sleeping soundly beside Sarafina in their queen-size bed. It gave Amber time—time to mull over what she'd learned about Edge the night before.

Dante and Morgan had turned one spare bedroom into a kind of "search-central" headquarters. Two computers with cable modems attached, a telephone with a line splitter, and a fax machine lined the room. If not for the bed, which had been shoved up against the far wall, it would have looked more like an office than a bedroom.

Amber spent a couple of hours there, reading the pages of information Dante and Morgan had gathered. There were file folders full of it. Nothing solid, though. Several out of focus photographs that might have been the scar-faced Stiles or a thousand other men. Numerous eye witness accounts that dragged on in painful detail and told her nothing. She found no pattern to the sightings, no one geographical area where Stiles seemed more likely to be. Paris, Albany, San Diego, Houston. She glanced up at the world map that was mounted to a corkboard and hanging on the bedroom wall, understanding now what all the colored push pins signified.

She went online, searching for clues about Stiles on her own, but again she came up empty. Finally she gave in to the sleepiness that was creeping up on her. She didn't require a lot of sleep. Had never needed the eight hours most people needed. And maybe that was part of what she was, or maybe it was the result of growing up with parents who were only awake by night. Whatever it was, Amber's habit was to nap, an hour here, two hours there. Her body seemed to know just how much sleep it needed, and she always woke up once she'd had it.

Right now, it was telling her to go to bed. So she did.

She slept soundly, and she dreamed erotic dreams of her and Edge, writhing and twisting around each other, with him whispering declarations of undying love along with all manner of dirty talk in her ear.

When she woke, Amber was sweaty and her heart was racing. She got out of bed, grateful that she'd had a dream about Edge that didn't include overwhelming feelings of grief and loss, and the presence of death looming over her. She headed straight into the shower, noting that the sun was still up and beaming brightly. Then she made herself a bowl of bran flakes with a sliced banana on top and sat down to eat it in her robe with a towel on her head.

"That looks good. Think I'll join you."

She looked up to see Willem limping into the kitchen. He wore jeans and a T-shirt. His feet were bare and his hair rather tousled. She got up immediately and hugged him, wrapping her arms around his strong neck, noticing the broadness of his shoulders and chest. It was hard to believe he was sick. Except that he looked haggard this morning, as if he'd put in a particularly rough few hours.

"It's good to have you back, Amber. We've missed you. And I gotta tell you, it gets lonely being the only human around here. Especially during the day."

"Tell me about it." She turned and pulled out her own chair, nodding until he took it. "Eat that, I'll get another." He started to argue, but she turned to the counter to fix a second bowl of bran flakes with banana slices, and since it took only a few seconds, he shut up and ate.

Returning to the table with her bowl of cereal, she sat down. "Of course, I'm not exactly human. Technically."

"You're awake and it's daylight. That's human enough for me."

She smiled, understanding that he was trying to keep

the conversation light. "You should get yourself some mortal help around this place. I don't know how I'd have survived without Susan and Alicia to keep me company."

He smiled. "They're a unique pair, though. You're lucky to have found people you can trust the way you trust them."

"They're family." She ate some cereal, let the comfortable silence stretch between them. Then they both said "So how are you feeling?" at the same time. She smiled at him, and he smiled back, and she said, "You first, since you're the one with the cancer."

"Blunt as ever, aren't you?"

"And I expect you to be the same."

His lips thinned. "I feel like I always have, most of the time. But once in a while I get these blinding headaches. Dizziness and nausea come with them, and they just about render me useless until they pass. Afterward I feel weak and shaky for a day or so."

"You're coming off one of them now," she said, stating it as fact.

He didn't deny it.

"How long do they last?" she asked, grateful that Will was being honest with her. Of them all, he was one of the few who didn't still insist on seeing her as a child.

"The first one was ten minutes. Then they started getting longer. A half hour, an hour. Two."

"And this morning's?" she asked.

He pursed his lips, glanced at his watch. "Four and a half."

"God. Isn't there anything they can give you for them?"

"They can give me enough morphine to knock me out until it passes. I don't like that option."

Pursing her lips, she nodded. Willem wasn't the kind of man who would enjoy being unconscious and helpless. He would rather bear the pain and remain in control.

"How often?" she asked.

"Like the duration, the frequency is increasing. I'm up to two a week now."

She reached out a hand, smoothed her fingertips over his forehead, his temple. "I'm so sorry, Will. It's not fair."

"Life isn't fair. I've had a better one than a lot of people, I'm not complaining."

"No, you wouldn't."

"It's 'Fina I'm worried about. Frankly, I don't think she'll do well, if I..." He met her eyes. "She's going to need all the help she can get. Even then, I'm not sure she'll make it."

"I'm worried about her, too," she admitted. "We'll all be here for her, Will. You know that. In the end, that's really all we can do. The rest is up to her."

"I know." He smiled at her. "Your turn. What's up with you?" Before she could speak, he added, "And I expect you to be equally blunt, Amber."

She thinned her lips. "Okay. Well...I'm not sure at all, but I don't think I've aged since Connecticut."

He frowned at her, seemed to look her over more closely. Then he tipped his head to one side. "It's not like there are all that many changes between eighteen and twenty-three, you know."

"I know."

"Still, there probably should be some."

"I've been watching Alicia. She's the only other person I've spoken to about this, by the way, so keep it between us." He nodded. "The changes are subtle. Really very subtle, but she has changed. Her face has changed. Her hips are a little wider, and it's not weight, it's adulthood. You know?''

"I know." He frowned. "You aged normally up to that point, grew from a baby to a little girl to an adolescent into a beautiful young woman. Why do you think you suddenly stopped?"

"I'm thinking maybe it was death."

He frowned.

"Stiles killed me several times while he held me. You know that. I don't think I've aged a day since." She shrugged.

"It's a solid theory."

"It's the only one I have right now."

He nodded, crunched a few more bites of cereal and finally pushed the bowl away. "So tell me about Edge."

She almost choked on a banana slice. Will leaned back in his chair, smiling, arms crossed over his chest, waiting for her to come up with an answer.

She got up, stumbled to the fridge for some orange juice, poured two tiny glasses and took a drink from one of them.

"You're stalling for time, right?"

She put the juice back, carried the glasses to the table. "You're too sharp for me." Sitting down, she added, "It's not that I don't want to tell you, just that I'm not sure yet what there is to tell."

"'Fina said you hit him with your car."

"Yeah, only I'm sure it was no accident. I got out to see if he was all right, and he said he was on his way to Salem. So I offered him a ride."

He nodded slowly. "You think that part was a coincidence? That you were both going to the same place?"

She shrugged. "I suppose it's not impossible. Last night I got him to admit that he deliberately bounced himself off my bumper, hoping to guilt me into a ride. Said his car had broken down and he wasn't looking forward to the walk.''

"At least he was honest with you, then.''

She licked her lips. "I have the feeling there's more.''

"You think he's dangerous to you?''

"Yeah, but not in the way you mean.''

He stared at her blankly for a moment, then his brows went up. "Oh.''

She had to avert her eyes.

"So you like him, huh?''

"Hell, Willem, I don't even know him.''

"But you're attracted to him.''

She nodded, not meeting his eyes. "Big time.''

"And it's mutual?''

She shrugged. "Either it's mutual or he's faking it because he's up to something, and I'm having trouble figuring out which.''

"You want me to kick his ass for you?''

She laughed at that, and Will made a wounded expression. "What, you think I'm not up to it?''

"I'm sure you'd manage, Willem. You're not untalented in that area, for a mortal. I was just thinking you'd have to stand in line behind your bride, my parents and Aunt Rhiannon.''

He nodded in agreement. "I doubt they'd leave me any scraps.''

"Pandora has dibs on the scraps. But frankly, I'd rather give Edge a chance to show his true colors.''

He nodded slowly. "That makes sense. So what's the plan?''

"He seems to want to see me. Keep me around. I can't imagine what he wants from me, but—'' She ignored the quick look he sent her. "But I think I'll figure it out, given time. And as long as he's here on the Rock, and I'm here, I may as well spend some time with him, see what I can find out.''

He licked his lips, saying nothing.

She met his eyes. ''What?''

He seemed uncomfortable, shifting in his seat. Then he said, ''Dammit, Amber, it's not my place. This is out of my field, you know. But…well, given what I know about your parents and your upbringing, I would guess you're not altogether…experienced. With the opposite sex, I mean.''

She shrugged. ''I'm psychic. I'm powerful. I'm strong. I've fought at my father's side more than once.''

''But you've never had a boyfriend.''

She licked her lips, averted her eyes. ''Well, there was Jimmy in high school. But the most we ever did was—''

He held up a hand, and she broke off there, then nodded. ''Okay, suffice it to say you're right. I'm not experienced in that area. But I can handle myself.''

''You think so?''

She nodded. ''I…think so. Besides, I think…I have to.''

Willem frowned. ''Have to?''

She turned her attention back to her cereal, but Will's hand came across the table and encircled her wrist, stopping its progress. The spoonful of bran flakes quivered in her hand.

''What aren't you telling me, Amber?''

She swallowed hard, blinked twice and finally met his eyes. ''I've been having…dreams.''

''About?''

''About him. About Edge.''

He sighed. ''Hon, it's normal. Don't let that worry

you. When there's an attraction, the subconscious some-times—"

"I've been having them for a year, Willem. I met Edge for the first time on my way here, when I hit him with my car. But I've been seeing him in vivid, recurring dreams for months and months. And I don't know why. I don't know what it means. But I think...I think it has to mean something."

He blinked slowly, licked his lips, his gaze turning inward, no doubt remembering dreams of his own. "You're right," he said softly. "You have to find out what it means."

She nodded, glancing at the clock. "There's still an hour of daylight left. I thought I might go out to his place, rifle through his things and see what I can find."

"You want company?"

She shook her head. "No. I think I need to handle this on my own."

"Just let me know if you need any help, Amber. And be careful. Where is he staying, by the way?"

She looked at him with her brows raised.

"Just in case you fail to come home one night, I'll know where to look."

"Oh. Uh, there's an abandoned church a mile up the beach."

"I know it."

She tipped her bowl to her lips to drink the remaining soy milk from the bottom, then put it on the table. "Guess I'll get dressed, then." She got to her feet.

Will did, too. He came around the table, put his hands on her shoulders. "Your father wouldn't like this."

"My father still thinks of me as a little girl. But you know I'm not."

"I know," he said. "Just...don't let this Edge character get the best of you. No matter what you decide to do or not to do, make sure it's what you want. Your decision, Amber. For your reasons. Remember what you know about him and be mindful of what you don't.''

She nodded, thinking there was a lot more she didn't know about Edge than that she did.

"If he hurts you, I'll take him out," he added, as if for good measure.

She smiled. "I'm counting on it." Leaning up, she kissed Will's cheek. "I love you, you know."

"Love you, too, Amber. Be careful."

"I will."

Amber took her time, walking along the edge of the rocky beach, barefoot, her jeans rolled up so the cold water could lap at her ankles as the waves rolled in. Guilt niggled at her for mistrusting Edge as much as she did. But only a little. She tamped it down by reminding herself how often her parents and their paranoia had turned out to be dead on target. There were bad people in the world. Edge might be one of them.

When she reached the church, the shutters were closed tight. She wondered where he was resting and sent a nervous glance toward the sky. The sun was still there, beyond the trees, hanging low, but not yet setting. She had time.

She stretched her arms, reached the very bottom of the shutters and tugged on them. They didn't move; something held them from the other side. So she yanked a little harder, popping them open, but only just slightly. She didn't want to let a shaft of sunlight in if he were lying within its reach on the other side. Pulling herself up, she peered through the crack she'd made and saw no sign of Edge, so she opened the shutters farther and climbed through. A little puff of dust rose from the floor when she landed. She quickly turned to close the shutters behind her, then faced in again as she brushed her hands against each other.

And then she frowned as she took in the changed appearance of the church.

The pews had been moved to one side, and in the large open space where they'd been, there was...equipment. A weight bench, with barbells balanced across its upright arms. A punching bag dangling from the rafters, a mat on the floor.

"What's he up to?" she wondered aloud, pacing through the church, examining the items, which were stamped with Salem Fitness Center, Salem, MA. She crooked an eyebrow. Edge had been busy.

She looked around for his duffel bag but didn't find it. The pew on the dais still held his strange little collection of keepsakes. There were more candles now than the three that stood on the pew. He'd affixed one on each windowsill. All unlit, of course. She wondered why he saw the need for candles, when he could see better than she could in the dark.

Where was he?

She went through a door at the rear of the church. It stuck a little, swollen from the weather and hanging by only one hinge, but she shoved it open and stepped into a dark, dusty storage room. There were shelves, a couple of disintegrating boxes with candles spilling out of them, and another door. Amber shoved that door open and stared down a rickety wooden staircase. Some of the steps were broken, others missing.

He was down there. Naturally he was down there. It would be the safest place to rest. No one in their right mind would attempt to navigate the broken-down stairs in the pitch-dark to invade his privacy. His duffel bag was apparently down there with him, since she hadn't located it anywhere else.

Drawing a breath, she started carefully, stepping past the missing first step, past the broken second step, and slowly lowering her weight onto the intact-looking third step from the top.

The distinct sound of wood splitting told her she'd made a serious mistake.

The sensation of plummeting through the darkness confirmed it, and the impact drove the point home.

6

Edge sensed something, just beyond the fringed edges of his consciousness, whispering to him. His face tightened, and his nose twitched. He smelled her—that soft, exotic scent that was neither human nor vampire, and every cell in his body came to screaming awareness, all of them craving her. That need circled through his brain as the clouds cleared slowly from his mind. His skin prickled and tingled. He felt her. She was close.

Gradually, other sensations returned. He felt the hard packed earth of the floor beneath his back and the softness of the blanket in between. He smelled the musty scent of the cellar, the dirt. He felt the cold, damp air and tasted the sea in it. Consciousness returned, and he opened his eyes, stretched his arms and sat up.

Amber lay on the floor a few yards from him, underneath the useless, skeletal staircase. Edge came fully awake then, rolling easily to his feet, hurrying forward. She wasn't moving. He smelled blood. And he saw the broken stair above that hadn't been broken before. She must have gone straight through. Dammit.

Edge knelt beside her. She lay on her side, hair covering her face. He moved the hair away and saw the ruby strand, stretching from her hairline across her forehead to her cheek. It was already drying. She'd been lying there a while.

"Alby?" he whispered. She was alive. He sensed the

life in her, felt her heart beating and the blood flowing through her veins. He heard her breaths whispering in and out. "Alby, come on. Talk to me now."

No response. Closing his eyes, Edge moved his hands over her. Out along her arms, over her neck, down her spine, not quite touching, just opening his senses, feeling for injuries. He examined her legs, then ran his hands up her sides to get a feel for the ribs. He didn't think she had any serious injuries. Gently, then, he rolled her over, scooped her up in his arms. He snatched his blanket from the floor, then stood by the foot of the broken stairway, bent his knees and pushed off.

When he landed at the top, she moaned.

Edge's throat went dry, and he swallowed hard, realizing that he really didn't want anything to happen to her. He told himself that was because he needed her. He needed her to lead him to Frank Stiles, and he needed her to reveal her weaknesses to him, so that he would know how to kill Stiles when he found him. And he needed, rather desperately, to get inside her, because if he didn't, he thought his head was going to explode.

None of that explained the sick feeling in his stomach on seeing her lying there, injured. It pissed him off a bit. He made a face at his own weakness, reminded himself she was no more than a means to an end, and carried her through to the main part of the church. He laid her on a pew, then tugged the blanket he'd slung over his shoulder and arranged it across her. Then he pushed the hair away to get a better look at the cut on her head.

His fingers found it; a rather wide gash and a lump the size of a jaw breaker.

"Owww."

He looked at her face, saw her eyes fluttering open.

She met his, sighed softly and let them fall closed again. "Oh, it's this again," she muttered.

"What again?" he asked, leaning closer to catch every word.

"The dream. Same old dream. Where's the box, anyway?"

He frowned deeply, tipped his head to one side. "Alby, listen up. It's me. It's Edge. You hit your head and now you're—somewhat delirious, I guess."

"It's not the dream again?"

"No, Alby, it's no dream."

Her brows bent closer, and her eyes opened to squinting little slits. "Edge?"

"Mmm-hmm."

One hand rose to her head, but as soon as she touched it, she winced and pulled her hand away. Her eyes opened a little farther.

"Awake now?"

"Yeah. What happened?"

"That's what I'd like to know."

"What do you mean?" She'd been looking around the church, but now she looked at him.

"I mean, what the hell were you doing creeping around my place by day, Amber Lily?"

She blinked, seemed to search her mind, then her eyes went serious again. "I came to see you—but I got here a little early and decided to come in and wait. I didn't think you'd mind."

He crooked one brow at her, just looked at her, because he knew damn well she was lying. She knew better. She'd been raised by his kind.

"Well, I mean, sure, any vampire would mind having someone invading their space while they were defenseless. But it's me. I mean, I thought you and I had a…connection.''

This time he arched both brows. "You thought so, did you?"

She shrugged. "Didn't you?" She sat up then, saving him the necessity of having to answer, pressing the heel of one hand to her forehead. "Damn, my head hurts."

"You came creeping into the cellar. A stair broke, and you took a tumble. Funny thing for a girl to do, when she only intended to come inside and wait."

She blinked up at him, peering from beneath her wrist. "What, do you think I was on my way down there to pull a Van Helsing on you? Did you see a wooden stake in my back pocket?"

He shrugged one shoulder. "What were you doing, then?"

She looked away, her hair black in the darkness, falling over her cheek and hiding her expression from him. "I told you, I arrived early and decided to wait." Edge honed his mind to hers, trying to be subtle, not too obvious about it.

She seemed to force herself to face him again, to look him in the eye and appear sincere. He wasn't fooled. "Can I help it if my curiosity got the best of me?"

He stared at her, and he felt something tugging at him, pulling him. A little shiver danced along his nape. Something inside her seemed to pulse with the gravitational pull of a black hole. There was a heavy emptiness there, and, consciously or not, she was aching for him to fill it.

He felt an answering demand from his own netherregions, forced himself not to act on it, though he couldn't exactly ignore it.

"You were curious," he repeated, breaking eye contact to keep from being sucked in. "About what? What

I looked like at rest?'' He let his lips pull into a sarcastic half smile. ''What I wear to bed?''

''You wish.''

He shrugged. ''What, then?''

She shook her head as if angry with him, then winced at the pain the action brought and got to her feet anyway. ''Look, if you don't trust me, I'll leave right now. You're the one who asked me to come back here.'' She took a step, swayed a little.

He gripped her shoulders. ''Not so fast, now. You're still shaky.''

''No kidding.'' She sagged closer to him, the movement imperceptible, and yet his body reacted, moving millimeters closer to hers at the same time. His hands tightened on her shoulders and let the gravity take over. She rested against him. He closed his eyes and told himself he was imagining the power that seemed to meld them together. It was silly, and completely counter to his purposes.

''Don't take offense, Alby. I don't trust anyone. It's nothing personal.''

''You sound like my father.''

He winced. Her father was the last person he wanted to remind her of. ''Why? He a suspicious sort, too?''

''I used to think my parents were the most paranoid, overprotective vampires in existence.''

''Used to?'' He forced himself to relax his hold on her, let his hands slide down her back to rest at her waist and peeled his body from her, putting healthy space between them.

She shrugged. ''Until Frank Stiles kidnapped me five years ago, pretty much proving my parents right.''

The reminder that Stiles had held her pricked his soul. He didn't like thinking about that. ''Used you as a guinea pig, did he?'' he asked, even as he tried to tell himself he could really care less, turning and pacing away from her.

''You know who he is, then?''

He looked back quickly. ''I've heard of him, yes. Former DPI, self-appointed vamp-hunter-slash-researcher. Have I got it right?''

''Pretty much.''

He nodded. ''He must have considered you his all-time prize catch.''

She smiled at him, flashed it so unexpectedly it temporarily dazzled him. ''Wouldn't any man?''

He shook the glitter from his head, rolled his eyes and grinned at her joke.

''So what's with the equipment?'' she asked, looking around at the items he'd acquired the night before. ''Vampiric strength not good enough for you? You aspire to something…bulkier?''

He smirked. ''I've got all the strength I'll ever need, Alby. Don't doubt that. I got this stuff together for you, not myself.''

''For me?'' She faced him, her pretty dark brows arching over those odd colored eyes. Blue-black as oil slicks, they were. ''What am I supposed to do with it?''

''Test yourself.''

She frowned, but when she turned to look at the equipment again, it was with a curious, interested expression.

''You talked to me in the car, remember? You told me you didn't know the full extent of your powers.''

''And you said you would help me find out.''

He nodded. ''So I thought to begin with physical strength.'' He smiled at her. ''And I thought I might teach you a few moves, while we're at it. You may as well learn to defend yourself, right?''

"You think I can't defend myself?"

He shrugged. "You said Stiles got you. He'd never get me."

"He had an army, weapons, tranquilizers. There was nothing I could have done. Believe me, I tried."

He looked doubtfully at her. "Tried what? Slapping him?"

She frowned, getting a little angry. "Why don't we play with these toys of yours, Edge? Then you can see for yourself what I can do."

He shook his head. "Not tonight, after that bump on the head."

She strode toward him, no longer the least bit unsteady on her feet, closed her hand around his wrist and brought his hand to her head. He frowned, but obliged her, probing the spot where the lump and cut had been. But the lump was nearly gone, and the cut itself was noticeably smaller. He shot her a look.

"Quick healing. It used to take a couple of days. I healed faster than a human but slower than a vamp. But since Stiles got through with me, it's been changing. A lot of things have."

"So you heal faster than we do now?"

She shrugged. "I don't have to wait for the day sleep. So it starts right away."

Edge nodded. "Why do you suppose your time in captivity coincides with these…changes?"

She pursed her lips, lowered her head. "I don't know." He knew it was a lie. She did know. Or thought she did. And he could guess her theory. Stiles had killed her, only to see her revive each time. Death and rebirth, even in myth, brought drastic change. Metamorphosis.

"What other changes have you noticed?"

She only shook her head.

He tipped his to one side. "Don't trust me yet, do you, Alby?"

She used his own words against him. "Like you, Edge, I don't trust anyone."

"I had that coming." He shrugged. "So you want to play?" He moved to the punching bag, braced his shoulder against it and framed it with his forearms. "Come on, let's see what you've got, love."

Sighing, she moved to the punching bag, gave it a couple of practice jabs.

"Come on, Alby. Like you mean it."

"I don't want to hurt you."

The laughter burst from him even louder than it would have if he hadn't been trying so hard to keep it in. He saw her face change, saw her draw back her slender arm, raising the opposite one in a defensive pose. He braced for the punch. She delivered it. The bag recoiled so rapidly that it picked him off his feet before he lost his grip and sailed backward, hit the wall and slid to the floor.

She walked across the church, and he looked up at her, standing there with her hands on her hips. "You okay?"

"Depends. Can you see the little birdies flitting around my head?"

She extended a hand. He took it and let her tug him to his feet. "Sorry about that."

"Hey, I asked for it." He brushed himself off, gathered up his pride. "So you're strong. We've established that much."

She nodded. "I'm strong. I can pick up my car, one end at a time, not the entire thing."

He could probably do the same, he thought. Yeah, he could do that.

"How about speed?"

"Dad had a treadmill custom-made for me, so I could clock myself in the privacy of our home, where I wouldn't be seen. I've hit sixty."

Then she couldn't move with vampiric speed, so fast she would blur human vision, appearing to vanish and reappear in a new place. He could. At least in this, he was superior.

"And then, of course, there's this."

He started to ask what, but before he spoke, she was looking across the room, and he followed her gaze. She jerked her head a little, and the pew she seemed to be focused on rose up off the floor and shot toward them. Edge ducked, flinging up an arm to protect his head, but the thing stopped in midair and landed heavily, tipping over.

He straightened, lowering his arm, blinking at her. "Unbelievable."

She shrugged. "That's me." Then she sighed. "Don't look so shaken, Edge. I can't control minds or hypnotize mortals or play with their memories. I can send and receive, if the other party isn't blocking. I'm not very good at eavesdropping on thoughts." She shrugged. "Psychically, that's about it. Except for the—"

She broke off there, but Edge heard the final word anyway. Her mind spoke it, though her lips didn't. "The dreams?" he asked. He searched her face, recalled her saying something about dreams earlier, in her delirium. She'd thought she was dreaming then. "What dreams, Alby?"

She shrugged, averting her eyes. "Sometimes I dream…things."

"Things that later come to pass?"

She nodded. "It's usually nothing significant."

"But…?" he prompted, sensing there was more to the thought, though she was shielding more effectively now.

She faced him squarely. "Why are you so interested in me, Edge? Tell me the truth. What do you want with me?"

He smiled just a little, deliberately opened his mind to her, filling his head with images of the two of them engaged in various acts. He made the pictures as vivid and shocking as he could, and he saw her eyes widen, her face redden.

She turned away and whispered, "Besides all that, I mean."

He brought his shields up again. "Nothing, Alby. Why can't you believe me?"

"I know better, that's why. I'm not stupid, Edge. You want to use me…."

"In every imaginable way." He moved up behind her, and when he spoke those words, his cold breath caressed her neck. "I haven't tried to hide that fact from you, Alby."

She shivered.

He stroked his hands down her shoulders, outer arms, all the way to her wrists, then closed his hands on hers. "It's all right. I can be patient."

"There's more. There's more you want from me. I know it."

"I swear there isn't."

"I dreamed about you, Edge."

He went very still, as stunned as if she'd hit him right between the eyes.

"I've been dreaming about you for nearly a year now."

"Really?" He didn't know how to react, what to say.

But he had to know; he had to ask. "What happens in these dreams?" he asked.

"Well, most recently…" she whispered. Then, suddenly, he could see inside her mind as she opened it to him, revealing the same erotic images he'd painted for her only moments earlier. He felt as if his blood turned to lava in his veins. His mind raced, and his hunger for her burned. "Jesus," he muttered.

"Oh, there's more." She leaned back against his chest, let her head fall to one side. He nuzzled her throat, let his lips slide over it, licked softly and felt the pounding beat in the jugular. God, he wanted to taste her.

"God, yes," he muttered against her skin. "What else?" he whispered, parting his lips against her neck to speak the words.

"A couple of things. I'm overwhelmed with feelings of passion, fear and grief. You give me something."

"Yes?" He sucked the skin of her throat just a little, scraped his teeth over it without allowing himself to bite down, and he felt the heat and the passion in her, rising to equal his own.

"Oh, yes. You give me death."

Edge froze. Slowly he lifted his head from her neck, and, hands to her shoulders, he turned her to face him. "I…kill you?"

She nodded. "I don't know. I only know you bring me a gift, and the gift is death. Now maybe you see why I'm a little bit wary about trusting you, Edge."

7

Amber watched him as carefully as she would have watched a coiled cobra. He'd seemed stunned when she told him about her dream. She thought his shock was genuine.

"I'm *not* going to get you killed." The way he said it, she could almost believe he was trying to convince himself as much as her. "I swear, Alby, I'm not. I wouldn't do that."

She shrugged. "That's a funny way to put it."

"What is?"

"You said you wouldn't get me killed. I didn't say you got me killed in the dream, I said you gave me death."

"It's the same thing, isn't it?"

"I don't think so. Not exactly."

He lowered his head, pacing away from her. "Hell, how could I kill you, anyway? I don't even know if anything can kill you. *You* don't even know."

She shrugged. "Well, no, but I know what won't. Drowning, electric shock, poisons, sunlight. Blood loss makes me pretty helpless, but who knows if it would kill me or not? I would imagine burning or beheading—"

"Stop it!"

She smiled, because he looked shaken by the images she'd painted in his mind. Turning away from him, she spent a few minutes pounding the punching bag with hooks, jabs, crescent kicks and back kicks. She was showing off, and she thought he knew it. When she stopped for a breather, he stood aside, hands on his hips, watching her. He said, "Do your dreams always come to pass?"

She sent him a glance. "So far? Always." She gave the bag one last kick for good measure. "Walk me back to the house?"

"And give me a chance to attack?"

"I think I could take you."

"I wish you would."

She smiled slowly.

He said, "Why aren't you running away from me as fast as you can? I don't get it."

"Neither do I. Partly because I want to know what the dream means. And partly…" She lowered her eyes, not finishing the sentence.

"Yeah, partly that. That I understand."

She brushed the comment aside. "I want you to spend more time with the others. Get to know them a little."

"I'm a loner, Alby."

She tilted her head. "It's okay, Edge. They don't know about the dreams. No one does, except Will, and he doesn't know the content. Only that I dreamed about you."

He pursed his lips, lowered his head. "Besides, they're better mind probers than you are, right? They might pick up on my ulterior motives. That's why you really want to drag me back there, isn't it?"

"You weren't lying when you said you didn't trust anyone, were you?" She sighed heavily. "Hell, Edge, if that's what you think, it's fine by me. So long as you have nothing to hide, why do you care?"

He seemed to mull it over for a long moment. Then he brightened a bit. "What's in it for me?" he asked her.

She was surprised, but less so as she examined the spark in his eyes. "You mean I have to resort to bribery to get you to spend time with me?"

"I'll spend every night with you, Alby, if you want. But with those others? Yes, it requires compensation. So what will you give me?"

"What do you want?"

He smiled, an evil smile. She knew, right to the core of her, what he was going to say. Sex. Or blood. Or both. He wanted to take her, own her, possess her, drink her, and God help her, the idea heated her to the verge of meltdown.

"A kiss," he said then.

She blinked at him as her brain registered what he had said, and that it did not match what she had been expecting. "I'm sorry?"

"A kiss. I want one long, passionate, uninhibited kiss."

"You've already kissed me."

He shrugged. "Doesn't mean I won't do it again, but that's beside the point. I want you to kiss me."

She frowned at him. "And if I do, you'll come back to the house with me?"

"And stay until a quarter to dawn, if that's what you want. But it has to be a real kiss. No little peck. Kiss me like you mean it."

She wasn't sure she would be capable of kissing him and *not* meaning it, but she wasn't about to tell him that. "All right, it's a deal. Pucker up."

He wiggled his eyebrows at her and sat down on a bench that had probably once belonged in front of an organ. "Just so you can reach," he explained. "Without standing on tiptoe."

"Mmm-hmm." She moved to the bench and turned to sit beside him, but he stopped her, hands on her waist.

"No, no. Here, like this." He moved her sideways until she stood right in front of the bench, facing him. Then he slid his hands down her sides, over her hips. His fingertips touched her backside as he moved his hands lower, to her thighs, then downward to the hollow behind her knees. Then he tugged gently, so she moved closer, until his knees were between hers and his head was level with her breasts. Pulling on one knee until she bent it, he brought it up, over the bench, around him. Then he tugged at the other.

Amber put her hands on his shoulders, and moved the other leg where he wanted it. He pulled her down, until she sat on him, straddling him.

"There. That's better now, isn't it?" he asked her. His voice had gone soft, rough. She felt him getting hard underneath her. Her belly twisted, and she wanted to do a lot more than kiss him and wasn't even bothered by the fact that his hands had settled on the curve of her ass, so they could keep her hips imprisoned against his. He moved his hips a little, rubbing his erection against her. "Yeah, that's much better. Now kiss me."

Amber licked her lips. His eyes followed the motion. She lifted her palms to his cheeks, tipped his head up a little and lowered hers. He didn't close his eyes but left them open, and she couldn't seem to break the grip they had and close her own. Not until she pressed her mouth to his.

He did not kiss her. He remained still, passive and expectant. She moved her lips over his, opening and closing, adding a little suction that tugged them into her, and she liked that. She experimented then with her tongue, pushing his lips apart and slipping inside. She traced his lips with her tongue, tickled the roof of his mouth with it, then slid over his teeth. She felt his incisors, long and razor-sharp. Then she played with his tongue until she managed to elicit the response she'd been craving.

He closed his arms around her waist, and he kissed her in return. His fangs scraped her lip, and he lapped the taste of blood from the scratch. His fingers tangled in her hair, and he seemed intent on drinking her very soul from her lips and her mouth. That was how deeply he kissed her, how much he took.

When he finally lifted his head away the blood lust was raging so strongly in him that his eyes seemed to glow. Amber was breathless, panting, her heart pounding like the bass-line of a rap song. Her entire body shook and trembled, and she felt light-headed. She twined her arms around his neck and lowered her head to his shoulder, resting against him, waiting for the high voltage charge pulsing through her to fade away.

"Alby?" he asked.

"Hmm?"

"Is this another part of your...you know, abilities?"

She lifted her head slowly. "What?"

He seemed to be searching for the correct way to rephrase his question. "Have you kissed other men?" he asked, finally.

"Of course I've kissed men before." Boys, she thought. No men. Not really.

"Did they...did it...was it like this?"

"Like this?" She smiled at him, realizing it had been as mind-blowing for him as for her. But she wanted to hear him admit that, so she put on her most innocent expression and asked, "Like what?"

"Like what," he repeated, giving her a look that told her he knew exactly what she was doing. "Did their eyes roll back in their heads, doll? Did their tongues loll out to their knees? Did they go into core meltdown?"

The smile broke wide across her lips; she couldn't prevent it. "That's what it felt like to you, too?"

He thinned his lips, averted his eyes. "I didn't say that." Giving her a little nudge, he moved her off his lap, onto her feet, and got to his own. "Let's go, then." He flashed into motion, and before she could speak again, he was out the window, standing on the beach and waiting for her.

Amber went to the window, too, vaulted the sill and landed in a crouch, bouncing quickly upright again. She walked to where he stood, slid her hand into his, laced her fingers through his and began walking along the beach.

He looked down at their hands, a deep frown etching itself between his brows. It wasn't exactly one of dismay or dislike. More like…confusion.

"It's never been like that before, Edge. Never, not with anyone."

He pursed his lips. "Then again, that's not saying much, is it? Given your lack of experience, I mean?"

She looked up at him, and thought, *You know better. It's got nothing to do with my virginity. There's something powerful here.*

He pretended not to have heard her, though she knew he had. And together, they walked back to the house.

"I don't like this. I don't like it one bit," Morgan said softly. She was sitting in a chair on the patio, a notebook computer open on her lap. It painted her worried face in a soft electric blue glow. "Where is she, anyway? Not with that Sting wanna-be, is she?"

"Sting?" Dante asked. He sat nearby in a reclining lawn chair, beside a glass topped umbrella table. The umbrella, of course, was absent. It would have shaded them only from the moonlight. Sarafina sat beside him, and Willem was at the fourth spot.

"I don't think he looks anything like Sting," Amber said, tightening her hand around Edge's as she walked him up the redwood steps to the patio overlooking the beach. "Billy Idol, maybe?"

Everyone looked their way. She'd felt Edge stiffen just a little when they'd first come up and overheard the conversation. He hadn't relaxed, even when she'd turned Morgan's comment back on her.

Dante rose at their approach. "I'm afraid I don't know either reference." He smiled, nodding hello to them.

"It's just as well, since neither is accurate, anyway," Edge said. He glanced at Morgan, and at the laptop. "Bad news, I take it?"

She pursed her lips, shot a look at Amber.

"I'll probably tell him anyway," she said, interpreting Morgan's look correctly.

Morgan sighed. Sarafina said, "If Amber trusts him, we should, as well. She's the one in jeopardy, after all."

Edge lifted his brows. "What makes you think Alby's in danger?"

"Amber Lily is always in danger," Willem said. "She's one of a kind, Edge. Prize quarry for certain hunters."

"Like Frank Stiles," Amber explained in an aside. "That's who they're worried about."

"And now someone has leaked word that she's here,

in Salem,'' Morgan said, and she speared Edge with her eyes when she said it. "It's all over the Internet."

"Well, don't look at me." Edge glanced from one of them to the other. "I'm not exactly a technophile."

"Edge doesn't even have electricity where he's been staying, much less an Internet connection." Amber tugged him by the hand to a thickly cushioned swing that hung from chains and a wood frame. She sat there, and he sank down beside her. She drew a breath. "So do you think Stiles has heard I'm here yet?"

"If he's alive, he's heard," Willem said softly. "I think you should leave, Amber Lily. Go down to Wind Ridge and join Rhiannon, Roland and your parents at Eric and Tam's place."

Edge looked at Amber. "If Stiles knows where you are, will he come for you?"

She smiled slowly as she thought about her answer, then let the smile widen as it came to her in full. "There's not a doubt in my mind," she said. "And that's not necessarily a bad thing."

"Not a bad thing? In what world?" Morgan asked. "Amber, he had you once. You, of all people, should know what he's capable of."

Amber looked at her. "We need him," she said. "He might be our only chance of saving Will. If my being in Salem will bring him to us, then I should stay right here. Let him come. It'll save us the time and trouble of hunting him down. Frankly, if I'd thought of it, I'd have posted that information myself."

Will met Amber's eyes. "I'm not going to let you act as bait, Amber."

She shrugged, not holding his gaze. "If I were to go join the others at Wind Ridge, what makes you think I'd be any safer? What's to stop whoever leaked this information from leaking that, as well?''

She knew when she looked to Willem again and saw his jaw tighten that she'd scored a point. Dante said, "She has a point, Will. We can't be certain she's safe anywhere until we know who's spying on us and why.''

Will nodded at the computer. "Can you track those posts back to the bastard who sent them?''

Rather than answering, Dante looked to Morgan. She nodded. "We can trace them back to the computer that sent them. Not necessarily the individual. And it'll take some time.''

"How long?'' It was Edge who asked the question, and it rather surprised Amber that he was this interested.

"A day, maybe two. There's a tangled mess of screen names and identities to wade through, but I'll get there.''

He nodded, then glanced at Amber. "Maybe they're right. Maybe you should go off to…Windy Hill or wherever that princess and the rest of your family are hiding out.''

"Wind Ridge, and they aren't hiding out, Edge,'' she told him gently. "Rhiannon doesn't believe in it.''

"Whatever. We could sneak you out of here quietly. As far as Stiles would know, you would still be here.''

She tipped her head to one side, searching his eyes until he looked away. "You trying to get rid of me, Edge?''

He slanted her a look, maybe caught the teasing light in her eyes, sent her a wink. "Trying to keep you around, Alby. Alive and kicking.''

She felt a little better, but she wasn't sure she believed him. It was odd, she thought, being so drawn to a man and second-guessing every word he said. "It doesn't matter,'' she told him. "I'm not leaving.''

She eyed the others. "I'm as capable of defending myself as any of you, and you know it."

Will nodded slowly. "We know it."

"Then let's move on to another topic."

"Such as?" Dante asked, a little light of admiration in his eyes.

"Well...Stiles may be on his way here. We should plan for that, figure out what we intend to do about it."

"Wait for him," Sarafina said softly. "We won't have to do much more than that. He'll come to us."

Will shook his head. "He'll come to Amber. By day, more than likely, knowing she'll have less protection."

Edge frowned. "I hadn't...thought of that."

"It's how he did it last time," Will said. "Came for her by day, with half a dozen thugs, all of them armed." He shook his head. "I just don't know how to prepare you, Amber, to withstand an attack like that. But I think you should stick close to me by day. At least you won't be alone."

She lowered her head, looked away. "The two of us could kick the stuffing out of Stiles, Will." Then she added, "Besides, we aren't even sure he's still alive. There's no point in panicking."

"I've put tracers on his social security number," Morgan said. "If he's foolish enough to use it, I'll pick up any credit cards he might try to obtain or existing ones he might use, jobs he might take, vehicles he buys or tries to license, and just about anything else he does." She pursed her lips, shook her head. "Though if he is alive, he's managed to remain all but invisible for the past five years. Still, if he thinks he's close to getting his hands on Amber again, he might get eager enough to slip up."

"I have more faith in the undead than I do in the computer," Dante said softly.

"What do you mean?" Edge asked.

Dante held his gaze steadily. "I've sent the message out to every vampire I could reach," he said. And Amber knew he was talking about a mental message, not a mass e-mail. "They know it's more important now than ever before to watch for Stiles, to contact us if he's spotted."

"Anything yet?" Amber asked.

He shook his head.

"I can keep an eye on the local hotels, inns, that sort of thing," Edge offered.

"There are dozens of them," Sarafina told him. She'd been uncharacteristically quiet, Amber thought, though she understood why. Her heart was breaking.

Edge only shrugged. "I'm a vampire. I can cover them in an evening."

"It's a good idea," Will said. "Stiles will need to stay somewhere, and he'll likely rush here without much prep time when he hears Amber is in town."

"Meanwhile, there's another problem we need to contend with."

"Another problem?" Amber searched Dante's face. "I can't imagine anything else dire enough to compete with Will's death sentence and Stiles's impending visit."

"Show her, Dante," Morgan said.

Dante's lips thinned, but he got to his feet and walked quickly down the steps and across the sloping lawn toward the shore. Amber followed him, Edge walking along beside her, his hands shoved into his jeans pockets. Waves rolled slowly, hypnotically over the rock and pebble strewn beach. Willem's small motorboat sat there, pulled up onto the beach. It had a rope extending from a metal ring on its nose to a large, darkly colored wooden post that had been driven deep into the ground. A tan-colored canvas covered it.

"Someone's been hunting in Salem," Dante said.

She blinked. "Hunting?" She wrinkled her nose, smelling something unpleasant and familiar.

Death.

The word whispered through her mind, and her heart turned over. The fear she always felt in the dream shivered through her soul.

Dante reached down, tugged the canvas back. Amber sucked in a breath when she saw the body lying there, turning her head away automatically.

"Hell," Edge muttered. "You might have warned her." His hands closed on Amber's shoulders as if to comfort her from the disturbing sight. But she sent him a look telling him she was all right and turned to take another look.

The woman lay in the bottom of the boat. She was in her fifties, gaunt and, of course, pale as porcelain. She wore a long black dress of sheer fabric over a satin underskirt. The sleeves had draping points at their ends. Her throat, Amber noted, bore two small punctures, right over the jugular.

She turned around again, staring at Edge, and realized Dante was doing the same.

He lifted his brows and his hands. "Why are you looking at *me?*"

Amber frowned, wishing she knew what he was thinking just then, but his thoughts were guarded.

"Sure," Edge went on. "Blame the new guy. This is Salem, for Chrissakes. It's probably crawling with vampires."

Blinking slowly, Amber turned to Dante again. "What was she dressed up for?"

"I don't know. I found her when I was in town earlier tonight, just getting the lay of the land. Smelled her and homed in. She was underneath a pier, lying on the rocks. No identification, no other marks."

"How long ago was she killed?"

"Last night sometime. No one's been reported missing—not yet, anyway."

Amber pressed her lips tight. Edge said, "Why did you drag her back here, anyway?"

Dante's face darkened, and Amber spoke before he could. "We can't have bloodless bodies with fang marks in their throats showing up in Salem, Edge. Do you know what the media would do with a story like that? It would be an open invitation to every vampire hunter in the country."

"In the world," Dante said. "You're a loner, aren't you? One of those solitary vamps who shuns his own kind?"

Edge shrugged, reaching down to tug the canvas back over the body. "I don't shun them. Don't seek them out, either."

"Until now," Dante said.

Edge met his eyes. "If you want to accuse me of something, stop dancing around it and step up."

Dante held his temper, in spite of the clear challenge Edge had laid down. "We don't kill humans."

"*We?* What, you're speaking for me now? *You* don't kill humans, Dante. *I* do what I damn well please."

Dante's eyes narrowed, and his fists clenched. Edge leaned in a little closer, and Amber stepped between the two, pressing a hand to each powerful chest. "That's enough. Dante, if Edge says he didn't kill that woman, then he didn't. Let it go."

She was all too aware, though, that Edge hadn't said any such thing.

"You could do with some manners," Dante muttered. He turned away, heading back toward the house. "Who the hell sired you, anyway? Satan?"

"He didn't stick around long enough to give me his name," Edge shot back. "But according to local legend, it was O'Roark."

Dante stopped walking, stood stock-still in the sand. "Donovan O'Roark?"

8

"We can take my car," Amber said, jarring Edge a bit from his contemplation of the ever-shrinking motor-boat. He dragged his gaze from the sea, fixed it instead on the woman who stood beside him on the pebble-strewn shore.

"To check the hotels in town, I mean," she added. "To see whether Stiles has checked into any of them."

"Right." He glanced at the sea again. "I'm surprised he's willing to dump the body like that."

"Why?"

He shrugged. "Figured this crew of yours to be more the notify-the-next-of-kin-and-hold-them-while-they-cry types." He shook a cigarette from the pack in his pocket, fired it up.

She lowered her head, so her dark, dark hair fell over her eyes. "They're kind, Edge, but they're not stupid. Leaving victims around only draws attention to our existence. It would be a dangerous thing to do, for all of us." She glanced behind them at the ocean. "I pity her family, though. Never to know what became of her…"

"She has no family."

Amber looked at him sharply.

He shoved his hands into his pockets, lowered his head. "Lost them in a house fire six months back. Husband, teenage twins."

Her eyes narrowed. "How do you know this?"

He didn't answer the question. "Then last month she was diagnosed with cancer. Inoperable. So she went to that bridge, tied a cinder block to her leg, and stood there trying to work up the nerve to jump."

"You killed her, didn't you?"

"I did her a favor."

Amber sighed deeply, lowering her head. "You shouldn't have done it."

"Do you believe in an afterlife, Alby? Some paradise where souls go when their bodies wear out?"

She started walking back along the beach toward the house, and he fell into step beside her, smoking, waiting for her answer.

"I suppose I do," she said.

"Then she's there now, with her husband and her girls. Better than where she was, facing a slow, lingering death with nothing but her grief for company."

They'd skirted the house and come to where Amber's car was parked in the driveway. She went to the driver's door, opened it, but didn't get in. Instead she looked over the top of the car at Edge. "Do you?"

"What? Believe in heaven?"

She nodded.

He took a last drag from his cigarette, then flicked it away. "Haven't thought about it, Alby. Why should I? I'm never going to die."

They visited every hotel and inn they could locate, stopping first at a visitors' center for a comprehensive list. They didn't go inside. Copping a look at guest registries or computers wasn't necessary. Amber knew Stiles—far better than she would have liked. She searched for him by opening her mind, her senses, listening, smelling, *feeling* for his presence. She was certain she would know if he were near.

Certainly her psychic powers were nowhere near as strong as those of a vampire. But they were good, sharp. Especially where her one-time captor was concerned.

Oddly, she could have sworn Edge was doing the same thing. And yet, he didn't know Stiles. Did he?

By the time they had finished, it was 4:00 a.m. She drove back to the beach house, which was quiet now. Apparently everyone had gone inside. When they got out of the car, Edge said, "No sign of Stiles, then. You must be relieved."

She met his eyes, sighed. "Not as much as you would think. We need him."

He nodded. "We'll find him."

She was certain they would. They had to. She licked her lips. "That woman, the one you—"

"What about her?"

She lowered her head, looked away.

"You want to know what kind of cancer she had. Whether it was like your friend Willem's." He came around the car and, to her surprise, closed his hand around one of hers, tugging her with him as he walked toward the shore.

"Was it?"

"No. Pancreatic. And it had spread to the liver, stomach. She was a mess."

Amber nodded. They were on the shore now, walking slowly back toward Edge's place. She looked at him, searched his face, wondering if he was a monster, wondering what the poor woman's final moments had been like.

He held her gaze as they walked, then stopped and turned her to face him. "I walked up on her, there on the bridge. Her grief was so loud I didn't even have to try to read her thoughts. They were pouring out of her. She looked at me, just looked at me, for the longest time. And she knew what I was. I don't know how, but she did.''

Amber felt caught in his eyes, mesmerized by them. ''Was she afraid?''

He shook his head slowly, left, then right. ''She pushed her hair back, tipped her head to one side. She said, 'Please.' Just that one word, nothing more. But it came with a rush of pain that was…unbearable.''

She saw the echo of that pain in his eyes, just for a moment.

''So I took her into my arms,'' he said, taking Amber into his arms as he did so. She relaxed against him, and he bent his head, nuzzled her neck. ''I held her, and I drank from her.'' His lips moved against her throat as he spoke. ''Her pain, her grief, her suffering, her despair— I took it all away, and I felt every bit of it as I did. But she felt…only ecstasy. A rush of relief and release.'' He let his lips part and close on the skin of her neck, gentle suction that made her knees weak. ''She thanked me with her final breath.''

''It was a better death than she might have had otherwise,'' Amber whispered. ''Then you truly only did what you did—to help her?''

He backed away from her neck, blinked down at her. ''I did what I did because it was a free meal.''

The spell was broken. Amber took a shocked step away from him.

''Don't try to think of me as one of your do-gooders, Alby. I make decisions based on what's best for me, and me alone. I'm nobody's hero. And I'm nothing like your friends back there at Chez Stone.''

She stood there for a moment, willing his mind to open to hers, but it was impenetrable. "I don't think I believe you," she told him.

"You don't want to believe me. You can't let yourself be taken by a man like me. You think you're too good for that. But you do want me to take you. So you're trying to believe I'm someone else."

"That's not what I'm trying to do."

"No?"

She shook her head slowly. "No. I'm just trying to— know you."

"And why do you want to know me, Alby?"

She held his gaze, decided to shock him by being straightforward with him. "Because I want you, and I can't let myself…be intimate with a man I don't even know. And because I'm not convinced our first meeting was an accident at all. I think you're up to something, and I can't let myself be intimate with a man I don't trust."

He smiled slowly. "You never know until you try."

"What would be the point?"

"The same thing that's always the point where sex is concerned, Alby. Pleasure. Screaming, trembling, mind-blowing pleasure." He ran a fingertip from her temple down her cheek to her chin. "What else is there?"

She held his gaze, shivering down deep, and she knew he was doing something to her with his eyes, with his mind, or trying to. He was making her want him. He had to be, because God, she'd never wanted this way before. Never!

"You're afraid of me, aren't you?"

She shook her head in denial.

"It's all right. That'll only make it better. Come on." He slid his arms around her waist, pulled her hard against him, so his hips were pressed to hers. He put his hands on her backside, squeezing it and holding her to him. He lowered his head, nuzzled her neck some more. She shivered, and he slid his lips around, tracing her jaw and finally finding her mouth. He kissed her, and she opened for him, let him lick and taste and probe her.

He held her so hard that when he let his knees bend and fell backward onto the sand, he took her with him. He was powerful. So strong. And yet, so was she. And she was on top of him now, and angry with herself for being so afraid of something as simple as sex with this man, when she wanted it so badly she burned.

She shifted her legs so that she straddled him, her knees in the sand bracketing his hips, and she threaded her fingers in his hair and kissed him back, just as deeply as he'd kissed her. His hips moved against her, and she rubbed him in return. He made a little growling sound, rolling her quickly onto her back, pinning her there with his body. Rising a little, he reached down to her blouse, hooked a finger at the neck and gave a tug, tearing it from neck to hemline, smiling while he did it.

She gasped at the feel of the chill sea air on her naked breasts, but it was his eyes on them as much as the cold that made them harden and ache. He put his hands on her then, flicking his thumbs over her nipples and making her suck in a breath with every touch. Then he bent, sliding lower over her body so his mouth could catch a nipple, while his fingers held the other.

At the touch of his lips, she cried out. At the tugging, pulling suction, she stopped breathing. At the pinch of his teeth, every cell in her body screamed in pleasure.

He slid one hand between them, down the front of her jeans, and he didn't take his time, didn't hesitate, didn't wait for permission to tug them open. He pushed her legs apart with his own and slid his fingers into the wetness there, rubbing, stroking, driving into her until she was writhing.

Then suddenly the hand was gone, and the mouth left her breast, wet now in the cold air, and he was kneeling between her parted legs, tugging the jeans off her so furiously she didn't have time to object. He tore the panties off and threw them to the wind, then pushed her knees up to her chest and bent his head to her center.

She heard herself screaming, begging, panting and moaning, and didn't even recognize the sound of her own voice. His mouth attacked, his tongue possessed, as he devoured her. When she twisted he held her still, when she pushed at his head he shoved her hands away and burrowed deeper. He bit and licked and sucked at her until her mind exploded and she shrieked his name aloud.

And even as the spasms racked her body, he was sliding up over her, shoving his own jeans down as he did. She felt the hardness of him at her pulsing center, and then he plunged into her, spearing her deeply. She felt resistance, no real pain. Her body was too busy screaming in ecstasy to allow her to feel pain. And even before the waves of the first orgasm faded, he was pushing her toward another, driving into her, possessing her, holding her to receive him.

When she exploded again, he did, too. She felt the rush of him filling her, the pleasure of his release as, finally, for the first time since she'd known him, the barriers around his mind dissolved and she could feel everything inside him. His pleasure. His confusion. His wondering what the hell it was about her that made the experience more powerful than any he'd ever had before. His wondering how soon he would be able to convince her to do this again. His regret that he had to use her....

Use me for what? she wondered, and the moment she did, the shields slammed back into place around his mind. Dammit, it hadn't occurred to her that she'd been as open to him as he had to her during those moments of intense union.

He rolled onto his back, pulling her with him, until she lay nestled in the curve of his arm, her head on his chest. She lay there, shivering with the aftermath of pleasure.

He said, "Still afraid of me?"

"Petrified," she admitted.

"Afraid I'm going to hurt you?"

"Try it and I'll kick your ass. I suppose I might be a little afraid of doing you permanent damage if I have to do that."

"Right."

She lifted her head, smiled at him.

"That's not what I meant, and you know it."

She looked away. "You think you could hurt me any other way? Emotionally? I don't intend to give you the power to do that, either. Don't flatter yourself."

He held her gaze. "You're a smart girl, Alby. Smart girl." Then he pulled her to him again, arching his hips to hers, hard and ready for more.

She kissed his chin and whispered, "The sun will be up soon, Edge."

He closed his eyes in frustration, fell back onto the sand, swore softly.

"Not too bad, hmm? If I could make a vampire forget the sunrise?"

He lifted his hips off the sand and tugged his jeans up. "Not too bad at all, Alby."

She pursed her lips. "You're a real romantic." She rolled to her back, sat up, and looked around the sand at her scattered clothes. Her jeans were within reach, so she pulled them on. Her panties and blouse were ruined. "How the hell am I supposed to walk back to the house like this?"

He rolled into a sitting up position, peeling his T-shirt over his head as he did, then handed it to her. "Put mine on. It's not like I need it."

She stared at him and tried not to let herself get distracted by the washboard abs, instead sending him a disapproving look. "You didn't even get undressed."

"I'd strip off every stitch if we had more time. I will next time," he told her. "Promise." He sent her a wink.

She scowled at him, held out a hand, and when he took it, she pulled him to his feet. "You're damn right you will."

His smile grew. "Wow."

"What?"

"I half expected you to tell me there wasn't going to be a next time."

"That would be pretty stupid, considering we both know there will be."

He waggled his eyebrows. "That good, was I?"

"That's not what I heard whispering through your mind a few minutes ago."

His eyes narrowed. "Thought I felt you listening in."

"It's the first time you've let your guard down since I've met you. I couldn't resist."

"Mmm. The euphoria of sex will do that to a man."

She shrugged. "So I was the best you've ever had, huh?"

"Everyone's the best one at that particular moment, Alby. Don't go reading too much into it."

"Don't worry, I won't."

He studied her face for a long while. She didn't hold

his gaze, though, as they walked along the shore. Instead she let hers fall and found herself studying his chest again. He had a great chest. Not huge, not bulky, but every muscle clear and hard beneath the taut, pale skin. He could have been a sculpture. She thought vaguely that it ought to be illegal to cover it up, ever.

Finally she looked up. "We're going the wrong way, if I'm still walking you home," she said.

"You're not. I'm walking you home." He stopped looking at her, sighed and slid an arm around her shoulders.

"Don't tell me you're getting protective instincts just because we had sex?"

He made a sound of disbelief. "Hell no. I never wanted you to walk me home in the first place. Just wanted to get you alone on the beach so I could make my move."

"I see." She glanced out at the paling sky. "You going to have time to get back home?"

"Have you seen my speed?"

"Yeah, just a few minutes ago on the beach."

His head swung around fast, eyes wide, until he saw her smiling. Still he said, "Is that a complaint?"

She lowered her head, put a palm on his chest and slid it slowly over his luscious pecs. "I enjoyed every second of it, Edge."

"But next time you'd like to go slower." He put a hand over hers on his chest, so she had to stop moving it around. She wondered why. He licked his lips, looked past her. "We're here."

All too soon, she thought. She turned, saw the house behind her, sighed and faced him again.

"I should go," he said.

"So go, then."

He started to turn away.

"Bye, Edge. Have a good rest."

He stopped moving and stood there, then turned half-way around, and she thought he was arguing with him-self. Finally, he sighed, swore under his breath and faced her again, only to wrap her in a fierce embrace. He took her mouth deeply, thoroughly, held her entire body so tightly to his own she wondered why they didn't meld. And she thought she felt him shiver.

When he let her go, he turned without a word and vanished. She knew he hadn't disappeared. It had only been a burst of speed.

She licked her lips, lowered her head, wondered why every cell in her body tingled and sang. She felt more alive than she had ever felt. Ever. Because of him?

No, she told herself. Not because of him. Because she'd experienced something she'd never experienced before, and it had been great. Better than great.

She couldn't let this feeling be because of him. She couldn't let herself fall for him, because he'd made it very clear to her that that would be a mistake. And be-cause she believed him.

She'd dreamed of him. In the dream, he'd been dark, tortured, frightening. He'd given her something, some-thing that terrified her. Death. What did it mean? That damned dream, what could it possibly mean?

She had to find out. And she had to be careful.

She walked along the beach, found a place to sit, with a boulder at her back and sank into the sand, drawing her knees to her chest. She watched the waves rolling slowly over the shore. Watched the deep indigo color of the sea slowly change to purple. The upper curve of the sun licked at the sky, painting the streaks of cloud above it in fiery red, neon orange, lemon-yellow.

"Beautiful thing, the sunrise."

She didn't take her eyes away from the spectacular sight when she heard Willem's voice or when he sank into the sand beside her. "I think people like us probably appreciate it more than most."

"I imagine we do. Being so intimately close to those who can never see it themselves."

"It's odd, isn't it? The very thing that ensures life can exist on earth means death to vampires."

"Mmm. Maybe someday we'll find a way around that."

She sighed, turning to study Will. He didn't look well, she thought. Paler than usual, and there were dark circles under his eyes. "How are you feeling?"

"Not great, but that's between us."

She nodded. "You can trust me."

"I know. I hope you know you can trust *me,* too."

"I do." She clasped his hand, leaning closer, so her shoulder pressed to his.

"Amber, Morgan managed to find the source of those Internet posts."

She lifted her head. "That's progress. So who sent them?"

He licked his lips. "We don't know who. But they were posted from a computer in the office of a local gym."

Amber's heart slowly formed a thin layer of ice.

"Salem Fitness Center," he said. "And the posts were sent after hours, sometime in the dead of night. We checked the police blotter in the local paper, found they'd reported a break-in that same night. A few pieces of equipment are missing."

She lowered her head very slowly. "Thanks for telling me."

He didn't say anything for a moment. Then, "Do you think it was Edge?"

She shrugged, knowing even that motion of uncertainty was a bald-faced lie. She knew it was Edge. He was using her—apparently as bait to lure Stiles. But why?

"Amber, I don't know this guy. What I've seen of him, I don't find particularly endearing, but…things aren't always what they seem."

She lifted her head, searching Willem's eyes.

"When I first met 'Fina, I thought I knew what she was. Bloodthirsty, cold-hearted, ruthless. I was wrong. There might be more to this Edge fellow than he's letting you see."

"I had the same notion myself."

"We might know a little more about him soon, at any rate."

"How?"

Will sighed. It seemed to Amber that talking was leaving him short of breath. And she thought he might be cold, as well. She rose to her feet, extending a hand to him. He pretended not to see it there and got up on his own, using the good leg and walking stick more than the bad one. Stubborn man.

They turned together, began walking back to the house. His limp seemed more pronounced than it had been earlier. "Dante said he mentioned the name of his sire last night."

"Yes. O'Roark. I think it's someone Dante knows."

"Someone Dante sired," Will told her.

She blinked in shock. "You're kidding me."

He shook his head. "He hasn't seen the man in centuries. Traveled back to Ireland several years ago hoping to renew the acquaintance, but it never happened."

She smiled a little. "Dante took an instant dislike to Edge. It's almost funny that it turns out they're related."

Will rolled his eyes. "I suppose, in vampiric terms, they are." Then he joined her in the smile, though his seemed halfhearted. "Serves Dante right. He's always been a little too full of himself, in my opinion."

"You just haven't forgiven him for hurting Sarafina all those years ago."

He shrugged, pausing at the bottom of the back steps, and she thought he was catching his breath.

"God, Will, it's worse than you've been letting anyone know."

He lifted his head. "Yeah. But keep that to yourself."

"You know I will, but how are you managing to hide it? Especially from 'Fina?"

"Hell, kid, I've learned a few things about shielding my thoughts from the graveyard shift."

She smiled. "How bad is it? Be honest with me, Will."

He pursed his lips, lowered his eyes. "I've been through worse."

"You've been through torture, so that's not really saying much."

He sighed and climbed the three steps to the deck, then crossed it. "It's not so much the pain—that comes and goes, and right now it's absent—it's this damned exhaustion. I can't stand being this weak."

"Maybe he did us a favor, posting that information on the Internet," she said softly.

"He?"

She shot him a glance. "Whoever it was, he had to be male. Women just aren't that obvious."

He knew perfectly well she thought it was Edge, but

he wasn't going to call her on it. "Typical reverse sexism."

She got to the door before him, reached to pull it open, then waited while he walked through. "You ready to get some sleep?" she asked him.

He nodded. "You?"

"Yeah, soon as I shower."

He closed and locked the door, flicked a button. "We've got an alarm system and it's armed. If anyone comes near the place, you'll hear bells and whistles. You come straight to me if you hear anything like that. All right?"

She nodded as she walked beside him up the stairs to the second floor, and they stopped outside the master bedroom. "All right."

"I mean it. I'm sick, not dead. I can still shoot straight, and my forty-five will stop an elephant in its tracks."

"I have *got* to get myself one of those."

He chucked her on the chin. "I'm well aware you're not without skills of your own, kid. But if Stiles and his goons come for you and you don't let me help fend 'em off, I'm gonna be mad as hell."

Secretly, she thought that if Stiles and his goons came for her, the goons would wind up dead or running for their lives, and Stiles would end up *her* prisoner for a change.

"Have a good sleep," she told Will.

"You, too."

She didn't, though. She had the dream again. The man, the beautiful man, with a face like an archangel, all dressed in black, came to her again, appearing from within a thick swirl of mist. He had a name now, her dark angel. Edge. And again he held out the box. Ornate, ancient looking, not a single inch of its rich dark wood face was smooth. All of it was carved, engraved, embellished, with swirls and symbols and shapes. She thought she saw eyes tooled into the wood. He offered it to her yet again.

As before, she told herself no. Don't take it. Don't touch it. Don't look inside.

But this time she could not stop her dream self from accepting the gift. She reached out, her hands trembling, sweat beading on her forehead, as her palms pressed to the sides of the box, and, slowly, she lowered her gaze.

She stared inside, and this time…she saw what was there.

Amber shrieked in terror. She sat up in the bed, coming wide-awake, and still screaming until she forced her jaws closed.

Her bedroom door burst open. Will stood there, wide-eyed, a handgun so big she was surprised he could heft it clasped in his hands.

"What is it?" he shouted. "What's wrong, Amber?"

She lowered her head, shaking it side to side, racking her brain, her memory. But the dream was gone. Whatever she'd seen, whatever had caused her terror, was gone like the morning mist when the sun comes out. What the hell had she seen in that box in her dream that had made her blood run ice cold and her mind whirl in shock and denial?

"My God," she whispered. "Nothing could be that bad. Could it?"

9

Amber refused to acknowledge the ache in her heart when she returned to the abandoned church just before sundown. The anger, that was all right. Acceptable. He'd used her, leaked her presence in Salem to the entire Internet-using public, just to lure Stiles here. For what purpose, she could only guess. He must have a grudge against the vampire hunter, like so many of his kind. It didn't matter why. And it didn't matter that she would have done the same thing if she'd thought of it first. It only mattered that Edge had put her life at risk to satisfy his hunger for vengeance.

Well, he wasn't going to get away with it. She would call him on it tonight. Tell him she knew damned well what he'd done. Put him on notice that he wasn't to harm one piece of twisted pink scar tissue on Stiles's face until she got the information she needed from the man.

After that, she could care less.

Dammit, why did it hurt so much? She didn't give a damn about Edge. She wouldn't be stupid enough to have any feelings for a man like him. Any emotional feelings, at least. She couldn't help her physical feelings.

Her insides turned wet and warm when she thought about that, so she banished the memory as she climbed through the window of the church. Landing on the floor, she brushed off her hands, and eyed the punching bag that hung from a rafter. Salem Fitness Center was printed on its side.

"Bastard," she said, punctuating the word with a jab to the bag. It felt good, hitting the bag, imagining it as his face. His chiseled, sharp face. With those cheekbones and that damnable sexy dimple. She hit it again. "You used me, you son of a—" Right hook to the temple, rattling that peroxide blond head. Uppercut, splitting those full, sexy lips. "Probably never even wanted me. Not really." She delivered a roundhouse blow, then a series of kicks that she thought would be rib breakers for sure. "It was all just a game, wasn't it, Edge?" The final blow should have taken off his head.

It didn't. Instead it tore the bag from its eye-ring. The weighted sack flew a couple of yards and hit the floor, cracking several floorboards and sending up a dust cloud.

She pursed her lips, sucking in a few breaths, enjoying the surge of blood in her veins and the release of her anger. Then she turned, noted the spreading darkness and, for the first time, the lack of brick-a-brack on the makeshift altar in the front.

Her brows drew together. She opened her senses but felt no hint of Edge nearby. His presence made her skin tingle; there would have been no mistaking it. "Edge?"

But she didn't need to wait, or listen to the echoing answer of her own voice. She knew. He wasn't there. He was gone.

Edge opened his eyes and stared up at the wooden ribs curving downward, around either side of him. For a moment the notion that he'd been swallowed by a large fish amused him with its absurdity, and then his head cleared and he remembered. His head was pillowed by his freshly packed duffel bag, and his back by the sand and grass surface where beach gave way to meadow. He'd arrived back at the church with enough time to gather his things and head out, but he'd had to settle for the first shelter he'd found, which turned out to be an over-turned rowboat. He'd hauled the thing inland far enough to be sure the tide wouldn't reach him and scrambled underneath for the night.

It was a good enough shelter. No sun made it through. And as he lifted one side now, he saw that the sun was long gone. He flung the boat over, sat up, ran his hands through his hair and instantly thought of the one thing he'd decided not to think of, the same thing he'd gone to sleep thinking of. Amber Lily Bryant.

By now, he thought, she probably had a pretty good idea of what he'd been up to, that he'd been the one to send the posts to the 'net, tipping off any who cared to know that she was in Salem.

Hell, he probably shouldn't have done that. And no doubt she was mad as hell about it. But it wasn't as if he intended to let the guy within a mile of her. She wasn't at risk. He wouldn't let her be at risk. He would nab Stiles long before Amber was in any danger.

And besides, this would be over soon. Stiles was on his way. Edge felt it right to his bones. He was making his way north, on U.S. 1., drawing closer with every tick of the clock. Odd he would take the scenic route, rather than the faster one, but Edge assumed the butcher had his reasons. The knowledge had come to him during his rest, clearly, sharply. He didn't question it. He'd been prepared to lurk around Salem, avoiding Alby and her expressive, soulful eyes for as long as necessary. It was just as well it would be over with soon.

He slung the duffel over his shoulder and began hiking into town. He didn't exert his preternatural speed. He didn't need to, he had time, and in fact, he was enjoying the walk, the night, the sea air.

In an hour, he was south of Salem, walking along the shoulder of the road, waiting for Stiles to show. It was going to be great, killing the bastard at last. He intended to make sure the son of a bitch stayed dead this time, even if it meant cutting him to bits and burning the pieces. He would relish every second of it.

Headlights came, grew brighter, passed by. He sent his awareness into each vehicle, until, eventually, he felt the approach of the one he'd been waiting for.

Stiles. He was sitting in the back seat, passenger side. Edge focused on him, homing in on his mind. He could see the backs of the heads of two men in the front seat. He could hear the strains of a baritone, booming out in Italian, and realized it came from a set of headphones. He felt the rub of a waistband slightly too snug, and the protests of muscles too long in the same position.

He waited, letting the headlights come closer, and then he stepped out into the center of the road.

The car didn't slow. Edge didn't move. He could play chicken with the best of them.

The driver stepped down harder on the accelerator, and Stiles yanked the headphones off and leaned forward. Shit. They were going to hit him. Edge braced himself for the impact, set his feet and waited. He wouldn't give easily, and that car was going to end up smoking in the ditch, at the very least.

It came faster, closing the distance between them.

He set his jaw.

And Alby stepped in front of him.

Even as his shocked mind registered her presence and his hands reached up to push her out of the path of danger, she set her feet and flung up her hands as if shooing a fly. Her hair blew behind her, tickling his face, but he saw the car all the same. Its tires skidded sideways, leaving black streaks of rubber on the pavement, and then it flipped up onto its side. Metal scraped the blacktop, and showers of sparks arched. Edge flung his arms up in front of his face automatically. But Alby still stood where she was, not moving, just watching until the car came to a stop in the dust on the side of the road.

She turned slowly.

Edge caught his breath. Her eyes glowed, blue-black, as if backlit from within.

But even as he searched them, the light faded. He found the ability to speak, said, "Jesus, Alby, what the hell are you doing here?"

"Came to tell you to go to hell," she said. "The timing was just good luck."

Turning, she started forward, toward the car.

Edge gripped her arm, tugged her around to face him. "How did you find me?"

She only smiled slowly and pulled free again.

Again he grabbed her, spun her around. "Dammit, Alby, get out of here. He'll hurt you if he can."

"Oh, and protecting me is right on top of your list of priorities, right, Edge? Just like making love to me was?"

"Alby—"

She flung her hand at him, and he thought she meant to backhand him across the face. But it was considerably more than that. While she never touched him, her energy did. He felt the impact like a blast of furnace-hot wind that lifted him off his feet and sent him flying backward a good ten yards.

When he landed, the breath was driven out of him. He lifted his head, shook it clear and focused on the woman.

God, she was raging. He felt it blasting from her in waves. She faced the car, jerked her head upward, then down, an exaggerated nod. The car followed the motion, rocking back down, so all four tires were on the pavement again. She swung her head to the left, and the front doors popped open. She pointed at the car, flicked her wrist upward, and the driver was yanked out as if by an invisible giant. He rolled and tumbled thirty feet along the road. She repeated the gesture and the other man was flung from the passenger side.

She got behind the wheel, slammed the door.

Edge dragged himself to his feet. He moved into the road, aware that Stiles was in that car with Amber, probably in the back seat. Jesus, what if he hurt her? What if he…?

She gunned the engine, and the tires spun, spitting dirt and rocks up behind them as the car fishtailed its way back onto the road.

Edge moved faster, putting himself right in her path.

And he heard her shout at him mentally, *Move it!*

You'll have to go through me.

Have it your way.

She gunned it, and she hit him. The pain exploded from his hipbone, where the bumper drove into him, to his head, when it connected with the pavement. He felt his skull split and was blinded by pain.

Jesus! He couldn't believe she'd actually hit him. Oh, God, it hurt!

He struggled to get upright, and that was when he felt the moisture, the blood oozing from the gaping wound. Dammit. It flowed too fast, and though he pressed his hand to the wound to stanch the flow, he knew it wasn't going to do him much good. He sat up, struggled to his feet, pressing his hand to his head and watching through the flowing blood as Amber drove by. And then his knees gave out, and he sank to the ground.

"Dammit to hell," she muttered, easing the car along the road, keeping her focus divided between the unconscious man in the back seat and Edge. "Don't do this to me again," she asked him. "It's an act, it's just an act. Damn you, Edge."

But she saw the blood oozing from between his fingers where they splayed against his head, and she felt the pain shooting like an electric current through his limbs. And beyond him, she saw Stiles's two henchmen stirring.

As Edge's eyes rolled back and he sank to the ground, she stopped the car. She couldn't leave him there. Not like that.

Hell. Twisting in her seat, she leaned over to examine Stiles. He was leaning sideways, seat belt on, body limp, not a mark on him.

Faking?

Beside him, a black bag, like a doctor might carry, rested on the seat. She smiled slowly, yanked it into the front with her and opened it up. It was jam packed with fun little toys. Vials of drugs, tranquilizer guns, handcuffs with keys taped to the chain, leg irons and even a snub-nosed .38 and a miniature first-aid kit. She took out the handcuffs, put one of them on his wrist and jerked him forward until she could snap the other around the steering wheel. Then she put the keys in her pocket and got out, taking the bag with her.

"Edge?"

She moved closer to him, certain he was faking her out yet again. Damn him, using her to lure Stiles here and then trying to beat her to the bastard.

She knelt down on the pavement, where he'd collapsed, and she touched him.

He moaned a little.

"Edge?" She rolled him onto his back and saw the blood pumping from the cut in his head. "Dammit, why the hell didn't you move?"

His eyes didn't open. But his lips moved. In a bare whisper he said, "Didn't think you'd really hit me."

"You deserved worse."

"Mmm. True enough."

She dug the first-aid kit out of the black bag and rummaged inside. It was almost useless, but she did locate a roll of gauze and adhesive tape. She tore off strips of the tape, then pinched the gaping cut together and applied them. He winced, and she knew that pain in him was magnified. Vampires felt it like no one else. And she ached for him, even though she hated him at that moment. She wouldn't have stopped at all, if not for the fact that he would have bled out before dawn.

When she finished her work, the bleeding seemed to stop. She added some gauze over the wound, holding it there with more tape.

"You'll be all right now," she said. "I have to go."

"No." He gripped her arm, even as she rose from his side. "Jesus, Alby, you can't leave me here. I'm weak as a kitten."

"You'll last until daybreak. Just find some shelter and then you'll heal."

"I won't last an hour. Look around you, woman."

She did. The two henchmen were up now, moving cautiously nearer, one from either direction.

"Go away!" she ordered, and with a snap of her wrists, they were both flung backward.

Edge lay there, not moving. She leaned over him, gripping his shoulders. "Come on, get up, I'll put you somewhere safe."

"I'll die if you leave me," he told her.

"You're the best liar I've ever met."

"I never lied to you. I'm not now."

"And I'm supposed to believe that?"

He closed his eyes, hesitated, opened them again, and when he did, he opened his mind to her, let her see and hear and feel inside him. *I need you, Alby. Don't leave me to die. Take me with you, wherever the hell you're going.*

She stared down at him. As she did, a single strand of blood made its way from beneath the bandage on his head to trickle slowly down his cheek. "Damn you for this." She tugged him up into a sitting position, then pulled his arm over her shoulders and got upright, taking him with her.

"Thanks," he muttered, grunting the word as she hauled him to the car. She opened the front passenger door without touching it and slung him into the seat. Then she went around to the other side to open her own door. She unlocked the handcuff from the steering wheel, then leaning into the back seat, knocked Stiles onto the seat facedown, pulled his hands behind his back and snapped the cuff around the free wrist to keep them there.

Finally she twisted face front in her seat, pocketed the handcuff key and slammed the vehicle into gear again.

Edge lifted his head, opened his eyes, tried to take stock as his awareness slowly returned. His head hurt. That was the first thing that made its way to his consciousness: pain. A sense of exhaustion, of being drained of energy, followed on its heels, and he wondered why, but only briefly. Memory returned slowly. The clash with

Stiles. Amber Lily's anger. He frowned, then, because the last thing he remembered was her helping him into the car. But he wasn't in a car now. He was in a pile of musty smelling hay, inside what must be a barn. She must have dumped him somewhere she assumed would be safe come sunrise and gone on her way.

Unfortunately he wasn't sure he was going to survive until sunrise, as bad as he felt.

"Awake, finally?"

He jerked his head toward the sound of her voice. She walked toward him, sank into the hay beside him.

"Finally?" Even speaking was an effort. "How long have I been out?"

"Long enough for all the coolant to run out of Stiles's radiator and the car to overheat, thanks to you."

"You're the one who ran me down."

"You should have moved."

"I didn't think you'd do it."

"You don't know me very well, then, do you."

"Not as well as I thought." He sat up, but waves of dizziness made it difficult. When he started to sway sideways, she gripped his shoulder, steadying him.

"How bad is it?"

"Bad enough so I didn't realize you were nearby." He pressed a hand to his aching head, felt the bandages she'd put there. "Given my usual reaction to your presence, it must be pretty bad."

"Oh, please. We're beyond that now, Edge. You can drop the act."

He lifted his head, searching her face.

She said, "We both know you were only using me to get your hands on Stiles."

He held her gaze until she turned her head away. Then

he touched her face, turning it back again. "I didn't have to make love to you to get my hands on Stiles, Alby."

She rolled her eyes, pulled free of his touch.

Edge sighed. "Where is he, anyway?"

"Stiles?" She looked across the barn, nodded toward a corner where the man lay, unconscious, his hands cuffed around a beam. "I found some of his favorite tranquilizer in his little black bag."

"You should just kill him and have done with it."

She swung her huge, dark eyes back to his. "I need him alive."

He held those eyes for a long moment, before looking away.

"Why do you hate him so much?"

He shook his head, saying nothing.

"I'm not going to let you kill him, Edge. I can't."

"You drag him around the countryside with you much longer, Alby, he's going to get loose. He's going make a try for you. You know he will."

"Not this time."

Angry, he surged to his feet, but the weakness slammed into him like a wrecking ball, and he found himself flat on his back in the hay again a second later.

It shocked him when Alby's hair tickled his face. She was kneeling beside him, leaning over him, and she looked worried, in spite of her apparent determination to hate his guts. He closed his eyes.

"The damage to your hard head will heal when the sun comes up, but you're not going to make it that long, are you, Edge?"

"I'm fine."

She shook her head. "You need to feed."

"Good idea." God, even his voice sounded weak now. "Drag Stiles over here and let me have at him."

"I don't trust you not to kill him."

"Yeah, well, it's him or me."

"Not necessarily."

He shot his eyes to hers.

She shrugged. "There's me."

"No."

"Come on, Edge. You're fading faster than snow in a heat wave. You need blood. I've got it, and I'm offering to share. It would be foolish not to."

He felt the hunger stirring inside him at the very thought of it. Of tasting her. And while his body was weak, he was turned on as hell. "You've...never let a vampire drink from you before, have you, Alby?"

"No. I've heard it's...pleasant."

"Pleasant."

"Mmm." She lifted her arm, pushing her sleeve back, looking intently at the veins in her wrist.

"When I made you come, back there on the beach, and you were shaking all over and screaming my name, would you have called that pleasant?"

"Edge, that's got nothing to do—"

"My drinking from you would be ten times as intense."

She blinked, clearly not believing him. "I think you're exaggerating."

He shrugged. "No one's ever tasted you. I've tasted plenty of humans, and even a vamp or two in my time. I know what it's like."

She met his eyes. "I'm not a human or a vamp. It could be entirely different with me."

And would be, he had no doubt of that. That was what worried him. God knew sex with her had been the most mind-blowing experience of his life. What would drinking from her tender veins be like?

He wanted it. He burned with wanting it. He wanted to be the first to devour her, just the way he'd been the first to take her body.

She was watching his eyes, which were no doubt beginning to glow with hunger by now. Trembling, she offered her forearm, extending it until her wrist hovered near his lips. "Go on," she whispered. "I can handle it if you can."

Still lying on his back in the hay, he lifted his hands, closed them on her forearm, and drew it to his lips. He let his lips and tongue taste the salty skin there but kept his eyes on hers. Saw them light just a little. She might pretend to hate him, he realized. But she wanted him. In every way.

He parted his lips, sucking at the skin, and then, tightening his grip, he bit down. His incisors sank into her flesh, popped through the tougher walls of her veins. He didn't bite deeply. Just enough to draw a thin trickle of her lifeblood into him.

But when it touched his tongue, he was completely unprepared for the force that hit him. A jolt so strong it made his entire body jerk in reaction. The power of it. God! Her eyes widened, and her mouth opened. Her head fell backward, and she shuddered.

He sucked a little harder, and her force arced through his body. Strength returned. Amber moaned, dropping backward into the hay, even as Edge sat up, dragging his mouth from her wrist so he could roll over onto her. Everything in him screamed for more, more than she'd offered. More than she'd given. He wanted all of her.

His hands found her blouse and slid underneath to find her breasts and close around them. She was shivering, her body begging him to take her. Her nipples were hard and hot against his cold touch. He pushed the blouse out of the way and bent to those peaks, sucking one of them and then biting it until she cried out in mingled pain and pleasure. He tasted her blood on his tongue and sucked harder.

She arched her back to tell him her cries were not protests. And he was hard, the furious hunger raging through him more powerfully than it ever had.

He wrestled her jeans off her, never releasing her nipple, and he freed himself from his own the same way. And then he was on her, pinning her to the hay and driving himself into her as deep and hard as he could.

She screamed and clasped his shoulders, then tore at the T-shirt he wore, peeling it off him. Her legs wrapped around his waist, locking at the ankles, and she tipped her hips up to receive him. He slid his hands to her buttocks, squeezing them hard, to hold her to him as he rose up, onto his knees, carrying her with him. As he knelt there, holding her, lifting and lowering her body over him again and again, he watched her head fall back, her hair slide sideways, baring her neck to him.

He pressed his mouth to her throat, kissing, preparing, and she whimpered what he took to be encouragement. So he sank his fangs into her jugular.

The blood flowed into him, and with it, everything she was feeling—and then everything she *was*. God, the power of this woman! It raged inside him, so shocking he surged to his feet, her legs still twisted around his waist. He staggered backward, slamming into a wall and feeling it crack behind him. Something crashed to the floor, a beam and several bales of hay from somewhere above avalanching from the ceiling, narrowly missing them, and he didn't care. He knew her, everything about her, everything she'd felt in captivity. Her furious love for her parents and her friends. Her grief for Willem

Stone and fierce determination to save him. And her passion right now, for him, for Edge, overwhelming everything else. What she felt for him was so intense it humbled him, shook him to his core, and with it he felt her denial, her resistance, her fear.

And then there was something else, something… separate. Beyond it all, he became slowly aware of something more inside her. Within her, and yet separate. It was something new. Small. Only barely there. Deep, deep inside her.

Life.

His orgasm broke through him at the same time as the shock of his discovery, and he jerked his mouth away from her throat to break contact with the impossible truth.

She was coming, clinging to him, shivering and moving and milking him right to his core. And he held her while it ravaged her with its power and his own ecstasy pumped into her. He held her until the pleasure ebbed. And then he carried her back to the hay, laid her down there, very gently, pushed the hair away from her face and saw tears on her cheeks.

She'd lied to him. And he supposed he would be angry about that…later. But right now, he was too overwhelmed by his suddenly much clearer view of who and what she was. He was not ready for her. Whatever he'd been thinking about her, planning for her, he'd been wrong, because she was way beyond what he'd expected. Everything about her was…more.

She was physically stunning, her beauty on the level one would attribute to an angel or a goddess. A demon or a witch. Unnatural beauty. Her power—it was intense, not greater than his own, but different. The telekinesis, the precognition—yes, she had that, too; he'd felt it when he'd tasted her. The jolt of her blood hit his brain the way he imagined crack cocaine hit an addict. And he wondered if he would be able to live without it. Her passion—it was above and beyond anything he'd ever known any female to feel, and his own had matched it.

Her emotions—God, they were intense. What she felt for him was shattering, and even the mere glimpse of it he'd been allowed was enough to put him on the edge of panic.

Beyond that, he felt he'd committed a sacrilege, defiled something sacred. He hadn't even begun to understand what she was, just how special she was, until now. His mistake. Whoever the other man was, he was probably far more worthy. So he supposed it was just as well. Or he told himself it was.

He touched the tears on her cheeks, absorbing them into his fingertips. "I shouldn't have…"

"Yes, you should."

He closed his eyes against the soulful look in hers. "Are you all right? Did I take too much?"

She nodded, but seemed sleepy, her eyelids heavy.

"God, what have I been doing with you?" he whispered.

"You didn't take that much, Edge. I'm fine."

"That's not what I meant."

She frowned at him, then nodded. "Oh." The word was icy, and suddenly she didn't seem as sleepy anymore. "Stop looking so worried, Edge, I'm not an idiot. I know it didn't mean anything. We both got carried away, that's all." She rolled onto her side, putting her back to him.

Probably, he thought, so that he wouldn't see the lie in her eyes. "Of course it didn't mean anything. How could it?" Given what he knew now.

His body was surging with more energy than he'd ever had. More power. It made itself known to him more with each passing second. Her blood was…different. Supercharged and potent. It sang in his veins, making his skin tingle with heightened awareness. His mind raced with sensations; his body itched with pent-up energy.

Alby dragged herself to her feet. She searched for her clothes, putting them on slowly, clumsily. He moved closer, wanting to help her in spite of himself, but she pulled away from his touch. She might be tired and dull right now—thanks to him—but her anger was as sharp as ever.

No doubt she, too, was finally becoming aware of the distance between them. Probably thinking about the other one, whoever he was. He was as far beneath her as he could be. He wasn't worthy of an angel, and, frankly, he didn't want to be.

"I'm going to have to find another vehicle," she told him. "Stiles's car is stranded a few miles from here where I left it when it overheated. And I won't get far on foot."

So she didn't even want to talk about what had just happened between them? Or the secret she was keeping?

It occurred to him then that maybe she didn't even know.

Hell, that was it. She didn't know.

"Where is it we're going?" he asked her.

"I have to take Stiles to Eric and Tam's place. Eric has a lab there."

"And when you get him there?"

"I make him talk, make him tell me about his formula for stealing immortality, and then we create our own batch."

"Using his blood?"

She buttoned her blouse without looking at him. "I wouldn't let him pollute Willem with his evil. No. We'll be using mine."

He nodded, understanding her reasons for that, but unsure it was a very good idea. He'd seen her worst nightmares—and they all involved Stiles and the time she'd spent as his prisoner. All the more reason to kill the bastard. The sooner the better. And why he should still feel that way, knowing what he did, was beyond him. He really was pathetic.

"You don't intend to let me go with you, do you, Alby?"

She glanced at him, smiled sweetly, though he could see the pain behind the smile. It swam in her blue-black eyes. "As soon as you curl up for a good day's sleep, Edge, Stiles and I are out of here."

"And you think I won't follow you?"

"You don't know where they live."

"Windy Ridge," he said. "Or something like that," he replied.

She made a face. "What state?"

He lowered his eyes.

"I really don't think my dear friends in Salem are likely to tell you. Especially not once I get to someplace where my cell phone can pull in a signal and call them."

"You have it all figured out, don't you?"

"Mmm-hmm."

"Only one problem, love. Right now, I'm stronger than I've ever been in my life. And you're a little on the weak side." And he was getting angrier by the minute, as well, he thought. Bad enough she'd lied to him; now she was acting as if he were the enemy, all in an effort to protect a pig like Stiles.

She shrugged. "So?"

He smiled his most evil smile, spun on his heel and strode across the barn to where Stiles lay limp. He gripped the man by his throat, shook him so that his head flopped on his shoulders like a rag doll's. "Wake up, you bastard. I've been waiting a long time for this."

Amber lunged toward him, grabbed his shoulder to jerk him away, but she didn't have the strength to make it work. He shook her off, but carefully. She staggered a few steps backward but didn't hit the floor.

"Let it be, Alby. Better I kill him now than let you risk your life on some insane, hopeless trek alone with him. Especially now."

"What I risk or don't risk is my own business, damn you!"

He ignored her, even when she pounded on his back, and gave the man another shake. "Wake up, Stiles."

Stiles opened his eyes, looking confused. But when his gaze fell on Edge, his eyes widened. "You!"

Suddenly Alby stopped beating on him, and Edge knew she was wondering just how he knew this man.

"Been a long time, hasn't it, Stiles?" Edge growled.

Stiles glared at him. "Came to try again? You can't kill me, and you know it."

"Oh, I'll make it work this time. I just wanted you awake enough to know who was going to take you out."

Stiles tugged uselessly on the handcuffs, but they didn't give.

"Edge, don't. Please, don't do this," Amber whispered.

Edge tightened his hand on the man's throat, even as Amber screamed at him to stop. She pummeled him, the blows delivered with her mind, not her hands. None of them were powerful enough to shake him.

He squeezed, and, oddly, the satisfaction of crushing

the life out of Stiles wasn't as good as imagining that
the throat he was wringing belonged to the man Amber
Lily had been with. Had slept with. Maybe even loved.
He felt the satisfying snap and crush of the bones underneath his hand and watched the light fade out of
Stiles's eyes. He held a little longer, crushing, making
sure there was no sign of life left, and then he let go, let
the limp body fall to the hay strewn floor.

"You son of a bitch."

He turned to look at her, saw the sheer hatred in her
eyes.

"Best burrow under that haystack, Edge," she said,
and her voice was ice cold. "Sun's coming up."

He looked beyond her and saw the first hints of dawn
peering through the cracks in the barn boards. He swallowed hard. "Don't go on without me," he said. "We
need to talk. And Stiles—"

"There's nothing you can say that I really want to
hear."

"Alby, there are things you don't know." He sent an
anxious glance toward Stiles as he spoke. Then pain siz-
zled in his skin, and he looked down to see smoke coiling
from his shoulder, where a beam of palest sunlight
touched him.

Alby shoved him out of the way, both hands flat to
his chest. "Get into shelter, dammit."

He stood there for a moment, all too aware of the sun
rising outside. It wasn't having its usual impact on him.
He felt sleep calling to him, but not overwhelming him
as it normally would have. His body didn't grow weak
nor his mind lethargic. He was as strong and sharp as he
would have been at midnight. And he credited her blood
with that.

The light moved, narrow beams of it, seeming to creep

toward him as the sun rose higher, slanting between the boards at an ever sharpening angle. "This isn't finished. Not until you hear me out. You have a lot of explaining to do, woman."

"*I* have explaining to do? You're the one who might have just signed Will's death sentence." She shoved him again. "Go."

"You'd care, then? If I were to stand here and burn?"

"I'd toast marshmallows and sing campfire songs."

"You're a liar."

Again he felt pain. Again light seared his flesh, his side, this time, just over the rib cage. And again Alby slammed him with her hands, shoving him out of the way. "Edge, will you just go?"

He shook his head. "Only if you'll wait for me. Go back to the house in Salem, where you're safe, and wait for me there."

"I..."

More light spilled in; his hair was starting to smolder. "One conversation, Alby. That's all. In Salem. After that I'll leave you alone forever." He felt increased heat, and suddenly she was smacking his head with her palms. Putting out tiny tongues of flame, no doubt.

"All right. All right, I'll do it."

"You promise?"

She shoved him full force, and he knew it cost her, knew she was still weak and tired because she had shared her blood with him. But she mustered her strength, and she shoved him hard, combining her physical and mental power. He shot backward, hitting a pile of hay. Then she lifted her hands, drew them sharply downward, her face contorted as if she was straining every muscle to do it. The next thing he knew, the mountain of hay was tumbling down on him. The weight pushed him to the ground. The battering continued, until he lay flat, choking on hay seed and dust, drowning in its musty scent, but utterly enveloped in darkness.

He sought her out with his mind, even as, at long last, the day sleep began to seep into him, stealing his consciousness.

Alby?

He felt her exasperation.

Promise me you'll do as I ask. Promise me.

If it will shut you up, I promise.

He sighed, finally letting his body relax and his mind surrender to the sleep.

Amber turned around slowly, because something had moved behind her.

Stiles's body lay limply, in a half-sitting position, suspended by his hands anchored to one another high above him, by the cuffs that were looped over a low slanting beam. His head hung very low, nearly upside down, with his neck twisted at an impossible angle.

But as she stood there, looking at him, he moved.

His head turned, and she could hear the sickening crunch of bones. His eyes were wide-open, unfocused, but seemingly fixed on her. That scarred half of his face, with its bright pink skin, never moved, but the other half twisted in a grimace as, slowly, he lifted his head, getting it perpendicular with his neck again. Bones popped and cracked like a favorite cereal she remembered from her childhood. When his head was upright, he turned it slowly, left, then right, making a horrible face as he did so, probably due to the pain. Then he shrugged his shoulders, tipped his head sideways once or twice, and, finally, got to his feet. He gave an experimental tug on the handcuffs that held his arms—at chest level now—around the nearby beam, and fixed his steady, searing eyes on her.

Amber swallowed her fear, took an involuntary step backward. She hadn't been certain he would revive—not until she'd seen it with her own eyes. Even now, she could scarcely believe it. She shivered.

Stiles only smiled.

10

―――――

"Mmm, you've drugged me, I see," Stiles said slowly as he tugged on the handcuffs that held him. "Good thinking, that. Normally, I could snap this chain in two."

Amber tried to shrug off the eerie sensation of seeing him return to life right before her eyes, tried to sound as nonchalant and unperturbed as he did. "Me, too. You were barely conscious when I first put them on you, but I figured once you came around, that would be a risk."

He nodded. "So you've turned the tables on me, then. May I ask what you plan to do with me, now that you have me? Killing me obviously isn't part of the plan."

"What makes you so sure of that?"

He shrugged. "I'm still alive. And a few minutes ago, you were begging Edgar not to do it."

She blinked slowly. "Edgar?"

He nodded. "Quaint, isn't it?"

"Oh, it's cute as hell." She lowered her head to hide her half smile. Edgar. Who would have guessed?

"So will you tell me what you intend to do with me?"

Drawing a breath, sighing slowly, she moved across the barn to the medical bag she'd found in Stiles's car, digging out some of the tiny vials from amid the other contents, which included syringes, a pint of saline solution, bandages, antiseptic, even a tiny suture kit. She filled an empty syringe before realizing most of them were already loaded. With what, she couldn't be sure.

As an afterthought, she emptied them all onto the floor and refilled them herself. She slid her first loaded needle into a pocket, her back to Stiles, and kept another one in her hand.

"I'm afraid leaving you conscious long enough for conversation wouldn't be very wise of me," she told him. Especially, she thought, when she was already in a weakened state. Though she was dying to hear how he knew Edge, Edgar. Still, she didn't suppose she could really believe a word this animal of a man might tell her. So there was little point risking her life by letting him stay awake long enough to talk.

It was a shame, she thought, that she wasn't going to be able to keep her promise to Edge—at least long enough to rib him about this Edgar revelation. Her smile faded as she recalled his stunned expression after what had just happened between them.

Clearly he'd been worried, once the passion had died down. She thought she knew what he was worried about. That she might be getting romantic ideas about him, or developing feelings for him, or that she would expect something more from him now that they'd been as intimate as it was possible to be. Sharing blood was a powerful act. More powerful than she'd ever expected. And one that tended, her mother had told her, to create unbreakable bonds between two people, or to intensify existing ones.

He must know those things. Obviously he didn't want any bond with her. He'd regretted it the moment the passion had cooled, so much so that he'd seemed angry at her over it. If he hadn't been so weak with hunger, she doubted he would ever have capitulated in the first place.

She shrugged. To hell with him.

And yet, deep down, she missed him already.

She returned to Stiles, taking the needle with her, wondering if he were as weak as he was pretending to be, watchful and wary. "Sorry about this," she said. "I am going to want you awake and talkative later on. But until I have more backup, I figure better safe than sorry."

She reached out to roll up his sleeve.

He snapped the chain on the cuffs as if it were a length of yarn, grasped her wrist and squeezed until she dropped the syringe. "Not quite safe," he muttered into her ear. "But I think we can definitely count on sorry."

As the sun sank, Edge drew his first breath of the night and promptly choked on it. The musty hay didn't agree with him, he decided, and he began digging his way out of the mountain of it. It occurred to him as he did that he'd come awake fast, and fully. The usual moments of slowly dawning lucidity and gradually returning power hadn't come. And when he stood free of the mountain, brushing bits of hay and dust from his hair and clothes, he knew the infusion of power Alby had provided hadn't faded. If anything, it had grown in intensity.

Incredible.

He located his discarded T-shirt, shook it hard, sending clouds of hayseed and dust into the air, and pulled it on before taking a look around. He didn't expect Amber to be there. She'd given her promise that she would return to the house in Salem and wait for him there. So he wasn't alarmed at her absence. Though he probably should be, given that he'd discovered her lack of honesty, at least where he was concerned. He supposed it was her only fault. But it was a hell of a big one. And it was one he never would have suspected, one that hurt his pride.

Still, he wasn't alarmed at her absence...until he

crossed the barn to the place where he'd left Stiles's body, lying limp and lifeless.

He'd never tried killing the man by crushing his neck before, and it had seemed to do the trick. Though it had troubled him that there had been no time to watch him, to make sure. Now, though, he wondered. Because there was no body.

He closed his eyes slowly. Had the bastard revived yet again?

Sighing, he forced himself to take a closer look at the area in search of clues. He found two things that terrified him. The handcuffs, their chain snapped neatly in two, and a spent hypodermic needle lying in the hay.

"Jesus."

His mind told him it might still be all right. If Stiles had revived while Alby was still here, even enough to break free of the handcuffs, she might have tranquilized him and taken him back to Salem with her.

And that had better be the way it had happened. Because if it wasn't, she was in trouble. Edge swallowed the rush of panic that tried to rise at the thought. It was an unaccustomed feeling for him, that exaggerated level of concern for another being. He hadn't felt this way since…since his fledgling band had been slaughtered. And yet it was real. He supposed, given the circumstances, it was understandable.

He tried to quiet his mind and to focus on Alby. He put her face in his mind's eye—it was surprisingly easy to do—and reached out mental fingers to feel for her. But there was nothing. No sense of her. Either she was blocking him—or she was dead.

Hell. He had to return to that houseful of busybodies in Salem, much as he dreaded the thought. It was the only way to learn what had happened to Amber Lily. And he still had unfinished business with Stiles.

He went on foot, but rapidly, pausing only long enough to get his bearings before exerting his full power. And he found himself moving at speeds he'd never before approached. When he arrived at the house on the shore, stiffened his spine and strode up to the door, it opened before he reached it.

Sarafina stood on the other side, and her expression was not friendly. Nor were those on the faces of the others who stood around her. Expectant, perhaps demanding, but definitely not friendly.

"Where the hell is she?" the vampiress demanded.

Edge didn't flinch from Sarafina's probing, accusing eyes. "I hoped to find her here."

For just an instant he thought she was going to lunge at him, but then Willem Stone gripped her shoulders from behind, moving her gently aside.

"Maybe you'd better come on inside and tell us what happened, Edge."

Sarafina nodded with a jerk of her head. "Yes, do come inside. We may as well hear the whole of it before I rip out your heart."

"May as well," he said, and he walked into what he perceived was a nest of vipers, wondering if he would walk out again. And then he reminded himself of the heightened state of his powers. They could have no clue as to the extent of his strength now. Hell, he had no clue as to its limits himself. He reached into his T-shirt pocket for his pack of cigarettes. "Mind if I smoke?"

"Willem has cancer, you ignorant whelp. What do you think?"

He took the pack out anyway, shook one loose and walked back outside onto the redwood deck to light it.

Then he took a seat in a lawn chair and glanced back at them, waiting.

With a furious sigh, Sarafina came outside. Willem followed, with Morgan and Dante close on his heels. They all sat. Morgan spoke first. "We know you're the one who leaked Amber's location," she said.

He shrugged. "I thought it was the best way to get Stiles here. That's what you all wanted, wasn't it?"

"We didn't ask for your help," Sarafina snapped.

Willem put a calming hand on her arm. "It isn't the help we mind. But we certainly had no intention of using Amber as bait."

Edge lowered his head. "And I had no intention of letting Stiles get within a mile of her. He wouldn't have, either, had she not taken matters into her own hands." He sucked on his cigarette while they waited, blew a few smoke rings before going on. "I was about to capture Stiles when she showed up and got in the way. She flung his car into a ditch as if it were weightless, then ran me down like a dog with it."

"Again?" Morgan asked, a flicker of disbelief in her eyes.

"For real, this time. She dragged me into the vehicle with Stiles and took off. I was…a bit out of it. I woke in a barn, with Stiles cuffed to a beam, unconscious. She stuck around long enough to make sure I'd survive, buried me under an avalanche of hay when the daylight came, and when I woke again, she and Stiles were both gone."

Willem was searching his face, as if he knew Edge was leaving out vital parts of the story. "You should have killed the bastard. My life isn't worth Amber putting herself within his reach again."

"I did kill him, actually. Crushed every bone in his

throat. But from what I found when I woke tonight, I'm guessing he didn't stay dead very long."

"What did you find?" Sarafina asked.

"The handcuffs were broken. And there was a spent hypodermic." When she frowned, he explained. "Alby must have taken Stiles's bag of tricks from his vehicle. The tranquilizer was inside. She kept him drugged for most of the time."

"Apparently not drugged enough," Dante muttered.

Edge shook his head. "I made her promise to come back here and wait for me. But obviously she didn't. What I don't know right now is which of them is the captive and which is the captor." His voice broke a little on the final word. He cleared his throat, took another drag of his smoke.

"We have to get word to Jameson and Angelica," Will said. "They'll want to leave immediately. It's more than a full night's drive from Wind Ridge."

Edge nodded. "I suppose the more of us there are searching for her the better."

"For her, perhaps. Not for you, Edge," Sarafina said. "Because if I don't kill you for this, Rhiannon will. And she's with Amber's parents."

"Yes, someplace windy with some vampire scientist and his bride."

"Eric and Tamara," Will said.

"That's where she planned to take Stiles," Edge told them. "If she's in control, that's where you'll find her."

"And if she's not," Willem added, "Angelica might be able to home in on her location."

Edge shook his head. "She's blocking. I tried that already and couldn't come close."

"Oh, aren't we full of ourselves?" Sarafina all but

growled. "To think your bond to Amber Lily could begin to compare to the one she shares with her mother."

Edge lifted his brows. "You might be surprised."

Her eyes narrowed. God, she looked for all the world as if she would like nothing better than to rip out his throat.

"There's something else," Will said. "What aren't you telling us, Edge?"

He studied the man and thought he wasn't a bad sort, for a human. Of the bunch of them, he found he hated Willem least. He shook his head slowly, though. "Whatever else there is, is between Alby and me. And that's where it will stay. For now."

The man's lips thinned, and Sarafina surged to her feet. "You arrogant little wretch, I'll wring it out of you!"

"No." Again Willem stopped her, simply by reaching out and clasping her hand in his own. He didn't even have to get up. "Unless it has some bearing on our ability to locate her?" He glanced at Edge.

"It doesn't."

"Then it's not our business."

She bared her teeth and didn't return to her chair but instead paced the deck. "We need a plan. We need to search for her."

"Call her parents. Tell me where this Eric Marquand lives, and give me your list of known locations for Stiles. I'll find her," Edge said quietly.

"As if we'd trust you with this mission!" Sarafina snapped.

He shrugged. "I'm going, either way. Armed with all the information or not. Your choice." He took a final drag, then flicked the cigarette butt over the rail and into the sand beyond.

"I'll get you what we have in my files," Morgan said,

getting to her feet. "Give me a second to print it up for you."

He nodded, and she hurried inside. Dante turned to Edge. "I'm going with you."

"The hell you are."

The other man shrugged. "Then I'll follow you. I don't trust you, Edge. If you find Amber Lily, one of us should be on hand. Sarafina and Will need to stay here, so Will can continue his medical treatments uninterrupted. Morgan can stay, as well, and continue working leads via the phones and Internet. I'm the logical choice."

Edge shook his head, rolled his eyes. "Right. Just the two of us."

"Three, actually," Dante said.

Edge frowned at him, not understanding.

"I made a few calls, mental ones as well as physical, while you and Amber have been away, Edge. Finally made contact with an old friend of mine I thought might have some input into this situation. He's on his way."

Edge shook his head. "I'm not waiting. You can catch up with me when this mystery guest arrives."

"He'll be here at any time, Edge."

"He's here now," a deep voice said from the darkness beyond the deck.

Something shivered down Edge's spine. An awareness he hadn't felt since he'd been newly made. A prickle, a connection like a live wire under his skin. He turned toward that voice, watching as the man came closer.

"You," Edge whispered. He was rocked, right to his core, as the vampire who'd sired him, then abandoned him, stood there, holding his gaze. "You son of a bitch."

Edge vaulted the rail and sprang on the man with all the fury he'd been carrying around for more than fifty years.

11

After Stiles jabbed her with the needle, obviously operating at full strength while she was feeling absurdly weak, Amber thanked the gods that at least her brains were still functioning at full capacity and sank to the floor.

Stiles, the handcuffs hanging uselessly from his wrists, their chain snapped in half, leaned over her. "I've been hoping to run into you again," he said softly. "The timing is…well, it's quite astounding, really."

She let her eyelids hang heavy, half shielding her eyes, as if there really had been tranquilizer in that needle he'd jabbed into her arm, instead of the saline solution she'd found in his little black bag. The hypodermic with the actual drug was in her pocket. She'd had a feeling he was faking—had guessed the drug would have been wearing off by now. Just as she'd had a feeling she would learn more by playing along than she would by fighting him and—given her state—probably losing. So she'd taken a few…precautions.

"What are you…talking about?" she asked, slurring her words.

He shrugged. "You took my journals. You know what I did with the blood I took from you."

She nodded, moving her head as if her neck were made of rubber. "You made some kind of formula… from my blood…."

He shrugged. "Among other ingredients. I call it Ambrosia. Clever, don't you think? The nectar of the gods, key to immortality?"

"Ambrosia," she repeated.

"Ambrosia-Six, actually. The first five tries were ineffective."

"You injected yourself. And now you're…you're… immortal?"

"Well, not exactly." He smiled down at her. "It wears off, you see. I've had to remedicate myself every six months, and I'm nearly out of Ambrosia-Six. So you can see how fortuitous our meeting again is for me. Thank you, Amber Lily."

He watched her carefully, expectantly, and she knew she should probably be unconscious by now, so she let her eyes fall closed and her head go limp. He went to the black bag, and she heard him when he returned, turning the handcuff key, dropping the cuffs into the hay. She tried not to cringe in revulsion when he hauled her up over his shoulder and began striding out of the barn with the bag in his free hand. He paused near the door, looking around the barn. "If I knew where that bastard Edgar was, I'd take the time to kill him. He'll keep coming after me until one of us is dead, I'm afraid. And I don't intend for it to be me." He sighed as if in sincere and deep regret that he wouldn't be able to murder Edge, then kept walking.

Amber could feel the capped hypodermic, the only one left with real tranquilizer inside, poking her thigh where she'd tucked it into her pocket. She thought about jerking it out and jabbing him with it, but it occurred to her that he was giving her exactly what she needed. He was taking her somewhere to extract some more of her blood, so he could use it to make the very same formula she needed in order to save Willem. If she were there, pretending to be his prisoner, she could get the formula, or even steal his supply of the elixir. Ambrosia indeed. In the hands of a man as evil as Stiles, it was more the nectar of demons than of gods.

Still, she needed to know how he'd made the stuff. So she continued to hang limp over his shoulder and let him carry her down through the woods until they reached a narrow, barely paved road. To her surprise, there was a vehicle waiting there. A black Lincoln, parked along the shoulder.

As Stiles approached it, a woman got out of the driver's seat and opened a rear door for him without a word. Through the slits of her eyelids, Amber saw flaming hair, in a "big-hair" style, that surrounded the woman like a red cloud. She wore sunglasses with rhinestones on the frames. Spandex encased her legs to mid-calf, and hot pink polish colored the toenails visible in the spike heeled sandals. Her tight black rib-knit sweater had fake leopard fur trim around the collar and cuffs.

Stiles slung the black bag into the car. "I see the homing beacon did its job?"

"You are so smart, Frankie," the woman said, her voice irritatingly high pitched. "Puttin' it into the heel of your shoe like that—fuckin' brilliant."

He grunted and bent low, flipping Amber off his shoulder and onto the back seat.

"So this is the one, huh?"

"Yes."

"She don't look so special."

"Doesn't she?" He sighed, then slammed the door and went around to get in the passenger side, while the redhead returned to her spot behind the wheel. "Head to the Boston Center, Brookie. It's the closest one."

"You sure you don't wanna drive?" she asked.

"I'm sure. I've had a trying evening, and I'm not sure I'm back to a hundred percent, even now. She drugged me, or I'd have been here sooner."

"She drugged you?"

"Mmm."

Amber felt the twit send an angry glance into the back seat and heard her mutter, "Feisty little bitch, ain't she?" prior to snapping her gum. She was driving by then, so she had to face front again soon. She said, "I waited all night. I would have come lookin' for you if you hadn't told me not to."

Amber almost laughed at the thought of the woman traipsing through the forest in those high heeled, open-toed, suicide shoes she was wearing.

"You did the right thing," Stiles assured her. "I hope it wasn't too awful for you." Gross. His voice had turned sugary sweet.

"It *was* pretty awful. It was dark, and I was all alone. I had to pee out in the bushes. I didn't like that one bit. And I saw a skunk."

"I'm sorry. I'll make it up to you, though. I promise."

Amber thought he was probably touching her then. Squeezing her hand, or something comforting and apologetic like that. Clearly their relationship was personal, intimate. Talk about an odd couple, Amber thought. A scarred, aging, evil genius and a beautiful young airhead.

Sighing, she told herself to just relax during the ride to Boston. It would give her body time to recover from her rather…energetic morning with Edge.

But as soon as she thought of him, she felt anything but relaxed. Feelings stirred inside her, as if he'd left a part of himself behind; a part that had taken up residence beneath her skin and deep in her bones. He was there, inside her, all through her. She could smell him, feel him, taste him again, just by thinking of him. She could hear his voice, see his sarcastic little smile, and sense the passion burning between them as if it were still there.

The drive took only a couple of hours—almost the exact distance she'd managed to haul Stiles before his car had given out. Boston, that was good. Close to Salem. Close to help, should she need it. But she wouldn't.

Amber calculated the amount of time the dose of tranquilizer she'd given to Stiles had lasted and determined she needn't feign coming out of it until six hours had passed. So she continued the phony state as they pulled into a long, curving driveway and up a hill to a stylish brick house in the suburbs, surrounded by what looked like ordinary mesh fence.

She let Stiles carry her inside, noticing the eerie silence of the place as he punched codes into electronic boxes to open the gate and then the door. It felt…empty. She opened her senses briefly, trying to feel for others in the house on the hill, but she sensed no one. Two presences made themselves known to her. The dark, black, oppressive and sharp-minded essence of Stiles, and another. An intelligent, determined, manipulative essence.

She blinked, because it didn't match up with what she'd observed about the redhead. But she didn't sense a third aura. Only two. And two people, moving through the house and into a bedroom at the end of a hall. Amber was dropped onto a bed.

"Bring me the kit, Brookie."

The bimbo hustled away with staccato steps and was back only moments later. Amber heard rattling, and then felt the pinch when Stiles tied a rubber band around her upper arm. She braced herself, compelled her body not to stiffen or react in any way, fully aware of what was coming.

Her arm felt the cold swipe of an alcohol pad. Then the sting of a needle.

"Are you sure you need to do this?" Brookie asked.

"I told you, I'll die without it."

"Of a degenerative blood disease," she said.

"Yes. I need transfusions, and she's the only donor with the same rare blood type as mine. And she refuses to help me."

He was lying through his teeth, Amber thought angrily. He didn't have any degenerative disease. He might die without her blood, but only of old age or natural causes. Obviously he didn't trust the redhead enough to tell her the whole truth.

Amber felt the strength leaving her as the blood flowed from her arm into the receptacle. Dizziness seemed to sweep in to fill the void. Weakness. Nausea. God, he couldn't be aware she was already a pint or two low.

The bag filled; he leaned closer. "Hmm, not flowing very fast today. I wonder." He rubbed a hand along her cheek. "Best just settle for one, she's pale as a ghost."

"What do you care?"

"Think, Brookie. If she dies, where will I get my transfusion the next time I need one?" He pressed a cotton ball to the puncture, as he pulled the needle from her arm. Then he bent it at the elbow, holding it there.

"How you gonna be sure you can get it from her anyway, the next time? She could get hit by a truck tomorrow. Or just get too smart to let you catch her again."

"Don't you worry your pretty head about that, Brookie. I have a plan."

"Huh?"

''Come on, Brooke. Come with me. We need to get the process going.''

''All right, Frankie.''

They left the room, closing the bedroom door behind them.

Amber opened her eyes the moment they were gone. He had a plan? Hell, that didn't bode well. Gave her chills, actually. But that wasn't where she needed to focus at the moment. She scanned the room, visually and mentally, all without moving. But she saw no cameras monitoring her, sensed no eyes observing. This place was not equipped to hold vampires captive. He was counting on the tranquilizer to keep her in line—for now. And that was to her advantage. She got to her feet, only to sink immediately to her knees. Damn, but she was weak! She pulled herself upright again, made her way to the door, tried the knob.

Locked. And given the electronics attached to every other lock in the place, she had no doubt her so-called captors would be alerted if this lock were to be tampered with. Though breaking it would pose no real challenge, once she got her strength back.

A meal would help. God, she was famished.

She took stock of her situation, examining the room. No windows. Solid looking walls. A tiny heat register. Ceiling panels. She licked her lips. Those ceiling panels might be a possibility.

But not in her current state.

The dizziness returned, and she doubled over as nausea washed over her. She barely avoided throwing up as she staggered back to the bed, crawled facedown into it, and clutched the bedding in fisted hands. What the hell was wrong with her? A second ago she'd felt starved to death. Now her stomach was rebelling.

She hugged the bed as if she could stop it from spinning around the room by doing so and gave herself permission to go to sleep. She wouldn't rejuvenate with the day sleep, the way a vampire would. She wouldn't regain her strength in the space of a few hours, and her wounds wouldn't miraculously heal as she slept. She healed faster than ordinary mortals—but not quite as fast as a vampire by day. Though she had an advantage, in that she didn't have to wait for the day sleep for the healing to begin. It could take a full day, maybe longer, to get back to her ordinary self again. But maybe she would be strong enough to do what needed doing a lot sooner.

She would probably have to be.

Edge landed one good blow to Donovan O'Roark's jaw before Dante gripped him from behind and flung him to the ground. He landed hard, back first, and the breath was driven from his lungs. Then he sat up slowly, as Dante towered over him.

"You need to learn some respect for your elders, boy."

"Leave him be." Donovan O'Roark stepped up beside Dante, rubbing his jaw with one hand. "I had that one coming." Then he reached a hand down to Edge.

Edge scowled at him, not taking it. Instead, he got to his feet on his own.

Shrugging, Donovan turned his attention to Dante. "It's been a long time, my friend."

"Too long," Dante said. He extended a hand, almost hesitantly.

Donovan didn't take it. Instead, he wrapped the other man in a bear hug that should have crushed him. For a moment Dante appeared stunned. Then he returned the embrace. "Dammit, Dante, why didn't you come back? For decades, I thought you were dead."

"I know. I'm sorry."

"I started hearing tales of you from others, accounts of you having lived for a time in one place or another. But always alone," Donovan said, his face full of questions.

Edge felt as if they'd both forgotten his presence. It angered him still further, and yet he was slightly interested in the discussion. Too much so to walk away just yet.

"At first I thought you'd died, as well, when the villagers burned us out of the castle. All because of my foolishness." Dante shook his head slowly. "I wanted no more to do with others of my kind, Donovan. And when I finally learned you'd survived, I..." He let his voice trail off.

"You assumed I would blame you for what had happened."

"I nearly got you killed, Donovan."

"You were betrayed. You should have known I wouldn't hate you for that."

Dante sighed. "Eventually my beloved Morgan convinced me of the same thing. I traveled to Ireland to look you up, but you'd gone. And still..."

"And still you're racked with guilt."

"I was your sire," Dante said. "My job was to teach you, to protect you. I let you down."

Edge finally spoke. "Funny, isn't it, how history repeats itself?"

Both men looked his way, and Donovan had the courtesy to lower his head. Dante started to speak, no doubt to reprimand Edge, but Donovan held up a hand. "No, he's right. I sired him and abandoned him all in the same night.''

"Damn straight," Edge said. "Do you have any idea how confused I was when I woke to my new nature? My God, I didn't even know enough to seek shelter from the sun until my skin began to blister with burns. And I was completely unprepared for the intensity of the pain. I didn't even know how to survive, because of you.''

Donovan nodded. "I owe you an apology."

"You owe me considerably more than that. Fortunately for you, I don't care enough to collect." He turned around, ready now to make his exit.

"There are things you don't know about that night, Edgar.''

He froze in place. "It's Edge now. And I don't *want* to know.''

"But you *do* want to find the Child of Promise, don't you?''

Slowly Edge turned and faced his sire once more. "I don't need your help to do that. I've managed to get by without it for more than fifty years, after all.''

Donovan sighed. Dante said, "Don't think of yourself and what you want or need, Edge. Think of Amber Lily. The more of us there are searching for her, the better our chances of finding her. And sooner than one alone might manage to do.''

"Yes, and the less time she's forced to spend as a captive of Frank Stiles, the better," Donovan put in.

When Edge looked at him questioningly, he added, "Your thoughts are less than well guarded tonight. And they've been mostly centered on Amber and her situation, with a few spare ones directed toward hatred for me.''

Edge said nothing.

"Edge may not want to hear your explanation, Donovan," Dante said. "But I do."

Nodding, Donovan turned to Dante. "I found Edge lying near death. He'd been part of one of Dublin's street gangs, and there had been a war of sorts with a rival group. I'd seen part of the battle, been impressed by his courage. He fought like a true warrior. Utterly fearless. I thought he deserved to live."

"So you changed me over and left me there in the street," Edge said softly.

"I changed you over and was attacked. Both the gangs set on me at once, no doubt in shock over what they saw me doing to you," Donovan explained. "I was beaten to within an inch of my life. And then your fellows dragged you off somewhere, no doubt thinking they were reclaiming their valiant dead."

"God, you're fortunate they didn't bury you," Dante said.

"I feared that same thing," Donovan replied. "I searched and searched for you, Edge. Even when I was being hunted, and it would have been better to leave Ireland altogether, I stayed and hunted for you. But I never found you." He smiled just slightly. "Until now. By God, it's good to know you survived."

Dante lowered his head, shaking it slowly. "It's little wonder you mistrust your own kind," he said. "Tell us what happened to you that night, Edge."

He shrugged as if it were of little consequence. "They took me to a side street, dropped me in a ditch when they heard someone coming. Intended to come back for me, I imagine. But I woke when the sun started roasting my flesh. Ran from it, my clothes in flames before I found a bog and submerged myself. It was an effort to cool the flames. I didn't know enough to hide from the sun, but fortunately, I lost consciousness at that point.''

"And woke again at sundown," Donovan surmised. "Wondering why you hadn't drowned."

Edge shrugged. "Whatever. It's over, doesn't matter."

"It matters to me," Donovan said.

The door banged open, and Morgan, the small, almost mortal-looking vampiress, came across the deck and down to the lawn where the three of them stood.

"You reached Amber's parents?" Dante asked.

"Yes. They haven't heard a thing from her tonight, and they're heading this way just in case. Eric and Tam are staying behind in case she shows up there. We can reach Jameson and the others by cellphone if we need them and they're too far out to reach telepathically." She handed him a card with a number scrawled on the back.

Edge closed his eyes in anguish, then jerked in surprise when Donovan's hand lowered to his shoulder.

"She hasn't had time to reach them yet. We mustn't think the worst."

"You must be Donovan," Morgan said. "You don't know how long I've wanted to meet you."

"I forget my manners," Dante said quickly. "Donovan, this is Morgan, my bride."

"I assumed as much." O'Roark reached for Morgan's hand, lifted it to his lips. "I'm so glad to know Dante has found you, dear Morgan. I only wish we could have met under more pleasant circum—"

"Oh, for Christ's sake, can we omit the formalities?" Edge interrupted. "A woman's life is at stake here." Shaking his head, he turned away, not to be stopped this time.

"Edge, you don't even know where to begin," Dante called after him.

"I'll begin where I last saw her," he barked. "Come along or stay and continue your happy little reunion. I don't care either way."

Amber slept. She didn't know for sure how long, but she knew when she awoke that night had fallen. She felt marginally stronger, and when she finally got around to checking her wristwatch, she cursed herself for letting so many hours pass beyond her awareness. Since when did she sleep so long at a stretch? What essential bits of information might she have missed?

She got up and went to the closed door, pressed her ear against it and listened with her entire being, mentally as well as aurally. She could make out a television in some distant part of the house, a crunching sound. Brookie, eating popcorn and watching the tube. Her thoughts were focused on the program.

Closer, she made out only occasional footsteps, the tap of glass against glass, and the pouring sounds of liquids. Stiles in his lab, no doubt. And his thoughts were carefully guarded, right up until the moment he said, "I can't believe it!" and a burst of surprise shot from his mind like a flash of light.

A door slammed, and his steps came her way. Amber flung herself away from the door and dropped back onto the bed, closing her eyes and willing her body to relax. Locks turned, and the door opened.

"Wake up. I need a word."

She blinked her eyes open, mentally counting the hours since he'd tranquilized her and deciding it had been long enough for him to believe it had worn off at this point. "I'm awake."

"Mmm. I guessed you would be. By now I assume

you've put two and two together and realize your situation?''

Sure she did, she thought. But did he realize his? Aloud, she said, ''Apparently I'm once again your houseguest. You took blood from me already,'' she added, glancing at the bandage on her arm. ''But I'm guessing you need more?''

''Considerably more.''

''I'm surprised you didn't drain me dry and have it over with.''

''Well now, that would be killing the only source, Amber. The only one at the moment, anyway. If I'm going to live forever, I need to keep the font healthy.''

''So you're just going to kidnap me once every few years or so and help yourself to a new supply?''

''That hardly seems practical, does it? You might get smart enough to avoid me after a while, and that would be the end of me.''

''Going to keep me your captive forever? Even you can't possibly think you could get away with that.''

''Oh, heavens no. Your gang of undead loved ones would hunt me to the ends of the earth.''

''Glad you've finally figured that out.''

''No, what I was planning was much more efficient. Harvest a couple of hundred egg cells from your ovaries, fertilize them with your own DNA, and raise myself a crop of baby blood donors.''

She felt her blood run cold, and the earlier nausea returned full force. ''I'm going to be sick.''

''I'm not surprised.'' He took her arm and tugged her out of the room, into a hallway. Then he opened the door to a bathroom and stood aside.

Amber stumbled to the toilet, and fell to her knees as she rid herself of everything she'd eaten the day before.

She let her head hang low, reached up with a trembling hand to flush.

Stiles gripped her arm, helped her to her feet and turned her toward the sink. She rinsed her mouth, washed her hands. "So you're talking about…cloning me."

"Mmm."

She shook her head. "You can't. You can't possibly have the expertise to do something like that."

"No, but I can draft someone who'd be willing. Geneticists tend to be more interested in immortality than your average humans are. I'm sure one would accept it as payment in full for helping me out."

"But you haven't found one yet."

He shrugged. "I've narrowed it down. There are a handful of qualified scientists on my short list. But it's not the selection of a scientist that's holding things up at the moment, Amber."

"No?"

"No, no, not at all. It's your blood. There's something there that wasn't before, and it certainly puts a delay on any egg harvesting I might have had in mind. Of course, it could work to my benefit. But I won't know for sure it's a perfect match for…oh, somewhere around nine months, I would guess."

Turning away from the sink very slowly, she stared at him. "What the hell are you talking about, Stiles?"

One eyebrow arched. The other eye had no brow, only pink scar tissue that puckered with the expression. "You really don't know?"

She rolled her eyes. "Stop playing games, will you? Either tell me or don't, I'm too dizzy and sick to stand here and play along."

"Oh, I'll tell you. What harm is there, after all? You'll find out on your own in due time. I ran all the usual tests on the blood I took from you, just be sure it hadn't altered or mutated—after all, it's been a while.''

''And?''

''And something...quite surprising showed up.''

''Food poisoning? Stomach cancer? What?''

He watched her eyes very closely as he replied, ''A child. You're pregnant, Amber.''

12

Amber closed her eyes very slowly as the shock washed over her but quickly got a grip on herself as she realized Frank Stiles was lying through his teeth. "Very funny," she said. "But I happen to know that's impossible."

"Now what makes you say that? You stole my journals when you left five years ago. You read the notes."

She shrugged.

"So you know you're perfectly fertile. That was one of the things I recorded there. Which means it's far from impossible. Unless you're trying to tell me you've never been with a man."

She spun away from him, heading into the hall. She thought maybe she should make a break for it then and there but chose restraint. She still didn't have what she'd come for, she thought. And she was supposed to be suffering the chemical hangover of the tranquilizer, a side effect she remembered all too well. "I'm not discussing this. It's absurd."

He shot after her, gripping her arm before she got far and hustling her straight into the bedroom. "Is this some kind of immaculate conception, then?"

"Leave me alone." She paced away from him, sat on the bed.

"I can easily put you on the table in my lab and examine you. Or you can give me a straight answer. Are you a virgin or not?"

She lowered her head. More than anything she would like to avoid undergoing any more of this man's "examinations." "No."

"Then you *have* slept with a man. Or men?"

She didn't reply.

"Did you use protection?" This time, when she failed to respond, he sighed. "Fine, I'll go and get the stun gun, if that's how you want to do this. I just hope it doesn't have some dramatic impact on the baby."

"There *is no* baby."

He rolled his eyes. "Five minutes. I'll be back in five minutes. Don't try anything." Then he slammed out of the room, locking the door behind him.

Amber sank onto the bed, holding her head in her hands as it spun with disbelief. Male vampires were infertile. Everyone knew that.

She looked up at the ceiling tiles, wondering if she should try now to get the hell out of here. But no. He would be back in five minutes, he said. She had to wait this out, give it some time, get the formula he used to make his Ambrosia-Six.

Stiles was playing head games with her. That was all. His five minutes turned out to be closer to fifteen, and she was pacing, eager to get past his return and get on with things. She was starved to death—again. At least the nausea had gone, and the dizziness. She still felt tired, weak.

Stiles unlocked the door, opened it and entered. He held a yellow plastic bag with a drugstore chain's logo on it, then handed it to her.

Frowning, she took it and glanced inside.

A home pregnancy test kit. She pressed her lips tight, swallowed a lump of fear. He was really taking this ruse to the bitter end, wasn't he? What she couldn't figure out was what he had to gain by trying to make her believe she was pregnant.

"It was a vampire, wasn't it?" he asked.

She blinked up at him.

"You've only been with one person, and that person was a vampire. That's why you keep saying it's impossible. Tell me, was it my old friend Edgar?"

Clutching the bag in her fist, she muttered, "That's none of your business."

"I thought I glimpsed his mark on your throat before we stepped out into the sunlight this morning." He touched her chin, turning her head to look at her neck. "No sign of it now, of course."

She pressed her lips tight, and he took her arm again, tugged her into the hall, shoved her into the bathroom. "Take the test," he said. "Convince yourself, so we can get past that and move on."

She shook her head. "What makes you think I'd trust this kit? How do I know you haven't rigged it to make me believe this insane notion?"

He shrugged. "I just went to the drugstore on the corner and bought it. Receipt's still in the bag. Check it out for yourself." He pulled the door closed but didn't walk away. She knew he was standing out there, waiting.

She glanced at the tiny single bathroom window and thought she could probably squeeze through it. But not yet. She didn't have what she'd come after yet. If she had to play along, take this stupid test, she would. But she wasn't leaving here without Willem's cure.

She took the boxed kit from the drugstore bag. It was shrink wrapped, and she checked it carefully for tears. There were none. When she took off the cellophane, she checked the box's seal. It was glued tight. She tore it open and found everything inside just as intact. Nothing seemed to have been tampered with. She even checked the store receipt, which included a date and time stamp.

Okay, okay. So it was *probably* the real thing.

Sighing, she read the instructions, made a face and followed them. Then she paced the bathroom, watching the second hand on her watch impatiently.

There was a tap on the door.

She opened it and faced Stiles. "Well?"

She looked at her wrist. "Thirty more seconds."

He pursed his lips and waited. The time ticked away slowly, dragging its feet.

Finally time was up. She picked up the indicator stick and looked at the symbol in its tiny green tinted window.

A plus sign.

Blinking in shock, she looked again. But it was clear, clear as day. A plus sign. She even double-checked the instruction sheet to be sure that meant what she already knew it meant. "It's not possible," she whispered.

Stiles took her arm, guiding her back to the bedroom. She moved in a daze, not believing, even now.

"It was Edgar, wasn't it?"

She said nothing.

"Amazing. Every vampire DPI ever tested was sterile—males from the time of the transformation, females within six months or so. Are you sure you haven't been with anyone else?"

She frowned up at him, hearing, but not processing his words.

"Of course you are," he said. "Otherwise you wouldn't be so stunned by this." He shook his head slowly as he silently mulled over the ramifications.

Amber lay down on the bed, letting her forearm rest over her eyes.

Sighing, Stiles left the room, but he returned a moment

later with a hypodermic. As he touched the needle to her arm, she jerked away.

He sent her his trademark smile, half natural, half a twisted grimace of scarred skin. "Don't worry, it's a half dose. And I've got no reason to believe it will be harmful to the fetus."

"You have no reason to believe it won't be, either." Then she caught herself. "Not that there is any fetus to be worried about." She looked past him at the floor, saw the small black bag, realized that was where he'd taken the needle from. Or at least she hoped it was.

Its slender sharp tip pierced her skin. She braced herself, waiting for the rush of dizziness and inevitable sleep, but it didn't come. Not for real. She thanked whatever sorts of angels watched out for her kind, whatever the hell her kind was, and let her arm go limp and her eyes fall closed.

Hours and hours passed before Amber finally felt the soft, heavy energy of sleep pervading the house. She was still tired, and her mind was spinning with the possibility that she might be carrying a baby. She really couldn't give it any credence, not now. Stiles was clever, clever enough to have a ready-made test kit on hand, or to fake a drugstore receipt. He had some reason for wanting her to believe something she knew to be impossible. She couldn't imagine what it was, but he had a reason. Maybe he thought she would be less likely to engage him in violence, or perhaps he thought he could hold the safety of her unborn child over her like the Sword of Damocles, using it to force her to cooperate with him.

She wasn't buying it. She *couldn't.*

Even so, she found her hands pressing to her abdomen. She closed her eyes and opened her senses. Her throat tightened until she couldn't swallow, because she felt something. Something so faint, so fleeting, that she couldn't be sure it was real. Was she picking up the essence of a new life or the effects of the power of suggestion?

She grimaced, got to her feet and arranged the covers over the pillows, thinking it probably wouldn't fool Stiles for a minute. With any luck, it wouldn't have to. She needed to keep her focus on the mission. She'd come here to get the formula Stiles called Ambrosia-Six and take it back to Willem to save his life. Stiles and his attempts at distracting her must not be allowed to work.

She could not allow herself to believe this insanity. Not even for a minute. Because if it were true…

No!

No.

She stepped up onto the bed and, from it, onto the top of the slightly higher nightstand. From there she could reach the ceiling easily, and she pushed one of its panels upward. It wasn't easy—there was insulation backing the thing, and she had to tear it apart with her fingers before it would allow the panel to move freely. She moved the panel to one side, then peered up into the rectangle of darkness, in search of a stud. There was one on either side of the opening, just as she'd guessed there would be—the panel's framework had to be attached to something, after all. She thrust her hands up through the hole, jumped just a little, and caught hold of the two-by-fours that flanked the opening; then, carefully, she pulled herself up into the ceiling. She made sure to lower her feet, one and then the other, onto the beams, not the panels. She would break right through those panels, and then she would give away her presence. So she straddled them, getting to her hands and knees, crawling along the two-by-fours, which stood up on their edges, left hand and knee on one, right on another, sixteen inches away. The narrow surfaces made balance difficult, and crawling on them was less than pleasant. Painful, in fact, by the time she'd moved a distance she judged would put her outside the locked bedroom door. She could have broken the lock, she thought. But so long as Stiles believed she was weak, kept tame by his tranquilizer, his guard would remain down.

She paused, pawing aside insulation and lifting a ceiling panel so she could peer below her. She was over the hallway now. She thought about dropping down into the hall but knew his lab would likely have a locked door, just as her bedroom did. If he were true to form, it would have an alarm on it that would sound when it was opened. So she would just keep moving.

She crept farther, certain there would be two inch dents in her knees by the time she finished. She slid her hands along until a sliver drove itself into one palm, making her suck in a breath.

"Dammit," she whispered.

The sliver was embedded in the fleshy pad beneath her forefinger. She tried to bite it and pull it out, but it was in too deep. She would just have to suffer.

She got moving again.

The next room she peered down into was a bedroom. She saw Stiles, lying sound asleep in his oversized bed, a sheet covering his torso. A naked arm and leg were flung over the woman who lay beside him. Brookie. She lay still, not quite stiff, but not relaxed, either. She was asleep, but not deeply.

There was something about her....

Amber lowered the panel into place again and moved on. She located a living room, an empty bedroom and a kitchen, before she finally moved a panel aside and saw a pristine laboratory.

She felt like shouting. But instead, she only lowered herself as far as her arms would reach and then let go, dropping to the floor.

She brushed her hands against each other, took stock of the room.

Utterly white. The walls, the floor, the cupboards, the countertops. Aside from the silver knobs on the drawers and faucets on the sink, the place wasn't broken by any other color. A refrigerator stood on one side. A desk and computer on another. She went to the PC, turned it on, then searched for the most recently accessed files.

The one he'd viewed most recently was called "Hilary Garner Journals."

Frowning, Amber clicked on the icon. The document opened in a word processing program, and as she skimmed the first few lines, she knew it hadn't been written by Stiles.

I should have believed Tamara, years ago, when she told me what DPI was really all about. I should have believed her, but I didn't. And now that I've seen the truth for myself, it's too late. If I try to leave—when I try, for I must—they'll hunt me down and they will kill me. I know that. And yet it's not fear that keeps me from making the move. It's their latest experiment. The female captive is pregnant. They inseminated her with the sperm of one of the Chosen—a male mortal with the rare Belladonna Antigen. Not just any male. But the little boy Tamara worked with so long ago, when we were best friends and she was still among the living. Jameson Bryant. Precocious little Jamey.

Amber blinked. My God, this was about her parents! It was about *her!*

Tapping the down arrow impatiently, she read on.

Hilary Garner had sent a letter, in secret, to Tamara and Eric Marquand, telling them about the prisoner and her pregnancy, knowing they would get word to Jameson and he would do something. But in the meantime, she wrote about how quickly Angelica seemed to become aware of her pregnancy, even before any symptoms should have been apparent. She would sit in her cell, her hands embracing her lower abdomen, caressing, stroking the child there as if she could reach it...

...and she would sing. God, the sound of her voice was like a choir of angels, I swear. I never heard anything so heart-wrenching, so sad or so full of love. I think part of the power of her voice is preternatural—she can sing like no human being ever could. But it's more than that. It's almost...magic. The other prisoners can hear her songs, all up and down the sublevels. And even the most violent, the most agitated, seem to relax at the sound of them. They stop pacing, lie back, close their eyes. It's the most amazing thing...and the guard dogs react, too. I've observed a few of them when her voice came floating on the air. The way their ears perk up and their tails wag. Some of them even begin to whimper, as if trying to sing along. I think they'd cut loose and do it, if they were less well trained.

She talks to her baby as if the baby can hear her and talk back. And I don't know, maybe it can. She knows it's a girl, she says.

I can't leave here yet. Not yet. Because I think maybe I'm the only one here who's willing to help her and her baby. She begs me to help her. Every single time I see her, she begs me with those eyes of hers. So imploring, so expressive. I try to tell her that I will, that I'll do whatever I can, but of course I can't say it out loud. I hope she understands. I hope she can read my thoughts the way DPI says they can. I hope she knows. I'm staying on here, continuing to work for DPI until that baby's born, and then I'm going to do something to help. Somehow.

She's not a monster. She's a mother. The only monsters here are Fuller and Stiles and the others.

Amber closed her eyes, and her stomach clenched tight. Her mother. That had been her own dear mother, singing her heart out from a prison cell, wondering what would become of her child. And a short while later a mob of vampires had surrounded that building and burned it to the ground. That was where Stiles had gotten his scars.

God, what if she were in the same horrible predicament her mother had been? Alone, imprisoned and unable to be sure she could protect her child?

"But I'm not," she whispered. "I'm no prisoner, and I'm far from helpless. I have the upper hand here. I say how long I stay. I say when I leave." Even as the thoughts crossed her mind, she looked toward the door and thought about running.

Then she swallowed hard, faced the computer again. "Besides, I'm not pregnant." She closed the file and opened the next most recently viewed document.

Edge arrived at the barn alone. He didn't know or care whether the other two were following. He had no time to focus his attention behind him. Only ahead of him. Only on Amber Lily...and that bastard Stiles.

He went to the barn where he'd last seen her, only this time, instead of going inside, he circled the place, moving slowly, his entire mind homed to pick up any trace of her.

"Look at him," Dante said. "He's like a bloodhound trying to pick up a scent."

"Mmm," Donovan agreed. "I read somewhere that bloodhounds on the scent will be so focused, so oblivious to everything else, that they've been known to walk right over cliffs, into canyons, even in front of speeding traffic."

"Then my analogy fits," Dante put in. "He's not even aware of our presence."

"Of course I'm aware of your fucking presence," Edge said, spinning around. "Now would you shut up so I can concentrate?"

Dante and Donovan exchanged glances. "There might be a better way, son," Donovan said softly.

Edge turned very slowly, pinned the man with his gaze. "Son? You're my sire, not my father."

"Is there really a difference?"

Edge stared so intently he thought the other man should have burst into flames. But apparently there was still only one in existence who could commit such a feat. A vampire named Damian—the first, according to legend. As for Edge's efforts, Donovan's hair didn't even begin to smolder.

"Dante has something for you, Edge," Donovan said.

Edge shot a look at Dante. "And I suppose you want me to address you as 'Gramps'?"

"Hardly," Dante said, seeming not the least bit amused. Still, he tugged a packet of papers, all stapled together, from the pocket of his black trench coat. "I went through the files of the old DPI. They had what were known as safe houses all over the country. Ordinary-looking homes, in ordinary neighborhoods, fitted with labs, computers and cells for the occasional prisoner."

"So?"

"So I got the full list. The Northeast Region begins on page three," he said, holding the sheaf of papers out to Edge.

Edge took it from him with a sigh, flipped the first two pages. "I don't see what good it will do. It's hardly likely Stiles would be using the former DPI safe houses."

"Why not? They'd have been put up for sale by the government when DPI was dismantled. They were, at the time, in a hell of a hurry to wash their hands of the entire operation, distance themselves from it."

"Probably in case word of the atrocities DPI committed ever leaked out," Donovan suggested.

Edge pursed his lips and skimmed the addresses under the header "Northeast Region." He slid his forefinger along with his gaze.

That one, someone said.

Edge frowned, lifting his head sharply. "Well, if you already know which one, why the hell are you asking me?"

Dante and Donovan frowned at each other, then at him. "What makes you think we know which one?" Dante asked.

"One of you just said so."

"I didn't say a word," Dante said.

"Neither did I. Niether mentally nor audibly," Donovan agreed.

Sighing, Edge returned his attention to the sheet, reading farther.

No, no, go back. It's that one, up there, I told you!

He jerked his head up again, eyeing the other two men.

Fourth from the top, that's the one!

Neither man had spoken. Nor did this voice seem like the ones he heard when he communicated with others of his kind telepathically. No, this voice seemed for all the world to be coming from someplace inside him.

"Surely you can hear that," he asked.

Donovan's puzzled expression changed to one of concern. "I hear nothing. Edge, are you all right?"

"Please, spare me the parental concern." He glanced down at the sheet again, fourth listing from the top, and read aloud. "One sixty-three, Poplar Avenue, Boston. Is that the one?"

"I don't know," Donovan said, still confused.

Yes, the voice said. It was a male voice, not as deep as Edge's own. Some other vampire, trying to offer assistance from afar? Or was it one of Stiles's newest tricks? Had he mastered telepathy now? Was he trying to draw Edge and the others into a trap?

He squeezed his eyes tight. "All right. That's the one."

"What makes you think that's where she is?" Donovan asked.

Opening his eyes, Edge lifted his brows and tipped his chin to the right. "That's what the voice in my head is telling me, all right?" Then he shrugged. "And I don't hear any better ideas coming from either of you."

"Fine. Boston, then."

The formula was not on the computer. Nor was it in the file cabinet she managed to open with the force of her mind. She found several vials of her own blood in the refrigerator, but that was all.

Dammit.

Finally she put everything back exactly the way she'd found it and jumped upward, tugging herself through the hole in the ceiling again. When she looked back down at the room from above, she saw a tiny bit of pink fluff lying on the floor—a piece of the insulation. She looked at it and turned her head just slightly. The fluff spun across the floor and along the wall, vanishing behind a cabinet.

Perfect. She replaced the panel and crawled along the two-by-fours again until she was outside the lab and over the hallway. Then she emerged, lowering herself to the floor, straightening the panel behind her, making sure she left no signs. Then she began walking through the rest of the house.

He must have had notes somewhere. He must have recorded his work as he developed the formula. And he must have the formula itself hidden in this house. He didn't have a photographic memory that she knew of, so there had to be notes, a recipe, something.

Hell, where would he keep it, if not in the lab?

She tiptoed through the hallway, searching the house room by room. It was nearly dawn, she realized when she crossed the living room and glanced at the clock on the wall. It crossed her mind that very soon he would move her to a more secure location. She would be out of reach of assistance. Maybe she should remove the blocks from her mind. Send a call out to her friends. To her mother. To Edge. Just to let them know she was all right.

She closed her eyes and reminded herself of all the reasons why she must not do that. They wouldn't let her stay here long enough to get the formula. If they knew where she was, they would home in on her like a flock of bats on a mosquito swarm. And they would know where she was if she lowered her shields. They would come charging to the rescue, just like they always did. Edge right along with them, she thought—though she imagined he would deny it with everything in him, if asked. If he found her, he wouldn't leave Stiles alive. She didn't know what his issue with the man was, but it must be a big one.

No, she couldn't let her guard down. Couldn't let any of them know where she was. At least not until she got the formula for Will.

She padded through the carpeted living room, past the sofa and television stand and coffee table. There was a file folder on the coffee table, and she scooped it up as she passed, glancing at its label. "Poe."

Frowning, she carried it with her into the kitchen, set it on the table and opened the fridge as her stomach growled. She thought about helping herself to some of the fruits and vegetables that filled the drawers. Apparently someone—probably Brookie—had been sent shopping since their arrival here. Amber wondered if they would notice if anything went missing and decided to risk it. She took an apple, a banana, a stalk of celery. Then she opened the cupboards and located a box of granola bars. Thankfully, it was already open, so she took one out. Lastly she took a single serving size bottle of tomato juice. She loaded her stolen booty into a plastic grocery back she found tucked under the sink and turned back to the file folder on the table, flipping it open.

"Poe, Edgar. aka Edge," the top sheet read. "Ireland, 1943. Sire, Donovan O'Roark."

She blinked slowly. Edge's name was Edgar Poe? God, his mother must have had one sick sense of humor. And Stiles must be worried about him, to have pulled his file.

Something made her jerk her head up sharply. Not a sound—a feeling. No, the absence of a feeling. Not everyone in the house was asleep anymore.

Hell!

She closed the folder and stuffed it into her bag, certain she could sneak it back out to the living room before anyone noticed it missing. Then she tiptoed quickly through the house, every sense on full alert.

She made it to her bedroom door, saw the dead bolt on the outside.

A dead bolt. Nothing else. Excellent. She turned the bolt and quickly jerked the door open, ducking inside. Then, closing the door behind her, she used the power of her mind to close the dead bolt lock again.

She heard it snap into place and knew she'd been successful. Standing on the bed, she shoved the plastic bag up through the now loose ceiling panel, into the crawl space above—ceiling panels had long been a favorite hiding place of hers—and then she carefully put the panel back into place.

Even as footsteps came down the hall, Amber dropped into the bed, wriggled her way beneath the covers and wrestled the pillows up to the top of the mattress where they belonged. Just as she hugged them to her face, the door lock turned, the door opened.

Only it wasn't Stiles who came in this time.

It was Brookie.

13

Amber smelled a hint of Brooke's perfume, left over from the day before, a sweet mix of bubble gum and tropical fruit. It was like something a schoolgirl would wear, something that probably came in a pink glass bottle shaped like a kitten.

The woman came farther into the room, her steps soft and padded rather than sharp and clicking. No heels. She was wearing slippers or socks this morning. Probably still in her nightgown. She crept up to Amber's bedside, pausing every couple of steps, as if she were approaching a sleeping tiger. Step, step, pause. Her breaths were strained, as if she were trying to keep them quiet, even while her pounding heart demanded more and more oxygen. Quick, short little breaths. Amber sensed her fear.

What the hell was she doing in here, if she was so afraid?

"Hey," she whispered. "Hey, wake up."

Blinking, Amber rolled onto her side and blinked her eyes sleepily. "What?" She frowned as if puzzled, rubbed her eyes.

"I just…wanted to check on you. See if you're okay," Brookie said.

Amber sat up in the bed, a hand to her head as if she were dizzy. No way was she giving anything away to this woman. Something was wrong about her, off. Studying her face, Amber said, "Who are you?"

"I'm Brooke. I…work with Frank. Sort of."

"Oh," Amber said. "You're one of my kidnappers."

"It's not like that." Brooke's coppery curls were in disarray, her green eyes huge and round as she shot a nervous look back toward the door. "I don't like what he's doing to you. But it's not like I can stop it."

"No, of course not."

"I saw the test kit in the bathroom, so I know you used it by now. Is it true? Are you…?"

Amber shook her head. "It's not possible."

"The test stick in the garbage read positive."

"It was a trick. Stiles has some reason for wanting me to believe this absurd notion, but I know better."

Brooke frowned at her. "How could he have tricked you? The test kit—"

"He had it made up in advance. Tampered with it so it would give a false positive. He must have been planning this for some time."

Brooke lowered her head.

"What?" Amber asked.

Copper curls moved as she looked up again. "He sent me to the drugstore for the test kit."

Amber felt her heart squeeze into a tight little knot.

"It was on the shelf with dozens of others, in probably ten different brands. He didn't tell me what brand to buy. Heck, he didn't even tell me which drugstore to use— there are three within a couple blocks of here." She shook her head slowly. "Unless he managed to tamper with every kit in all three stores. And since we've never even been to this place until the day before he took you, I don't see how…"

"The day before he kidnapped me?"

She nodded. "We were here for one night. Just long enough to set up the lab, fill the cupboards and turn up the heat. Then we headed to Salem to hunt for you. I had to keep a distance, following along by using the homing device, and just wait until he came to me.''

Amber pursed her lips. "Why are you telling me all this?"

"I...you asked."

"He told you to, didn't he? He told you to try to make nice with me, to win my trust so you could try to convince me to believe in this insanity he's trying to sell me."

Brooke took a few steps backward, toward the door. "If he catches me in here, I'm in deep trouble. I just— I just felt sorry for you."

"You felt sorry for me?"

"Young, pregnant, alone. Being held against your will." She sent another glance back at the door. "Is there anything I can get for you that will make this easier?"

"Sure, several things. A key to that door would be great. I'd also like the blood he stole from my veins returned to me."

Brooke pursed her lips. "I could get you some prenatal vitamins."

"I'd prefer a machine gun. Although that wouldn't kill him anyway, would it?"

"So you know about that," Brooke whispered.

"Do you?" Amber asked.

Looking up slowly, Brooke nodded.

"What will kill him, Brooke? How can he die?"

She shook her head, backing nearer the door. "He doesn't know I know."

"I don't want to kill him," Amber said quickly. "In fact, that's the last thing I want to happen. That's why I stopped Edge from killing him." She didn't even know if the woman was aware of anything that had happened until now. Not until she said it, at least. As soon as she did, she saw the acknowledgment in Brooke's green eyes.

"I've wondered...why you did that."

"Then he told you."

She shook her head. "I read some of his notes about it. I'm not supposed to know any of this."

"Stiles is the only other person in the world who's like me," Amber said. "Do you have any idea what it's like, not knowing what can kill you?"

Brooke licked her lips, her hand turning on the doorknob.

"Please," Amber asked, knowing she was about to lose her best chance.

Brooke met her eyes. "Incineration." She spat the word quickly as she jerked the door open. "Till there's nothing left but ash. It's the only way." Ducking out the door, she closed it softly behind her and turned the lock.

Licking her lips, Amber sat down to digest the information she'd been given. And yet, she couldn't really trust any of it. There was no way to be sure Stiles hadn't put Brooke up to this entire little visitation.

She was hungry. She thought about her hidden snacks and the file on Edge, wondered if Stiles would be in to check on her anytime soon and decided to risk it. She climbed onto the bed, reaching up into the ceiling, and retrieved her bag. Then she sat on the bed, opened the file folder, peeled the banana and kept her senses alert for Stiles's approach.

"Right there, see?"

Edge stood in brilliant sunlight, beside a gaunt, tough-looking kid of about seventeen. It shocked him to be standing in the sunlight and not burning. But after a mo-

ment he accepted that it simply was and focused on the
boy. The kid wore faded jeans, with straight legs and
worn-out knees. The hems were frayed. His hair was too
long, dark and straight, and tended to fall into his eyes.

"Right there," the boy said again.

He was pointing, and Edge looked. There was a small,
ordinary looking brick house, on a hilltop. Steps land-
scaped into the lawn zigzagged up the hill to the front
door. There was a wrought-iron fence around the place,
but it looked more ornamental than functional.

"That's where she is?" Edge asked.

"Yeah."

"How do you know?"

"What difference does it make? She's in there. You
want to see?"

Edge felt his heart contract. "God, yes."

The kid smiled a little, gave a nod.

Edge felt his brain twist and whirl as if being sucked
into a whirlpool. He pressed his hands to the sides of his
head, grimacing in pain. And then just as suddenly there
was a pop and a rush of relief. He blinked his vision into
focus, gave his head a shake. "Jesus, what the hell was
that?" At least the pain was gone. He lowered his hands
to his sides and looked around.

He was in a tiny room, and right in front of him, Alby
sat in a bed, under the covers, with her back braced
against the headboard and her knees bent. An open file
folder rested against her thighs. She was staring at something inside it. A banana peel and an apple core lay on
the bed beside her, and she was working on devouring a
granola bar and sucking down a bottle of tomato juice.

"Alby!" He moved closer, noting her color was still
pale, but otherwise, she looked well. God, he wished he
could sustain his indignation, his anger. But right now

all he could feel was relief at seeing her again. "Are you all right?"

She didn't move, didn't react in any way, and when Edge reached out a hand to touch her, to shake her out of her apparent stupor if necessary, his hand moved right through her. As if one of them were made of smoke.

"This is a dream, Edge. She doesn't even know you're here," his companion told him.

"The hell she doesn't. Alby!" He shouted her name with his entire being, with his mind, with his soul.

She blinked, frowned, and looked up from the file folder, glancing around the room as if she'd heard or sensed something. Edge focused everything in him on her. *I'm coming for you.*

She continued to look around the room, then sighed and focused again on the pages she was reading so intently. Curious, Edge moved around until he could see what had her so engrossed.

The left side of the folder held a line drawing that bore a striking resemblance, Edge thought, to himself. It showed a lanky young man in a leather jacket, sitting on the hood of a '69 Mustang, a cigarette dangling from one hand.

Wait a minute, that was *his* Mustang.

He glanced at the facing page and saw a thick sheaf of papers, line after line of typed words, telling his story—or Stiles's version of it, anyway.

Again he was sucked headfirst into the vortex, and this time when he popped out the other side, he found himself returning to the warehouse on that horrible night in 1959.

Hell, no. No, I don't want to see this.

But he couldn't control the scene playing out in front of him, and he knew, somehow, through gut instinct, why. This was Alby's mind. He was seeing what she imagined as she read Stiles's account. Watching himself. Things didn't look exactly as they had been. The warehouse was cleaner, neater, the windows unbroken as he moved through it. And he looked different, too, more as he was today and less as he had been then.

He tried to withdraw from Amber's consciousness, but it wasn't possible. This wasn't like reading her thoughts, trespassing inside her mind. He didn't know what the hell this was. It was different, beyond his control.

He closed his eyes, and still he saw. He saw himself walking into the warehouse, heard himself calling out to Scottie and Bridget and the others. "I'm back. Didn't find Billy Boy. Has he come home yet?"

But only his own voice echoed back in answer. He remembered the dread, the certainty that something was terribly wrong.

He kept moving, and then, suddenly, he smelled it even stronger than before.

Death, rank and bloody, tinged the air with its reeking stench. It was coming from here, from inside the warehouse. "God, no," he heard himself whisper, and he ran forward, across the warehouse's floor, around the corner. Then he skidded to a stop and fought down the bile as he saw what awaited him there.

They hung upside down, suspended from the rafters high above, by ropes wrapped around their ankles. Their throats had been cut. Every one of them. Bridget, her little girl face streaked in blood. It had soaked her red curls, dripped from them into the pool on the floor. Her terror still echoed in the air.

He heard his own voice crying out in denial, felt the weakness that overwhelmed him until he sank to his knees, felt the hot tears welling in his eyes and spilling over.

Dead. Gone. All of them. And he was alone.

Staggering to his feet, he gathered his wits, leaped upward, to the loft, and looked at the items on the floor. Items that identified the killer clearly, just by the ones that were missing. Stiles. Frank W. Stiles. He would remember the name for the rest of his days.

He tugged out his pocketknife. One by one he cut the ropes, gripping them and lowering the lifeless shells of the vampiric children to the floor below, gently, with great care. His kids, he'd called them. His fledgling gang. The closest thing he would ever have to children of his own. When he jumped down from the loft again, he knelt beside them, shaking his head, touching their faces, washing them with his tears, speaking to them.

Edge spoke to his past self. "You idiot, shake off the grief and realize he's still there somewhere. He's watching. You could get him right now, right there! Wake up!"

But of course he couldn't change the past. In the past, he'd been too overwhelmed with grief and horror to think about opening his mind to the space around him. He watched as his former self went for a pail of water and a washrag, and proceeded to bathe the blood from his orphans. He watched as the past Edge went to wash the streaks of it from Bridget's delicate face.

Stiles. The name whispered through his mind with a certainty that couldn't be denied. Anger rushed through him, like fire through his veins. His blood turned to lava. He would find the bastard, wherever he was, and he would kill him.

But first...

The old Edge went through the kids' belongings, locating clothes for them, dressing them. Then he chose one item from each of them, to keep in their memory.

He lit a cigarette then. Sat on the floor, their bodies all laid out before him, smoking, talking to them.

"I'll get him," he said. "I'll get him for what he did to you. I promise you that. He'll pay."

And finally he got to his feet and flicked his cigarette into the pool of kerosene he'd poured around them. Then he left his home for the last time.

It was only as he stood outside, watching it burn, that he felt the presence. Someone was there…watching him. *Stiles!*

He whirled, honing his senses to locate the man. Bastard! The nerve to hang around and watch him suffer! Watch him grieve!

He opened his mind, searching, casting a wide net, and sensing, even as he did, the man fleeing, escaping, slipping out of Edge's reach.

And then the images ended.

Edge's brain was nearly crushed under the pressure as he was sucked out of the consciousness he'd been inside and found himself back in the bedroom again, watching her, watching Amber Lily.

She closed the file folder, but the drawing was no longer inside. She held it, staring at it as tears flowed down her cheeks. "No wonder," she whispered. "God, no wonder you hate Stiles so much."

He shook off the excruciating pain of the memory. *Never mind that,* he thought at her. *It's over. It doesn't matter anymore. Just stay alive. I'm coming to get you.*

He jerked his head around—and so did she—at the sound of footsteps in the hall. She quickly jumped to her feet, shoving the file folder and banana peel and granola bar wrapper up into the ceiling. Then she dropped into the bed again and instantly went limp.

Her strength wasn't what it should be, but it wasn't

seriously waning, either. The speed with which she'd moved was proof enough of that. Good.

The locks turned, and the door opened.

Edge's eyes narrowed as the bastard, Stiles, entered the room. Instinctively he lunged at the man, reaching for his throat, only to move right through him, bodily, which left him feeling sick and dizzy. He shook himself. Then the man moved closer to Amber, and Edge was surprised his anger didn't knock Stiles on his ass. It didn't, though. Stiles reached for Amber, lifting her hand, and letting it go. It dropped limply onto the blankets. He tapped her cheeks, moving her head back and forth.

"Amber Lily. Come on, wake up. You should eat something. We want to keep the baby healthy, now, don't we?"

Edge reeled. God, it was true, then, what he'd sensed before. Amber Lily was pregnant. She knew it now, if she hadn't before. She knew what he'd only sensed inside her, what he hadn't even been certain was real. More importantly—more chillingly—Stiles knew, as well. Where the hell was this child's father? He should be here, taking steps to protect his offspring. But he wasn't. Edge resented it. He resented being the only one who cared when the child wasn't his own, couldn't be his own. Which was utterly stupid, since the last thing on earth he wanted was a child. He never wanted to be responsible for anyone ever again. Only for himself.

He resented Amber Lily for not telling him she'd been with someone else before him. She'd just let him believe she was a virgin. Why? It burned like hell to know she'd been with someone else. Some other man had touched her, kissed her....

Hell.

She blinked her eyes open, and in a slurred voice said, "Stop it. There's no baby."

Stiles smiled, shaking his head. "You're a stubborn one, I'll give you that." He set the tray of food on the dresser. He started to say something else, but Edge was suddenly jerked out of the scene, jerked from everything, and sucked back into his own body. When he woke in the barn, which was as far as they'd managed to get last night before having to seek shelter from the sun, he realized that night had fallen.

Dante and Donovan were standing over him, brushing hay from their clothes and looking worried.

"What the hell…?" Edge's head was pounding, and he pressed a hand to it, closing his eyes tightly.

"You were thrashing around in your sleep," Dante told him. "Muttering, clutching your head."

"For a while we didn't think you were going to wake," Donovan put in. "Damn strange. The day sleep is too deep for dreaming."

"It was no dream." Edge sat up slowly and lowered his hands from his head. "I think it was more like a—I don't know—it felt as if my spirit left my body." He looked from one man to the other, seeing curiosity rather than blatant disbelief. It gave him the nudge to go on. "There was a guide of some sort. He took me to Amber."

Dante lifted his brows. "Is she all right?"

He nodded. "Yes. For some reason Stiles's tranquilizer isn't affecting her, but she's pretending that it is. He's holding her in a house, in Boston. I saw it clearly." He could have kicked himself for wasting time, coming here, to where he'd last seen Amber, only to find she'd been a half hour from Salem the entire time.

"We'll have her out of there before this night is out," Dante said.

"What else?" Donovan asked. "Edge, what the hell is it you're keeping from us?"

Edge sighed, shielded his mind and lowered his head. It was up to Amber Lily to tell them about her little secret. It wasn't his place, had nothing to do with him. "Nothing. We should let her family know where we think she is, and that we're going after her."

"Good idea," Dante said. "They're bringing two vehicles, they said. Can't be more than a couple of hours out by now."

"Can you reach them telepathically? Tell them where to meet us?"

Dante nodded.

"Then let's go get Alby," Edge said.

Amber didn't trust the meals Stiles had been bringing her throughout the day, though she had to admit she was surprised by his changed demeanor. He was treating her almost...tenderly, checking on her often. Too often. It had taken her most of the day to get through the file he kept on Edge, because his constant visits kept interrupting her. Edge had been hunting him since 1959 but had only had luck locating him since the destruction of the DPI. Prior to that, Stiles theorized, the protection of the organization had kept him too well covered for anyone to track him down. Edge had tried to kill him twice, Stiles had written. Smashed his head in with a brick once, and stabbed him once—more than twelve times. But both times Stiles had revived.

She supposed Stiles hadn't had the chance to add the latest attempt to this set of notes, with the neck crushing back in the barn. There must be other notes somewhere; the ones Brooke had seen.

Stiles set the latest plate of food he'd brought, a bed-time snack she supposed, on the nightstand beside the bed and leaned over to plump her pillows.

"How are you feeling?"

"Queasy as hell. I'm not sure I can eat this."

He nodded. "That's normal early in a pregnancy, according to what I've been reading."

She lifted her brows. "You've been reading about pregnancy?" She almost asked him if bloating were common. Her jeans were feeling awfully snug. Even if this pregnancy were for real—which it was not—she wouldn't be swelling at this early date.

"I sent Brookie out for some books today. Though I doubt any of them deal with this particular sort of gestation."

She licked her lips as he set the tray on her lap and pulled up a chair. "Why would you do that, Stiles?"

He shrugged. "Sure you can't manage to eat just a little?"

"You're planning to keep me here a while, aren't you? Long enough that you feel you need to know about pre-natal care." She picked at the food, not eating any. Not because she wasn't starved to death, though.

"Nothing this noteworthy has happened in vampire research since…well, since your own birth. Naturally, I want to record it."

"And you need more of my blood, as well. To make the serum, the Ambrosia-Six."

He shook his head slowly. "What I took yesterday is enough for my next round of injections. I'm not taking any more of your blood, Amber, not until the child is born. I don't want to put it at risk, and besides, I don't even know the serum will work the same way as before. Your blood is different now that you're pregnant.''

She resisted the urge to deny it yet again. He was determined to keep pushing this fantasy, so fine. She would go along with it. "Have you tried? Making your serum from the blood you took from me, I mean?"

He nodded. "I finished it this morning," he said. "Since your blood is different, this will have to be Ambrosia-Seven." Then he looked at her sharply. "Why do you want to know?"

She shrugged and averted her eyes. "I want to know everything...about me, about what I am, how I...work." She dared to look at him again.

He still seemed slightly suspicious.

"It's frustrating, not knowing simple things...how long I'll live, whether I'm still aging, how I can die."

His face altered, a hint of sympathy appearing in his eyes. "Whether your baby will be normal?" he asked.

Deciding to play along, she nodded hard. "That most of all."

He shrugged. "The serum's effect lasts six months. When it begins to wear off, I tend to age rapidly, but it stops the moment I inject more. I don't know how those things apply to you. You've always aged normally. Chances are your child will, as well."

She had aged normally, she thought—but only up to the first time Stiles had killed her, just to see if she would revive. That memory was a sharp reminder of this man's true nature. He was evil. Any sympathy he showed now was only an act. A ruse. He was trying to gain her trust for some sick reason.

If she didn't know better, she would think he wanted to keep her calm and happy long enough to get his hands on her baby. But she did know better. Because there was no baby.

"Have you tried the new serum yet?"

"I don't need it yet. Won't for another five or six weeks. And I do have one more vial of the A-Six remaining. Although I have to admit, I'm eager to see how the new formula works. Your blood seems...enhanced somehow from what it was before. It might be even more potent than the last batch."

"Really?"

"Mmm. Ambrosia-Seven might just be my greatest work yet."

"Then again," she whispered, "it may not work at all."

"I'm afraid that's all too true."

At least it was made, Amber thought. All she had to do now was get her hands on it and get out of here. The second he slept, she thought. The very second...

He got to his feet. "I'm going to move you soon, to a more secure location. That way we can dispense with the tranquilizer, just to be on the safe side."

He paused, as if expecting her to thank him for that. She didn't.

"For now, though..." He took a hypodermic from his lab coat pocket.

She flinched as he jabbed it into her arm but told herself it was all right. It was only salt water.

Only it wasn't. He must have restocked the little black bag, or taken this batch from another source. Her head swam, and she cursed under her breath.

"Just relax. Get some sleep," he said, taking the food from her lap, setting it aside, and then putting his hands on her shoulders to ease her gently onto the pillows. "There now. Don't fight it."

The sleep rolled in like the tide, covering her consciousness, sweeping it away.

She had the dream again. It unfolded in its familiar way. She saw Edge, standing across a darkened room, facing her. In his arms, there was the ornate little box, like a miniature treasure chest. He stared down into it, his face stricken. Then he turned, to bring it across the room toward her.

"No," she whispered. "I don't want it."

Again he bent lower as he approached the bed, so that she could look inside.

"I don't want to look," she heard herself saying. "Please, don't make me look." But she had no choice. And this time, when she looked at what the box held, the dream didn't fade as it had all the other times. It didn't black out. It didn't change. She saw it very clearly. It was a bundle, something small, wrapped in soft blankets.

She felt her heart begin to pound in her chest, because of what that bundle looked like. And yet she couldn't see beyond the blankets. Her gaze shot to Edge's face, and she caught her breath. A single teardrop rolled slowly down his cheek. She looked to the bundle in the box again. It was still. No movement, no motion.

Edge moved nearer, lifting the box closer to her.

And now she could see the tiny elfin face. The closed eyes. The blue-tinted skin. The deathly stillness.

Death. She was looking at the face of death. And her own child was wearing it.

The sound of her screams woke her.

Edge heard Amber Lily scream and sprang from where he was crouched behind a parked car. Donovan's hand on his shoulder stopped him from racing forward. "Easy. We have to wait for the others."

"The hell we do!"

"Edge, don't be foolish," Dante said sharply. "We'll have a far better chance of rescuing her unharmed once Rhiannon and Roland arrive with her parents."

"Unharmed?" He sent the man a look of sheer disbelief. "Did that scream sound to you as if she were unharmed?"

"There's strength in numbers."

"I've got all the strength I need." He shook off the hand that held him, ran for the house, vaulted the fence and kicked in the front door.

Some kind of alarm went off, emitting short, earsplitting shrieks. He heard someone running toward him, saw Stiles's shocked expression as he appeared in front of him, dressed in pajama bottoms and a T-shirt, a tranquilizer gun in his hand.

Edge hit the man so hard and so fast he never had time to pull the trigger. Stiles sailed bodily through the air, hit the wall, splitting it, and then slid to the floor. The gun landed on the floor at his feet, and Edge stomped it to bits as he strode through the house. He wasn't worried about Stiles. The other two men would be on his heels, and they would handle him. For now. "Alby! Where are you?"

There was nothing, no reply. He walked down the hall, smashing every door he came to with the flat of one hand. Each one flew open, crashed into the wall behind it and bounced back at him. Each room was empty.

Until the last one. And that was where he found her.

She lay in the bed, barely conscious, her eyes bleary and unfocused, her hair tangled and damp with sweat. Edge went to her, stripping back the covers and gathering her into his arms. She wore a nightgown of soft white muslin. She was weeping, trembling all over. Straightening, Edge turned to take her out of this place.

"No," she whispered.

He stopped. She was pointing at the ceiling. "Get the...file."

"Screw the file." He carried her through the open door into the hall.

"Edge, please!" She lifted her head, spoke as if forcing power into her words. "The lab. The serum." She closed her eyes slowly, clearly under the influence of a powerful narcotic.

"Where?" he asked.

She lifted a weak hand, pointing, and he carried her through the house, spotting Dante and Donovan leaning over Stiles's motionless body.

"Take care," Edge called to them. "He'll revive." Then, to Amber, "Which way?"

Again she pointed, and he crossed the room, entered another hallway, and kicked open yet another door. The spotless white laboratory stood there, immaculate as before. And empty. The refrigerator door stood open, and there was nothing inside. File drawers were likewise gaping and void. Amber looked around, then let her head fall limp against his shoulder.

"Oh, no."

"Who else was here?"

She licked her lips. "A woman. Brooke." Her eyes opened again. "The computer...?"

He looked where she was looking, saw an empty desk. "Gone. As we should be."

He carried her back into the living room, where Donovan was securing Stiles's hands behind his back. Dante came in from another room. "The house is empty."

"Amber says there was a woman here."

Dante lifted his brows. "If there was, she left before we ever arrived."

"Well, she took Stiles's notes and his serum with her," Edge told them. Then he nodded toward Donovan. "Those cuffs won't hold him once he revives."

"Then we'd best see to it he doesn't revive, don't you think?" a woman's voice asked. Everyone turned to see Rhiannon entering the house. Behind her, another woman, one Edge had never seen before, raced toward him. And he knew, when he looked at her face, she had to be Amber's mother. She had the same penetrating eyes and sculpted cheekbones. She was stunning, and yet she didn't compare to her daughter.

She ran her hands over Amber's face, stroked her hair. "My darling," she whispered. "Tell me you're all right."

"I'm okay," Amber said, her voice weak, strained. It was fully obvious she was far from all right. "Stiles... has a device. Heel of his shoe. Homing beacon," she managed to tell them.

"I'll take care of it," Donovan said.

Amber's mother shot a look at Edge, obviously worried about Amber's drowsy, drunken state. He said, "It's the tranquilizer." He guessed its effects were the reason he'd been unable to sense Amber, to know which room she was in. "It'll wear off soon enough."

A man came in from the back of the house, apparently having entered that way. He strode right up to Edge, gathering Amber from his arms and into his own. "It's okay, hon. I've got you now."

Edge hoped, for the man's sake, he was Amber's father. Otherwise...

"I take it you're the fellow who used my daughter's life as bait for Stiles?"

"Easy, Bryant," Dante said. "He's also the man who led us to her and got her out."

"I can walk," Amber said, her voice still slurred. "Please, Dad, put me down."

Jameson Bryant looked at his daughter for a long moment, then hugged her fiercely before setting her on her feet. She looked at Edge, and her eyes seemed to pierce his soul. "Edge had reasons for what he did," she said, speaking to her father but never looking away. "And he had no intention of letting Stiles get anywhere near me."

"It was a mistake," Edge said. "If I could undo it, I would."

"I think you just did," Angelica said softly.

Rhiannon gripped Stiles by his shirt collar. "Let's get out of here. No doubt that alarm was heard beyond these walls." Turning, she dragged Stiles across the floor, his body bumping down the steps behind her.

The others followed, but Amber faltered with her first steps. Edge reached for her, but her mother was faster, gathering her close and helping her walk. And then, suddenly, Angelica stopped. Her eyes went wide, and she looked at her daughter.

"What? What's wrong?"

Angelica opened her mouth, closed it again, shot a look at Edge, and then at Jameson, who followed behind them. She licked her lips and seemed to battle tears. "Nothing. Never mind." Closing her eyes, she tucked Amber's head onto her own shoulder. Then she started forward again.

She knew. Edge had seen it in her eyes. She knew. Hell, if they thought he was responsible for Amber's condition, he would probably be dust by this time tomorrow.

Her family would stake him out in the desert to await the sunrise.

Fortunately for him, everyone knew such a thing was impossible. Male vampires were sterile. Amber's child could not be his.

14

"We need to search the place thoroughly before we leave here," Jameson said as he eased her onto the couch. She could still smell faint traces of Brookie's popcorn. "Amber, rest here, on the sofa. You're safe here."

"I'll stay with her," she heard Edge say quickly. Then there was a prickle of tension in the air, but it passed.

She opened her eyes to find him sitting on the sofa beside her, his gaze fixed on her face, as if searching…for something.

"I didn't need rescuing," she managed to say. "I let him bring me here on purpose."

"And it was working well, love. Right up until he dosed you with that drug."

She thinned her lips, nodded. "I filled some of the syringes with water. Faked him out the first couple of times."

"Think he caught on?"

"Nah, just grabbed the wrong needle." She drew a breath, sighed. "You seemed…mad at me after we…"

He shrugged. "More at myself than you." Then he tipped his head to one side. "A little at you, though."

She pursed her lips. "You tried to kill Stiles, even though I begged you not to."

"Okay, so I was more than a little mad at you. Do you blame me?"

She frowned, unsure what he was talking about.

"Jesus, Alby, isn't there anything you want to tell me here?"

Very quickly, she averted her eyes. Obviously he sensed she was keeping something from him. He couldn't know what, of course. But—God, she wasn't ready to talk about this. Not here, not now. How did you just blurt something like this out to a man who thought himself sterile? She imagined herself saying it. "I might be carrying your child, even though you and I both know that it's physically impossible. And oh, by the way, don't worry too much about it, because it's going to be still-born."

No.

"Alby?"

She sighed. "Look, there is something, but it's…"

"None of my business?" he asked.

She frowned. "That's not what I was going to say."

"Why not? It's true. I'm sorry, Alby, you're right. I've got no right to press you on this. It's…not my place."

"The house is clear," Amber heard her father call. "Let's get Amber the hell out of here."

Someone lifted her from the sofa. It wasn't Edge. She needed to talk to him, to tell him he had things all wrong. But the drug was fighting her every step of the way.

"Rhiannon and Angelica will take her back to Salem. It's the closest, safest place for her," her father said.

"And the rest of you?" Edge asked.

"Roland, Dante, Donovan and I will transport Stiles to Eric's lab, in Wind Ridge. It's in Southwestern Pennsylvania, near the West Virginia border. Which group you go with is up to you, Edge."

Amber tried to open her eyes, get her voice to cooperate. She wanted to tell Edge to stay with her, that she did have something to tell him. But before she could manage to win the battle of wills with the drug, she heard him say, "I'll stick with Stiles. Alby's in good hands. She doesn't need me hanging around."

Her heart seemed to contract and shrink in her chest. He sounded so angry, so…hurt. Amber gave up the fight, feeling she'd lost more than just the battle, and sank into sleep.

She felt as if she should be in a state of panic, but she couldn't seem to work up to it. Everything was happening in a soft haze of slow motion bliss. Her head and limbs were heavy, her eyes too tired to stay open. And yet, when they did fall closed, the dream returned—or the memory of it did.

Her eyes flew open. "What—where—"

"Take a breath, honey," her mother said softly. "You're all right. I've got you."

She was, she realized, in the back seat of a car, snuggled in the curve of her mother's arm.

"Where…are the others?"

"The men took the other car back to Pennsylvania," Rhiannon told her softly. She was driving. "Stiles is in their trunk."

"What about Edge?"

Her mother looked at her gently, probingly, one hand stroking her hair.

"Oh, *he's* not in the trunk," Rhiannon said, deadpan. "Though I think he might have been safer there." She turned slightly, just enough to send Amber a sneaky smile.

"He shouldn't be with them," Amber said. "He wants Stiles dead. He'll kill him if they turn their backs."

"Darling," Angelica said, "there are four powerful

men with him. Dante, Donovan, Roland and your father. They're not going to let him hurt Stiles."

"They won't stop him."

"Of course they will. Meanwhile, we're taking you back to Salem, where you can rest and recover from your ordeal."

Amber sat up. "Mother, the only thing I need to recover from is that one dose of tranquilizer Stiles managed to get into me. Other than that I'm fine."

"Are you?" her mother asked.

Amber frowned at her, searching her face. "What are you getting at?"

Rhiannon glanced over her shoulder as she drove, curious.

"Did you think I wouldn't know, Amber? As close as we are, did you think I wouldn't feel it the first time I touched you, see it the first time I looked into your eyes?"

"Mom, I don't know what you're—"

"You're pregnant, Amber."

Rhiannon hit the brakes so hard the tires squealed and hot rubber scented the air. She jerked the wheel to keep the car pointed straight ahead and brought it to a stop in a cloud of dust on the shoulder.

Then she turned around in her seat, getting up on her knees to stare fully at Amber, a question in her eyes.

Amber released the death grip she had on the armrest, glad they hadn't crashed, forced herself to look Rhiannon in the eye, and then her mother. "Obviously Stiles managed to spin his fairy tale for you before he was knocked unconscious."

"Stiles?" Rhiannon asked. "Is he responsible for this?"

"He made it up," Amber told them, even though she

was no longer sure it was the truth. "He's been trying to convince me of it for some insane reason. I can't imagine why. Much less why he'd try to fool you."

Rhiannon rolled her eyes. But Angelica only lowered her head. "Stiles didn't tell me this, Amber Lily," she whispered.

"Then were *did* you get such a ludicrous idea?"

Angelica lifted her head again, and there were tears brimming in her eyes. "I told you. I saw it in your eyes, felt it in your touch." She pressed her hand to Amber's belly. "Can't you feel it, Amber? There's life inside you."

Amber felt the blood drain from her face as she shook her head in denial. "It's impossible. He made it up. It can't be real."

"It is real."

"But...but..."

"Who is the father?" Rhiannon's voice was short, clipped, deep and vibrating with menace. "I'll eat his liver."

"No, you can't hurt him. God, I don't even want you to tell him." She shook her head. "Let him go on his way. He's a loner, always has been. He wouldn't want this."

"You don't know that for sure, darling," Angelica said. "Give the young man a chance."

"No, you don't understand. All he wants is vengeance on Stiles. That's all."

The two women met each other's eyes, then, slowly, they both looked at Amber again. Angelica whispered, "Darling, you sound as if you think Edge is the father."

"Haven't you explained this to her?" Rhiannon asked. "Amber, vampires can't reproduce."

"Apparently they can," Amber said. She drew a breath, lowered her head. "He's…the only one."

Angelica searched her eyes, then sent a similar look to Rhiannon. "How is this possible?"

"I don't see that it matters," Rhiannon said. "Except as it concerns the methods I can use to kill him."

"Rhiannon, you aren't going to—"

"I say we douse him in gasoline, give him a head start and then see which of us can be the first to hit him with a lit match." Rhiannon smiled. "It'll be like a game of tag. Only, you know, better."

"Rhiannon, you're upsetting her."

"No, she's not." Amber sat up straighter in her seat and fixed Rhiannon with a very serious stare. "If you want to hurt him, Aunt Rhiannon, you're going to have to go through me first. And I promise you, I'm way tougher than any of you give me credit for being."

Rhiannon looked surprised, then angry. "You dare—"

"You wanna go right now?" Amber jerked her car door open, got out, waved a hand at the driver's door and watched it fly open, as well. She was dizzy, unsteady on her feet, and her jeans were so tight they hurt. But she was mad as hell and ready to fight.

Rhiannon got out of the car slowly, gracefully, like a queen alighting from a chariot. Amber stood ready. She kept her stance wide, knees bent, arms loose at her sides.

"I suppose," Rhiannon said slowly, "raging hormones and Stiles's tranquilizer could be to blame for this."

"Or maybe she's in love," Angelica said, getting out of the car, as well. She stood beside her daughter, put a hand on her shoulder. "Don't be ridiculous, Amber. Rhiannon is not going to fight you."

Rhiannon shrugged. "Not while you're pregnant, anyway."

"You'll have to, if you want to hurt Edge."

"So he gets to keep breathing for a few months longer." Rhiannon shrugged. "Suddenly defending your honor has lost its appeal. Ungrateful little whelp." She spun around and got back into the car, slamming the door.

Angelica shook her head. "You hurt her terribly, Amber."

Amber lowered her head. "She had it coming." But she regretted her tough talk with her aunt. No one loved her the way Rhiannon did. "I don't want Edge to know," she told her mother, deciding to deal with Aunt Rhi later. "Not yet."

Her mother shrugged. "He has a right to know. But you have a right to be the one to tell him." She shook her head. "But don't expect me to keep this from your father. We don't deceive each other."

"Then stay away from him for a while. In Salem, with Willem and Sarafina. Morgan's there, you know."

"Dante's Morgan?"

She nodded, knowing her mother would welcome the chance to get to know the vampiress-screenwriter. "I suppose. That's where you'll be, so I'll stay a while." She stroked Amber's hair. "A girl needs her mother at a time like this." Then her face split into a smile. "A baby," she said. "I can't believe we're going to have a baby in the family again."

Amber accepted the hug in order to keep her face hidden. But the memory of her dream returned, menacing and dark, with the image of the still, pale child in the ornate, almost coffinlike, box.

She closed her eyes to block it out. Please, she thought. Not that.

A car passed, followed by a bus so large it rumbled the highway.

Amber felt something and looked up, turning to follow the bus's progress. Then she yanked open the car door, pulling her mother in behind her. "Follow that bus, Rhiannon!"

"What?"

"The woman who took the serum is on it. I felt her as it passed. Brooke, her name is Brooke, and she's got the cure for Willem."

The voice in his head kept telling him he was going in the wrong direction. It was loud, so loud Edge couldn't believe the other men in the car couldn't hear it. And it was insistent. After arguing silently with the damn thing for several minutes and struggling to keep his thoughts shielded, he barked, "Where the hell do you want me to go, then?"

The other men stared at him, blatantly stunned.

"Hell," Edge muttered, and leaned against the seat back as if trying to catch some rest. In truth, he only wanted a rest from the insistent voice and from his own growing guilt. He'd left Amber in a fit of temper based on nothing more than jealousy. He was an idiot. God, it wasn't as if he were in love with the woman. He had no right to be jealous. Must be a male ego thing. Still, he'd made the wrong decision, for the wrong reasons, and he knew it.

Jameson looked from Dante, in the front seat beside him, to Donovan and Roland in the back with Edge. "Is he all right?"

"Hears voices," Dante said. He drew circles near his ear with a forefinger.

"We *all* hear voices," Donovan corrected. "Voices, thoughts—both from each other and mortals." He turned to Edge. "Are the voices like that, Edge?"

"Oh, God, he thinks he's a vampire therapist," Edge groaned.

Donovan thinned his lips. "If you'd tell us what's happening, we might be able to help." He looked to the front seat, to Jameson. "It even happened during the day sleep."

Jameson frowned. "That's not normal. Probably not a sign of insanity, either. It would take more than mental illness to penetrate the day sleep. Could it be someone outside you, Edge? Deliberately sending these messages?"

He shook his head. "I don't know."

"Well, what do the voices sound like?"

He pursed his lips.

"Don't bother, Jameson. He's a loner. Far too manly to share his problems with us."

Edge glanced at Dante, who seemed to detest him, and perhaps just to prove the man wrong, he said, "It's one voice. Male. Young, though not a child. It feels as if it's coming from within me. But I can't control it, can't silence it."

"Can you converse with it?" Roland asked.

Edge frowned. "Yes."

"And what does it tell you?"

He sighed, shaking his head.

"It told him where to find Amber Lily," Donovan said, his eyes on Edge. "Didn't it?"

He nodded.

"And what's it telling you now?" Jameson asked.

Edge sighed. "That I'm going the wrong way."

"That's it?"

Edge nodded.

Jameson glanced at his watch. "It's nearly dawn. We're going to have to stop soon, seek shelter."

Edge nodded. "Alby can drive all day. She could put an awful lot of distance between us while we rest." God, why had he given in to his temper and left her side? It didn't matter that she was carrying another man's child. She was in danger, and he had to get to her. He felt it with everything in him, wanted to kick himself for ever leaving her in the first place.

Jameson was studying Edge's face intently. "You're awfully concerned about her."

"You should probably get used to it. God knows I'm starting to."

Jameson's brows went up; then his face darkened a little.

Donovan spoke quickly as if to diffuse the tension. "I wouldn't worry about her getting too far, Edge. After all, she'll stop once she reaches Salem."

She's not going to Salem!

Edge blinked, gave his head a shake, but couldn't ignore the voice. "She's not going to Salem."

"What? Why the hell not?" Jameson demanded.

"I'm damned if I know." He shook his head, heard words whispering through his mind. *Canada. Edmunston, New Brunswick.* He felt an urgency tugging at him. Dammit, he hated to leave Stiles. The bastard would escape him yet again, and it was high time he extract the vengeance that was his only priority. Or…used to be his only priority, anyway. Hell, when had that changed?

They passed a sign showing a bus icon.

"Take the next exit," Edge said. "There's a bus station. Get me there."

"You can't get on a bus this close to daylight," Donovan argued.

"No, not on one. Under one." He glanced at Jameson, who was studying him without blinking.

"The luggage compartment," he said. "It's not first class, but it gets you where you need to go." He nodded to Dante. "Don't pretend you won't be glad to be rid of me."

"I wasn't planning to." He steered onto the exit ramp, followed the signs for the bus depot.

"The four of you can handle Stiles all right without me," Edge said as he got out of the car when Dante pulled it to a stop outside the terminal. It was more an effort to convince himself of it than a statement of fact.

"Three of them," Jameson said, getting out of the front seat.

Edge looked at him.

"Don't even think of arguing. She's my daughter."

Sighing, he lowered his head. The man was right. He had ten times the right to go after Alby as Edge did. If it had been his own daughter—

Son.

Edge's head came up fast, and he looked around, but like every other time, there was no one there. He blinked hard, felt his throat getting tight. Of all the things the voice had said to him, this one made the least sense of all.

"What? What is it?"

Amber was going to have to tell her father about her condition sooner or later. Edge wasn't the least bit afraid of telling him—hell, he had no reason to be. But it wasn't his place. Right now, though... Right now, he didn't know what the hell to think.

The two men walked to the area just outside the terminal, where buses were lined up in angular parking slots, some with their engines running. Jameson approached a driver, just ambling down out of his vehicle, moving as if it were an effort.

"Is one of these buses going to Canada?"

The driver glanced at his watch, gave a nod. "Woodstock, Grand Falls, Edmunston," he said. "Three slots down. But he won't be leaving for a half hour yet." Then he glanced at the ticket window. "Ticket window isn't open until nine, but you talk with the driver, he can take care of it for you."

"Thanks."

Edge led the way to the large, silent bus. "Half hour," he said, with a glance at the sky.

"The sun will be up by then," Jameson said.

"Driver will come out before then," Edge said. "Warm up the engine, open the baggage compartments."

"And we just...what? Climb in and hope no one notices?"

"We can move faster than human eyes can perceive. Getting in unnoticed won't be a problem."

"And when the driver goes to toss a few passengers' bags in, and there are two bodies inside?"

Edge met the man's eyes, a hint of mischief in his own. "Have a little faith. It's not like I haven't done this before, you know."

Jameson looked doubtful, but he sat down on a bench outside the station. "I'll just sit here, then. Fortunately, this bench faces east, so I'll be able to see the sun a split second before I burst into flames."

"Such an optimist."

Minutes ticked by. Jameson seemed to be growing more nervous with every one that passed. Edge, meanwhile, stood near the bus and smoked.

Eventually a few passengers showed up, cars and taxis dropping them off, then leaving. They invariably went first to the ticket window, then grew anxious when they found it closed. Then they gathered around the bus.

But not around Edge. His smoke created a buffer zone. It was a secondary benefit of smoking—kept nonsmokers from invading your space. Oh, there was always a wheezing mealymouthed type who would come close enough to get a whiff and then make a big production of waving his hand in front of his face and sending Edge a dirty look. Just to make a point. The point, Edge guessed, was that smoking out of doors should be made illegal.

He smiled to himself as he wondered if the passive aggressive idiots ever caught a clue who—or what—he was.

Inevitably, it happened. One pale, scrawny mortal broke from the cluster gathered near the bus, walked a few steps in his direction, then began to cough. He tugged a handkerchief from his pocket and held it to his mouth, scowling over it at Edge.

Edge growled at him, softly, so the others couldn't hear, baring his fangs just for an instant.

The man gasped and backed away so fast he bumped into one of the people standing behind him. When he looked again, though, Edge was gone, having moved to the far side of the bus. Maybe the little prick would remember his manners next time, he thought a little darkly.

He heard the sound of the bus engine starting, then, moments later, the luggage compartments being opened. The driver slung bags in, heavily and none too carefully, one after the other. Edge moved around to the front of the bus, crossed to where Jameson was still sitting, pondering the sky, which had lightened alarmingly to a pale gray near the horizon.

"Ready?"

"As I'll ever be," Jameson said.

He got up, followed Edge back around until they stood near the rear of the bus. The driver's back was toward them, and the passengers were focused on climbing aboard the bus, picking out seats, wrestling with their carry-on bags.

Edge waited until the driver was reaching for one last bag and the final passenger had stepped aboard to knock several bags back out of the compartment with a quick grab.

Swearing and looking as surprised as a toddler when Jack pops out of the box, the driver bent to begin retrieving them—some had shot several feet from the bus, so he was kept distracted.

"Let's go, then," Edge said. And he dove into the compartment, on top of the bags, shoving them aside until he'd made room for himself behind them. Jameson joined him within a heartbeat and assisted him in redistributing the luggage into a neat stack in front of the two of them. There was just room enough to sit up. Not to lie down, and not to stand.

"Grand accommodations, Edge."

"Mmm. Fortunately, we'll be unconscious for most of the trip."

"We'll be more than that, if he doesn't hurry up and close the compartment door."

Beyond the luggage, Edge could see the light beginning to filter through. Not direct sunlight, not yet, but the daylight creeping just ahead of it.

The compartment rocked as the driver slung bags into it. Then, finally, he slammed it closed. Edge heard a latch turn.

Jameson sighed in relief. "About time. I guess we're home free now."

Edge shrugged. "Barring a rollover or flaming wreck, yes, I suppose we are."

"You're just full of happy thoughts, aren't you, Edge?"

"Always."

15

Amber frowned at the sky, irritated that the extended layovers the bus had made had taken up so much of the darker hours. "We're going to have to stop soon. It'll be daylight."

Rhiannon looked back at her. "You forget whose car you're riding in, dear. There will be no need to stop."

"But...the sun."

Rhiannon shrugged. "Climb up here, child."

Frowning, Amber climbed into the passenger side of the front.

Rhiannon set the cruise control. "Take the wheel."

Amber took hold of the steering wheel, holding the car on course while Rhiannon climbed into the back seat. Then Amber slid over into the driver's side. The car wobbled a bit, veering over the broken white lines briefly, before Amber straightened it out again.

"I think it would be better to stop," Angelica said. "Amber can get some rest, find herself something to eat while we sleep."

"It would cost us precious time," Rhiannon said. "God knows this bus with its roundabout route, endless stops and long-term layovers, has already cost us enough. Why people ride those things I will never know. Besides, we'll be perfectly safe back here. I've installed certain...precautions."

"It's not us I'm worried about," she replied, sending a worried look at Amber.

"I'll be fine, Mom. If I'd wanted to rest, I would have during one of the layovers. And I've been grabbing junk food at every one of them. I just don't want to risk losing Brooke."

"You need to start taking better care of yourself, Amber. It's not just you you're driving to the point of exhaustion. It's your baby."

Amber closed her eyes, the words effectively dragging the impossible situation to the forefront of her mind again. But then, who was she kidding? It had never been far from there.

She glanced into the back seat, ignoring her mother's warnings. "So where are these safety features of yours, Aunt Rhi?"

"Are you sure you're all right to drive?" Angelica asked before Rhiannon could reply. "The drug—"

"Has worn off. I feel better."

"Amber, I just don't like this. I don't want you confronting the woman on your own."

"She's only a mortal," Amber said.

"So was Stiles."

Amber frowned. "If it were Dad dying slowly of something horrible, and the cure was rolling along the highway just ahead of us, would you be willing to stop?"

Angelica tipped her head skyward, then finally shook it slowly. "I don't suppose I would be."

"Then think of Sarafina. Think of Will. He saved my life, Mother. And yours."

"And mine," Rhiannon added. "There's no point in arguing with her, Angelica. She's going to do as she pleases the moment we're asleep anyway." She shrugged. "Much as I hate to admit it, in this case, I believe she's right."

"The sun is rising. Will you get into the trunk or do whatever it is you're planning to do back there before you both go up in smoke?"

Rhiannon nodded, then hit a button on the armrest that Amber had taken as the window control. The tinted glass side windows remained still, but panels rose up inside them—shining black sheets of what looked like acrylic. Rhiannon hit another button, and a similar sheet slid smoothly upward, covering the rear window. Amber could see through them, though they were very, very dark.

"You can see out, but nothing can penetrate within. No light. It's also bullet-proof, fireproof and airtight," Rhiannon said, sounding proud.

"Leave it to you to have a custom-made coffin on wheels," Amber said. "And a Mercedes, at that."

"Then you approve," Rhiannon said.

"Assuming there's another partition that slides up between the front seat and back…"

"Of course."

"Then yes, I think it's ingenious."

Rhiannon pursed her lips. "Kissing up isn't going to make me forget your bad manners, Amber Lily."

Amber sighed. "I'm sorry, Rhiannon. Chalk it up to the drugs, the stress, the fear and the fact that you were threatening to disembowel the father of my…baby." She had to force that word out. Saying it aloud was like—like making it real, somehow.

"I would do the same should someone threaten Roland," Rhiannon said slowly. "But only because I love him beyond reason. Beyond comprehension. Beyond life, death, sanity or madness. Beyond anything. Is that the way you feel about this...Edge character?''

"Don't be ridiculous," Amber said, the words spilling out automatically, without her giving any thought at all to her answer. "I'd be an idiot to feel anything for a man like him."

Rhiannon shrugged, hit another button, and the partition between the seats began to rise. "Well then, I cannot accept your apology. You're going to have to do better."

Amber sighed, wondering just how much groveling and ass-kissing she was going to have to do to make things up to her honorary aunt. "Sleep well," she told them as the partition neared the top.

"Be careful, Amber," her mother said. Her voice already heavy with sleep.

"I will."

The partition closed. Silence engulfed her. She sensed the two most important women in her life slipping far from her reach, into the day sleep, and felt utterly alone. Thoughts she'd been holding at bay came rushing in on her. A baby. God, a baby—one she feared would never live to draw its first breath.

Amber's dreams had never, ever been wrong. Not once.

Tears rose up in her eyes, even as she told herself that maybe, so long as she never let herself think of this child as real, as alive, as her baby, but instead just as a mass of cells destined to live for nine short months and then die, she would be able to bear it. You couldn't lose what you had never had, could you?

But I do have it. I have it now, alive and growing inside me. A baby. My own living child.

She hit the radio button. Classical strains filled the car, but only until she found a station playing hard driving

Godsmack. She cranked up the volume, and let the sexy, growling voice and heavy bass drown out the unwanted thoughts.

When the night whispered to his senses, rousing him from the impenetrable day sleep, Edge felt the weight of a dozen pieces of luggage pressing down on him. A corner of a suitcase was jabbing him in the rib cage; a large heavy object that bounced with every bump in the road kept knocking him on the head.

He groaned and shoved and wriggled until he'd managed to move the worst offenders and allow himself a modicum of breathing room.

"God," Jameson muttered, his voice muffled. "I feel as if I've been beaten all day with a club." Some more cases shifted, and his face appeared in the hole they'd left behind. "This is torture."

"Maybe for an old guy."

Jameson scowled. Edge grinned at him, and then almost gasped in surprise when the other man returned a half smile. "Very funny."

"I do what I can."

"So will this barge be stopping anytime soon?"

Edge glanced at his watch. "Another hour. But we don't need to wait."

"No?"

"We're close."

"To Amber?"

Edge nodded.

Jameson's eyes narrowed on him. "How is it you're so connected to my daughter, Edge?"

Edge averted his eyes. "I don't know that I am. After all, it's not her voice that refuses to stop shouting at me."

"Are you sure this…voice…is on our side? I mean,

it could be a trick. Someone trying to lead us into a trap.''

''I've thought of that.'' Edge shrugged. ''Frankly, it could be just that. I've got no frame of reference for this type of thing. You?''

Jameson shot him a look. ''You're asking my opinion?''

''I figure a man who fathered a woman like Alby can't be all bad.'' He sighed. ''So what do you think? You ever have voices in your head like this?''

Jameson shook his head. ''Not like the one you describe, no. But…what kind of feelings does this voice stir within you? Is there a gut reaction? Anger, trepidation, fear?''

Edge shook his head. ''More like…a call to battle. Makes me want to go charging in like some kind of mythical hero.'' He sighed heavily.

''And that worries you?''

''Greatly. It's not me. It's not what I do.''

''Not the heroic type, hmm?''

''Heroes tend to die young. I intend to live a long time.''

Jameson nodded. ''And yet you're here, following a voice you're not sure you can trust, into what might be a life-threatening venture.''

''Yeah.'' Edge smiled self-deprecatingly, shaking his head. ''Go figure, huh?''

''Why?'' Jameson asked.

''Damned if I know.'' He shoved some more cases out of the way, making a path to the compartment door.

''Is it because you'd rather risk your own life than hers?''

Without looking back at him, Edge said, ''More likely because the damned voice screaming in my ears will drive me insane if I don't do what it's telling me.'' He got to the front of the compartment, turned so he was sitting down, and braced his feet against the door. ''What do you say we quit with the analysis and get on with this?''

''Ready when you are,'' Jameson said.

With a nod, Edge shoved with his feet, and the compartment door gave way. He saw the pavement speeding by beneath him. ''This is going to hurt like hell.'' He glanced back at the other man. ''Sure your old bones can take it?''

''Enough with the age jokes. I may have been older than you when I was remade, but you've likely been a vamp longer.''

''Mmm. So I have both mortal youth and vampiric power on you.''

''I won't hold it against you.'' Jameson made his way to the front of the compartment, put a hand on Edge's shoulder. ''Ready?''

''Aim for the grass along the roadside,'' Edge said. ''It'll be kinder than the blacktop.''

Edge leaped from the bus, Jameson at his side. They hit the ground hard, rolling down the grassy hill that ran along the roadside. The ground pummeled them, until they came to stop. Jameson sat up slowly, brushing dirt and twigs from his clothes, wincing in pain. Edge did the same, even while inspecting himself for cuts or gashes.

''You bleeding anywhere?'' Jameson asked.

Edge shook his head. ''You?''

''Don't think so.'' He got to his feet, then extended a hand down to Edge.

Edge hesitated, then took it, let the other man pull him upright. ''Thanks.''

Jameson nodded, then turned, and seemed to focus inward. He was silent for a moment, then he sighed. ''I can't feel her,'' he said at last.

''She's blocking. Has been right along.''

Jameson shot him a look. ''Trying to protect us, keep us from following her and getting into trouble.''

Edge thought it more likely she was blocking to keep something of a far more personal nature from her father—hell, from the both of them—but he wasn't about to say it aloud.

''If her mother were here, she'd pick up on her,'' Jameson said.

Edge lifted his brows. ''Even if she's blocking?''

''Sometimes. They have a connection that's…it's powerful. I haven't seen anything like it, even among our kind. It started before Amber was even born. Angelica could communicate with her in the womb, could tell how she was doing.''

''Amazing.''

''I've always been just a little envious of the bond they share.'' He sighed. ''It sure as hell would come in handy right now.''

Edge shrugged. ''It would, but we don't need it.'' He looked off in the distance, lifted a hand and pointed. ''She's that way.''

By the time the sun set, Amber had parked Rhiannon's customized Benz on the tree-lined lane outside the towering gates of a miniature castle. The building was made of pale, rust-tinted stone blocks and included two towerlike structures that flanked the entryway. Matching stone blocks formed a solid, ten-foot boundary fence around the entire property and held an iron gate in place that sealed off the driveway.

The sign mounted on the gate read Athena, and there were sculptures of large owls atop the stones on either side.

Amber squinted at it, willing it to give up its secret meaning to her, but the only thing she heard was the soft hum of the motor lowering the dark glass partition.

Rhiannon stretched and yawned. Angelica smoothed her hair away from her face. "What I wouldn't give for a shower," she muttered.

"Amen to that, sister," Rhiannon said.

Amber shot her a look, then glanced at her mother.

"Sorry," Rhiannon said quickly. "That was not a jibe at your former calling, Angelica. Just a slip of the tongue."

"I know."

Amber opened the car door and stepped out, putting her hands on her lower back and arching. Angelica got out, too, and paused in the midst of inhaling the night air to stare at the building beyond the gate across the street. "What is this place?"

"Yes, what have we missed, Amber? Fill us in," Rhiannon said, as she exited the car.

Amber got out, taking the keys with her, dropping them into her pocket. "Well, we're in Canada. Crossed the border a while back. I don't know what this place is. But it's where Brooke went. She took a cab from the bus station—must have cost a fortune, too, because it was fifty miles, at least. I followed her, of course."

"Were you seen, Amber?" Rhiannon asked.

"Of course not. I didn't even stay within sight of her. And the car is blocked from sight by that little copse of trees and the stone wall."

Rhiannon nodded. "So they have no idea we're out here."

"None." Amber glanced at her mother, then frowned. She was staring into the place as if transfixed. "What is it, Mom?"

Blinking and giving her head a shake, she said, "I don't know. It feels...familiar."

"You've been here before?" Amber asked.

"No, never. But the feeling..." She looked in at the house again; then her brows went up. "It feels like a convent," she said suddenly.

Rhiannon blinked in shock. "Oh, joy. This Brooke person has taken refuge in a nunnery?"

"I don't think they're nuns," Angelica said. "But there's that same kind of energy here."

Amber slid a hand over her mother's shoulder. "What kind? Tell us."

She narrowed her eyes. "A sisterhood. That place is filled with women who share a powerful bond and single-minded devotion to...something."

"To what?" Rhiannon asked.

"That I can't tell you."

Amber swallowed hard. "Somehow, I'd feel safer sneaking into an army barracks."

"You should," Rhiannon told her. She pursed her lips, frowned. "So what's the plan?"

Amber looked at the two women. "Alicia called me on the cell, just after daybreak. She'd driven out to Salem to join me there, and when I told her where we were, she insisted on coming up here. Said she had a feeling we were going to need her. She's on her way. Once she gets here, we have to get inside."

"Amber, we have no way of knowing what sort of security they have," Rhiannon cautioned. "And we can't just show up at the door. If they're tied to Stiles or the former DPI, they would likely recognize your mother and me for what we are on sight.''

Angelica nodded. ''I've seen the inside of far too many of their prison cells,'' she said. ''I'd hate to end up hurled into yet another.''

''And this Brooke person has seen you, Amber,'' Rhiannon went on.

Amber bit her lip, eyeing the gate, the wall. ''Alicia was right, then. We *are* going to need her.''

''How far out is she?'' Angelica asked.

Amber glanced at her watch. ''She's got her 'Vette, and was driving straight through, so she'll get here a lot faster than we did. A couple more hours, at most.'' Her throat went tight. Why should the thought of seeing Alicia choke her up so much? She'd only seen her a few days ago. But it felt more like a lifetime.

Her mother read her face. ''We'll just wait for her, then.''

''Do you think it's too risky, Mom? I don't want to send her walking into a nest of vipers.''

Angelica looked just as worried. ''I don't know. Rhiannon?''

Rhiannon waved a hand. ''Oh, please, what threat is a houseful of mortal women to us? I'll fry up the fat ones for a snack and use the skinny ones to pick my teeth when I've finished.''

Amber made a face.

Rhiannon smiled a little sheepishly. ''Sorry to offend your vegetarian sensibilities, dear. Can I help it if my mind is on food? I'm famished.''

''Me, too,'' Amber said. She'd been irrationally starved for days now, and her waistline was showing the results all too clearly. ''We passed a diner a few miles back. I'll call Alicia, have her meet us there. There was a medical clinic not far from it. Maybe you two can find some sustenance there.''

''A blood supply or a nice young doctor,'' Rhiannon said with a twinkle in her eye. ''At this point, either would do.''

16

This is the place. This is it! This is the place. You're here! She's here. She's here. She's here! She's—

"What do you think?" Jameson asked, staring through the barred gate at the mansion beyond.

Edge was crouching on the ground, holding his hands to the sides of his head, trying to silence the damned voice that had grown steadily louder and more powerful. "I think she must be here. Somewhere." He squeezed his eyes together. "Shut up, dammit!"

Miraculously the voice went silent.

Edge felt a hand on his shoulder and looked up to see Jameson staring down at him, his brows etched into a worried frown. "It's getting worse, isn't it?"

Edge shrugged.

"I could feel the pain from ten feet away," Jameson said. "It's stopped now?"

"Yeah." Edge got slowly to his feet, massaging his temples. "First time it's responded to my shouting at it."

"I'm sorry, Edge. If I knew what the hell this was, how to stop it—"

"You wouldn't do a damn thing," Edge said. "Neither would I. It's the only thing we have to go on."

Jameson thinned his lips but acknowledged Edge's words with a sigh. "I suppose you're right." He looked around. "I don't see Rhiannon's car."

"No. Still..." Edge got to his feet, looked at the stone wall.

Jameson nodded. "Shall we?"

"Let's do it while my head's in between explosions."

The two vampires leaped easily over the wall, strode up the walk to the front door of the massive place, paused outside. "You going to knock?" Jameson asked.

Edge pursed his lips, gripped the knob, gave it an experimental twist. "Doesn't look like it's necessary. Door's open."

He met Jameson's eyes. Jameson gave a nod, and Edge opened the door. Then the two of them stepped inside, Edge looking right, Jameson left, before they both moved silently into a great hall that belonged in a castle.

"I don't feel her," Jameson said.

"Neither do I," Edge whispered. And he should, he thought. If he were this close to her, he should damn well be tingling all over with the sense of her being near him, the way he always did. God, he missed her, and it had only been a matter of hours. What was wrong with him?

That thought was chased away by another. A niggling sense that there was something terribly wrong here.

And then he did pick up someone's energy—but it wasn't Amber's. It was other people, women, many of them, all around him, hiding, watching, waiting.

It sent a shiver up his spine. He glanced at Jameson, saw that he felt it, too, and the two of them turned to slip right back out the door again.

But they never got there.

The women sprang, dozens of them. Blows rained down on Edge's head and body, driving him to the floor like a blade of grass in a hailstorm. The last thing he heard was the voice in his head, laughing like hell.

* * *

Alicia arrived at the small all-night diner twenty minutes ahead of schedule. Amber saw her cherry-red Corvette pull in from the window beside her booth, and forced herself not to spring up and sprint across the diner to meet her. It wouldn't do to create a scene, and besides, it would scare Alicia senseless.

Still, she rose from the booth as Alicia pushed open the glass entry door. Her friend spotted her, smiled broadly and hurried to wrap her in a hug. Amber's arms tightened around Alicia in return.

When they broke the embrace, Alicia's smile was gone and a searching look had replaced it. "Okay, give. What's wrong?"

"What makes you think anything's wrong?" Amber said, sliding into her seat at the table, averting her eyes.

"You hugged me hard enough to crack a rib, and you're shaking. And your eyes are big. And you're not looking at me." She frowned, glancing around the diner. "Where are Angel and Aunt Rhi?"

"They went out to get something to eat."

Alicia lifted her brows. "One of the locals piss them off?"

Amber smiled. "Nah, we passed a clinic ten miles out. We need them strong."

"Okay. So what's got you so off your game?"

"You mean besides the fact that someone I love is dying?"

"Yeah," Alicia said, matching her friend's sad but sarcastic tone precisely. "Besides that."

Amber lifted her head, met Alicia's eyes. "It's a long story, 'Leesh."

"Then talk fast."

Amber nodded. "It's got to do with that dream."

"The recurring one? The one where the vampire with the sexiest, most intense eyes you've ever seen gives you something that scares the hell out of you?"

Amber opened her mouth to object, but Alicia beat her to the punch, holding up a hand. "Hey, that was exactly the way you described it to me."

Amber sighed, lowering her head. "It's actually a pretty accurate description. He's real."

"You met him?" Alicia's eyes widened.

"Gave him a ride to Salem."

"Holy cow. You mean it was Edge?"

Amber frowned.

"Will and Sarafina told me about him. So? What happened? Did he give you anything?"

"You might say that, yeah."

Alicia tipped her head to one side, studying her. Amber met her friend's eyes, saying nothing. Then Alicia clapped a hand to her mouth. From behind it she muttered, "You slept with him."

Amber nodded. "Yeah. And now I'm pregnant."

Alicia frowned. "You're panicking, that's all. You can't be. You know male vamps can't—"

"This one can."

"But…are you sure?"

"I took a test when I was with Stiles, but I couldn't be sure he wasn't faking it for some sick reason. But he wasn't. My mother knew it as soon as she saw me. No test needed. It's for real, Alicia, and I'm scared."

"Does Edge know?"

"No, and I'm not sure I want him to. This is my issue. I don't need him involved."

"Well, he's kind of already involved, sis."

Amber made a face. Alicia smiled a little crookedly. "God, I'm going to be an aunt."

Shaking her head slowly, Amber reached across the table. "I had the dream again, 'Leesh. This time I could see what it was Edge was giving me."

"Was it a baby?"

Amber nodded. A tear surprised her by swelling and spilling over without warning. "Yeah, but...it was...it was..."

"What, honey? It was what?" Alicia slid out of her seat, coming around to Amber's side of the booth, sliding in beside her.

"It wasn't moving or...or breathing."

"No," Alicia whispered.

"I think it's going to be stillborn, 'Leesh. I think there's something terribly wrong with it, and it can't survive."

Alicia wrapped Amber in her arms, held her hard, stroking her hair. "No," she said again. "You're overwrought, you're scared to death, you're confused."

"My precog dreams are always on the money, Alicia. You know that."

"Yeah, well, I also know that male vampires are sterile. Apparently there really is a first time for everything, Amber. A first time for a male vampire to be fertile, and a first time for the Child of Promise to misinterpret a precognitive dream. It's not so far-fetched."

She sat back a little, pushing Amber's hair behind her ears gently. "And I know you. You're afraid to let yourself believe it might be all right. You think you're protecting yourself from being let down. You're being all strong and practical and tough, just like always. God, you're afraid to love a man so much you can't live without him—how much more scary must it be for you to let yourself get attached to your own baby?"

Amber licked her lips. "I suppose you're right."

"Honey, you're carrying a baby. And right now it's alive and well, isn't it?"

"It feels as if it is. My mother...she seems to think it is."

Alicia nodded slowly. "Well, you want my take on this?"

"I need it, 'Leesh. I barely held it together when I found out. I don't know which way is up right now."

Alicia nodded. "For a freaking borderline genius, you can be a real dope, you know that?" She drew a breath, sighed. "Listen, if this baby doesn't make it, you're going to be crushed right to bits. It isn't gonna matter one bit if you let yourself get your hopes up or not, or how practical or realistic you try to be. It'll destroy you. You know it, and I know it."

Amber leaned back in the chair and closed her eyes. "So far, not being so helpful, pal."

"No, I'm being honest. It's not going to make any difference if you let yourself believe or not. It's gonna hurt just as much."

"Still not feeling cheered up."

Alicia ran a hand over Amber's hair. "The point is, it's not doing you any good to refuse to acknowledge this baby. It's not doing you any good to refuse to love it, or be happy about it, or excited, or any of those things. It's not doing you one bit of good, Amber. You'll be devastated anyway if you lose it. So what the hell is the point? Let yourself be happy about this. Let yourself be excited, and think of names and sing lullabies and pick out baby clothes. Let yourself be overjoyed. It's not doing you any good to go into mourning nine months early. There will be plenty of time for that later. Maybe. Because maybe there won't be any mourning to do at all. Deal with that when it gets here."

Amber opened her eyes, staring at her friend in wonder. "How did you get to be so smart?"

Alicia shrugged. "I hang out with a really brainy crowd," she said. She pressed a hand to Amber's belly. "Ohh, gosh, I could swear you're swelling up already. I wonder if it's a girl or a boy?"

She met Amber's eyes and smiled so hard Amber couldn't help but smile back. And it wasn't a fake smile. It was an outgrowth of the joy she'd been too afraid to allow herself to feel.

"What would I do without you, Alicia?"

"I don't know. You sure wouldn't have any fun, that's for sure." Then she blinked, and her eyes widened. "Does your father know about this?"

"No. If he did, Edge would be dead by now."

"Oh, hell. We're going to have our work cut out for us."

"You can say that again." Amber saw Rhiannon's Mercedes pull in. "Mom and Aunt Rhi are back."

"Oh, God, does Rhiannon know?" Alicia's eyes were even wider.

"Yes, she threatened to eat Edge's liver, and I told her she'd have to go through me to do it." Amber licked her lips. "I really hurt her feelings. She's still pretty mad at me."

"She'll get over it."

"'Leesh, neither Mom nor Aunt Rhi knows about the dream. I want to keep it that way."

"All right. I'll be really careful not to think about it without shielding."

"Thanks."

"So what's the deal with the cure for Will?"

Rhiannon blew the horn once. Amber got to her feet,

grabbed her chocolate milk and headed for the door. "I'll explain on the way. Let's go."

Voices, whispering. Eyes, staring. Women, all of them, all around him.

Edge lifted his head, wincing at the pain that shot through it when he did. He pressed a hand to the most tender spot and blinked his vision into focus.

He was in the center of a very large concrete room. There was a white line painted on the floor, like the boundary line on a basketball court. It outlined a ten-foot square around him.

"What the hell?" He started to get to his feet.

"Don't step outside the line or you'll be destroyed," a woman's voice said.

Edge frowned, staring into the darkness, but the bright light glaring down on him and his little square prison from above made it impossible to focus on the darkness beyond.

He shielded his eyes, looking down, spotting Jameson lying on the floor near his feet. A rush of real concern rose up, catching him by surprise even as he knelt beside the other man, rolling him onto his back, smacking his cheeks.

"What did you use, some of Stiles's tranquilizer?" he asked, his voice flatly accusing them.

"We don't need it," a woman said. "Repeated blows to the head will render a vampire incapacitated just as effectively, but for a shorter period and with far fewer side effects."

"That's real considerate of you, bashing our heads in rather than using that nasty, relatively painless other method. I should probably be thanking you."

"You're welcome."

The woman, whoever she was, didn't seem to have any sense of humor. "So what is this place? And exactly what's going to happen if I step over the white line? Besides my draining you dry, I mean?"

"Sarah?" the woman said.

Another woman stepped forward, into the edge of the pool of light, right up to the white boundary line. She was tall, slender, dressed in a blazer and skirt, with her hair pinned up and a pair of plastic framed glasses perched on her nose. All business. She held a broomstick by its neck. "Watch," she told him.

He watched. She held the broom's business end over the white line, and in a flash, flames shot from both the ceiling and the floor, meeting in the middle. When she jerked the broom back, it was blazing. She lowered it to the floor, dipping it into a waiting pail of water. Smoke rose in ribbons, stinking up the place.

Edge was still swearing under his breath when the one called Sarah explained.

"The nozzles line the entire border, from both the ceiling and the floor. Any movement sets them off, and they go off too fast for even a vampire to beat them."

He lifted his brows.

"Yes," said the other woman. "We know what you are."

Edge swallowed hard. "So I take it you're the headmistress of this…Academy for Brutal Bad Girls, is that it?"

"I'm in charge, yes."

"Do you have a name?"

"Not that you need to know."

"Are you going to tell me what you're doing with us? Why you're holding us?"

She shook her head. "We're holding you because we

don't yet know what sort of a threat you pose to us. What we'll do with you—well, we'll let you know as soon as we've made a decision on that.''

She remained out of the light. It drove him mad that he couldn't see her face, the better to remember it and exact vengeance later.

"You won't be harmed. Just so long as you don't try to get out, you'll be fine.''

"I'm afraid I have urgent business to attend to, head-mistress.''

"Yes, and I'd like to know what that urgent business might be,'' she countered. "Why did you come here? What are you looking for?''

He frowned, searching her mind. He found she'd made an effort to guard it, but she was no professional. He saw no hint of Amber or other vampiresses in her thoughts. She knew nothing about them. He wasn't about to tell her.

And then, just then, he became aware of that tingling sensation that heated his blood and tightened his loins. Alby was here. She was close. She hadn't been, but she was now.

"I came here out of curiosity,'' he told her. "I heard a group of beautiful women lived here, and I, being a red-blooded male, wanted to check it out.''

"Or perhaps you thought to feast on us tonight,'' she said. "Or perhaps you heard other things about this place.''

"That implies there are other things to hear. You're piquing my curiosity, headmistress.''

"Melina, someone's at the gate,'' another woman said.

"Melina, hmm? That's a very pretty name.''

"You're wasting your time,'' she said. "Everyone, back to your duties, with the exception of those on guard duty. Guards, don't talk to them, don't engage them in any way. Keep your minds shielded. And if they give you any trouble, page me.''

''Yes, ma'am,'' several voices said in unison.

''Good God,'' Jameson moaned, opening his eyes. ''What the hell is going on? Where are we?''

The women were filing out of the room. Edge couldn't see them, but he could hear their steps, feel their retreat.

''I think we've landed in some sort of dominatrix boot camp,'' Edge said. ''Could be fun, don't you think?''

''Stop fidgeting. They'll see you,'' Rhiannon whispered, as the three of them crouched in the bushes across from the lush, rolling lawns of the mansion.

''I can't see her!'' Amber tried again to crane her neck so she could see beyond their shrubbery shelter, across the street, past the gate that had swung slowly open to admit Alicia after she'd spoken to someone through an intercom. Alicia stood now in front of the open door, pouring out the story she'd rehearsed to the woman who stood on the other side. The gate behind her closed with a finality that made Amber's heart trip over itself.

''She'll let us know if she needs help,'' Angelica said. ''She's nearly as capable telepathically as you are.''

It was an exaggeration, Amber thought. But her mother had a point, Alicia could send a mental shout for help if she needed to. Amber strained her ears to hear the conversation, but even her honed senses couldn't pick it up from this distance. She knew what Alicia was saying, though. That her car had broken down a mile away. That she'd been fleeing an abusive lover and feared he wasn't far behind her. They would let her use the phone to call her auto club. And it would take a few hours for the tow truck to be dispatched, so they would let her stay there, safe behind the stone walls, until it arrived.

Maybe.

From her crouched position, Amber could see the woman as she stepped out onto the stoop, looked around beyond Alicia and, finally, nodded and put a hand on Alicia's arm, guiding her inside. The door closed.

Amber sank to the ground. "Well, that's it," she said. "She's in."

Angelica nodded. "She'll be fine, Amber. She's smart."

"Smartest mortal I know," Rhiannon put in.

Amber nodded. The worry for her friend's safety, and the constant questioning in her mind as to whether she'd done the right thing by letting Alicia take this risk, were things she would rather not have clouding her mind, but she welcomed the distraction, all the same. Ever since they'd come back here from the diner, Amber had been getting niggling feelings, like tiny sparks being set off in her nerve centers. The sense of Edge, that instant feeling that came over her whenever she was near him—that feeling of being drawn inexorably closer to him, that irresistible tug of his invisible tractor beam, pulling her. But the prickles of awareness were brief and only lasted an instant. They did bring him to mind, though, and so much else with him.

She shook herself, reminded herself that Edge was far away from here, escorting Stiles to Eric's lab, along with Donovan and Dante and...

"Dad," she whispered. Her frown deepened.

Her mother clasped her shoulder. "You felt it, too, then?" she asked.

Rhiannon frowned at her. "Felt what?"

Amber gave her head a shake. "I just got the oddest feeling Dad was nearby. And Edge…"

"It's faded now," Angelica said. "But for a moment, I felt your father, as well. As if he were standing behind us." She closed her eyes for a moment, then shook her head when she opened them. "It's gone now, whatever it was."

"They probably called Salem to check on us," Amber said. "They probably found out we'd taken a detour and got worried. Maybe it was just their worry we sensed."

"Their attention and focus, rather than their actual presence?" Rhiannon asked. Then she shrugged. "It's possible, though I think you would know the difference."

"It was so fleeting." Angelica frowned. "And almost…muffled."

"Diluted was the word that came to me," Amber said.

Rhiannon sighed. "Don't let it distract you. We need to focus on the job at hand. We have no idea when Alicia will manage to slip away from them long enough to…" She stopped then, arching one brow and looking toward the house.

Amber and her mother followed her gaze to see the outdoor light flash off, then on again, off, then on again.

"That's three," Rhiannon said. She nodded hard. "She works fast, that one."

"The faster the better, as far as I'm concerned," Amber said. "I hate her being in there alone. Come on."

They skirted the stone fence, finding the spot that seemed least likely to be visible from within. Amber crouched low and sprang, pushing off with her feet, catching the top of the wall with her hands and using them to propel her the rest of the way over, swinging her legs to the side like a gymnast on a pummel horse. She let her knees bend low to absorb the impact of the landing, then remained crouched there, palms pressed to the cool grass as she looked up, her senses open wide.

Her mother and aunt hit the ground on either side of her.

"This place has a half dozen doors," Rhiannon whispered. "Which one?"

Amber peered through the darkness, looking for a signal. Then... "There," she said, pointing to a glass enclosed annex. "That sunroom or greenhouse or whatever it is, attached to the back of the house. See the door there?" She waited for the others to spot it, to notice Alicia's trademark pink sunglasses dangling by their beaded chain from the doorknob.

"Come on," Amber said.

Staying low, the three of them raced forward, moving fast and silently. The glass structure sloped downward, its ceiling and walls entirely made of glass panels supported by a green metal frame. The door was glass, as well. Amber felt utterly exposed as she opened the door, sensing beyond it and snatching Alicia's sunglasses from the knob before stepping through.

The first thing that hit her was the humidity. It was steamy and moist, incredibly warm. And yet the glass was barely steamed up. Everywhere she looked, there were exotic plants, vines dangling from above, trees and ferns all around. Here and there, she spotted wicker tables, chairs, benches. A fountain bubbled and splashed in the center, and in one corner, a hot tub was the source of the steam. It looked as if it were made of stone, though the inside was clearly smooth and man-made.

Alicia lounged within it in a borrowed bathing suit. A dewy glass sat close to her hand.

"Workin' hard, 'Leesh?"

Her head came up fast, eyes popping open. She looked

around, spotting them, then shooting a quick glance toward the double doors on the opposite side—doors that must lead into the main part of the house. "Shh. Lock the door behind you."

"Already did," Amber said. She tossed the sunglasses to her friend. "Good thinking."

"What did you expect?" She caught the glasses and draped the beads around her neck. The women moved closer, keeping an eye on the doors. "I haven't figured out what sort of sorority this is yet, but they seem genuinely nice."

"Sure are hospitable." Rhiannon splashed a hand in the water. "Putting you right in the hot tub out here."

"I got the feeling they'd be going through my clothes and purse while I was distracted. Little do they know I'm the one trying to distract them."

"Is there anything in there that will give you away?" Amber asked, alarmed.

"What difference does it make? You're in." She rose from the water, reaching for a terry robe that was slung nearby, pulling it on. "Through that door is a hallway. Kitchens are off to the right, pantry to the left. After that, there are libraries—I counted three—and offices on the east side of the house. The west side has a formal dining room, a sitting room, and a living room. The entire front is foyer. That's where the stairs to the second floor are, but I'm sure I spotted a second set off the pantry, right next to another set that goes down below."

"You *are* good," Rhiannon said.

"What did you think I'd been doing, soaking in a hot tub sipping fruit punch the whole time?"

Amber said, "I'll go below. Mom, you take the ground floor and offices, and Rhiannon can go upstairs and check the bedrooms. See if you can find out what kind of place this is, what these women are up to. But remember, the main objective is the serum. It's probably in some kind of vials or syringes, and most likely refrigerated. If it's labeled at all, it will say something like 'Ambrosia-Six.'" Rhiannon's brows went up in question. "That's what Stiles calls it."

"Clever."

"What about me?" Alicia asked. "What should I do?"

"You need to keep playing the role you've been playing, 'Leesh. Keep them from getting suspicious while we creep through this place."

She sighed but nodded. "Fine, then. If you insist." She shucked the robe and stepped back into the water. "Just don't forget me when you take off, or I might decide to stay." She sent Amber a wink, which for some reason brought a shiver of something else along with it.

Footsteps approached, and Amber, Angelica and Rhiannon ducked behind a nearby bush, melding into the greenery as the door opened and a woman came through. Green silk lounge suit, flat shoes, short blond hair that was ultraneat. She exuded class and a sort of easy grace as she crossed to the hot tub and sank into a wicker chair nearby.

"How are you feeling? Calmer now?"

Alicia nodded. "This place just oozes calm, Melina. I don't know how to thank you," she said. "Has the auto club called back?"

"No, not yet. But you're more than welcome to stay until they do. They said no more than two hours, didn't they?"

Alicia nodded. "But I'm taking advantage of your hospitality." She got up, again reaching for the robe and pulling it on.

"You're no trouble at all."

"So what is this place, exactly?" Alicia asked. "I'm guessing it's not a spa, since there's just the one hot tub."

The woman called Melina smiled. "It's just…where we live."

"How many?" Alicia had slid her feet into slippers now. They were pink terry cloth and matched the robe.

"Twelve, at the moment."

"All women?"

"Mmm-hmm." She slid an arm through Alicia's and walked her toward the double doors.

"And you just threw in together, bought this place? I don't get it. Are you like a commune?"

"More like a sisterhood. We…share the same interests."

"What kind of interests?"

The woman smiled gently, leading Alicia through the double doors. "Mary made some of her famous turtle cheesecake for our nightly snack-and-coffee break in the sitting room. You have to try some."

"Cheesecake? Oh, honey, you don't have to try too hard to talk me into that."

They both laughed softly as they walked together back into the house.

Amber crept out of her foliate cover. "I don't like this."

"She obviously doesn't intend to tell Alicia what this place is really about," Angelica said.

"I couldn't read her," Amber put in. "She knows how to shield. Ordinary mortals don't."

Rhiannon lifted her brows. "There's something a little more ominous than that going on," she said softly. "I have the distinct feeling there are other vampires in this house."

17

Amber squeezed her mother's hand before she let go and veered to the right, Rhiannon at her side, while Angelica moved straight ahead, toward the offices and living areas on the ground floor. Amber and Rhiannon entered a large room lined in shelves and cupboards, every visible space filled. On one wall, two doors stood side by side, like sentries. Amber gave the doors a slow motion wave, and they opened slowly, silently, to reveal two sets of steep, narrow stairs. One led up, the other down.

Amber nodded once to Rhiannon and started down the stairs into the basement, while Rhiannon headed up the other flight to the second floor. The basement stairs were less than sturdy, old and unkempt looking. It didn't fit, Amber thought, as she moved lower, step by creaking step. The rest of the house, though obviously old, was in perfect repair. The place might be old, but the owners kept it looking like new. This, though...this was different.

Almost...deliberately so.

She reached the bottom, a dirt floor cellar with stacked stone walls.

"This is just odd," she muttered, stepping into the cellar, slowly crossing the floor, examining everything from the breaker box to the furnace, both of which looked brand-new. And then she felt it—something that stopped her in her tracks.

She frowned, searching the atmosphere. "Edge?"

Alby!

God, he was here. Down here somewhere. Dull and muffled, but not by distance. *Edge, what are you doing here?* She asked the question with her mind, hoping to keep the fragile connection open. As he answered, she moved around the basement, searching for the place where the signal was strongest, like moving a radio antenna around in search of the strongest signal.

Came looking for you, what else?

Without Stiles? I thought he was your top priority.

Jealous, are you?

She stuck her middle finger up at him and hoped he knew it. When she felt laughter coming back at her, she was certain he did.

You're still mad at me, then. Even though I rescued you from Stiles?

My hero. She loaded the thought with as much sarcasm as she could manage.

Truth is, kitten, I couldn't stand to think of you off playing warrior princess games in your condition.

Amber went still. He knew?

What, no reply to that?

His signal was stronger, near the back wall. She went to the spot and ran her hands along the stones.

I...was going to tell you.

She detected a fissure—not a natural crack in the stone, but a barely discernible linear break that, though uneven, formed a rough-edged boundary in the shape of a door. Its edges zigged and zagged with the shape of the stone, an extremely effective concealment. Except to eyes as powerful as hers.

Don't apologize. It's not my business, after all.

She blinked. *What the hell is that supposed to mean?*

Well, I'll admit, I was wildly jealous at first. Petty of me, I realize that now. I thought I was your first, you know. I believed you about that....

"You son of a..." Amber drew her knee up to chin height, then fired off a kick at the door. It crashed inward, from the top down, and she stomped over it into the huge room. Then she spotted Edge, sitting in the middle of the floor, her father sitting beside him, close by, oblivious to the mental conversation she and Edge had been having. Both men sprang to their feet when she entered.

"Amber, watch out!" her father shouted.

Too late, though. Two women had been standing at either side of the door, and they were on her instantly, gripping her arms and trying to force her to the floor.

Amber rolled her eyes, ripped herself free of their hands and jerked both fists up and back, smashing the faces on either side of her. The women crumpled to the floor, and Amber strode forward to the odd little white line painted on the floor around the men.

Edge flung his arms out in front of him, hands making stop signs. "Don't!"

"Don't come any closer, Amber!" her father said at the same moment.

She frowned at them, glancing at the floor. The toes of her shoes were at the edge of the white painted boundary. She rolled her eyes, shook her head. "But there's nothing there." She reached out a hand, half expecting to touch an invisible force field.

Edge hit her, hard, flat of his hand to her chest, sending her reeling backward. She hit the wall, then the floor, even as she saw the flames, closing on his arm from above and below like the jaws of a trap. Edge howled, jerking his arm back. His shirtsleeve was blazing. Jameson tore off his jacket and wrapped Edge in it, arm and all, smothering the flames.

"Oh my God, Edge, what the hell...?" Amber asked.

He sank to the floor, letting her father's jacket fall away, hugging his arm to his chest. The shirt sleeve was gone, nothing but bits of blackened fabric left. His skin was just as black, just as tattered. "Didn't want you gettin' burned." He ground the words out. His jaw was tight, his entire body shaking now with the pain, which had to be excruciating. "Wouldn't be good for the little one."

Jameson was kneeling over him, telling him to stop trying to talk, but he stopped in midsentence. "Little one?"

Her father looked at Edge, then slowly turned his head to stare at his daughter. "What the hell is that supposed to mean?"

"This is hardly the time," she said quickly. "We've got to find a way to turn off the damn flame throwers so we can get you out of here." She picked herself up from where Edge had flung her and moved close to the boundary again, knelt beside it, saw the harmless looking jets lining the floor. Lifting her gaze, she saw them in the ceiling as well, all neatly lined up and camouflaged within the white stripe. They were spaced every six inches or so.

Licking her lips, she said, "I have an idea."

"Amber Lily..." Jameson whispered. "Are you...are you..."

Edge winced in pain, bit his lip. "Sorry, love. I lost my head for a second." He let his head drop to the floor with an involuntary moan.

Amber ignored them both, even though Edge's pain was like a hot poker in her chest, and she dug into her pockets, praying she would find what she needed. And she did—a stick of chewing gum.

"Amber?"

"Yes, Dad. It's true. Apparently I'm pregnant. I'm also twenty-three years old. This is not a catastrophe." She crammed the gum into her mouth and chewed.

"B-but how…who…?"

Amber looked past him at Edge, who was perhaps unconscious by now. She hoped he wasn't dead. Enough pain could kill his kind, or that was what the lore said. Lore, however, was proving to be a rather unreliable resource.

Her father followed her gaze, and his eyes widened. "But—"

"I know. It's not supposed to be possible." She plucked the chewed gum from her mouth and broke the pink wad in half. "But it is possible, because that's what happened. I can't explain it. I can only hope you know me well enough to know I wouldn't lie about something like this."

"God, Amber, you can't think I would doubt your word."

"Then it looks as if you're one up on our friend there."

Her father seemed as stunned as if she'd hit him between the eyes with a sledgehammer. Until he looked again at Edge, and then he just looked murderous. "I should have let the bastard burn."

"Now you sound like Aunt Rhiannon." She shrugged. "Actually, I haven't exactly told him it's his yet. I think he's making the logical assumption. Even though I thought he knew me better."

"Amber," her father began, his voice tender.

She held up a hand to silence him and eyed the floor,

choosing a spot halfway between two of the jets. "I'm betting the sensors are within the jets themselves, since I don't see anything else that could hold them. I'm going to toss this piece of gum in to you, between the jets, so the flames shouldn't react. Don't reach out for it, Dad. Just wait for it."

He nodded. She tossed the gum, and it moved cleanly between two of the jets, hitting the floor inside. Jameson picked it up. "As my little girl once said about her parents' liquid diet, 'Ew. Gross.'"

She smiled at him. "I'll always be your little girl."

"Are you all right, honey?"

He was getting emotional. This was not a good sign. Sympathy and tenderness from her father right now would turn her into a blubbering basket case. Already her throat felt tight, just from the look in his eyes and the catch in his voice. So instead of answering, she just nodded, and managed to swallow and clear her throat.

"Here's the plan. I'm going to stick my gum over the nozzle on the bottom. You're going to jump up and stick yours to the nozzle on the top. We have to do it at the same time, or one of us is going to get burned. Fortunately, we can both move with pretty impressive speed. I'll give you a beat to get up there."

"Half a beat," he said.

She nodded. "On three. Ready?"

Her father bent at the knees.

"One, two, three!"

He jumped, and as soon as he left the floor Amber slammed her wad of gum over the gas jet's nozzle and jerked her hand out of the line of fire. By then, Jameson was back on the floor inside the square.

No flames shot out. "It worked," Jameson said. Amber shot forward, but he held up a hand. "Let me test it first." He picked up his jacket, the one that had put out Edge's blazing arm, and held it out over the gas jets. Nothing happened. He nodded. "Stay there, Amber. I'll bring him out."

It nearly killed her to do what her father told her, but she forced herself. She stood still while he bent to pick Edge up off the floor and turned toward the boundary line.

Amber shook her head, moving a few involuntary steps closer. "Dad, no. The two of you together are too wide. There's only a twelve-inch space here." Dropping to her knees, she held her hands to either side of the opening, to show him how much room he had to pass through.

Sighing, Jameson put Edge down. "Take his hands," he said. "You pull him slowly out, and I'll keep him steady." As he said it he lifted Edge's arms over his head, laying them gently on the floor.

She reached in, gripped his right wrist, then winced as she nearly grasped the burned left one. "I have to pull him by one arm, Dad. The other one's too damaged."

He nodded. "If he wakes up, we'll be in trouble."

"He won't wake up." She willed it to be true and slowly began to pull, dragging Edge through the opening. He twitched once, and Amber spoke directly to his mind and as powerfully as she could, said, *Don't move, Edge. Lie still. Trust me.*

Her face beaded with sweat as she pulled him out of the trap. Not from exertion, but from fear. Fear for Edge.

Finally his feet cleared the white boundary line. Jameson walked out behind him, as tense as she was, only sighing his relief when he stood in the clear. Then he closed the space between himself and his daughter, and hugged her gently.

She hugged him back. "Mom and Rhiannon are upstairs. 'Leesha, too."

He nodded. "You see to Edge," he said. "I'll go clear us a path, gather the troops and give you a call when we're ready."

"Make it a loud one, Dad. There's something about this room that seems to…insulate telepathy."

He nodded. "No wonder we couldn't sense you clearly."

She was staring down at Edge even as her father held her, thinking how she'd felt him, wondering if he'd felt her, too, in spite of whatever force was at work here.

"Honey…"

She swallowed hard. "I can't talk about it. Not now, Dad." She pulled free of him and bent down beside Edge, one hand smoothing over his face. "How long till daylight?"

"Eight hours," her father said. "But he's tough. He'll pull through."

She nodded. "He will."

Jameson sighed and left the room, gripping the two fallen guards by one arm each and dragging them along with him—to put them out of reach of his daughter, Amber guessed.

Amber leaned over Edge, drinking in the sight of him so eagerly it stunned her. "Hey," she whispered. "Come on, wake up for me."

His eyelids tightened but quickly relaxed again.

"Edge, come on. I know it hurts. Just try."

Nothing. Nothing at all.

Pursing her lips, Amber said, "Fine. I'll do it myself then." She patted him down, found his ever-present pocketknife and flipped it open. Then she made a little slice on her forearm, sucking air through her teeth as she

did. The knife clattered from her hand, and she watched
the blood well up in the cut. Nodding firmly, she cradled
Edge's head in her other hand, lifting him up a little, and
held the wound to his lips.

At the first contact, his body jerked in reaction, awareness. His tongue darted out, snaked over her flesh, and
made her skin come alive. But then, just as suddenly, his
eyes flew open, and he lifted a hand to push her arm
away. "Amber, no," he whispered. "You can't, the
baby—"

"You have to, Edge. You need it. Let me do this."
She tried to press her arm to his mouth again, and again
he flung up a hand to push her away.

This time, when he did, she saw a tiny puff of white
smoke rising from his arm. "Edge!" God, he couldn't
be burning, not again. The fire was out, how could he...?

Amber went still then, as a drop of blood from her cut
forearm landed on Edge's blackened flesh, and another
puff of white smoke rose up. "What the hell?"

"What?" Edge lifted his head to look, but it moved
as if his neck were made of rubber and fell back to the
floor again with a little thud.

Amber leaned closer, squinting at his poor burned arm.
But the spot where her blood had landed...was fading.
The black was paling, and a tiny, droplet shaped patch
of pink, healthy skin appeared in its place.

"I don't...I don't understand."

"Alby?"

"Shh. Lie still. Just lie still, Edge." She extended her
cut forearm and, grating her teeth in sympathy for his
pain, let the blood drip slowly onto him. Carefully she
used her fingers to spread those drops over his burned
skin. Again the white smoke rose from his flesh.

"What are you... God, that feels odd."

"Does it hurt?"

"Tingles. What are you doing, Alby?" Again he tried to lift his head.

This time she helped him. Then she watched his face as he stared at his arm. It was healing, right before his eyes. Everywhere her blood had touched, he was healing. As he watched, she squeezed her wounded arm again, harder this time, forcing the blood to trickle rather than just drip.

"Alby, stop!" Edge closed his hand over the wound, and she knew it was an impulse. Apply pressure, stop the bleeding and all that. But he used his burned hand, and the process kept working. She watched as her blood oozed between his fingers, leaving healthy new flesh in its wake.

He released her, staring at his hand, fingers splayed, turning his palm. The front, perfect, flawless. The back, blackened, burned.

She touched the burned part, her fingers moistened by her own blood.

Edge lifted his eyes to hers. "How is this possible? How can you…?"

She shrugged. "Damned if I know. You're my first."

He averted his eyes so fast, she knew what he was thinking.

"That makes twice now," she said. "You being my first."

He lifted his gaze slowly, met her eyes, searched them. "It's not important enough to…I was being petty, Alby. It doesn't matter."

"Mattered enough so you were furious with me back at Stiles's place."

He shrugged. "Male ego. Fragile thing, you know?"

She sighed. "Well, for what it's worth, Edge, I didn't lie to you."

He frowned; then his eyes widened and filled with some unidentifiable emotion.

"You were the first. The only man I've ever slept with, Edge."

"But it's not supposed to be possible...."

"Like this, you mean?" She ran her fingertips over his forearm, up and down his skin, making him look down quickly. His eyes widened as he stared at the new, flawless skin. Even the tiny hairs had grown back. His hand, his arm, were completely restored.

"Lots of things I used to think were impossible have been happening lately, Edge. This baby, for example. I thought it was impossible for a vampire to father a child." She shrugged. "But apparently it's not."

Blinking in shock, he stared into her eyes. "The baby...is...mine?"

She held his gaze, nodded once, and didn't look away.

Edge knew she was expecting something, some reply to leap from his lips, but none did. He was completely speechless. And he wouldn't have been, if he hadn't wanted so badly to believe her. Hell, he *did* believe her. But there was this twice-burned cynic in the back of his mind telling him he was a blind freaking idiot.

Everyone knew vampires couldn't father babies.

Except...maybe for him.

Or maybe it wasn't him at all, he thought, glancing again down at his arm and hand, turning them this way and that. Maybe it was all her.

His pain was gone. He could flex and open his palm without so much as a twinge.

Amber turned away, stung by his silence, maybe. "I really don't care if you believe me or not."

He snapped his attention back to her. "It's just…a lot to process," he said, but he thought maybe he'd waited too long to speak. The moment was gone. She'd been hoping for something, and he hadn't given it to her, and now she'd closed her hands.

"Tell me about it," she said, her voice thick with sarcasm. She shook her head. "It doesn't mean anything. It's not like we're ordinary mortals, after all. I'm not expecting you to marry me and put up a picket fence, and it wouldn't matter even if I was."

Edge got up off the floor. Amber was pacing away from him now. "And why wouldn't it?"

She stopped walking with her back toward him. "I don't know."

Edge frowned, staring at her back, sensing…something. Fear. Almost…grief. "What are you keeping from me, Alby?"

"Nothing."

He moved forward, clasped her shoulders and turned her around to face him. That she refused to look him in the eye confirmed what he suspected. When he clasped her chin and tipped it up, he saw a glistening in her eyes that made his heart turn over. "Tell me."

She closed her eyes. "The dream…the baby…" She lowered her head, closed her eyes. "I finally saw what it was you were giving to me in the dream, the one I've been having."

"Death," he whispered. "You said I gave you death."

She nodded. "In a small wooden box. I could never see what was inside, only knew it was something horrifying. Frightening. Devastating."

He narrowed his eyes on her, aching with her pain.

"I didn't know what it meant. I thought—if I got to know you I might figure it out."

"And now you have?"

She nodded. "The other night I had the dream again, but this time I could see what it was you gave me. It was a baby. A small, still, lifeless baby."

Edge felt his stomach twist and lurch. He actually doubled over, hands to his middle, staggering a few steps backward. Mouth open, he gulped in a breath, wondering at the power of the blow.

"Edge?"

He looked at her, confused. He didn't understand this. It was as if he were a child again, with his father's fist in his belly. His back hit the wall, and he tried to straighten, to breathe.

Amber ran to him, gripping his shoulder, touching his face. "Are you all right?"

He stared into her eyes, still moist and so incredibly hurting. "No. My God, Alby, are you?"

She lowered her head. "I thought you should know. It's better to be prepared, you know?"

She sounded so cool, so practical about the whole thing. And yet he could feel the storm roiling inside her. "There's no way to be prepared for something like that," he said. "Alby…"

She turned away from him, pacing across the floor. "Maybe it's for the best," she whispered. Her voice was strained, aching. "We don't even know what it would be."

"How can you say that?"

She shrugged, still pacing. "Suppose it's born a vampire? God, can you imagine? An immortal blood drinker, trapped in the body of a newborn forever?"

"Suppose it's not? Suppose it's normal?"

"Come on, Edge, it's mine and yours. There isn't a normal gene in its entire pool."

"Why are you acting this way?"

"What way?"

He went to her again, moving in front of her so he could study her face. "Cavalier. As if you don't care when your soul is bleeding."

"I'm not—"

"I can *feel* you bleeding, Alby. This is killing you. God, carrying this knowledge around, all alone…"

When he touched her, tried to pull her close, she tugged away. "Don't. We don't…have time for this. Not now."

His mind was racing. So many things rushing around inside it, but mostly one. "This dream, this vision of yours—it doesn't have to come true."

"I've never had one that didn't."

"Ever had one you tried to change?"

She closed her eyes, lowered her head.

"Well, think about it. Remember. In all those precognitive dreams you've had, have you ever once tried to change one of them?"

"No. Not until now. I dreamed about Will being…gone. Not dead, just—no one could find him." She shrugged. "I'm trying hard to change that."

"Then you can try to change this."

"I can't." She closed her eyes, bit her lip. "I can't."

"You can." Edge gripped her shoulders. "Dammit, you have to."

Her eyes snapped open, staring into his. "Edge, I'm so afraid."

And he heard and felt and sensed all she was feeling as the floodgates of her mind opened, swamping him utterly in her feelings, her fears. She was afraid to let herself hope, only to face disappointment. Afraid to try, only to fail. Afraid to love...only to lose.

She was even afraid to let him hold her right now, because she was only barely holding on to her self-control, and a touch from him, an embrace, would shatter her.

He wanted, right then, to hold her—maybe more than he'd ever wanted to do anything. But he held himself back, because that was what she needed. For now.

"Alby, you don't need to bear this alone, not anymore. I'll help you get through it. Whatever happens, it'll happen to both of us."

She stared into his eyes, her own slightly shocky. "I thought you didn't believe this baby could be yours."

"Hell, Alby. That was before you told me it was."

"And you believe me?"

He tilted his head to one side. "You *do* remember the last time we were alone together, right? When I was damn near dying and you made me drink..."

"So?"

"So something happened, Alby." Something major, he thought. She was inside him now, a part of him. Maybe she had been even before. He only knew that since that moment...

"What? What happened?"

"I saw inside you," he said. Then he shrugged, because the words sounded so heavy with meaning. He tried to lighten them with a look, an attitude. "I know you, that's all."

She was staring at him as if she'd never seen him before. Hell, no wonder. She hadn't tasted him, probably didn't have a clue what he was talking about.

"It never entered my mind you would lie to me about this. I know you."

Her tears spilled over, running down her face. "Thank you for that."

He swallowed hard. "Come on, let's get upstairs. I'm antsy as hell down here, and there's no need to wait on the sidelines now that you've performed your little healing miracle. Is there?"

"No, I...guess not."

"Then let's go." Taking her arm, he turned her toward the door, walked up the stairs and straight into the razor-edged iron bolt of a crossbow.

"It's powerful enough to take off your head," a woman said softly. "So don't even *think* about trying anything."

18

Amber counted her heartbeats, shocked when she felt Edge's hand sneak back to her hip, nudging her sideways until she was directly behind him.

"No need to get violent now." He didn't even seem rattled, just offered the woman his most charming smile. How any woman could withstand it, Amber couldn't figure. But this one didn't flinch.

"Come on, you might as well join your friends."

"Don't have any friends, love. I only came for the cheesecake."

Her eyes widened as she shot him a look.

"That is cheesecake I smell, isn't it? Don't tell me I'm mistaken."

"Move," she said, jerking the crossbow.

He moved, keeping that one hand behind him, on Amber's hip. *Don't worry, kitten. We'll get out of this.*

Who said I was worried?

He shot her a look, admiring and mildly amused.

The woman herded them through the house, into one of the rooms off the side, where Amber saw other women, armed to the teeth with various weapons, all of them pointed at Angelica, Rhiannon and Jameson. Amber and Edge were shoved into the midst of them.

"I think it's about time you told us what you're doing here," one woman said at last.

Rhiannon smiled at her. It was a smile that should

have chilled her to the bone. "You would think a mortal woman would choose what might be her final words with a bit more care, wouldn't you?"

The woman faltered just a little. She swallowed hard. "You're the ones who broke into our home. You owe us an explanation."

"I *owe* you?" Rhiannon asked.

Amber put a hand on her shoulder. "I followed a woman here," she said. "Her name is Brooke, and she has something that doesn't belong to her."

From among the others, Brooke herself emerged. But this was a different Brooke. The big hair look was gone, her red locks smooth and slicked back now. She wore a no-nonsense suit and sensible shoes. She met the eyes of the woman in charge. "That's the one, Melina. That's her."

The one called Melina moved a step closer. But Edge stepped into her path. "Oh, no, you don't," he said, even as Jameson pulled Amber backward and the others closed ranks around her. "You're not getting near that one. Not without going through me, at least."

"Through all of us," Jameson added. He moved up to stand shoulder to shoulder with Edge.

Melina went still. "You've got this all wrong. We don't mean you any harm."

"Can't prove that by the lumps on my head," Edge said. "Or that cute little firepit you were holding the two of us in earlier."

Another woman entered the room. "The other girl is gone. I can't find her anywhere."

Melina nodded. "Alicia. Was she with you?"

"Never heard of her," Edge said.

She looked at him as if she knew he was lying, then

turned back to the other girl. "What about Keisha and Kelly?"

"We found them locked in the storage room in the basement. We put them upstairs, in their rooms. They're hurting, but they'll be all right."

Edge nodded. "Those would be the two you had guarding us below. Of course they'll be all right," he said. "If we'd wanted them dead, they would have been." He reached into his pocket, and every weapon in the place jerked toward him. Then he held up a calming hand and took out a cigarette, stuck it between his lips. "Nervous bunch, aren't you?" He glanced at Angelica while digging for a lighter. *Did you find out anything about them?*

She kept her eyes on them as she replied. *They call themselves Athena. Fancy themselves some kind of vampirologists.*

An all-girl DPI? Edge asked silently.

"Not by a longshot," Melina said.

Amber sucked in a breath, and everyone stared at Melina.

She shrugged. "I'm a bit psychic. Clairaudient, to be precise." She sighed. "We don't hunt vampires, we study them."

"That would be a little easier to believe if you weren't currently aiming a small arsenal at us," Edge said.

She seemed to think on that for a moment. Then she looked at the other women in the room. "Lower the weapons."

"Melina, I don't think—"

"Lower them. Go on back to your work, and see if you can locate Alicia and bring her in to join us. Brooke, you can stay."

Slowly the weapons lowered, and the women filed out,

though they looked unhappy about it. Amber breathed a sigh of relief and moved to a comfy looking chair to sit down. She heard Edge swear under his breath, and then he was tossing the unlit cigarette aside, kneeling in front of her, grasping her forearm.

"Damn thing is bleeding again." He looked toward Melina. "Can you—"

Before he finished the sentence, Melina was at the door, calling to someone to bring some bandages and ointment. A moment later she was passing a roll of gauze and some tape to Edge.

Amber sat still, surprised at this turn of events, as Edge tenderly wrapped her forearm, his face a grimace of shared pain and worry. "Got to thinking, I'll have to get used to not lighting up around you, won't I? Wouldn't be good for the little one."

She saw the looks her parents exchanged, and Rhiannon's raised eyebrows, though Edge didn't seem to notice.

"Can I get you anything else?" Melina asked.

"A pint of A-positive would be welcome," Edge muttered. Glancing up at Amber, he winked. He was trying, she thought, to lighten her mood.

"Perhaps an explanation would do just as well," Rhiannon said. "You, Brooke, or whatever your name is. What were you doing with Stiles?"

Brooke glanced at Melina. Melina nodded. With a sigh, Brooke said, "I was working under cover."

Amber was amazed at the change in her, not just her appearance, but in her voice and demeanor. She was no longer the bubblehead devotee of Frank Stiles. She seemed self-assured, confident, intelligent.

"We'd heard Stiles had developed a formula that imbued him with immortality. That he used the blood of…'' She looked at Amber. "The Child of Promise to do it.''

"And why was that of interest to you?" Rhiannon asked.

Brooke again looked to Melina. Melina said, "Because it's against the supernatural order. It couldn't be allowed."

"The *super*natural order?" Angelica asked.

"Yes. Things that can't be explained are considered supernatural, even though they aren't really. They're perfectly natural, just beyond human comprehension." She sighed. "When mankind interferes, however, things…go wrong."

She glanced at Amber as she said it.

"Things…like me, you mean," Amber said softly. "I'm the result of man tampering with the supernatural order, after all."

Melina shook her head. "We determined that you could have been conceived with or without man's intervention," she said. "Your mother was artificially inseminated, but it could have happened just as easily the other way."

"So you decided to let her live, is that it?" Rhiannon asked.

"We're not killers. We're protectors. The Sisterhood of Athena has been guarding and protecting the supernatural order for centuries. Always secretly. We go unseen, unknown. We observe and protect, that's all."

"Then what were you planning to do with Stiles?" Edge asked.

She lowered her head. "Stop him. Destroy the formula, so no one else could ever make use of it. Keep him from creating any more, until he died a natural death."

Brooke nodded and picked up from there. "But when I learned of his plans for the Child of Promise, I decided I couldn't just take the formula and leave, as planned. I had to stay, to be sure he couldn't use her to make more."

Amber shot to her feet. "But in the end, you did take the formula and leave."

"Yes," she said. "Your rescuers were at hand. I slipped away as soon as I saw them gathering outside."

"What did you do with it, Brooke?" Amber demanded. "What did you do with the Ambrosia?"

Brooke looked at Melina, who looked at the floor. "We destroyed it. As well as all of Stiles's notes and computer files. Everything. It's gone."

"Oh, God. No," Amber whispered, sinking back into the chair.

Edge knelt in front of her, gripped her shoulders and spoke intently. "We still have Stiles, love. And I think between your aunt Rhiannon and I, we can convince him to talk." He turned toward Melina. "Thanks for the info. Since you don't have what we came for, we'll be leaving now."

Melina stepped in front of the door. "I'm sorry, but…it's just not that simple."

Rhiannon's eyes narrowed. Edge rolled his, rising slowly to his feet and turning to face the woman fully. "Why am I not surprised?"

"We're a secret society," Melina said. "Your kind must never know of our existence. We can't function effectively if we become common knowledge."

"It's a little late for that, don't you think?" Angelica whispered.

Jameson closed his hand around hers. "If you wanted

to keep us here, you probably shouldn't have had them put the weapons away."

"You're very untrusting, aren't you?" Melina said softly. "Though I don't suppose one can blame you for that. I was only going to ask for your word that you will keep our existence to yourselves. That's all we want. Just a simple promise."

Edge stepped forward. "No."

"Edge, what harm would it do to—" Rhiannon began.

Edge held up a hand toward her, and she stopped speaking. "I was thinking more along the lines of a trade."

Melina frowned at him. "What kind of trade?"

"We'll keep your secret…if you'll keep ours." As he said it, he looked at Amber. "The only person outside this room who knows about Amber's condition is Stiles. I think it would be best to keep it that way."

"On that, we're in agreement." Melina turned to Amber. "I'd give my right arm to know how it happened, whether it can happen again."

"We don't know that ourselves," Amber said softly.

The other woman nodded. "I hope…it goes well for you."

Amber tilted her head to one side. "I think I believe you."

With a sigh, Melina moved aside from the door, reached for the knob. "Will you…let me know?"

"Probably not," Edge said, taking Amber's hand in his, and walking her toward the door. "Nothing personal, though."

Melina nodded rather sadly. "I'll walk you out." She started to pull the door open, but just as she did, something hit it from the other side, slamming it open wide.

And there in the doorway stood Alicia, with a shotgun the size of a small cannon pulled up to her shoulder.

"Nobody move!" she shouted.

Brooke and Melina shot their hands skyward and stood motionless, while the others stood there gaping at her.

"Come on, you guys. Let's go!" Alicia said.

Rhiannon lowered her head, pinching the bridge of her nose. Edge looked at Amber, grinning broadly.

"Well, what are you waiting for? Come on, I'm busting you out!"

Amber laughed out loud then, even got up and went to gently take the gun from her friend's arms. "It's okay, 'Leesh. They're not trying to keep us here."

"They're not?"

Melina and Brooke lowered their arms as Amber leaned the shotgun against the wall. "God, where did you get that thing? It must have been all you could do to hold it up."

"I found their weapons room." Alicia shrugged, then smiled a little. "Thought I was finally going to get my chance to play hero."

Amber looked at her dear, dear friend. "Anyone with half a brain would have been long gone by now. You really thought you could take on an entire houseful of armed women? One little mortal with a shotgun?"

She shrugged, looking a little sheepish, then sending a meaningful glance at Amber's midsection. "I had to try."

"Do you have any idea how much I love you, 'Leesh?"

Alicia met her eyes and smiled. "Me, too."

Amber turned to the others. "Let's get out of here." She slid an arm around Alicia's shoulders, waited for Melina to lead the way to the front door.

As they filed out, Edge turned around. "Don't forget our deal now," he told Melina. "You don't want me to have to come back here."

She held his gaze, nodded. "I never break my word."

They walked to the front gate, all of them, and no one followed. No one. The gate swung open at their approach, then closed behind them after they walked through. Amber looked up at the concrete owls perched atop the gateposts. Then, finally, she lowered her head and gave way to the tears of disappointment.

Edge squeezed her shoulder. "It's going to be all right," he promised.

"How? They destroyed it, Edge. They destroyed everything. And it was Will's only hope."

"Not exactly," Alicia said.

Everyone looked at her. She smiled and pulled something from a pocket. A tiny glass vial, with a clear liquid inside.

"Guess I get to be the hero after all," she said, handing the vial to Amber.

"Is this…but…how?"

"I found it hidden in Brooke's bedroom, along with this computer disk," she said, pulling the disk from another pocket. "She must have given them all of the serum except for this one vial. And if my guess is right, she kept a copy of some of Stiles's pertinent notes, as well."

Edge muttered, "That two-faced little—"

"Don't be too hard on her, Edge," Angelica said. "Immortality is a very tempting thing."

Amber took the vial, looking at it. "This is the old stuff, the last of his original batch of Ambrosia-Six. Stiles said he had only one dose left." She narrowed her eyes.

"She must have turned over the newer batch. But she kept the last vial of the old one."

"How can you be sure?" Edge asked.

"He was calling the newer batch Ambrosia-Seven," she said, tapping the label with her fingernail. She frowned. "I suppose we should probably let Melina know that Brooke is less than trustworthy."

"We do that, we'll also have to tell her what we did with the formula," Rhiannon said. "And who knows what her little gang of women might do if they suddenly deem Willem to be in violation of their precious 'supernatural order.'"

"You think they might harm him?" Jameson asked.

Rhiannon sent a narrow-eyed look back at the place. "I don't trust them."

"Any reason for that, or is it just a gut instinct?" Edge asked her.

She met his eyes. "They're mortals. That's reason enough." Then she bit her lip and shot a look at Alicia. "I've met very few of them who are trustworthy. Even fewer who are as exceptional and brave as our dear Alicia," she added quickly.

Alicia lowered her head, her cheeks blushing red.

"We have to get this back to Willem," Amber said.

"Half of it," Jameson said. "The other half should be in Eric's lab, so he can duplicate the formula. Otherwise, we'll be right back where we are now when this batch wears off."

"How can we know half is enough to keep him alive," Amber asked.

"We can't," her father told her. "We can only hope."

Alicia tucked the diskette back into her pocket. "I tried to open this to get a glimpse of its contents on the computer in Brooke's room, but it's password protected."

"Can you get to it, Alicia?"

Alicia nodded. "If I can't, Morgan can. We should get this to her in Salem, then we can e-mail the file to Eric."

"Guess it's time to split up," Amber said. "So who's going where?"

Rhiannon's Mercedes still sat where they'd left it, and Alicia's Corvette was parked nearby. Edge stepped up beside the 'Vette and stiffened his spine in preparation for a battle, though he hoped like hell it wouldn't be necessary. He said, "Nice little car, Alicia. Bucket front seats, no rear." He held her eyes. "No room for passengers, though. It only holds two."

The little blond mortal seemed to pick up on his meaning immediately. She pulled a set of keys from her pocket and tossed them to him. "Why don't you and Amber take it?"

Jameson opened his mouth to object. Edge saw it clearly, then saw, too, the way his tender little wife put a hand on his shoulder, silencing him. "I think that's a good idea," she said, before anyone else could object. "The rest of us can fit quite comfortably into Rhiannon's Mercedes."

"Good, then," Edge said. "We'll take the half that's going to what's-his-name's lab."

This time Jameson did speak up. "I'd prefer you take the dose of serum to Will in Salem. I don't want Amber within reach of Frank Stiles."

Edge lifted his brows. "I have unfinished business with Stiles. And believe me, I'm not going to let him get his hands on Alby again."

Amber cleared her throat. "Is everyone conveniently forgetting to ask me what I prefer to do?"

They all looked at her. Rhiannon seemed to be restraining a smile.

"I think Edge is right, we should go to the lab. Eric and Tamara, Donovan and Dante, and even Roland are there to back me up should Stiles try anything. And it's imperative I be on hand as Eric runs his tests." She nodded at the vial. "This is the last of Stiles's original batch. We need to know how to duplicate it, and my blood is the key ingredient."

Edge tipped his head to one side. "You make a good point."

"Yeah. Way better than your petty need for vengeance," Amber told him. "You're going to keep your hands off Stiles until I say so. If you won't agree to that, here and now, you can just leave and I'll go alone."

One corner of his mouth pulled into a grudging grin. "You'd turn me out, here, on foot, alone?"

"So fast it would make your head spin."

Edge sighed, turning to face her father. "As I think you can see, your daughter and I have some things to work out." Then he wiped the smirk from his face, turning serious. "You can trust me, Bryant. I won't let any harm come to her."

"I believe you, Edge." Jameson sighed. "Just remember, if you do, you'll answer to me."

"Understood."

Amber looked surprised, maybe because he didn't reply to Jameson Bryant's threat with sarcasm or lip. Actually it surprised him a bit, as well. But he understood the man completely, even respected him for his devotion to Amber Lily. He opened the car's passenger door for

Amber. With thinned lips, she got in, pulled on her seat belt and slammed the door.

Jameson handed him the vial. He'd already sucked a portion into a syringe he'd found in Rhiannon's emergency first-aid kit, in the trunk of the car that had everything, to take to Willem Stone. "You're hauling precious cargo, Edge. Don't forget it."

"Not for a minute." He took the vial, held the man's eyes for one extended heartbeat. Something passed between them. They understood each other, Edge thought. Then, finally, Edge turned and went around the car to the driver's side. There he glanced at Alicia, offered her a warm smile. "Thank you for this," he whispered.

She nodded. "Be worth it, Edge."

He got in, started the engine and pulled the car into motion. And all of a sudden, the notion of several long hours alone with Amber seemed less appealing than it had before. She was angry, though he was uncertain why. And he had no idea what to say to her.

She finally looked at him after the first few miles of silence. "Well?"

"Well, what?" he asked.

She rolled her eyes. "You obviously wanted to get me alone so you could talk to me. So talk."

He slanted her a look. Smiled a little. "Now when did I ever give you the idea that talking would be my reason for wanting to get you alone? Hmm?"

Her face colored a little, and she looked away.

"Don't pretend to be offended, Alby. You've never played games with me before, don't start now."

"I'm not playing games. And I am offended if you think anything could be more important than—than what I'm facing right now."

He reached out to trail the backs of his fingers over her cheek. "What *we're* facing, you mean."

She shook her head slowly.

"What, you don't believe me? You think I'm going to take off and leave you to it?"

"Not until you get what you want," she said softly.

"And what is it you think I want?"

She frowned at him. "You've been pretty up-front about what you want all along, Edge. At least, once you decided to stop lying about it. You want Stiles. You want your revenge on him. That's all you ever wanted."

"No," he said. "Not all." He drew a breath, sighed deeply. "I don't suppose I get any points for leaving Stiles and coming after you when I thought you might be in trouble?"

She said nothing.

"Come on, please? Just enough to cancel out the black marks I earned for choosing to go with him rather than you in the first place?" He turned those eyes on her, flashed that blasted dimple. "It was a stupid mistake, Alby. I knew it the minute I was away from you, and I've been kicking myself for it ever since."

"When are you going to get it through your head that I don't care what you do?"

"When it's true, I suppose. It isn't. Not now, at least."

She shrugged. "It's going to be daylight long before we make it all the way to Wind Ridge."

"Yeah, well, I've got no intention of getting into the trunk again, lady." He eyed her. "Besides, you look exhausted. When's the last time you slept?"

She thought about it, realized she didn't remember. "I don't know. Since before we left Stiles's place."

"Curl up, love. Take a nap. I'll drive until I have to stop."

She blinked slowly, shook her head. "You don't even know where we're going."

"You can tell me before you rest."

She flipped open the glove compartment, took out a pocket-sized road atlas, flipped pages. He watched her. Not her finger, tracing a path along the map. But her face, as she frowned in concentration. The little lines between her bent eyebrows and the shape of her nose. Her tongue as she licked her full lips.

"You can pick up the highway about fifteen miles ahead. You'll probably have to stop before we need to turn off."

He nodded, only half listening, darting quick looks at the road ahead. "How are you feeling?" he asked.

She looked up quickly, startled, perhaps, by the abrupt change of subject. She mulled for a moment, then shrugged. "All right, I suppose."

"You're as pale as alabaster."

"You should talk." She said it with a slight smile.

He grinned back at her, relieved to have her teasing him. It was, he thought, a good sign. "Well, I have reason to be."

"So do I, although the way I've been feeling, I would think green would be a more accurate skin tone than alabaster."

His smile died. "That bad?"

"I can't be more than a few days pregnant," she said. "I can't believe it's already giving me symptoms. And when I'm not queasy or puking, I'm eating everything I can get my hands on. I seem to be getting fat just for the hell of it." She looked away, seemed suddenly nervous, and spoke rapidly. "I mean, it has to be from all the food I've been shoveling in," she said, her hands on her belly. "It can't be the baby. It's only been a few days."

"Just gives a man more to explore, love."

She looked away. "I've begun to wonder if...maybe there's something about me that makes things happen...sooner. I know it seems farfetched, Edge, but I suppose Eric could confirm that, with a few tests and—"

"Wait a minute, wait a minute," he said quickly. He frowned at her, searching her face. "God, you're still thinking I don't believe you."

She didn't look up, kept her eyes focused on her hands in her lap.

"Alby, look at me."

Licking her lips, she forced her head up, met his eyes.

"I have no idea in hell how this could have happened. No more than you do. But I don't for one minute think you're lying about it."

"I'm not sure I'd believe it, if I were in your place."

He sighed hard, hit his hand on the steering wheel. "This is about my initial reaction, isn't it? Hell, Alby, naturally I *assumed* the child wasn't mine. As far as I knew, there was no possible way it could have been. And you didn't tell me differently, don't forget. You didn't give me a chance."

She shrugged. "So you really don't...question this?"

"Of course I question it. I question how the hell it happened, why it happened, whether it's something about my body chemistry, or something about yours, or some chemical reaction that happens when the two meet. God knows there's something pretty damned explosive between us, after all. But I don't question *you*, Alby. I won't. And I don't need your friend the science geek running any tests to prove it, either."

She stared at him, her eyes wide, for the longest time.

She didn't say anything, just stared. He glanced at her a few times, but every time, it was only to see her staring back at him.

He drove on in silence for several hours. Eventually Amber tipped her seat back as far as it would go and curled onto one side, still facing him. He was beginning to wonder if he'd sprouted a second head or something by the time he looked at her to find her eyes had closed at last, dark, thick lashes resting on her cheeks. Her lips, full and moist, were slightly parted. Her breaths flowed in and out of her like waves rolling up onto the beach and then slowly back out to sea again.

He knew the instant she fell into a deep sleep. He felt the shields she'd erected around her mind slowly dissolving. The resistance melted away, and he could not quite resist the urge to tiptoe through her mind, to look in on her dreams. It wasn't ethical, but he'd never been the most upstanding citizen of the dark realms, anyway.

He slowed the car to a crawl, so he could focus more easily on her, on her mind, on her dreams. He saw it unfold, all of it...so clearly in her mind's eye.

He saw her lying in a large bed, her hair tangled, her face damp with sweat. He saw himself, on the other side of a strange bedroom, picking up a small, ornately carved wooden box, carrying it toward her.

He could feel her whispering in her mind, *No, no, please, I don't want to see this again!* And yet the dream unwound, unfurled, spun its images for both of them to see.

His dream self brought the box to her bedside, lowered it toward her, and then he could see, through her eyes, what was inside. A tiny, beautiful baby, with stunningly dark lashes and eyebrows and pale golden hair. It was still, still and white as porcelain.

A black veil slammed down on the dream images, but he could still hear Amber's thoughts swirling through her mind.

I'll lose the baby, she whispered, frantic, panic-stricken. *And even if I could bear it, it's only the beginning, because I'll lose him, too.*

He frowned, jerking his attention back to the road, realizing he was sending up a cloud of dust, having veered onto the shoulder.

I can't love him. I can't love the child. I can't let myself hope, because none of it matters.

"Dammit, Alby, that's just not true."

A car blew its horn, snapping him back to reality. Edge jerked the wheel, pulling back into his own lane and narrowly avoiding the oncoming car. Amber sat up straight, startled wide-awake.

He got the car stopped safely on the shoulder of the road. Amber sent him a questioning glance. "It's all right," he said. "I...I just got distracted for a minute."

She blinked at him, and he could see the trauma in her eyes, the grief, the worry. But then she went cold, pulling that curtain down over her emotions, over her feelings. And he understood it now, that sudden pulling back, the distance she seemed determined to put between them. He understood it—but he was damned if he knew what to do about it.

She looked past him, toward the sky, then turned to scan the area where they'd come to a stop. "At least you picked a good spot for it," she said.

He was so distracted that he didn't get her point, until he followed her gaze to the wooden sign, swinging in the breeze.

"Haven Inn, Bed & Breakfast," he read aloud. Then he lifted his brows. "As good a place as any, I suppose."

"If the room's too sunny, we can always stick you under the bed, or in a closet or something."

He smiled at her. "Gee, thanks. That sounds so inviting."

"Doesn't it?" she asked, slightly teasing.

His spirits rose, because hers seemed to be a bit lighter. "I can only hope they have room service."

"Going to order up a pint?" she asked.

"I was thinking more of just eating the waiter."

She sent him a smirk, and he smiled at her, then pulled into the driveway and up to the inn. Aside from the imitation gas lamps outside, the place was pitch-black. "I hope we'll be able to rouse the innkeepers before the sun rises," he muttered, killing the engine and headlights, getting out of the car.

Amber got out her side. "Worse comes to worse, there's always the trunk," she told him.

He shot a look at her over the top of the car, then hit the lock button on the keyring. "You *are* feeling a little better, aren't you?"

She averted her eyes, shrugged. "Let's get inside, Edge."

He nodded, and when she came around the car, slid his hand around hers and walked with her to the door.

19

The innkeeper was a small, round woman of indeterminate—but likely beyond middle—age. She came to the door in a flannel bathrobe that was cinched tight around her middle, with pink fuzzy slippers on her feet. Locks turned, the door opened, and the woman blinked up at Amber from amid a mass of artificially red curls.

"I'm so sorry to bother you at this hour," Amber said. "But we were hoping you might have a room available."

She wrinkled her nose, looking from Amber to Edge, who stood back a little, keeping to the shadows. He sent her a smile. "Just a pair of weary travelers, ma'am," he said. "We'll pay full price, even though the night's all but over."

Pursing her lips in thought, the woman hesitated only a moment, then finally gave a nod and opened the door wide. "Oh, come on in," she said. "You look too sleepy to do any more driving tonight, anyway."

She stood aside while they entered. The foyer was dimly lit by the small table lamp she must have flicked on when she heard them ringing the bell. She moved behind the large desk that occupied a corner, took her seat and pulled a large book down from a shelf on the wall beside her. "Well, welcome to Haven Inn. I'm Mrs. Monroe, but my guests call me Sally," she told them.

"It's the only rule. And your names are?" She stood there, with her pen poised over the page.

"Smith," Edge said quickly. "Mr. And Mrs."

The woman had pulled a pair of rectangular bifocals from her top drawer and was in the process of putting them on when she stopped and looked up at him, the glasses held halfway to her face. "Smith?"

"No one ever believes me," Edge said. "It's the curse of having such a common name."

She smiled, turning the book toward him. "Just sign in, and add the make, model and license plate number of your car."

"Of course."

"And I'll need a credit card."

"We'll be paying cash," Edge said as he scribbled down some blatantly false information in the book. He set the pen down, pulled his wallet from his back pocket and flipped it open. He took out a stack of ones, pulled out six of them and slid them across the counter to the woman.

Amber saw the bills and frowned, then she shot a glance at Edge, caught the intensity in his eyes, the gleam. He was messing with the woman's perceptions.

She smiled and took five of them. "The rate is only $80 per night," she said. "Plus tax, of course. Total comes to $86.40. I'll get you some change." She unlocked a drawer in the desk.

"Edge…" Amber said, a warning tone in her voice.

He sent her a wink. "Come on, love, I'd let her keep the change, but I'm damned if we won't need it for gas and things along the way."

We can use my plastic, she told him with her mind.

Too easily traceable. Stiles has friends, don't forget. It's not worth the risk.

The woman handed him a ten, three ones and some change. More money than he'd given her in the first place. He'd managed to get the room for free and make a tiny profit.

Amber sighed, shaking her head at him in disapproval and vowing silently to mail a check as soon as she got home. The woman smilingly handed over a key. "Top of the stairs and off to the left. Breakfast is served at eight."

"We're not going to want to be disturbed, Sally," Amber said. "After driving all night, we'll probably sleep until sundown. Though I might creep out for a snack at some point in between. Can you make sure no one bothers us during the day?"

"Well...well, yes. I suppose I can do that."

"Thanks."

"Do you need help with your bags?"

"I'll get them later. Right now, I just need to sit down and rest my eyes," Edge said. He sent her a smile. "Go on back to bed, Sally. We promise not to disturb your sleep again."

She gave him a shaky little smile, succumbing to that irresistible charm like every other woman in creation would do. Herself included, Amber thought, as she followed him up the stairs. He'd been right when he'd said she seemed to be feeling a bit better in the car. She *was* feeling better, in spite of the persistent dream. Being with him again was the reason for it. She knew that, even though she couldn't quite figure out why. She responded to him the way the sea responded to the tug of the moon, and she felt like a fool for it, but that didn't change the facts. She felt warm all over when she was near him. Even the threat of an impending grief too big to bear seemed to fade when he was with her.

Idiot.

They didn't need to use the key. Unoccupied, the bedroom was unlocked, the door standing open. The room was almost too cute to bear, with its pink and blue quilt on the bed, its pillow shams and canopy and the curtains in the windows, all made of the same fabric. Plush pale blue carpet lined the floor. The dresser sported an antique replica clock and a lamp that could have been a prop from *Gone with the Wind.*

Amber walked in, then went straight across the room and through the door at the far end to the bathroom, closing the door behind her. While she was in there, she started a hot bath running in the claw-foot tub.

When she returned, Edge was lying on the bed, arms folded behind his head, looking relaxed and comfortable.

"Thoughtful of you, running me a bath," he said without looking at her.

She pursed her lips, moved to the bed and sat down beside him. "I suppose you're welcome to it. There's not all that much time before daylight. I can take mine after."

"Or we could take one together."

She shot him a look. He was still lying there, still looking completely at ease.

He shrugged at her scowl. "Hell, the damage has already been done, love. It's not like you can get any more pregnant than you already are." He shrugged. "Not much more I can do to you, is there? Besides…the good stuff."

"Edge, I just don't think…"

He sat up, one hand sliding around her nape. His touch silenced her, and reluctantly she closed her eyes, let her head tip backward.

He leaned closer to her, his lips near her ear, so that she felt his cool breath when he spoke. "I want you, Alby. Have since I set eyes on you."

She pursed her lips, tensed up. "I thought it was make believe."

"What, I wasn't convincing enough?" He put his mouth on her ear, nibbled the lobe. Shivers and heat ran through her all at once. "It was never an act, love. Never. I thought it would ease up once I'd had you. Forbidden fruit is sweeter and all that. But it only got worse." He slid his hand slowly to the small of her back, moving it there in gentle circles that tingled and burned.

"So you want me," she said.

"And you want me," he replied.

But I want more, she thought against her will. She closed her eyes, told herself not to let the thoughts swirling around in the depths of her mind leak out where he could see them. She didn't just want him. There was something else, something so deep it penetrated her soul. She knew him. He was inside her, a part of her. Had been since before she'd set eyes on him. Sharing blood had intensified the feelings, and she imagined carrying his child did so even more. But it didn't matter why she felt the way she did. It only mattered that she felt something about a million times more powerful than desire for him. She didn't like being the one who cared, the one who was bound to be hurt. She would have far preferred being the object of adoration and knowing all the time that she could take it or leave it. Never be the one to care the most. How many times had she given that advice to Alicia? Never need a man more than he needs you. And never, *never* let yourself need someone so badly that the thought of being without him becomes paralyzing.

"Let me hold you, Alby," Edge said softly. "Let me take away some of the worry, just for a little while. Hmm?"

Damn her, she didn't have the willpower to say no. She let him turn her toward him, let him kiss her, felt her entire body tremble in bone-deep reaction that was as much emotional as physical. He was rain to her parched, thirsty desert. He threaded his hands in her hair, and she drank in his kisses, his touches, his essence. And then, suddenly, he lifted his head away.

When she blinked her eyes open, it was to find him frowning at her, studying her face. "You're...you're crying," he whispered.

She sniffed and lifted her hand to wipe the errant tear from her cheek. "A combination of sleep deprivation and raging hormones," she told him. "Ignore it."

."Alby, there's nothing about you I can ignore." Tenderly he swept her hair off her forehead, tucking it behind an ear. She'd never seen him look quite the way he looked right then. "What can I do to make it better?"

She blinked her eyes dry, told herself it didn't matter what she did or didn't do in the hour before dawn. It couldn't possibly make her love him any more. It was too late for her. Swallowing her certainty that she was in for a heartache of preternatural proportions, she leaned up to him and pressed her mouth to his. "Make love to me," she told him.

He wrapped his arms around her, kissed her, even as he scooped her off the bed and rose to his feet. He carried her across the room and into the bathroom, set her down on the edge of the tub and broke the grip of his mouth on hers long enough to shut the water off. Then he dragged a hand through the water a few times.

"Nice big tub," he observed, unbuttoning his shirt, peeling it off.

God, he had a chest to die for. She ran her hands over it. "You were always into working out, weren't you?" she asked. "Even as a mortal. That would explain your penchant for stealing expensive workout equipment."

He shrugged. "It was pretty much a job requirement, back then." He unbuttoned her blouse, peeled it off her, slung it over a towel rack beside his own.

"As part of a gang, you mean?"

He nodded. "It wasn't like it is today. We weren't a group of malicious thugs, just a bunch of kids who did what we had to to get by." He tipped his head to one side. "You read the file Stiles kept on me."

She nodded. "How did you know?"

"I saw it. While I slept, I was there with you, Alby. In your head, inside that room where they kept you. It was the damnedest thing."

She frowned, but he only pulled her close for a lingering kiss, undoing her bra in the back while he was at it. And in a moment she was no longer able to focus on wondering what the hell all of this meant, or whether it might be possible he felt more for her than just wanting.

By the time Edge had worked her out of her jeans and himself out of his, she was entirely focused on sensation, on the moment. On the way his hands felt on her backside, his mouth on her throat and breasts, his body pressing against hers.

Edge slid his hands down her thighs, pulling them up and around his waist, an act that opened her to him, let him rub against her. Then he stepped over the edge of the tub, into the water, and sank slowly down, until he leaned back and she knelt on top of him.

Her breasts dangled over him, and he stretched up, catching one in his mouth, tugging at the nipple with his teeth until she moaned. Then she moved herself over him and lowered her body, taking him inside her. He closed his eyes in apparent ecstasy, and that encouraged her to move. To raise and lower herself over him, to drag her nails over his chest to make him feel the way he was making her feel.

God, it was good.

His hands clasped tight on her buttocks, drawing her hard and tight to him, and then he shifted his hips, moving inside her, but slowly. She threw her head backward and muttered his name.

But he kept to the slow pace, exploring her body with his hands and his lips. He ran his fingers over her spine, curled his hands on her shoulders, ran them down her arms. It was as if he were memorizing every inch of her. When he ran his palms over her abdomen, she looked down, seeing the little mound her belly made, how hard and tight it was. His hands trembled there.

She met his eyes, wondering what it meant. A pregnant woman didn't show in the first few days. Did he doubt her now, when her very body seemed to be insisting that she'd lied to him?

No. She saw only wonder in his eyes. Wonder, and something more.

He moved his hand lower then, until his thumb found the nub of sensation so close to the place where they were joined. He rubbed her there, and she shivered. He suckled her, hard and then harder, increasing the pace of his movements inside her. Then she was moaning his name as he drove her over the edge.

Edge held her until the ripples of pleasure began to fade, then pulled her upper body down so she lay on his chest in the warm water. He stroked her hair, kissed her neck. "Is it better now?" he asked her.

She closed her eyes, loving the feel of his body against her, his arms around her. "Yes," she lied. "Lots better now."

Amber might have felt better, Edge thought, but damned if he didn't feel worse. He didn't know what the hell the woman was doing to him. She'd crept into his veins and was spreading through his system somehow. She was changing him. He didn't like it. It wasn't fair, and it wasn't what he wanted.

Hell. He didn't know what he wanted anymore. Life had been so simple before he'd decided to cross paths with this woman. He'd known exactly what he wanted. His priorities were limited: self-preservation and revenge. Now those things seemed to have been displaced by other things—her safety, her well-being, her happiness. And that of her child.

His child. Imagine that.

Those things had first risen up to become as important as his own goals and desires. Then they'd become more important. Now they seemed to have shoved his own need for vengeance and sense of self-preservation right off the chart. Those things paled in comparison to her. To the baby.

Beyond that, there were all these other changes happening inside him. The newfound power and strength and psychism. The voice in his head that no one else could hear. The one that led him to Amber, even when going to her proved less than healthy for him. The one that thought it was funny to see Edge beaten down by a gang of mortal women. Not that he didn't find it mildly amusing himself, in retrospect. And it was all because of her. Somehow or other, her blood, her taste, her touch—all of it had changed him. In every possible way.

He didn't question the tight little pouch of her belly. She'd said herself that she'd been eating nonstop lately, and she could be bloated. Any number of things could explain it. Not that she'd lied to him. That wasn't even a possibility. The child was his. He knew it with a certainty he could not—would not—question, and he thought he should have sensed it all along. Should have known it at the very moment of conception. How could a man not notice when his universe was inexorably altered?

She'd taken him over.

He wondered if she knew, sensed, his need for her. God, he hated this feeling. He was utterly at her mercy.

And yet she sat in the tub with him, as fresh, hot water rose around them, even while the cooling batch drained. She washed him, lathering him with soap and scrubbing him down with a loofah. She worked on his arms and shoulders, arm pits and then his chest, where she lingered a long while.

She liked his chest, he thought, feeling it swell with the notion. She seemed to pay a lot of attention to it.

Finally he settled his hands over hers. He didn't speak, just pried the soap and sponge from her grip, and began washing her the way she'd been washing him. She was the one carrying the child. She was the one who was half mortal. The female, the weaker of the two of them. At least, he liked to think she was. Even though everything she had shown him had denied those notions.

He washed her chest, thinking he understood her obsession with his. Then he reached all the way around her and pulled her against him on the pretense of scrubbing her back. So small, so delicate she felt in his arms. Snapping her like a twig would be no challenge, and that knowledge frightened him in ways he'd never imagined. He stopped scrubbing for a moment and just held her against him, waiting for the soul-deep shudder that had worked through him to fade. He didn't like pondering how fragile she was, or how delicate the life she cradled within.

"Edge?" she whispered.

He swallowed hard, forced himself to release her. "Morning is coming," he said, as if that explained his momentary lapse.

"Finish up," she said, and she rose from the water like Venus rising from the foam. Rivulets ran down her skin as she stepped out of the tub, pulled on one of the complimentary, emerald green plush terry robes. "Haven Inn" was embroidered on the front in gold thread, beneath some kind of crest. "I'll go make sure the windows are all covered."

"You didn't wash your hair."

"I can do it later."

"But I wanted to do it."

She looked puzzled, her head tipping just slightly, her smile wavering and unsure.

Edge shrugged. "I've never washed a woman's hair before." Nor had he ever wanted to, he thought. He was pathetic. He thanked his stars she was pregnant. It seemed to be reason enough for her to let him hang

around a while. Bask in her light. God knew he wasn't
worthy.

She tugged the robe tight, took one of the towels from
the big stack nearby and went to the bathroom window
to hang it over the glass before drawing the curtains.
"That's not a tight fit, Edge, so don't linger."

"I'll be out in a flash," he promised.

She nodded and left the room.

Edge finished his bath quickly, then wrapped himself
in a towel and joined her in the bedroom. She'd managed
to seal the room's two tall windows already, and he
looked, then gave his head a shake and looked again.
"Where did you get the duct tape and trash bags?"

She smiled. "Downstairs. I did a little snooping
around the kitchen while you finished your bath."

"I was only five minutes."

"Closer to ten. And I can move almost as fast as you
can, you know."

He nodded, walked to the canopy bed, eyeing it, then
lifting the spread to glance underneath the bed. "You
think I should play it safe?"

She tugged the covers out of his hand, then turned
them down and shed the robe, crawling into the bed.
Smiling at him, she patted the spot beside her.

"Hell, yes." He dove into the bed, then gathered her
close to him. "Ah, this is way better than sharing space
with dust bunnies."

"I thought it might be."

"Do you think it's safe, though?"

"What's the matter, Edge? Don't you trust me?"

He kissed her hair. "Course I do."

"I'm not going to let anyone get near you while you

rest. The door is locked up tight, including the bolt and chain on the inside. Just relax.''

He lifted his head, glanced at the clock. ''Maybe I'm not ready to relax yet.'' She sent him a questioning look, and he wiggled his eyebrows. ''Twenty minutes to sunrise. Think it's time enough?''

''For you or me?''

''Ouch!'' He clutched his chest as if wounded, then grinned and pulled her closer.

''I'm only kidding, you know,'' she whispered. ''You're an incredible lover, Edge. You take me to places I never dreamed of.'' She shrugged as he touched her. ''Not that I have much of a frame of reference for comparison, mind you.''

''And never will, if I have my way,'' he heard himself mutter as he pulled her into his arms. What shocked him was the realization that he meant it.

Amber fell asleep in his arms, and by the time she woke again there was life in the house around her. She could feel people moving around, hear their voices. Ordinary people. Nice, ordinary people. It was kind of comforting, in a way, to be surrounded by folks who knew nothing about her.

She took a quick shower and was delighted to find brand-new cellophane-wrapped toothbrushes and a sample-sized tube of toothpaste in the bathroom drawer, along with other comforting items, like deodorant, a hairbrush, a tiny sewing kit and a map of the nearby town. Gosh, that Sally really did want her guests to feel welcome.

Once she finished primping, she left the room, putting the Do Not Disturb sign on the door; then, as an afterthought, she decided to refasten the chain, just to be safe. From outside the door, she focused. Moving tiny things in precise motions was harder work than hurling large objects in a general direction. She used her forefinger to direct her energy, ran it along the door, lifting the chain on the other side and sliding it into the slot. Then she tried the door, just to make sure.

Finally she turned and headed down the stairs.

A couple were just heading out the front door, arm in arm, laughing all the way. Amber followed her senses to the kitchen, where she found Sally, garbed in a floral print dress and a full white apron, chopping vegetables on a cutting board. Beside her, in a row on the counter, were seven individual-sized pie tins, each of them lined in a perfectly trimmed crust.

"Pot pies for supper?" Amber asked.

Sally looked up quickly, startled. Too startled to stop the knife from continuing its downward journey. She hacked into her finger, shrieked and jumped. The knife clattered to the floor as she clutched her now bloody hand.

"Oh, geeze! I'm so sorry!" Amber raced forward, yanking paper towels off a roll and gripping the woman's hand to press the towels to her finger. "Hold this here. I'll get bandages," she said.

"In the bathroom, through there, down the hall, to the left," Sally said, nodding in the direction, because she couldn't really point. Tears were welling up in the woman's eyes. God, it must hurt.

"And don't apologize," Sally added quickly.

"I could just kick myself." Amber headed to the bathroom in search of the bandages and antiseptic ointment. But then she paused with the items in her hands. She recalled the magic her own blood had worked on Edge's burned flesh. Was it just him she could heal? Was it only vampires? Or would it work on anyone?

Licking her lips, she rummaged in the cupboard some more, locating a safety pin at length. Then she took all the items back to the kitchen with her. She got fresh paper towels, wet them at the sink and turned to Sally. "Sit down now. I'm very good at this."

"I hope so. I'm afraid it's deeper than I thought at first. I think I might need stitches."

"Let me take a look." Amber took the woman's hand in hers, turning it palm up, and with her free hand lifted the paper towels away. The cut was midway up the fore-finger, and it was gaping. As soon as the pressure was off, blood started flowing again.

"Oh, mercy," Sally said.

"You shouldn't look at it. It'll make you queasy." The sight of all that blood was making Amber queasy, too. But she fought past it. "Lean back in your chair, close your eyes, and hold your fingers tight, right here." She showed the woman the pressure points on either side of the base of her forefinger. "Squeeze hard. We have to get the bleeding stopped."

The woman did as Amber told her, closing her eyes and squeezing. Amber lifted the paper towel, replacing it with the cold, wet ones, wiping the blood away. The bleeding slowed. Glancing quickly at Sally to be sure her eyes were still closed, Amber grabbed the safety pin, flipped it open and jabbed herself in the forefinger with it.

When the blood welled up in the pinprick, she again moved the paper towels aside and quickly squeezed a few droplets of her own blood onto the wound. Then she lowered the paper towels again.

"Hold them there for me," she told Sally.

Frowning, Sally did so. "It feels…funny, dear."

"Funny how?" Amber asked, unwrapping adhesive strips that had roses decorating them. Better than cartoon characters, she thought.

"Kind of tingly, icy cold and burning at the same time." She opened her eyes, looking worried. "You don't suppose I've sliced into a nerve or something?"

"It's going to be fine. Close your eyes now. I'll be finished in a minute."

Sally obeyed, leaning her head back. Amber lifted the paper towels again. She watched but saw no fresh bleeding, and as she dabbed away the blood that was already there, she could find no cut. Only a pale pink line where the cut had been.

She bit back the exclamation that jumped to her lips, and instead washed the finger clean of blood, applied a little ointment to a bandage, and then stuck it around the place where the cut had been.

"There," she said. "Done."

When she looked at Sally's face, the woman was staring at her, an odd look in her eyes. She said, "It…doesn't hurt anymore."

"Well, this ointment must have some topical pain reliever in it."

She frowned at her finger, bent and straightened it. "But it doesn't hurt at all. It's like I never cut it."

"What can I say? I'm good at bandaging." Amber smiled. "Now, how about we clean up this mess, and then I'll help you finish those pot pies."

"You're a guest, dear. I wouldn't dream of it."

"Nonsense. I'm a guest who just made you darn near hack off a finger. I owe you one."

"You haven't even had breakfast."

"Oh, don't worry. I plan to snack while I help. Why do you think I came wandering into the kitchen in the first place?"

Sally smiled. "I kept two plates of breakfast aside for you and your husband this morning. You can help yourself." She nodded toward the fridge.

Amber opened it and found two plates wrapped in tinfoil. She took the foil off the top of one and saw stacks of French toast, fluffy scrambled eggs, home fries and sausage links. She flipped the tinfoil over, took the sausage links off the plate and dropped them into the foil, then did the same with the second plate. "I'm a vegetarian," she explained as Sally looked at her quizzically.

Then Sally nodded. "Ah, I had one of those here last summer. No worries, hon. The home fries were cooked in vegetable oil, and not even in the same pan."

"That's a relief. God, I'm starved." She took both plates out, set one inside the microwave and the other on the counter, and hit a button.

"You going to take a plate up for your husband?"

"Oh, he won't be awake before dinnertime. I'm going to eat them both."

Sally grinned ear to ear, carrying paper towels and bandage wrappers to the garbage, washing her hands at the sink. "My goodness, I would have guessed you to be one of those young women who eats like a bird. You're so tiny."

"I don't usually have this kind of appetite," Amber admitted.

Sally let her gaze roam down Amber's body, and it

stopped on her belly. "Is there a reason for it?" she asked with a smile.

Amber licked her lips. "The truth is, I'm kind of eating for two."

Sally looked up, eyes gleaming, a smile on her face. "You're expecting!"

Amber nodded. "I've only known for a couple of days."

"Oh!" Sally clapped her hands together, rushing back to her pies at the counter. "You eat. I'll put these together and set them aside. Then you and I are going into town for some first-class baby shopping."

"We are?"

"Oh, dear, yes. Trust me now. Go on, eat."

The microwave beeped. Amber took out the first plate, inserted the second, grabbed a fork and a bottle of maple syrup, and dug in.

20

Edge kept to the shadows while Amber thanked Sally for the huge basket of food she had made up for them to take along. He shouldn't be surprised, he figured, that Amber had won the woman's affections within the space of a single day. She'd won his in a heartbeat.

He smiled, waved goodbye, took the heavy basket from Amber and headed out to the car. Amber opened the passenger door for him, and he set the basket inside. Then he frowned at her. "It's chilly tonight. We'll be running the heat in the car. You think the food would be better off in the trunk?"

"No." She said it quickly.

Edge frowned at her, tipping his head to one side. "You hiding another vampire back there, Alby?"

She rolled her eyes, moving around to the driver's side. "Don't be ridiculous."

"Well, I know your penchant for shutting us up in your trunk. And you obviously don't want me poking around back there."

She crammed the keys into the switch and started the engine. "You coming with me or staying behind?"

Pursing his lips, Edge got in. He looked at her as she pulled away, then looked again. "You're wearing different clothes," he noted.

"Mmm-hmm. Sally took me shopping today. God knows I needed a change."

He nodded, noticing the loose fitting cotton sundress, white with lilac and yellow pansies all over it in honor of the impending springtime, and the long yellow cardigan sweater she wore with it in deference to the chill of winter still lingering in the air.

"It's pretty," he said. "Awfully timid for you, though."

"What, I'm not timid?"

He shot her a look. "You're vivid. You should wear jewel tones, not pastels. Satin and velvet, not cotton." He frowned a little. "You're not trying to change, are you?"

She shrugged. "Why would I?"

"The pregnancy. Do you think you need to behave in a manner befitting an expectant mother, Alby? Respectable, discreet...toned down?"

She didn't look him in the eye, which told him he might just be onto something.

"Don't mute your colors, love. It won't work, anyway. They're too bright to be covered in paler shades. They'll only bleed through."

She pursed her lips, seemed to think for a moment. Then she said, "I figured I should get used to it. I was looking at maternity clothes, and they really tend to be mostly muted pastels and sunny floral prints. Besides, I've been eating so much my jeans barely buttoned this morning."

"Maternity." He digested that. "God, I hadn't thought that far ahead. You're going to swell up like a hot air balloon before long, aren't you?"

She swung her head his way so fast he thought she must have wrenched her neck. "You have a *problem* with that?"

He grinned at her, looking her up and down and trying

to imagine her tiny body stretched around a baby. Her little belly swollen to beach ball size. It made his insides feel knotted up to picture her that way.

He jerked out of his imaginings when her fist connected with his shoulder hard enough to make him wince, and he forced his eyes up to hers again. "What?"

She looked wounded, refused to speak to him and kept her eyes dead ahead.

He reached out, cupping his palm over her belly. "Hard to believe it can happen. You're so tiny. I mean, there's not enough of you to stretch to that size, is there?"

"Oh, you just wait and see," she said. And she said it like a threat. As if she expected it to upset him or bother him, which, of course, it didn't.

"I intend to." His hand warmed there where it rested on her belly. Warmed and tingled. "I saw this sculpture of a goddess once. She was as green as the forest, and her belly was huge. Her breasts, too. She looked like a wild woman, an earth mother, and yet she had this expression of…serenity. I thought at the time that she was the most beautiful thing I'd ever seen." He smiled at her. "That's what you're going to look like, Alby. Like an earth mother, a nature goddess."

When he dared a glance at her face, she was gaping at him, blinking as if she'd never seen him before.

He shrugged. "Yeah, you're right. That was the sappiest thing I've ever said. I think your pregnancy hormones must be spilling over into me. Probably seeped in with your blood."

Her smile was tentative but finally real. "You have a sweet side," she accused.

"Don't let it get around."

There was a sharp popping sound, like a gunshot, and

the car jerked suddenly to the left. Amber gripped the wheel for all she was worth, her foot jamming onto the brake in a reflexive motion as the car skidded sideways. Edge gripped the wheel, as well, to help her hold it. A rush of panic hit him. What would have once seemed to him an amusing little thrill ride now scared him senseless, his mind jumping to thoughts of the tiny life inside Amber's womb. How easily it might be snuffed out.

The car finally came to a halt in a spray of gravel on the road's shoulder. Edge turned to Amber, hands to her belly, eyes wide as they searched her face. "Are you all right? Were you hurt? Is the baby…?"

"Fine, I'm…we're fine."

He let his eyes fall closed and sighed his relief. He'd never known fear like that. While self-preservation had always been his top priority, he thought, he'd never really cared if *he* lived or died. Oh, he'd decided he preferred living on, but he had no fear of death and what lay beyond its veil.

Now…God, now he was a quivering wreck of a man. To panic over a little skid. Is this what fatherhood did to men? He would never have believed himself capable of falling this far.

Sighing, he backed away, opened his door and got out to survey the damage. The driver's side front tire was flat, with a large, jagged tear in it. Amber got out, as well, and came to stand beside him.

"What happened?"

"Blowout," he said. "It's no big deal. I can fix it. Keys?"

She slapped them into his hand, and he aimed the key ring and thumbed the button with the open trunk icon. The trunk opened as if by magic, and Edge went to the rear of the car. Amber gasped and raced after him, right on his heels.

"Wait!"

He didn't heed her. And then he was standing there, looking down into the trunk, at the semitransparent pink and blue shopping bags, each bearing a teddy bear logo. He glanced up at her, and she lowered her eyes. Then he returned his attention to the bags, tugging one open and reaching inside. He pulled out a brown plush bunny with floppy ears. A tiny quilt in bright yellow checks with happy little ducklings all over it. A stack of tiny white T-shirts, and an assortment of minuscule pajamas in the softest fabric he'd ever touched and every color of the rainbow. They had little feet at the bottom. He couldn't believe any baby could be small enough to fit these things.

He lifted his head again, met her eyes, the little pajamas still in his hands. "You bought baby things today."

She nodded.

"And you didn't want me to see them?"

Pursing her lips, she seemed to have to make an effort to hold his gaze. "I don't know why I bought them. Given the dream, it's not like the baby is going to get the chance to use them."

"Don't say that."

"Sally took me into town, to the baby stores. I saw these things and I got...foolish. I forgot what I know. I let myself believe..."

Edge gripped her shoulders and turned her to face him. "You have to believe. Dammit, Alby, if you don't believe, who the hell is going to? If you don't believe, what hope can this baby possibly have?"

She blinked up at him, tears brimming in her eyes.

"Forget about protecting yourself from heartache,

Alby. You already know you can't. If it's going to come, it's going to come. But you can't just lie there like a doormat and wait for it. You can goddamn well fight it."

She stared into his eyes. "That's basically what Alicia said."

"Alicia's a smart girl."

Amber licked her lips. "The visions have never been wrong before."

"Damn the visions, then. Nothing is certain. Any tiny change you make can alter the future. You know that."

She blinked at him, seemed to gather herself, swallowed hard. "I so want to believe that."

"Don't *want to*. Just do it." He gave her a little shake. "Do it, Alby. I am. And I'll tell you what else, that baby is, too. No kid of mine is going to go down without a fight."

"I'm just not sure I'm strong enough to bear it, Edge, if…"

"I'll be strong enough for the both of us," he told her, even though he doubted his ability. He pulled her against him, pressing his mouth to her hair, holding her hard.

He felt her relax in his arms after a moment. Felt her melt against him and go soft and pliant. And then he felt the soft sobs shaking her back and shoulders as she wept. "I…wasn't sure what colors to get. So I…I bought everything."

"You don't have any sense of whether the baby is a girl or a boy, then?" Edge asked.

She sniffled, straightened a little, and looked at him, smiling through the tears on her face. "No idea at all."

I'm a boy. J.W. Mom calls me Jimmy. Tell her I like blues and greens, and especially red. I really like red.

Edge frowned, because the voice in his head was back.

And it hadn't been, not since it had directed him to where Amber was.

"My mother said she had this powerful sense of me from very early on. She knew I was a girl. She knew what I would look like."

I have my mother's hair, almost black with that blood-red rinse effect. But my face and my eyes, those are all yours. By the time I'm nineteen, people who see us together will mistake us for brothers.

"What the hell…?" Edge whispered.

He tucked the blanket sleepers—that was what the pajamas were called, according to their tags—back into the bag and shoved it aside to reach for the spare tire and jack.

"Mom says there was even some kind of…communication going on between us when I was still inside the womb," Amber was saying. She stood by herself now, hands cradling her belly as if holding her child. "And afterward, as well. Hell, it's still pretty strong. I can shield from anyone else, but it's almost impossible to keep her in the dark for long." She licked her lips, sighed. "It worries me, Edge. It scares me that I'm not feeling those things for this baby. I keep thinking maybe it's just another sign that it's not meant to be."

"Or it could be because in this case the baby's psychic bond is to its father."

He rolled the tire out onto the ground, stood there holding it upright with one hand, the jack in the other, as she blinked up at him.

"What do you mean?"

"I just figured it out," he told her. "That voice in my head, the one that told me where you were, both when Stiles had you and again when you went to Athenaville."

He shook his head, only barely believing it himself. "It was the baby."

Her eyes widened. "Edge?"

"I wouldn't lie to you about this, Alby. He's a boy. He says he likes blue and green and especially red, and that he has your hair and my eyes." He frowned a little. "He also got a hellish kick out of his old man getting beaten up by a gang of girls—though I don't imagine he saw it coming."

"He…spoke to you?"

Edge nodded. "Yes. And more than that, he spoke about his future, about how he'll look at nineteen. Don't you think that suggests there's a hole in your vision, Alby?"

"I…I don't know."

"Well, he knows. He knows what we're thinking, hears what we're saying when he's tuned in. And it can't do him a hell of a lot of good to hear you thinking he's doomed from birth."

"No. No, it can't."

Edge nodded firmly and rolled the tire around to the front of the car. He leaned it against the fender, then knelt to put the jack underneath.

"Edge, why are you bothering?" she asked softly. And he realized she was in a hurry to be on the road again.

He shrugged, looked both ways, saw no traffic and straightened, lifting the car up with one hand. Amber crouched down and spun off the lug nuts with her fingers. She yanked off the old tire, slid the new one into place and quickly spun the nuts back on.

As she stood up, brushing the dirt from her hands, Edge lowered the car.

"Why do you suppose he doesn't speak to me?" she asked.

Edge picked up the demolished tire and the jack, carrying both of them back to the trunk and putting them inside. "I don't know. Why didn't you speak to your father before you were born?"

She shrugged.

"Is it because you love your mother more?"

"Of course not! I adore my dad. He…oh, I see what you're doing." She smiled a little. "Thank you for that."

"Listen, next time I get the little runt talking, I'll let you know. You can try to listen in, through me. I mean, you and I seem to have a pretty strong bond ourselves, don't we?"

"I think that's an understatement."

"Then you probably know I want to take a turn driving."

"Yes, I do," she said. "And you know I'm starving and need to stop somewhere for a veggie sub soon or die."

He smiled. "Yes, I do. What's wrong, are you sick of the things in the goodie basket Miss Sally packed?"

She made a face. "I polished that off an hour ago."

He smiled. "I'll pull off at the first spot I see."

Edge pulled into the driveway of the Marquand Estate just after midnight. He whistled softly as he cut the engine. "Some place. Looks like a miniature of the White House."

"Eric always lives in style. Though this place is a lot more modern than what he normally prefers."

"Yeah?"

"Mmm, stone castles are more to Eric's taste."

"Maybe he got sick of living the cliché." He opened

his door and got out, then came around to open hers, as well, but Amber was out of the car before he got there.

"There's Tam," she said, waving as Tamara came out the front door, onto the curving, elegant front steps, framed by twin pillars. Amber hurried forward, hugged Tam hard. Tamara wore jeans and a lacy white blouse, her long black curls draping over her shoulders like a shawl. Amber sighed, glad to see her dear friend again.

"It's been so long, honey. How are you?"

"I'm good. I...there's a lot to talk about, Tam. So much." She lowered her eyes briefly, then brought her head up again as she heard Edge's footsteps. She glanced his way. "Tamara, this is Edge."

"I've heard a lot about you," Tam said, reaching out a hand.

Edge took it briefly. "Not as flattering as the things I've heard about you, I'm sure. Hope you'll give me the benefit of the doubt, though."

He smiled a little when he said it, but Amber picked up a little undercurrent. Was he really concerned what these people thought of him? That would be a switch.

"I heard you saved Amber's life—a couple of times now, according to my last talk with her mother. That's good enough for me." She stepped aside. "Come on inside. Everyone's waiting."

Edge walked beside Amber into the house. She glanced up at him, wondered if he were nervous, or if there was something else wrong with him. He seemed off, somehow.

Tam led them into an elegant sitting room, every piece of furniture an antique. Eric had always had a penchant for oversized, chunky wooden pieces from various ages and cultures, and it showed here. Four men sat waiting. Dante and Donovan, Roland and Eric. All four rose to greet them. Of them all, Roland was the only one who was formally dressed. He wore a dark suit, crisp white shirt underneath with a tab collar.

Amber didn't sense any underlying animosity in any of them, and suspected her mother hadn't told them her little secret. Probably just as well.

She took the little vial from her shoulder bag, held it out to Eric. "This is a sample of the formula Stiles made from my blood the last time he held me. We sent an equal amount back to Salem, for Will. But…this is all there is."

Eric took it, nodding. "I've been running tests on Stiles's blood since Roland, Donovan and Dante brought him here. But…"

"No luck?"

Eric shook his head. "Oh, there's been luck. All of it bad. The man's blood is deteriorating. Rather rapidly, I'm afraid. Whatever changes had occurred in him are reversing themselves. In other words, he's aging."

Amber frowned. "He told me it would be several more weeks before that happened."

"He likely thought that was true."

"He told me he only needed the formula every six months or so," Amber said.

"This time…something's different."

Amber frowned. "What?"

Eric shook his head. "I don't know." He held up the vial. "With this I may be able to duplicate the process he used, though."

"And when you do, we'll create a fresh batch for Willem."

He averted his eyes. "We'll cross that bridge when we come to it." He glanced at Edge. "You're famished."

"I'm way ahead of you, my friend," Roland said.

He'd slipped away, Amber realized, and she'd been too caught up in her talk with Eric to have noticed. But he'd returned now with a cut crystal goblet on a silver tray. He offered it to Edge.

Frowning, Edge took the glass, sniffed at it, then drank the contents down. "Fancy," he said, replacing the glass on the tray. "Thanks, I feel better already." Then he turned to Eric. "Where are you keeping Stiles?"

"Edge…" Amber began.

He met her eyes. "I'm not going to kill him, Alby. Yet. I just want to see him."

She held his gaze, trying to read him. Did she dare believe him? Donovan stepped between them. "I'll take you to him. He's in one of the bedrooms upstairs."

"Has he given you any information about how all this works?"

"No, nothing," Donovan said. "Come on, it's this way." The two of them went up the stairs.

Sighing, Amber turned to Tam. "He's got a very old grudge against Stiles. He's been hunting him for more than forty years."

"Do you know why?" she asked.

Amber nodded. "Edge was kind of…mentor and protector to a small group of fledglings. Street kids who'd been transformed young and abandoned by their sires."

"Just as he was," Tamara whispered. Then she met Amber's eyes and clarified. "Donovan explained the circumstances."

"Edge loved those kids. He hasn't told me so, but I've felt it. Stiles butchered them. All of them."

"Oh my God." Tamara closed her eyes, shook her head. "Do you think Edge will try for Stiles again here?"

Amber swallowed hard. "I don't think he'd lie to me. But…just in case…"

"We'll keep an eye on Stiles, Amber. Don't worry," Dante promised. "Go on. Go to the lab with Eric. You two have your work cut out for you."

Sighing, Amber nodded and followed Eric through the depths of the house and into his lab. "Have a seat, Amber. I suppose the first thing I ought to do is take another small sample of your blood."

She felt her lips thin, knowing that within a few moments Eric would likely know the secret she was keeping. Still, she took off her long sweater.

Then she went utterly still, staring down at herself, at her belly. "Oh my God," she whispered.

Eric turned, stared at her with wide eyes, and blinked slowly. "Is there…something you forgot to tell me Amber?"

Edge walked into the bedroom with Donovan at his side and took a look around. Plush carpet, elegant queen-sized bed laden with plump, soft bedding and pillows, soft lighting, a crystal water pitcher and glass on an antique stand near the bedside.

"Who's idea was this?" Edge asked bitterly.

"Sorry?"

"Well, when he takes one of ours, they get a dungeon or a cage. Who decided to give him the presidential suite?"

Donovan sighed. "Vengeance isn't the Marquands' style, Edge. Besides, they don't have cages or dungeons here."

"Aren't they worried he'll escape?"

"Go on. Go take a look at him."

Edge rolled his eyes, but he moved forward to the

bedside. He stopped when he could see the man's face. The plump covers had blocked his view from the doorway, but now he saw it.

Stiles lay in the bed, his face pale, creased with lines that hadn't been there before. And his hair had gone utterly gray. He opened his eyes weakly, spotted Edge and didn't even look panicked. He muttered, "Good. I've been hoping you'd show up. Kill me and end this."

Edge pursed his lips, ignoring Stiles as if he were a piece of the furniture. "He looks twenty years older. What the hell happened?"

"We don't know. It's more than the elixir wearing off, though, but I think Eric was trying not to send Amber into a panic. If the Ambrosia-Six had worn off, then, according to the notes we have, he would have begun aging again, but only up until he reached his true chronological age. That's not what's happening here. Within just a short time he's aged beyond that, and there's no end in sight."

Edge tilted his head, probed into Stiles's mind. "He knows what caused this," he said at length.

"Yes, we sensed the same. But he's not talking."

"Oh, he'll talk."

"Edge, I can't let you..."

Edge looked at the man in the bed again. "At this rate, he'll be dead in a few weeks anyway. Surely you don't intend to stand by and let him take his secrets with him."

Donovan lowered his head. From behind them, Tamara's voice came softly. "No, Edge," she said. "We don't intend that at all."

Both men turned to face her.

"We only hope we can discover what we need to know without resorting to violence. Or torture."

"And if you can't?" Edge asked.

Tamara lowered her eyes. "We still have time."

Edge pursed his lips, turning to look at Stiles and addressing him for the first time. "Well, old man, it looks as if you have a bit longer to decide to tell us what you know. But not much longer. I don't have the qualms these people do."

Turning, then, he strode out of the room, but he'd only gotten into the hallway when he felt the rush of pure panic hit him. Not his own…but Amber's.

"Alby?"

Something was wrong, terribly wrong. He lunged down the hall to the staircase, down it and through the sprawling house, following his sense of her. He didn't slow down, even when he realized others were following. He didn't have to think, to look into empty rooms, to wonder which door would lead to her. He just knew, and then he found that door and flung it wide.

She turned slowly to face him, her lips forming soundless questions, her eyes wet and frightened…her belly swollen so much that the fabric of the loose fitting sundress was near to tearing.

"Oh my God," Tamara whispered from behind him. "Amber…Amber, are you…pregnant?"

Amber held Edge's eyes, never looking away, and he held hers. "Yes," she said. "I have been for almost a week now."

"A week? But—" Tam didn't finish the sentence, ending instead with a little gasp.

"I thought I was just getting bloated. And maybe a little fat, since I've been eating nonstop…but this…"

"I don't understand," Edge said softly.

Amber whispered, "Something's wrong, Edge. Something is terribly, terribly wrong."

He shook his head in vehement denial and moved forward, pulling her into his arms and hoping to God she couldn't feel the paralyzing fear inside him, or the trembling that was starting down deep in his bones.

21

She let him hold her for the space of a heartbeat, but then suddenly she ripped herself away, turned and ran through the house. Edge took a single step, but the sprite-like Tamara stepped into his path and placed a soft hand on his chest. "She needs to cry it out, Edge. And she's not going to do it in front of you."

"Why the hell not?"

She smiled softly, as if she knew things he didn't. Myriad things he didn't. "I'll go to her…for now. Maybe you can stay and figure out just what it is my husband thinks he's on to."

Edge spun around to stare at Eric, who was hunched over a computer screen, hitting the scroll button rapidly. He wasn't idly browsing; he looked like a man in search of something specific.

"What? What is it?"

Eric shook his head. Tam was already gone, on her way up the stairs again. Donovan and Dante withdrew quietly, maybe to give him some space. But Roland came farther into the room, clapping a hand on Edge's shoulder. "Give Eric a moment. He'll tell us as soon as he's figured it out. Meanwhile, my new friend, I suppose congratulations are in order. This is nothing short of a miracle."

Edge shot him a glance. "Might be a bit premature for that, Roland."

"Not if you've won Amber's heart, my boy."

He glanced up at the man, about to say he hadn't even come close, but then decided that it wouldn't be exactly flattering to Amber to tell her family that she'd slept with a man she didn't love. "What the hell can be going on? How can she be that…that big this early?"

Roland shrugged. "Are you certain about the date you…er, that is, you and she…"

Edge nodded. "She was a—" He bit back the words, started over. "It was her first time. There can be no mistake. And it's not something I'm likely to forget."

"Here it is—here. Right here." Eric shot to his feet, reading aloud from the computer screen. "Alicia sent this e-mail while we rested. It's some of Stiles's most recent notes, taken from a disk she found at the Athena house. Listen to this. 'Ambrosia-Seven is ready to be tested, and even though I shouldn't need another treatment for several weeks, what better test subject than myself? In truth, I've been convinced for some time that more frequent treatments might increase my physical strength and psychic powers. I only hesitated putting it to the test due to the limited supply of Ambrosia-Six. Now, with a source in hand and plans to…' Oh my God."

"What?" Roland asked, alarmed.

Edge only stood still, his face grim, jaw tense.

Eric met his eyes briefly before reading the rest. "'Now, with a source in hand and plans to clone all the future sources I will ever need, there's no longer reason for delay. Tonight I begin the new treatment.'" Eric looked up from the computer screen and met Edge's eyes once more. "This entry is dated the night you and the others rescued Amber from him." He searched Edge's eyes. "Did Stiles do it? Did he inject himself?"

Edge shrugged. "How the hell would I know? What

difference does it make, anyway? It has nothing to do with what's going on with Amber and my son.''

''It has everything to do with Amber and your…'' Eric paused there. ''Son? You…already know?''

Edge nodded, turned to pace away, pushing a hand through his hair. ''I'm sorry I barked at you. I'm a little…''

''On edge?'' Roland asked.

Edge grimaced but knew the lame attempt at humor was only an effort to lighten the mood. Sighing, he faced Eric again. ''The man was in his bed, in his pajamas, when we kicked the doors in. Anything he had planned to do that evening, he would have already done. So chances are, if he didn't change his mind, he had already injected himself with this…Ambrosia-Seven.''

Eric nodded. ''Makes perfect sense.''

''Not to me.''

''I'm afraid it's as lost on me, as well, Eric,'' Roland said. ''Explain, please.''

''Stiles is aging at an accelerated pace. The baby also seems to be developing at a faster than normal pace.'' He shot Edge a look. ''You're sure this is your child?''

Edge must have looked murderous, because Eric quickly held up a calming hand. ''I mean, are you certain this pregnancy isn't the result of Stiles implanting her with a cloned embryo?''

Edge calmed himself, nodded. ''I'm sure. She was pregnant before he took her.''

He met the man's eyes. ''Don't bother asking how I know, just trust that I do.''

''All right.'' Eric frowned hard, so hard that Edge thought his brain must be processing ideas and thoughts and information as fast as a computer.

"So something about Amber's blood speeds up the aging process?" Edge asked, eager to be clear on this.

"Yes, apparently, but that wasn't the case before. Her blood...it must be different now than it was before the pregnancy."

"Could the pregnancy be to blame for that?" Roland asked, while Edge's mind reeled.

"Could be. I'd say it's the most likely bet."

Edge shook his head, holding up his hands. "I was burned—badly burned—the other day. Alby cut herself. Figured she could revive me with a sip, you know? But a drop fell on my arm and..."

"And what? What happened?" Eric had come across the room, was leaning close to Edge, listening with every part of him.

"It healed. My skin tingled and burned and...healed. Just like that."

"Amazing," Roland whispered.

"Makes sense, though. Her blood is speeding up physical processes, cell regeneration, healing."

Edge shook his head. "What does this mean? Will my child be born in a week, only to reach old age within a couple of years?" He shot Eric a look, fully expecting the man to say it didn't mean any such thing.

Instead Eric lowered his gaze. "I wish to God I knew."

"Jesus, this can't be happening." Edge tipped his head back, facing the ceiling and the grief raining down on him from Amber, somewhere above. "She can't go through this."

"We'll get to the bottom of it. I just...I need more time." Eric held up a hand. "I know, I know. Time is the one thing we don't have."

Edge licked his lips. "I have to go to her."

"Go," Roland said. "She has to know the situation, and it ought to come from you." He glanced at Eric. "I'm going to call Jamey."

He turned and left the room.

"Jamey?" Edge asked. He stood in the doorway, his back on one side of the frame, his hand braced on the other. He'd closed his mind to Amber's heartache, because it was damn close to crippling.

"No matter how old Jameson gets, nor how many grandchildren he acquires, Edge, he'll always be Jamey to Roland. He practically raised the boy, you know."

"No. I didn't know that." Edge straightened, turned to face the direction he had to go. "How the hell do I tell her this?"

"We don't know anything for sure, Edge. It might be better if you...wait until we do."

"I don't know if it's possible to keep this from her. I don't know." He started out of the room, heading toward the foyer and the stairs to the second floor.

"She'll be in her favorite guest room," Eric called after him. "Fourth door on the left."

Nodding, Edge went up the stairs.

But Amber wasn't behind the fourth door on the left. Edge opened it and stood there, looking inside at the rumpled covers of the bed, the box of tissues on the stand. The room was empty. Without forethought, he let the veil fall away, opened his mind to hers, and felt her. The grief washed over him again, but it was no longer crippling or paralyzing. It was active and angry. Lashing out.

Turning, he moved back up the hall, past the stairs. She drew him to her as surely and swiftly as a supermagnet would draw a shard of steel. He opened the door of the bedroom he'd been in earlier, and took in the scene swiftly, in the space of a heartbeat.

The pretty porcelain table lamp, shattered on the floor. Its power cord had been wrenched from its base. One end was plugged into the outlet, and the other end, with two bare wires emerging like the forked tongue of a venomous viper, was in Amber's grip. She held it a hair's breadth from the quivering old man in the bed. Tears of pain streaked Stiles's scarred face.

"Tell me what's happening to me," she said, her voice dangerous, low, trembling with passion and power. "Tell me, damn you." She jabbed him quickly, briefly, with the wires, and his body jerked and spasmed in the bed.

"Jesus, Alby!"

She straightened, turning to face him, even as Edge crossed the room and jerked the wire out of her hands. "Give me that before you fry yourself." He yanked the cord from the wall to render it harmless, then turned to see Stiles shaking, weeping. A helpless old man. Shaking his head, Edge took Amber's arm. "Where the hell is Tamara? I thought she was watching over you."

"I don't need watching over. I sent her downstairs to find me a cup of tea." She nearly spat out the words. "As if tea could help anything."

"I don't—"

"He knows something. Don't you see that? He knows, and he's going to die without telling us."

"No, he's not. I'm not going to let that happen, Alby." Sighing as he faced her down, Edge noted the lines of tension around her lips, the tight set of her jaw, the way she was holding herself so stiffly she was all but shaking.

Gently he touched her cheek. "This...this isn't you. Hell, woman, this is more my style than yours."

"I can't...just let this happen. I can't let him die, Edge. I can't let our baby die."

The stiffness of her body fled all at once. She collapsed like a flag when the wind goes still. He closed his arms around her, pulled her against him. He held her, and his gaze wandered to the eyes of the old man in the bed. He read them, knew and understood what Stiles wanted, and in that moment, his own need for vengeance melted away. He knew what he had to do. He nodded, the movement barely perceptible. But the old man saw it and acknowledged it with a nod of his own.

So be it, then, Edge thought. *So be it.*

Carefully, he scooped Amber up, turned and carried her back down the hall to the room Eric had described as her favorite. It was a modern room, painted a soft lilac hue. Its curtains and bedspread were white, patterned with purple pansies, and sheer violet scarfs draped lazily from the top of the curtain rod, and over the dresser and bedside stand.

He tugged the covers back with one hand, then lowered her into the bed. "Listen to me, Alby. You have to stop the hurricane of grief that's raging in your mind long enough to listen to me."

She lifted her eyes to his, and he held them with everything he had. "I am going to take care of Stiles. And I promise you, I'll find out all he knows. Every morsel. I swear it. On the memory of my long dead family of fledglings, I swear it to you."

She sniffled, nodded in jerky motions.

"And Eric will take care of the scientific end of this. He'll put all the information Stiles gives me to use. If there's a way to solve this, we will. We'll do it."

"What if there's not?"

"But what if there *is?* What if there *is* a way, and we

find it? Alby, you have only one job here. And that's to take care of our son. Take care of yourself, so he has a warm, safe, nurturing place to grow. Banish the stress. Chase it away, because it's toxic. It's poison to him. Understand?''

"I don't...I don't know if I can."

"You have to try. Try, Alby. You wouldn't smoke a pack of cigarettes or drink a quart of whiskey or inject yourself with heroin while you were carrying him inside you. This is just as bad. You've got to let it go."

Tears welled in her eyes, spilling over onto her beautiful cheeks. "Tell me how."

"Put your trust in me," he said. "I know I'm not what you probably thought of when you pictured the perfect man in your childhood dreams. I'm no one's knight in shining armor, Alby. God knows I'm aware of that. But I'm not going to let you down in this. I'm not going to let our baby down. I've got this. Let me deal with it. Trust that I can, and will, and just focus on doing what you have to do to keep little J.W. safe inside you."

She blinked. "J.W.?"

He nodded. "That's what he goes by," he said, smiling softly, stroking her hair in soothing, slow movements. "But he tells me his mother calls him Jimmy."

"He...he told you his name?"

He nodded. "I thought the initials stood for Jameson Willem, at first, in honor of your father and Will, but it doesn't feel quite right." He closed his eyes, put his palm on Amber's abdomen. "Shh, listen. Touch my mind and speak to your child, Alby."

Amber lowered her trembling hands over his and closed her eyes.

And Edge heard the voice that had become familiar

now. *I'm all right. Stronger all the time. Why is my mother so sad?*

Amber's eyes flew open, fresh tears pooling. "It's really him."

"Yes. It's really him."

She licked her lips, focusing, and then she whispered, "It's James William. That's his name, for my father and Will, but different enough to be his own."

Edge let the slight smile pull at his mouth. "That's it. That feels right."

"And he's okay. For now, right now at this moment, he's all right. Healthy and strong."

"Yes. And that's what you have to focus on. If there's grieving to be done, Alby, then we'll do it when the time comes. Not before, not one damn minute before."

She nodded, harder, firmer, this time.

"Trust me, Alby. I'm going to take care of everything. You. J.W. Everything."

I trust you, Dad.

"I trust you, too," Amber whispered.

She opened her eyes, and looked up into his, and Edge felt a white hot blade slide neatly between his ribs to pierce his heart. He lost his breath for just a moment. God, how could he ever live up to such a promise?

The only person who had ever looked at him with that much trust in her eyes had been his precious Bridget. And he'd let her down. Let Stiles cut her throat. Let her die. He was terrified of having someone so precious— even more precious—depending on him again. God help him, he'd better come through this time.

"Thank you, Edge," Amber whispered. "Thank you." Her eyes fell closed again, much needed sleep stealing over her. Her body relaxed beneath the covers, and her breaths became deep and rhythmic.

"No, Alby," Edge whispered. "Thank *you.*"

He slid his hands from beneath hers, heaved a sigh, and turned toward the door, only to see Tamara standing there, a china tea cup balanced on a saucer in her hands, tears dampening her cheeks.

When Amber opened her eyes again, the sun was shining in through the bedroom window, and Alicia was sitting in a chair beside her bed.

Frowning, she blinked her friend into focus. "How did you manage…?"

"Edge called me last night. Said he didn't want you alone while everyone was at rest. Your father chartered a flight for me, so I could get here by sunrise."

Amber sighed. "How is Willem doing? Did they give him the Ambrosia-Six?"

"As soon as we got back with it." She shrugged. "Sarafina thought he looked better."

"But what did you think?"

Alicia averted her eyes. "It's really too soon to tell."

She didn't think the formula had worked. Amber knew Alicia too well not to read her face. "Even if it did work," Amber said, "it's not a permanent fix. A few months, at most, and then—"

"Stop it. If it worked, that's a good thing. Let's not start borrowing trouble or worrying about what happens next. God, you've got enough to worry about." Her eyes wandered down the bedcovers, to the bulge of Amber's belly.

"Did Eric make any progress last night?"

Alicia averted her eyes. "Edge says I'm to keep you from focusing on anything negative."

"Are you *his* best friend or mine?"

"Amber…"

"Tell me. I need to know what's going on, 'Leesh."

Alicia's lips thinned, but she answered. "They can't duplicate the formula with your blood. Ambrosia-Seven was apparently a whole lot different than Ambrosia-Six, and maybe not in a good way. Eric says your blood is different now. He thinks maybe after the pregnancy it will change again, but there's no way to be sure."

Amber closed her eyes.

"He managed to run his tests without destroying the sample you brought him, though," Alicia said quickly. "That means we can give the second part of that to Will."

"That one tiny vial. That's all that's left. And there might never be more."

"Then again, there might be. God, Amber, when did you turn into such a pessimist?"

Amber sighed. Her stomach rumbled so loudly it made Alicia smile.

"Hungry?"

"Famished. It seems to be a constant state." She frowned, sitting up in the bed and pushing back the covers. "At least I'm not throwing up anymore."

"No, I'd say you passed that stage already." She nodded at Amber's belly as she said it.

Amber looked down, ran her hands over her middle. "I'm even bigger than I was last night. It's happening so fast, Alicia. God, I don't know what to think anymore."

"Well, lucky for you, I'm here to tell you what to think. And right now, I want you to think about taking a shower, putting on some clean clothes and doing something with your hair. By the time you finish, I'll have whipped up the biggest breakfast I can think of."

"Good luck finding food in this house."

"Hey, come on, you think I came empty-handed? I stopped at an all-night grocery on the way here from the airport. I like to eat, too, you know."

Amber smiled and clasped her friend's hand. "You're too good to me."

"Well, I'm gonna be an auntie. I have to be worthy." She squeezed Amber's hand, then turned toward the door. She paused there. "Tam left some of Eric's clothes in the closet for you. And…Edge said to tell you he had them move Stiles."

"To where?" Amber asked.

Alicia shrugged. "He wouldn't say. Only that it was someplace you won't be able to find him." She sighed. "I was kinda disappointed. I'd have liked a crack at that scar-faced bastard myself."

"You're turning into a regular warrior woman, you know that?"

"I'm turning into a lot of things. Change is good. Now go on, go take that shower."

Amber did as Alicia suggested. But as she stood beneath the shower spray, she found herself amazed at the new shape of her body. She would have stood naked in front of a mirror, had there been one in the house. She ran her hands over her belly, and as she did, something jabbed upward.

Amber went still, keeping her hand where it was. The baby kicked again, and she smiled, then laughed out loud. "Hey, in there. Guess you're awake, huh?"

She wondered if that meant anything. The baby being awake and active during the daylight hours. God, so many questions. How had her own mother ever managed to get through the uncertainty, the worry?

She got dressed, pulling on her own jeans but leaving them unbuttoned and unzipped, the fly folded inward.

She wore one of Eric's white button down shirts and her own bra, though she had to loosen the straps. She and Alicia shared a tower of pancakes, a luscious omelet and a pot of coffee, and then Amber fetched the packages from the trunk of the car and showed Alicia all the baby things she'd bought. They talked all day, and Alicia rubbed lotion on Amber's swollen belly to ease the rapid stretching of her skin, which was beginning to burn and itch.

By sundown, she was feeling a bit more optimistic—no doubt thanks to Alicia's constant positive conversation, on top of Edge's promises of the night before. She believed in him, in spite of herself. Maybe…somehow, everything really would be all right. Maybe Edge could somehow get the truth out of Stiles, and Eric could use it to solve the mystery of her blood.

Maybe.

She sighed, looking up from her comfy seat in the living room when Edge came in, moments after dusk. He stopped in the doorway, met her eyes across the room. It hit her then that she was doing what he wanted her to do. Trusting him, believing in him. Depending on him. It was something she'd never intended to do, and something that frightened her. She liked being in control, taking care of herself, needing no one. This…this was different.

She was completely in love with him. And that scared her even more.

22

Edge took Amber by the hand and led her out the house's back door. The lawn there was fenced in, and sported an antique lawn swing and a wide-open view of the stars.

He sat down on the swing, and she sat beside him. He slid an arm around her shoulders, drew her close. "Beautiful night," he said.

Amber looked up at him. "It is."

"You're hurting, though."

She started to deny it, but the knowing look he sent her made her realize he wasn't buying it. "How do you know?"

"I feel you. More and more, it seems. What hurts, Alby?"

"My back, mostly."

He drew her down until she was lying across his lap, then ran his hand over her back, exerting gentle pressure, rubbing in small circles. "Wish I could make it better."

"You are," she told him, closing her eyes. "Just by being here, you are."

"That's a relief."

"It won't be long, Edge," she said. "At this rate, this child could be born at any time, and I..."

"You're scared to death."

She nodded.

"I'll make it all right."

"Do you really believe you can?" she asked, relaxing a little more.

"I have to believe it. I can't accept the alternative. But whether I believe isn't important. The question is, do you?"

Amber opened her eyes and stared up into his face. "It seems a little insane, but I do."

He nodded, pleased, she thought, by her answer. "Then hold on to that."

"I'll try."

Edge bent over her, pressed his lips to hers, kissed her slowly, tenderly. "You do that," he said.

Amber heard the back door open, sensed others coming out into the yard. She sat up, self-conscious, saw Tamara on her way across the lawn.

"I'm going to go check on Eric's progress," Edge said. "Relax out here a while. Enjoy the night."

"All right." She was confused, wondering at his tenderness, the look in his eyes. Wondering what it might mean and trying not to let herself hope...

Edge rose from the swing, nodding to Tamara on his way back into the house. Amber watched him go, tears welling in her eyes. God, why did he have to be so wonderful? It made her hope for things she'd already decided could never be.

Or could they?

"Don't you ever take a break?"

Edge asked the question after walking into the lab to find Eric bent over a microscope, peering into its lenses. Eric straightened, rubbed his eyes. "With everything else running at such an accelerated pace, I don't dare slow down." He removed one slide from the microscope, inserted another. "How is Amber?"

"Terrified. Pretending not to be, for the sake of everyone else."

"And Stiles?"

"Still in that attic bedroom, still aging. I don't see much change." Eric nodded at the dark glass vials that stood in a little rack near Eric. "Is one of those the Ambrosia-Six?"

"No, those are all fresh samples from Amber Lily. This one's a duplication of the serum Stiles called Ambrosia-Seven."

"But it's useless."

"For our purposes, yes," Eric said. "I packed the A-Six in foam, put it in the cooler. It'll be safe there until someone takes it back to Willem."

"Good thinking. We wouldn't want anything to happen to it," Edge said, looking at the fridge in the corner of the lab.

"No. Though, from what Alicia's told me, I don't think he's going to survive long without it. The first treatment doesn't seem to be doing a lot of good."

Edge lowered his head, swallowed his guilt, kept his thoughts sealed within his own mind. "You should probably go take a look at Stiles," he said slowly.

Eric was already back to peering through the microscope, but he straightened then. "I thought you said there was no apparent change?"

"No, not apparent to me. But the aging is progressing. I can't make a guess at how much time he has left. I was hoping you might be able to. After all, we have to find some way to make him talk before he expires, taking all his secrets with him."

Eric nodded thoughtfully. "You're right about that." He peeled off the latex gloves he was wearing and started for the door. "All right. I'll look in on him." He headed for the door, and Edge followed him out of the lab. When they went through the hallway, into the large sitting area, Eric frowned. "Where is everyone?"

"Outside. It's a beautiful night, Eric. Very warm for so early in the year. Amber's expecting her parents and Rhiannon to arrive soon."

"It's good that her parents will be here for her."

"Yes, it'll do her good to have her mother with her," Edge said. "I think I'll go on out and join them."

Eric nodded, and continued across the room and up the stairs. As soon as he was out of sight, Edge turned and hurried back up the hallway and into the lab. He went to the mini-fridge, opened it, pried the flat square of foam off the top of the foam box and reached inside. The vial was there, nestled in bubble-wrap. He took it out, removed it from the wrappings. Then he found an empty vial to replace it and put everything back, just as he'd found it.

No one would ever know. At least not until the box was opened again. And then Amber would probably hate him for this. Hell, they would all hate him. What surprised him most was that he actually cared.

The others might forgive him in time, if his plan worked. If it didn't, they never would. But Amber—Amber would never forgive him, even if he succeeded. He closed his eyes, held the vial of precious fluid in his fist. It didn't matter if she hated him. He had to do this. For her. And for his son. But God, how he wished there were some other way.

Amber rocked slowly in the cushioned seat of the antique lawn swing, Tamara swinging beside her. The stars above her twinkled as brightly as if all was right with the world. As if her baby's life wasn't hanging in the balance, while Willem's waned to nothing. Alicia hadn't been honest with her about Will's condition. She'd tried to sugarcoat it. But Amber knew. She felt it in her soul. Willem was fading.

"It's a beautiful night," Eric said, stepping out onto the lawn to join her there. He looked around.

"Alicia's gone to the kitchen to make some dinner for the two of us," Amber told him. "Donovan and Dante decided to walk the perimeter. Make sure no one's lurking about the place."

He nodded. "Not a bad idea. Stiles still has a lot of associates. Roland?"

"I think he's off somewhere waiting for Rhiannon. He misses her terribly," Tamara said softly.

Eric met her eyes, and a silent exchange passed between them. Amber lowered her own eyes and pretended not to notice, but it did make her ache a little for the object of her own ill-advised affection.

"Where is Edge?" she asked, wondering why he wasn't still with Eric.

"He's not out here with you?"

"No. Last I knew he was going to the lab to check on your progress."

"That's odd," Eric said. "He told me he was coming out to join you."

Amber's heart skipped. Edge had told her he would take care of everything, that he would find a way to make Stiles talk before he died. What if...?

Tamara met her eyes, read her thoughts there. "He wouldn't harm Stiles. He's completely set aside his desire for vengeance, Amber."

She licked her lips. "I know that. But still..." She got to her feet, belly first. It had swollen even larger during the course of the night. "Tell me where you're keeping Stiles, Eric. I have to make sure."

"We'll come with you," Tamara said, rising as well, and taking Amber's arm as if she needed help.

Together they went back into the house, up the stairs and all the way down the ornate hall to the very end. Eric opened a door there, onto another staircase, this one old, looking seldom used. He led the way up these stairs and through yet another door at the top, into the giant house's attic.

"You hid him up here?"

"Edge said to get him our of your reach," Eric said as he led them across a plank floor. "Though I found it pretty odd that he'd have any desire to protect him."

"He wasn't protecting Stiles. He was protecting Amber," Tam said.

Amber sniffed. "Stiles is in no condition to be any threat to me."

"Not physically, no." Tamara squeezed her arm. "But emotionally. Amber, if you lost control, if you took his life, I'm not sure you'd ever get over it. Not you. You're not a killer. You have a gentle soul, despite your tough exterior. Edge has seen it. He knows."

Amber thinned her lips and kept her eyes forward as she picked her way through the attic, over dust bunnies and stacked boxes, through a door at one end, where a bedroom had been set up. Bed, nightstand and lamp. A peaked wall, with a window in it. Not much more. The covers on the bed were rumpled, but no one was in it. And the window was open.

Eric stared for a moment, then turned to face the two of them. "Stiles is gone."

"And so is Edge." The voice came from behind, and Amber turned to see Roland standing there. "I found

Stiles gone moments ago, and I've searched the place for Edge. He's not here.''

Amber had to grab the foot of the bed to keep herself upright.

Eric lowered a hand onto her shoulder. ''I know, Amber. I know it's disappointing. God, I was so certain he'd put his need for vengeance aside for your sake, but—''

''That's not what this is,'' she blurted.

Everyone stared at her, no one speaking. But she knew what they were thinking. That she was one of those pathetic women who fell in love and then went blind. Who refused to see the faults that glared at everyone else like neon. And for a moment she wondered if it was true.

''Amber, dear child,'' Roland said gently, ''I know it's difficult to accept that someone you care about might not have your best interests at heart, but—''

''If Edge took Stiles, he took him to try to get the truth out of him. Not to kill him. He wouldn't.''

The men looked at each other. Tamara slid an arm around her. ''She's right. The man wouldn't abandon her. Not now.''

''Tam, it might be best not to nurture false hope,'' Eric began.

''Oh, for God's sake! Listen to you. I know a man in love when I see one, and that man is completely out of his mind in love with Amber.''

Amber shot her eyes to Tam's.

''Come on, dear. You're pale as wraith. You need to lie down.''

''I need to eat,'' she said.

''You two get going. Go fetch Dante and Donovan, and then all of you go out and try to find Edge,'' Tam said.

The two men left in a hurry. Tam and Amber followed

more slowly, and when the men were out of sight, Amber said, "He's not, you know."

"Not what?"

"In love with me. Edge is a free spirit. A loner. He's not a romantic, not the kind who falls in love."

Tam smiled at her. "Is that what you think?"

"It's what I know."

"And you think you know him pretty well?"

"Inside and out," she said. "Sometimes it's like we're inside each other's minds. I understand him."

"I can see that."

"And I know he's not in love. But I also know he wouldn't have made the promises he made to me if he were going to break them at the first opportunity. He's up to something, Tam. He must think he knows a way to get Stiles to talk."

Tam nodded. "Keep on believing in him, Amber. No matter what the others may say. You know him best."

"I do."

They reached the ground floor, and Tam led her to the sofa in the large sitting room, the one near the gas fireplace. Amber let herself be coddled, feeling fragile, drained and overly emotional. She leaned against the pillow-padded arm and drew her legs up beside her. "He'll come back, Tam," she whispered. "I know he will."

Tam nodded. "You hold on to that."

She tried. But it wasn't easy. The night wore on, and the men returned from searching having found no sign of Edge or Stiles. They made less and less effort to conceal their anger. When Amber's parents and Rhiannon arrived, with Morgan in tow, Amber was beside herself, worrying they, too, would jump to the wrong conclusions and believe the worst about Edge.

That worry faded slightly, though, with her surprise

when Sarafina and Willem came in through the entryway behind them. Will was ashen, bent over, dragging his feet and leaning heavily on his walking stick, one arm slung around 'Fina's shoulders.

Amber came off the sofa in her shock at his appearance. How could he have worsened so drastically in such a short time?

She rushed toward him, only to stop short at the shocked look on his face. And then she realized he wasn't the only one looking at her that way. Her parents seemed stunned, and Rhiannon gaped at her. "My God," she said. "This is even worse than we imagined."

"Oh, it gets better," Eric called. "Jameson, join us in the library, won't you? We need a word."

Jameson lifted his brows, then nodded. "I'll be back, honey."

"Dad, wait."

"Just…give me a minute."

"I'm coming, too," Rhiannon said, and the two of them strode off to the library, following Eric. Donovan, Dante and Roland were already in there.

"It's as if they think I'm already dead," Will said, his voice weak, hoarse, but laced with humor. "How are you, Amber Lily?" He held out his arms, though Sarafina kept one of hers anchored around his waist.

Amber moved into them, hugging him gently. "You look like hell," she said.

"And you look like you swallowed a beach ball."

She backed away, smiling at him.

"Well, I'll be damned if I'll be left out of the deep dark meeting in the next room. Think you can get me that far, my love?" Will asked.

Sarafina smiled up at him. "Not until we get what we

came for, darling.'' She looked to Tamara. "The second dose?''

"It's in Eric's lab. Go ahead and take him to the library, 'Fina. I'll get it and bring it right in.''

Nodding, Sarafina pulled Will's arm around her. Amber placed herself on the other side of him, but her mother held up a hand and took that spot for herself, though she couldn't seem to tug her gaze from Amber's swollen middle.

"I'm huge. I know.''

"You're beautiful. Glowing, but you look exhausted, too.'' Angelica smiled. "I'm just so shocked. Tam's phone call didn't prepare us for the sight of you.''

"Well, she probably gave you the accurate account at the time. I seem to expanding exponentially.''

Her mother sent her a worried look.

"Edge has forbidden me to think about that,'' Amber said.

"About what?''

"What happens if this rapid development continues after he's born. Will he be twenty by this time next year? Will he die of old age before he starts school? What if he can't even survive the birth itself?''

"Amber, stop it,'' Will said. And he put more power behind those words than anything he'd said since he'd arrived. He shot her a stern look. "Edge is right. What earthly good can thoughts like those do either of you?''

"None, Will. I know that. But knowing it doesn't stop the questions from echoing constantly in my mind.''

They'd made it nearly to the library. Will moved very slowly and needed to stop every few yards to rest before moving on.

"What do you suppose the big meeting is about?'' Angelica asked.

Amber sighed. "It's about Edge. He's vanished and taken Stiles with him."

Angelica's eyes widened.

"Eric and Roland seem to think Edge decided to have his revenge on Stiles after all. But I know better." She opened the library door, then stood aside so that Sarafina and Angelica could help Will inside.

"The bastard," Rhiannon was saying. "If he harms that man before we learn what we need to know I'll—"

"Don't be ridiculous, Princess." It was Jameson who interrupted her. "You're all being ridiculous. I spent time with the man, more so than any of you did. If he took Stiles out of here, then it was because he thought he knew how to make him talk."

"I'd like to agree with you, Jamey," Roland said, his voice sad. "But if making him talk were the lad's goal, he could have done it right here."

"It's not his fault," Donovan said. "Don't forget, he had no one to teach him, no one to explain things."

"That was more than fifty years ago, Donovan. For God's sake, you explained what happened. If he's using that as an excuse—" Dante began.

"I haven't heard him use any excuse at all!" Jameson exploded. "God, you're all tossing around explanations for an evil that doesn't exist in the man. I'm telling you, he's taken Stiles to make him talk."

"Just what method could he employ elsewhere that he couldn't have employed here?" Eric asked.

Before anyone could answer, Tamara burst into the room. "The Ambrosia-Six!" she cried, a white foam box in her hands. "It's gone!"

"No," Amber whispered. She clutched Will's arm. "Please, God, not that."

Will nodded slowly. "Well, I guess that answers your

question," he said. "As to what method Edge could use to make Stiles talk that he couldn't use here. He's bribing him—with life."

Jameson closed his eyes. "Will's right. Stiles is the kind of man who craves immortality at any cost. He'd have given anything for that last dose of A-Six. Even if he knew there was a possibility it wouldn't work. Edge likely knew it was the only chance to get the truth out of him."

"No," Sarafina whispered. "By *Devel,* no!"

Will pulled her against him, though he had to brace his back against the wall to remain standing. "If Edge can get information that can help Amber and the baby, it's well worth it. I would have done the same."

She moaned against him, crying openly.

"Don't you hold this against him, Amber Lily," Willem told her. "Don't you do it. You know I'm not willing to live at your expense—or that child's. You know it. If he hadn't done it, I'd have found a way myself."

His knees bent a little. Sarafina lifted herself away, clutching him around the waist. She turned to the others. "We need to get him into a bed. He has to rest."

Nodding, Jameson strode forward, lifting Will easily and carrying him out of the room, with Sarafina right behind.

"I'll go see if they need anything," Tamara whispered, hurrying away.

"Donovan, you and I should continue to search for Edge until dawn," Dante said. "You, as his sire, would have the strongest bond to him."

He was wrong, Amber thought, sinking into a chair. She had the strongest bond to Edge. She'd been right to believe he wouldn't exact vengeance on Stiles at her expense. She'd been right to believe he had only taken the man to try to extract his secrets.

But had she been wrong to trust him? Had he just signed the death sentence of her best friend?

Tears welled in her eyes, and then more came when it felt as if a giant fist closed around her lower back and abdomen. The pressure was intense. She screamed, and thought the entire household probably heard it.

"So, here we are. Just the two of us. Ironic, isn't it? That of all people, I'd be the one with you at the end?" Edge sat in a rickety wooden chair, smoking a cigarette and studying the old man, who lay on the floor, a tarp over him for a blanket. Edge had carried the old bastard on his back until he'd located an abandoned farmhouse. He was using a shed out back. The house would have been too obvious. And hell, he didn't need too much time, anyway. This shouldn't take all that long.

"We both know," Stiles said slowly, "this isn't the end."

"Isn't it?"

"You aren't going to let me die."

Edge shrugged, took a slow drag and blew out the smoke. "I think that depends on you, Stiles. I'd like nothing better than to watch you die. Maybe even help you. But lucky for you, I've found something else to live for, besides vengeance." He nodded. "And your notes are somewhat…incomplete."

He pointed to his head, tapped it with a forefinger. "Some things, I keep right here."

"What sorts of things?"

"The formula, for one."

"Oh, we've figured out the formula. That Marquand, he's quite the science buff, you know. You're going to have to do better than that if you want the little present I brought you.'' As he said it, Edge drew the vial from his coat pocket, held it close enough to Stiles so the old man could read the label, though he had to squint to focus.

His eyes brightened with hope; he licked his lips. ''You'll give it to me?''

Edge nodded. ''If you tell me what you know about Amber. And the baby.''

''How do I know you'll keep your end of the bargain?''

Edge shrugged, reached into his pocket, pulled out a syringe, and tore off the cellophane wrapper. He stuck it into the vial, piercing the stopper and drawing all of the fluid up into the hypodermic. ''I'll let you hold the needle. How's that?''

He offered it to the man. Frowning, Stiles took it, and immediately turned it toward his arm.

''Ah-ah-ah,'' Edge said, and he pinned Stiles's hand to the floor at the wrist. ''You can't inject yourself until you've told me what I want to know. I'm not stupid. I let you inject it now, you won't tell me a thing.''

''You may not let me anyway,'' he said. ''You're far stronger than I am now.''

''I'm also the only chance you have, Stiles. Now, are you going to start talking, or are you going to keep wasting time?''

He frowned, nodded. ''Where do you want me to begin?''

''At the beginning,'' Edge said. ''As in, conception.''

''Ahh.'' Stiles nodded. ''Well, it's got to be her blood. It has healing properties, you know. Always has had just a hint of that, even as a girl. That was one of the things I learned about her the first time I held her. One of the things I didn't put in my notes." He shook his head slowly. "But it was nothing like the degree it possesses now. I believe that when your sperm cells entered her body, they were...healed. Revivified by that slight healing energy she's always possessed. They were brought back to life. She made you fertile again. Probably only with her, though."

"She is one of a kind," he muttered.

"What's that?"

"Nothing." Edge told himself to focus and returned his attention to Stiles. "Her blood chemistry changed once she became pregnant."

"Yes. I was running tests on her blood the night you all came bursting in on me. It's far more powerful now, but volatile. Unpredictable."

"What do you mean?"

"I mean, I can't predict how it's going to react to any test. One sample of plasma injected into a rat made it grow to twice its normal size in two hours. Another rat died, and a third gave birth."

"It was already pregnant?" Edge asked.

"It had been sterilized," Stiles told him.

Edge frowned. "What are you saying?"

"Sometimes the blood healed, sometimes it caused... inexplicable things to happen. There was no pattern, no rationale. And yet it was obviously the most powerful fluid imaginable. So I made the formula. Ambrosia-Seven. And I...I couldn't resist the allure of so much power."

"So you injected yourself," Edge said.

Stiles nodded. "And immediately began to age."

"You think the A-Six will reverse the process?"

"It's the only thing that might."

"What if it only stops it?" Edge asked. "Suppose it

only makes you stay as you are, right now, for years and years?''

''That's a chance I'm willing to take.''

Edge shook his head.

''Can I take the injection now?''

''Just one or two more questions, old man. Then you can do whatever you want.''

He nodded. ''You want to know about the baby. About what its chances are, what it will be. I don't know those things. I have no way of knowing those things.''

Edge nodded, believing the man for once.

''And what about Amber? Will her blood chemistry return to normal once the baby is born?''

Stiles nodded. ''Her mother's did.''

''What?''

''DPI held her mother throughout her pregnancy. Kept close tabs on her. Her blood chemistry was altered drastically during her pregnancy, though not in the same way as Amber's was. We took another sample right after the delivery. And it had returned to prepregnancy condition. I have no reason to believe Amber's won't do the same.''

''You were there when Amber Lily was born?''

''I was there.''

''Were there any...complications?''

The old man nodded. ''Yes. We almost lost her, in fact.''

''Amber Lily or her mother?'' Edge asked, leaning forward.

''The mother. It was due to the intense pain of the delivery. Your kind...don't do so well with pain.'' He shrugged. ''Not that anyone cared about the mother at that point.''

''Of course not. She was just a means to an end to you.''

"If not for us, your precious Amber Lily wouldn't even exist."

"I think maybe she would. I think maybe fate had more to do with that than you or DPI or anyone else."

"Fate." Stiles spat out the word.

Edge lit another smoke, leaned back, releasing Stiles's wrist but remaining close enough to grab it faster than the old man could move it six inches. He knew that Stiles realized it, as well, because he didn't even try. "You have a theory, don't you? About why Amber's body chemistry has changed so drastically? About why her blood suddenly has this volatile healing power?"

Stiles held his gaze, nodded.

"Then you tell me what it is. And don't leave anything out. Then you can have your injection," he told Stiles.

Stiles nodded, took a breath and kept on talking.

23

Amber hugged her belly and sank to her knees as everyone came running.

Everyone, she noted, except Edge.

"God, no. Not yet!" she cried. "Not yet, I still don't know what to do. I still don't know...ahhhh."

"Easy, baby. Easy now." Her mother's arms were around her, gentle but strong. "Come on, let's get you up to bed. Tam? Rhiannon?"

"Right here," Rhiannon said. They helped Amber to her feet, and then her dad was there, picking her up and carrying her, just the way he'd carried Will only moments ago. Not because her mother couldn't have done it herself, but because he was her dad. As he carried her up the stairs, he gazed down at her face. "I wasn't there when you were born," he said. "It's almost as if I'm getting the chance to make up for that now."

"It might not be the happy occasion you're hoping for," she whispered. "Prepare yourself, Dad. I don't know...ahh!"

He picked up the pace, and soon she was in her bed. It felt different, and she realized vaguely that someone had run ahead to line the mattress in something. There wasn't time to discover what. The contractions came fast, hard. She closed her eyes, focused on Edge in her mind. *It's time,* she thought desperately. *Edge, where are you? I need you!*

* * *

Edge listened to Stiles's theory about what was happening in Amber's body, which had all the earmarks of a madman's delusion—except that it explained everything. And he could think of nothing else that could. So maybe it wasn't so farfetched after all.

And then he heard Amber's call like the cry of a wounded siren, reaching across space to touch him. His body tingled with nervous energy, and he looked at Stiles. "And that's it? That's all you know?"

"That's all I know." Stiles looked down at the hypodermic he held in his hand. "Are you going to keep your word?"

Edge nodded once.

Stiles moved the needle toward his opposite arm, pressed the tip to his skin, then paused and looked up at Edge, as if surprised Edge had let him get that far. And then his face clouded. "How do I know this isn't a trick? That this is really the Ambrosia-Six?"

Edge shrugged. "How do you know it's not? What's the matter, Stiles, getting cold feet?"

"No. No, this is my only hope. Living on—it's worth any risk."

"Trust me on this, Stiles, it's not all sunshine. Hell, for me, none of it is." His pun seemed lost on the old man.

Stiles took a breath, drove the needle into his arm and depressed the plunger. Then he pulled the needle out again and dropped it to the floor. He laid his head back, closed his eyes, waited.

"Do you remember all those years ago?" Edge asked. "The way you killed my family?"

"Family. Hell, Edge, that wasn't a family. It was a street gang."

"They were family to me."

"Fledglings. No age, no power. No experience. Almost too dumb to live."

"I've always wondered, all this time. Why? Why did you do it?"

Stiles narrowed his eyes, staring at Edge. "Does it matter?"

"To me it does."

"They were street criminals. You all were."

"That's how we got by. Lifting wallets here and there, stealing what we could, when we got the chance."

He nodded. "One of your little 'family' members cornered me in an alley. Took my wallet, took my blood..."

"Yes, Bridget told me about it. But she didn't take your life," Edge said. "She let you live." Then he studied the man's face. "Ah, but she terrified you, didn't she? Scared you so badly you pissed yourself." He tipped his head sideways. "She laughed at you, humiliated you. Showed you to be the coward you truly are."

Stiles frowned, his attention no longer on Edge's words. "Something's...wrong..."

"So you went back, probably with a gang of your own, since you've never been man enough to do your own dirty work."

"I'd made some new friends," Stiles said. "A group called DPI. They'd been trying to recruit me. Leading them to your lair was...sort of my initiation."

"So you tortured them, and then you killed them. All of them."

"God, something's wrong!" the old man said.

Edge watched as Stiles's face began to change. It puckered and wrinkled, right before his eyes. He said, "You were right before, Stiles. That wasn't Ambrosia-Six in the vial. It was Ambrosia-Seven."

"No..."

"'Fraid so."

Stiles clutched at his throat, twisting and writhing as his face contorted. The pain must have been intense, Edge thought. Good.

The man thrashed, convulsed, as the formula did its work. He aged right before Edge's eyes, rapidly, amazingly.

"Consider this payment in full," Edge said. "For Bridget and Scottie. For Billy Boy and Ginger. For everything you did to Amber in the past. For all the vampires you've ever tormented, Stiles. It isn't half what you deserve."

Stiles's eyes widened, bulged, and then suddenly he went still, his face frozen in a terrible grimace. Within seconds, even that faded as his skin crumbled and flaked away, leaving only bones. And those, too, became dust, until all that remained of him was a pile of powder in the vague shape of a human form.

Edge rose and opened the door. A stiff wind blew in, and the dust scattered, swirled. Good. Edge left the door standing wide and sprinted with all his power through the night. Amber needed him, even though she probably hated him right now.

"Ah, God, it hurts!" Amber panted, followed her mother's breathing instructions, even while wondering how a vampiress, in whom every sense was magnified a thousand times, had ever gone through this kind of pain without losing her mind. She clutched her mother's hand.

"It'll be over soon, Amber."

"I know. If you survived this, I can."

The men had been banished from the room. Tamara,

Rhiannon, Alicia and Angelica surrounded her, Tam at the foot of the bed, Rhiannon pacing.

Alicia said, "Rhiannon, isn't there something you can do?"

"I'm not a doctor," she said. "Nor have I ever given birth." Amber detected a hint of regret in her voice when she said it.

"You were a priestess, though. I've read about the priestesses of Isis. You've got…real power. And women came to you when they were ready to give birth."

Rhiannon came to a stop in her pacing, met Alicia's eyes. "You've been dabbling in the magical arts, haven't you, child?"

"Maybe. A little."

Rhiannon drew a breath, sighed. "Well, it's true. There was a childbirth ritual that seemed to ease the pain of the women in labor. By the Gods, it was so long ago…." She turned to Angelica, to Amber. "Do you want me to try?"

"Of course," Angelica said, looking to Amber for confirmation.

"I'll try anything at this point," she said.

Nodding, Rhiannon climbed into the bed, lifting Amber into a sitting position and sliding in behind her, kneeling. She put a pillow over her thighs, then lowered Amber's back to them, so she lay at an angle. Then she pressed her fingertips to Amber's temples, closed her eyes and began chanting—strange, foreign words that at first seemed awkward but soon fell into a gentle cadence and rhythm.

Angelica watched Amber's face, a question in her eyes. Amber nodded, because despite her initial doubts, she felt something. A warmth, soothing through her body like liquid heat.

"Tam, get some candles," Alicia whispered. "Incense, too. Sandalwood, if you have it. I'll dim the lights."

Within a few moments the room's entire atmosphere had changed. Tamara returned to her position at the foot of the bed, keeping track of Amber's physical progress. Angelica sat in a chair right at Amber's side, holding her hand, coaching her through the breathing. Rhiannon remained where she was, stroking Amber's forehead and temples with her graceful hands, and chanting in that deep, powerful voice. Alicia moved around the room, placing candles and lighting them, then wafting the incense smoke around with smooth, graceful hand motions. Scarfs and veils had been draped over the lights. And Angelica was whispering Hail Mary's at her side.

The door opened, and Sarafina came in. She took in the scene, nodded her approval and joined in, adding her own Gypsy chant to the mix.

"It's time to push," Tamara said softly. "When the next contraction comes, bear down for a count of ten. All right?"

The contraction came all too soon. Amber bore down. All the women stopped their chanting, praying, songs, and joined in counting, all with one voice. "Ten, nine, eight, seven..." When they reached zero, they each returned to their individual techniques, only to return to the count the next time Amber had to push.

"The head's coming. It's coming, Amber."

The bedroom door burst open suddenly. Amber looked up and saw Edge standing there, his eyes wide, sweeping her, the women around her, and then focusing on the place where a new life was struggling to emerge from her body.

"Oh, God," he whispered. He looked as if he might be about to faint.

Panting, breathless, coated in sweat, Amber said, "Where the hell is Stiles?"

"He's dust."

Pant, pant, pant breathe. "Then—then you did it? You killed him?"

"Not exactly. Jesus, Alby, all this can wait."

"No, it can't! Ahh!"

"Push now, push." The women all began counting, and Edge came farther into the room, taking the spot at Amber's side, on the opposite side of the bed from her mother.

They reached zero, and Amber collapsed back onto Rhiannon's lap, panting. When she could breathe enough to talk, she said, "Tell me what happened, Edge. Where's the A-Six? What did you do with Stiles?"

He nodded, holding her hand, drawing it to his lips to kiss it, then speaking. "The Ambrosia-Six is still safely in Eric's lab. Just in an unlabeled vial."

Sarafina's song broke off abruptly. "You didn't give it to Stiles?"

"I'd planned to, but I knew Amber would never forgive me. It occurred to me I might be able to fool Stiles, so I told him I would, but what I gave him in exchange for his information was the Seven, not the Six."

Sarafina closed her eyes. "Thank the Gods," she whispered. "I have to—"

"Go," Amber told her. "Get it and inject Will. Do it now."

Nodding, Sarafina ran from the room as Edge called out after her, telling her where to find the precious elixir.

"What did Stiles tell you?" Amber demanded.

Edge shook his head, as if to clear it. "That your blood

has always had healing properties. He discovered it when he held you captive the first time. That it somehow revivified my useless sperm cells, making them viable again. And that the conception of the baby caused a chemical reaction in you that will likely be reversed as soon as our child is born.''

She gulped in air, nodded. "What about the baby?"

"He didn't know. Amber, he had some wild theories, but he just didn't know. I don't..."

"Ah, God!" She bore down again with the contraction.

Tamara leaned over her from below. "A little more, a little more, that's it! The head is out!"

The next contraction came with barely a heartbeat in between. Amber pushed again, and she felt the sudden whoosh of relief. A moment later Tamara was rising, a towel-wrapped bundle in her arms. Amber clutched Edge's hand hard, staring, whispering, "Please, please..."

And then the bundle wriggled. A soft, hoarse cry, muffled, gurgly, came from within it. Tamara lowered the baby into Amber's arms. She held her son, staring down at his pink, white-smeared face, his bright, open eyes, sobbing. "He's alive. God, Edge, he's alive."

"Not only alive, but big and strong," Tamara said, smiling.

Amber sighed. "The dream was wrong."

"Dream?" her mother asked.

Then Amber felt it, another mind-bending contraction. She cried out and pushed the baby toward his father. Edge took his son, holding him gently, gazing down at his tiny face with rapture on his own.

"Hey, J.W. Good to finally see you." His words were mere whispers.

"Oh, God, what's happening?" Amber cried.

Edge looked up, his face suddenly worried.

Tamara, at the foot of the bed, looked up at the two of them. "There's another baby," she said.

Edge felt his knees go weak. Angelica rose to her feet, leaning over the bed, reaching out. "I'll take him. It's going to be all right. Come here, little one."

Edge let her take the child from his arms. She left the room with the baby, and all his attention returned to Amber and the events unfolding before his eyes. He couldn't bear to see her in so much pain. Racked by so much fear. He was confused—if there were two babies, why had he heard only one voice?

Amber pushed, the women chanted and counted, and Edge held on to Amber, telling her softly that it would all be okay, but he had no idea if he believed the words he spoke to her. He only knew she needed to hear them.

Angelica returned. She'd lined what looked like the drawer of an ornate dresser in thick blankets. She'd cleaned and dressed the baby boy, wrapped him in one of the blue receiving blankets and laid him inside. She placed the makeshift cradle on a stand to await the second child, then gathered the wriggling baby from it and returned to the bedside to hold him, cooing softly.

Amber let her body go limp. "God, I can't. I can't push anymore. I can't..."

Angelica leaned closer, and Amber touched her newborn son's hand. Edge watched as the baby wrapped his tiny fist around Amber's forefinger. And suddenly she seemed stronger. Able to go on.

She pushed when told, panted in between. Her face was red, her hair sweat-soaked. She was utterly exhausted, and Edge felt it. He felt everything, the pain, the tiredness, but above it all, the fear.

"Here we go, one more push, Amber," Tamara said.

Again she pushed, forcing her second child into the world.

"A girl," Tam said, gathering the baby as she had the first one, wrapping her gently, rising to her feet. But her face wasn't smiling as it had been before. "Come on, baby girl. Come on now." She put her hand to the baby's chest, shaking it gently. "Come on, honey, take a breath."

But the bundle didn't wriggle, and no cry emerged. "I'll get Eric," she whispered, turning. She laid the baby in the prepared makeshift cradle, reached for the door, stifling a sob.

No, no way.

Edge looked up sharply. That voice. That familiar voice.

Bring my sister to me!

And suddenly, Edge knew what to do.

24

Amber watched in horror as everything in her dream came true, like a slow motion film reel playing in front of her. Edge crossed the room, picked up the dresser drawer and stared down into it. His chest heaved, and he turned toward the bed.

The drawer's front was ornately carved. From this angle, it looked like an elaborately engraved box. Just like the one in the dream. She jerked her eyes up to Edge's, saw the single tear, the same one she'd seen before, rolling down his face.

"No," she whispered. "No, Edge, this can't be happening…"

"Shh. Hold on, Alby." He came closer, to the side of the bed where her mother stood, holding the boy child, her face wet with tears. "Put him in here. Lay him beside his sister."

"But, Edge, she's—"

"Please," Edge whispered, so much emotion in his voice that it was choked and hoarse.

Rising to her feet, Angelica gently placed the healthy, wriggling baby beside the still child in the box. Edge knelt on the floor beside the bed, even as Amber sat up so she could see. She stared down into the face of her daughter. It was already tinged with pallor, a slight bluish tint to the skin. She was so small, so much smaller than the boy child. But even as she stared, her heart slowly being crushed by the weight of her grief, her baby boy's tiny little hand began to wave back and forth, almost aimlessly. When it touched, as if by accident, the still, lifeless hand of the tiny, frail child beside him, his hand opened and closed reflexively. He clasped his sister's fingers just the way a newborn child would clasp anything placed into its tiny fist.

The door opened, and Tamara and Eric burst into the room, followed quickly by the others. Even Will had managed to get himself this far. They crowded into the bedroom, then went still as, one by one, they took in the scene before them.

Amber knew they were there. But she couldn't take her eyes off her babies.

"Edge?" she whispered. "Her face... Am I imagining it?"

"No, she's getting more color. I see it, too."

"She's moving," Angelica whispered. "Look at her little foot...."

Suddenly the silence of the room was broken by a tiny, hoarse cry, like the bleat of a newborn lamb. The little girl in the makeshift cradle began to wriggle and squirm, as her scrunched-up face made her impatience clear.

Amber stretched out her arms, laughing and crying and shaking all over.

Edge leaned over the cradle, gathering both the babies into his arms. Rising again, he placed them into the bed with their mother, one nestled in the crook of each arm.

She gazed down at one baby, then the other, her tears flowing like rivers.

Edge stood there staring down at them for just a moment; then he sank into a nearby chair, as if he no longer possessed the power to stand.

"How...how did you know what to do, Edge?" Jameson asked, moving to the chair where Edge sat and hunkering down in front of him.

"J.W. told me. I think he...I think he healed her."

Eric nodded. "It actually makes sense. His mother's blood already had healing properties. Combine those with the enhanced powers of vampiric blood, and you get a powerful healer."

"Maybe." Edge shook his head. "Stiles had this insane theory that somehow the baby was controlling some things from within the womb. That's why Amber's blood suddenly had so much more power. That it wasn't coming from her...but from the baby. He even thought the child might have some control over how the power manifested. I didn't believe it...but now...I'm not so sure."

"Maybe we should give this new little family some time alone," Angelica said. She stood behind Jameson, her hands on his shoulders. "Not too long, though. I'm eager to start the spoiling process as early as possible."

Jameson rose to his feet with a nod; then he moved closer to Amber, leaned down and kissed her on the forehead. "You were right all along to believe in him, even when everyone else doubted."

"You didn't," she said.

"I trust your judgment."

One by one they came to the bed, kissed the babies. Alicia was sobbing so hard she couldn't talk. Will only stroked their silken heads. Amber thought he looked better and noticed the bandage on his arm from the fresh injection. A half dose hadn't been enough, but now that he'd had the rest, the serum appeared to be working.

"Do you think it worked?" Amber asked him, searching his face.

"Does it matter? If it didn't, I'll just let J.W. here grab onto my finger."

She didn't argue with him, didn't say that they couldn't be sure J.W.'s healing power would work on others the way it had worked on his sister, and that they had no reason to believe it could bestow immortality. Even before she finished the thought, though, Will gave her a wink. "It worked, Amber. I'm sure of it."

He straightened away from the bed, walked slowly to the door. When he left the room and closed it behind him, she looked at Edge. He looked as exhausted as she felt. But he met her eyes, rising slowly from the chair, coming closer. "Can you part with them for a minute, do you think?"

"I don't want to stop touching them," she whispered. "But I can barely hold my head up."

He took the little girl from her arms. "She's going to need a name."

"How about Bridget?" Amber asked softly.

Edge looked up suddenly. Fresh tears came into his eyes as he met hers. "Thank you for that."

"You're thanking me? Edge, you did this. You kept your promise. You got the information from Stiles and made sure you did it without robbing Will of his cure. And you saved our little girl."

"Her brother did that."

"You both did it."

He snuggled the child for a moment, then laid her in the cradle. Next he took the little boy and hugged him, kissed his cheek and placed him beside his sister. "He's going to be a handful. He actually laughed at me when that gang of mortal females at the Sisterhood of Athena beat me down." He tickled the baby's chin. "I owe you for that, J.W."

Then he straightened and sat on the mattress, close to Amber.

He took her hands in both of his. "With all that's been happening, Alby, I haven't managed to get around to talking to you about...us."

She lowered her eyes. "You don't have to."

"Don't have to what? Talk?"

"Stay," she whispered. "You don't have to stay. With me, I mean."

He smiled slowly. "That's enough dancing around this already, don't you think?" She frowned at him. He said, "Just give in, Amber, and tell me you love me."

Her heart turned over, and she searched his eyes. "What?"

"Tell me you love me, Alby. Even though I'm not the prince you dreamed of, even though I'm not worthy of you by half. Tell me you love me anyway. But only if you mean it."

She held his gaze and stopped pretending. Pressing her hands to his cheeks, she said, "You are worthy. And you are exactly what I dreamed of. And I've loved you from the first time you kissed me. Even though you warned me not to."

"Did I?"

She nodded. "You told me you were not a romantic, not the kind of man who was going to fall in love or stick around or mate for life. And like an idiot, I ignored all that and fell in love with you anyway."

He smiled at her. The dimples in his cheeks, the light in his eyes making her breath catch in her throat. "It's just as well. It was all bullshit anyway."

"It was?"

"Hell yes. You haven't figured that out yet? Alby, I'm nuts about you. I've even developed a ridiculous attachment to that bunch of meddlers you call family." He kissed her lips, gently, slowly.

When he lifted his head away, she was still searching his eyes, and her own were full of questions. "I'm still not... What are you saying, Edge? Is it...if it's the babies, then—"

"It's not the babies," he told her. "It's not the situation. It's not the others. It's you, Alby. You are...the only woman in all creation for me. You've got my heart imprisoned inside yours. You own my soul. If I had to live without you, I think I'd wither and die. I love you, woman. Is that clear enough for you?"

Her throat tried to close off, and she couldn't talk. It was real. Everything she'd dared not hope for but hoped for anyway was real. He loved her.

She tried to tell him what that meant to her, but there were no words powerful enough. So with tears of joy streaming, she kissed him again instead.

Epilogue

Golden-haired Bridget wore a flowing skirt, a dozen bangle bracelets and big silver hoops clipped onto her ears. She was imitating her aunt Sarafina, who was teaching her to dance like a Gypsy while playing her new tambourine. It was the twins' second birthday, and the huge party had become an annual event by now. The family had agreed to take turns hosting it, and this year it was at Sarafina and Willem's home in Salem. The pony rides had been Rhiannon's contribution, and the bonfire and authentic Gypsy costumes were 'Fina's idea. There were cakes, ice cream, music and scads of adoring attention. Every gift the kids tore open was more elaborate than the one before. And yet J.W. was ignoring them all, spending his time running around the beach with his Uncle Willem in search of dying starfish. Every time he found one, he picked it up, held it in his hands long enough to heal it and then tossed it into the water again.

Amber reclined in a comfy chair on the redwood deck, surrounded by the women in her life. Her mother and best friend. Her aunt Rhiannon and Tamara. Morgan was there, and Donovan had finally brought Rachel around to meet everyone. Alicia's mother, Susan, was there, as well. It felt good; it felt right.

She watched as her husband talked with the other men. She saw how they looked at him, with respect in their eyes. They loved him, every one of them. Amber's father would lay down his life for the man who had saved his grandchildren, and Eric and Roland felt the same. Edge had even formed a new and tender bond with Donovan and Dante.

As for Will, well, Will would always be grateful. He was healthy, vital again. The cancer had died, and he had healed. And when he needed more of the formula, Amber could provide it. As predicted, her blood had returned to its original state. Rhiannon had "borrowed" some of the new batch of A-Six, to "test" it on her cat, Pandora, who was behaving like an animal in its prime again.

Laughing, Sarafina danced Bridget, with her mass of golden curls, closer to the deck, then sank onto the steps breathlessly, hugging the two-year-old in her arms. Dante parted from the group of men and came closer to her. "It's like we have our tribe back again, isn't it, 'Fina?" he asked.

She nodded. "Except no one here would betray us. Not ever." She stared out at Willem, romping now in the surf with J.W., his jeans rolled up to his ankles. "Will doesn't even have the limp anymore."

"I know," Amber said. "It's wonderful to see him so healthy. We came so close to losing him." She sighed. "I used to feel so alone. Such an outsider. Because I was different from the rest of you. Different from Alicia and Susan, too."

"Ahh, but the gang of outsiders is growing," Angelica said softly. "Now there are Will, and the babies."

"Now there's Edge," Amber whispered. "I'll never feel alone again."

Edge looked up, caught her eye from near the central fire. None of the vampires stood too close to it. And there was water everywhere, just in case. But life was risk, and having a fire, as in times long past, was a very small risk,

Sarafina had insisted. So long as none of them were stupid enough to get too close.

Hearing his whispered message, Amber got up and went to him, and he met her halfway. "Think they can handle the rugrats for an hour?" he asked.

"I trust them like no one else. Why? What did you have in mind?"

He smiled. "A little walk along the beach. I thought we could visit that spot we found once before. You remember it, don't you? That isolated little cove—"

"Where our babies were conceived?"

His eyes darkened, and Amber tingled all over. She sent Alicia a look, and Alicia replied with a nod, understanding perfectly. Then Edge slid his arm around Amber's shoulders, and they walked up the beach together, arm in arm.

"Are you happy?" he asked her.

She looked up into his eyes. "I've found bliss," she whispered. "Running you over was the best thing I ever did."

"I can think of several things you've done since that I enjoyed more."

"Mmm. Can you?"

"Yeah. Standing up for me with your family. Giving birth to those two little bandits back there. Healing Will. Healing me."

"When you burned your arm, you mean?"

He turned her to face him, stared into her eyes. "No, not my arm. My soul. My heart. You healed everything in my life, Alby. All just by loving me. You really are the Child of Promise. You're a miracle, and I'll cherish you until the stars fall."

He wrapped her in his arms and kissed her. And Amber knew she had found her place at last.

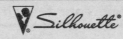

Carnival Elation
7-Day Exotic Western Caribbean Itinerary

DAY	PORT	ARRIVE	DEPART
Sun	Galveston		4:00 P.M.
Mon	"Fun Day" at Sea		
Tue	Progreso/Mérida	8:00 A.M.	4:00 P.M.
Wed	Cozumel	9:00 A.M.	5:00 P.M.
Thu	Belize	8:00 A.M.	6:00 P.M.
Fri	"Fun Day" at Sea		
Sat	"Fun Day" at Sea		
Sun	Galveston	8:00 A.M.	

TERMS AND CONDITIONS

PAYMENT SCHEDULE:
50% due upon booking. Full and final payment due by July 26, 2004.
Acceptable forms of payment are Visa, MasterCard, American Express, Discover and checks. The cardholder must be one of the passengers traveling. A fee of $25 will apply for all returned checks. Check payments must be made payable to **Advantage International, LLC and sent to: Advantage International, LLC, 195 North Harbor Drive, Suite 4206, Chicago, IL 60601.**

CHANGE/CANCELLATION:
Notice of change/cancellation must be made in writing to Advantage International, LLC.

Change:
Changes in cabin category may be requested and can result in increased rate and penalties. A name change is permitted 60 days or more prior to departure and will incur a penalty of $50 per name change. Deviation from the group schedule and package is a cancellation.

Cancellation:
181 days or more prior to departure	$250 per person
121—180 days or more prior to departure	50% of the package price
120—61 days prior to departure	75% of the package price
60 days or less prior to departure	100% of the package price (nonrefundable)

U.S. and Canadian citizens are required to present a valid passport or the original birth certificate and state issued photo ID (driver's license). All other nationalities must contact the consulate of the various ports that are visited for verification of documentation.

We strongly recommend trip cancellation insurance!

For further details call 1-877-ADV-NTGE or visit www.GetCaughtReadingatSea.com

For booking form and complete information
go to **www.getcaughtreadingatsea.com**
or call **1-877-ADV-NTGE**

Complete coupon and booking form and mail both to:
Advantage International, LLC
195 North Harbor Drive, Suite 4206, Chicago, IL 60601

Harlequin Enterprises Ltd. is a paid participant in this promotion.

THE FUN SHIPS, CARNIVAL DESIGN, CARNIVAL AND THE MOST POPULAR CRUISE LINE IN THE WORLD ARE TRADEMARKS OF CARNIVAL CORPORATION. ALL OTHER TRADEMARKS ARE TRADEMARKS OF HARLEQUIN ENTERPRISES LTD. OR ITS AFFILIATED COMPANIES, USED UNDER LICENSE.

Visit us at www.eHarlequin.com

GCRSEA2

MAGGIE SHAYNE

66886	TWILIGHT HUNGER	___ $6.50 U.S.	___ $7.99 CAN.
66737	THICKER THAN WATER	___ $6.99 U.S.	___ $8.50 CAN.
66668	EMBRACE THE TWILIGHT	___ $6.99 U.S.	___ $8.50 CAN.

(limited quantities available)

TOTAL AMOUNT $_____
POSTAGE & HANDLING $_____
($1.00 for one book; 50¢ for each additional)
APPLICABLE TAXES* $_____
<u>TOTAL PAYABLE</u> $_____
(check or money order—please do not send cash)

To order, complete this form and send it, along with a check or money order for the total above, payable to MIRA Books, to: **In the U.S.:** 3010 Walden Avenue, P.O. Box 9077, Buffalo, NY 14269-9077; **In Canada:** P.O. Box 636, Fort Erie, Ontario L2A 5X3.

Name:_____
Address:_____ City:_____
State/Prov.:_____ Zip/Postal Code:_____
Account Number (if applicable):_____
075 CSAS

  *New York residents remit applicable sales taxes.
   Canadian residents remit applicable GST and provincial taxes.

MIRA®